THE SAGA OF ICHIRIN

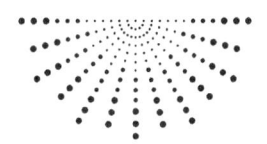

THE SAGA OF ICHIRIN

THE COMPLETE SERIES

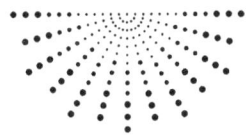

DYLAN BIRTOLO

Thank you Jaym, for putting up with me.

PART I
SHAPES IN THE SMOKE

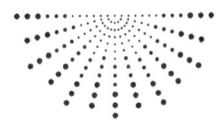

CHAPTER ONE

The light streaming in through the window landed on Ichirin's face, a better alarm clock than her phone. Groaning against the near-blinding glare, she reached up and covered her eyes, but it did little to stop the light from boring into her skull. Her arm flailed in an attempt to grab the cord to drop the blinds. At one point, she felt a brush against her fingers, but it danced away before she could grab hold.

Now growling, the young woman rolled over and opened her eyes, suffering the punishment from the morning sun, but at least she saw her target. She snatched the blind cord.

And her hand passed through the string.

That was when her sleep-burdened brain noticed her hand was no longer covered in pale flesh, but appeared made of gray-black smoke. Her eyes widened as her gaze traveled down her arm, and she realized the same substance comprised her entire body.

Ichirin screamed, trying to throw the sheets off her body and jump out of bed, but the fabric fluttered as if brushed by a breeze coming in through the window. She tumbled over the side and drifted to the ground rather than falling like years of dealing with gravity made her anticipate. For a moment, she laid on the floor of her bedroom and tried not to panic.

Slow deep breaths helped her relax and pull her mind back from the edge of fear. She needed to take stock of the situation, and giving in to reckless emotion would solve nothing. Tentatively, afraid that her own body might fall apart, she lifted a knee and slid it across the floor. It was a relief to find that she could still feel the carpet underneath her, even if it felt rougher than usual.

Ichirin paused as a revelation struck her. The carpet remained the same, but now she felt each fiber as her body sank into and around the threads of the fabric. She was still feeling the same surface, just more of it and to a greater intensity than her normal body permitted.

For the next few minutes, she swam in the wave of sensation that came at her through her entire body. It felt like acquiring a sense she had been missing her entire life. With this new awareness, the world seemed textured, like adding a new dimension. Reaching up with her arm, she rested her hand against the wall and dragged it across the surface, feeling every ripple and bump in a euphoric case of information overload.

She also noticed the black streaks left on the white wall in the wake of her fingers.

Curious to see how her other senses fared, she sniffed at the air. Nothing. She tried using her tongue to lick her lips and see if she tasted anything and was rewarded with the odd sensation of pressing her tongue through her lips.

The woman-turned-smoke pulled her feet underneath her and stood up, taking care to touch as little as possible. Looking down, an ashy smudge decorated the floor where she impacted it. Curious, she held out her arm, but nothing dropped from her new form.

What she needed right now was to talk to Taka, the *Sae no Kami* who served as her guide. He might have insight or techniques to help her control her manifesting abilities. She reached up to her chest to feel for the locket holding the rock containing the kami's essence. She wasn't quite sure how it worked, but she knew the small stone served as her connection to the spirit.

Her fingers passed through her own chest without feeling any other physical objects. Her head jerked to the bed, and she lurched forward, reaching out as she searched for the piece of jewelry. Seeing the locket resting on the bed with the rest of her clothes made her lower her arms and take a deep breath. It appeared that none of her belongings made the transition when she changed her form. Her hands went to cover her body before she realized the foolishness of such a motion. Her shape didn't have much to reveal, and she lived alone.

As comfortable as she could be with her situation, she tried to pick up the locket, but that resulted in a smudge across the sheets and her clothes. She tried again, but the black streaks darkened. On the third attempt, she inched her hand forward and paid careful attention to when she felt the locket in her hand. Closing her eyes—although she could still see through them, just behind a darkened haze—she tried to focus on picking up the locket and tightening her fingers around it. For a moment, it felt like the metal shifted under her palm, but then it slipped through her fingers.

Ichirin pressed her lips together and grunted. It sounded more like a hiss of steam escaping from a cracked pipe than a growl.

As entertaining as this could be, watching you fumble in an attempt to pick me up, I'm worried at some point you'll walk away in frustration. You don't need to have contact in order to communicate. As long as you are close enough, we can share thoughts.

Taka's voice in her mind relaxed her, and she started to sit down on the bed before she caught herself. Her hands flexed into fists for a moment as she realized Taka could've spoken up earlier. His voice was tinged with sardonic amusement, and she imagined if he had a face, he'd wear a grin mischievous enough to make Loki envious.

I have very few forms of amusement available to me. Considering the safety of your situation, I hope you'll forgive the few minutes of my indulgence.

The kami had a point, a concession that Ichirin had given multiple times. Over the months of their relationship, Taka demonstrated infallible logic, or at least logic that she could never dispute. His approach lacked subtlety or compassion, but she had grown to appreciate it over time.

At the moment, she needed to understand what exactly had happened and how to control it. A new monster had appeared, one that could turn into smoke or ash, but that exhausted her knowledge.

Smoke, not ash. I have seen creatures like this before. They are called enenra *and are nasty beasts. They are living entities made of smoke that exist only to kill. You know what you have to do. If you don't hunt it, no one will, and it will wreak havoc on Seattle, maybe all of Washington. Whatever brought it into existence must be nearby for your powers to manifest.*

Enenra? Ichirin hadn't heard that term before, but that didn't say much. Before she found the kami and became a hunter of mythological beasts, she hadn't studied much history. Her situation necessitated a change in that habit, but Japanese lore was rife with creatures and entities, far more than she could hope to learn even if she had years.

And that's why I'm so damned useful and you keep me around.

Of course, it would be more helpful if Taka gave her more details about the creatures or how to defeat them. But that argument had been covered more times than she cared to count. Right now, she needed to control her abilities and shift out of her insubstantial form.

Focus. Turn your will inward and picture your body. Remember it. Remember how it feels and how the air tastes. Remember seeing true darkness when you close your eyes. Feel your lungs swell as you take in a breath. Search for your heartbeat, and grasp it in your mind, being aware of every pulse of blood sent rushing through your system. You know you have a heart, and it must be beating, or else you'd be dead.

Focus on those things and feel the smoke and ash slough off you like a snake sheds its skin.

The hunter stood up straight and took a deep breath as she allowed Taka to lead her into a form of meditation. She pictured the things he described, so much that her eyebrows knit together. Her hands clenched into fists, and she felt the sting of her nails digging into her palm.

Never had pain felt so wonderful. She seized it in her mind, grasping tight and refusing to let go. Ichirin clenched more, trying to pierce her skin and draw blood. The pain grew until she gasped and stumbled forward, opening her hands and catching herself on the bed to keep from falling on her face. But her body was solid, and she kept herself upright.

At first, she could only stare at her hands. She pushed herself up from the bed and ran her fingers over her arms and legs, so glad to feel the smooth skin underneath. With a soft laugh to release the tension, she collapsed on the bed, relishing her dulled sensation of touch.

Now that you have a handle on your physical form, it's time to start hunting. There's no time to waste.

Even though she knew what she had to do, she still took a few moments to enjoy feeling like herself again. She could spare that much. Besides, it wasn't like she knew where to start. Seattle was not a small town, and even if she found the creature, she had no idea how to fight it. Knowing that it could turn into smoke summarized the extent of her information.

I know you think I'm withholding information, but a lot has changed over the centuries. It used to be as simple as "Oh look, people in that village are dying and screaming about bonfire smoke attacking them." While the modern world does have many advantages, it isn't easier to track these things down. As for killing it, that's your job. You're the soldier or assassin. I'm just the information broker.

She liked the thought of being an assassin, but soldier was a better term considering her role in this hunting ground she never knew existed. Grumbling, Ichirin rolled over and snatched her phone off the nightstand. She sent a quick text to Hemingway to let him know that it had happened again. He'd know what she was talking about. He was one of two people that she trusted with her secret, and he was the first one she opened up to about it. Only with his support was she able to bring someone else into her confidence. In the past, he proved invaluable in helping to ferret out the creatures. She didn't know if he was up yet but wanted him to get the message as soon as possible.

Then she called Corey, putting the phone on speaker so she could get dressed and reattach the locket around her neck.

"What's up?" Corey answered in a clipped voice, somehow managing to sound energetic and chipper even while rushed.

Her former roommate shuddered as she got flashbacks to their days living together when Corey would zip around the apartment before she could remember what day it was.

It's true. That woman can't be human considering how she's constantly stuck in overdrive. I wouldn't be surprised to find out she made some magical pact to avoid sleeping.

A large horn sounded in the background that seemed more like a train or tractor trailer than a car. Corey's voice came through muffled as she shouted at someone.

"Sorry about that. Stupid truckers."

"It happened again," Ichirin said. "Something's here."

"No shit!" Corey shouted, accomplishing the near-impossible feat of sounding even more excited. Ichirin had a mental image of her friend bouncing up and down as she spoke. "What are we dealing with this time? What can you do? How... Hey! Watch where you're going! Jackass. Anyways, how do you know? I'm ready to go!"

"I just woke up and messaged Hem. Where are you? How long would it take you to get to Redmond?"

"I'm down at the pier but packing up. Traffic's gonna suck, but I could be there in about thirty, maybe forty-five if traffic's really bad."

Her phone dinged to let her know she received a message. Logic said it had to be Hemingway. Few people texted her at all, especially before 8:30 on a workday.

"Sounds good. Come to my building and text me when you're here. We'll meet in my office so we have some measure of privacy."

"See you soon!"

That part handled, the tech manager finished getting her clothes for the day together and then checked her phone. Her assumption proved correct—Hemingway let her know he was at work and ready to meet as soon as she got into the office. She told him Corey's ETA, and then went about her morning routine, preparing to face the day.

The fact that a new creature emerged meant she needed to be ready to run or fight at a moment's notice. If she didn't dress for it, she should not have bothered doing all the extra cardio work with Hemingway over the past few months. Their last scrape with an ice demon stressed the importance of stamina. So she pushed aside the business suits in the closet and opted for a sensible pair of slacks and blouse. Her upbringing and lessons learned throughout the years as a woman in tech wouldn't let her dress as casual as either of her friends. The image she presented mattered, even if she was only at the office for a few minutes. Whether or not she liked the situation didn't change the reality.

Not wanting to take too much time, she brushed a few tangles out of her dark hair and then just let it hang behind her, the tips grazing her shoulder blades. She applied as little makeup as she felt she could get away with, just enough to cover the red splotches made all the more obvious with her pale skin.

I've never understood humans' obsession with appearance. Maybe because I don't—you know—actually have a body, but it always seemed like a waste of effort and time to me.

Within twenty minutes, the hunter stepped out the door and climbed into her car. Another ten and she found herself in her office. Living in Redmond could be expensive, but not as pricy as living in Seattle itself. Plus, the benefit of being that close to her place of employment had a value that made it more than worthwhile.

She'd just put her bag down when she got a text from Corey saying she had parked. Walking through the lobby, she was not surprised to see her friend bouncing on the balls of her feet in place as she stared at the locked doors. She had a Starbucks cup in her hand and drummed her fingers against the lid in rapid beat.

Oh great, she's had coffee. Because that one needs more caffeine.

Corey wore an Under Armour long-sleeved compression shirt with a faded Deadpool tee over it. Her leggings were recognizable from college, with stars and planets scattered across them. Her short blond hair was tucked up into a hat that covered her ears.

As soon as Corey noticed her friend, she looked her up and down with narrowed eyes, as if trying to determine what was different based on sight alone. She even tilted her head to the side and chewed on her bottom lip. Ichirin squirmed under the scrutiny, but she expected no different from Corey. She brushed it off as best as she could.

"Hey, how's it going?" Corey asked as she stepped closer, the smile returning along with a glint in her eyes.

"Good. We can talk about it in a second. Hem's on his way over."

"Gotcha."

The two of them walked over to the receptionist and checked in the visitor. That business handled, they went up to the third floor and sat in Ichirin's private office.

"So what happened?" Corey asked before the door closed. She tossed her cup into the recycle bin across the room.

"You can wait a minute. Hem's almost here, and then I only have to explain it once."

"Right, right," Corey said as she dropped into one of the chairs resting against the wall.

She sat there, bouncing her knees for a full ten seconds before getting up and pacing over to the shelves and picking up a book seemingly at random. When Hemingway knocked on the door, she threw the book back onto the shelf hard enough for it to bounce against the wall.

Hemingway wasn't a large man, but he still stood a head taller than Ichirin. Yet despite that, he always took care to never look down over her, even when she was sitting—a fact she appreciated about him. He took the casual dress code far more casual than her, wearing shorts and a "This is what a feminist looks like" t-shirt.

She gestured for Hemingway to enter, then reached up and closed the blinds. Hemingway took a seat, picking up his ankle and resting it on his other knee, looking up at his coworker and waiting with a somber expression on his face. In contrast, Corey resumed her bouncing, as she looked about to burst with anticipation.

"So, this morning, I woke up, and my body was smoke. I could see through my eyelids and when I tried to grab the cord for the blinds to close them, my hand passed right through." She decided to leave out the bit about falling out of bed. "I started to panic because I couldn't touch or grab anything. But thanks to Taka's help, I was able to calm down and get my body back."

"Are you saying you went all Kitty Pryde?" Corey took a step forward, her grin widening. "Like you could walk through walls and stuff like that?"

Ichirin shook her head. "Not quite. The floor stopped me well enough. I didn't sink through it. In fact, I could feel more of the floor, like my body penetrated the carpet, but every single piece of the smoke was still me, and I was still aware of it."

Hemingway shuddered at her description and leaned back in his chair, his dark skin paling a noticeable amount.

"Can you show us now?" Corey asked.

"I can try."

The hunter closed her eyes and focused, thinking about what it felt like that morning. She imagined her body breaking apart and becoming small pieces of smoke and ash held together more by force of will than any natural force. Light filtered through her eyelids, and she heard Hemingway gasp. Opening her eyes and looking down, she saw that once again she had turned into an insubstantial creature.

She also saw her pile of clothes at her feet.

Forgot about that part, didn't you?

"That's cool. Can I touch you?" Corey stepped forward but kept her hands at her sides.

"Sure."

Corey reached up and passed her hand through the smoke woman's shoulder. It was a strange sensation, feeling the warmth of Corey's hand not just on her skin, but rather penetrating through her body and still being aware of every inch of it along the way. When Corey removed her hand, she whistled and held it in front of her, the fingers all blackened.

"That's so cool. What's it like?"

"It's weird. It feels like you're shoving your hands inside me, but it doesn't hurt. It's hard to describe. Now... um..." Ichirin paused as she brought her arms in front of her body, covering herself. "If you don't mind turning around so I can get dressed?"

Hemingway got up and took position in front of the door, facing away and barring the entrance with his body. Ichirin appreciated that, just in case someone decided to walk in without knocking. It wasn't a typical occurrence, but she didn't relish the thought of explaining why she stood naked in her office with two of her friends. Corey also obliged, turning to face the wall while still studying her hand. She reached out and rubbed a finger against the wall, transferring some ash and making a faint black line on the plain surface.

Realizing that was the extent of the privacy she could get, Ichirin forced herself back into her physical form. She snatched her clothes from the ground and jerked them on, slamming her hip into her desk in the process and sucking in air through clenched teeth. Hemingway started to turn but stopped.

"You okay?" he asked.

"I'm fine. Just give me another moment. There, you can turn around now."

She was still making adjustments to appear professional, but at least she was decent. Hemingway glanced at her out of the corner of his eye before committing to fully turning around. Satisfied that she was fully clothed, he sat back down in the chair.

"Do you know what kind of creature we're dealing with this time?" He pulled out his phone and looked at the screen, fingers poised over the keypad ready to type away.

"Taka says it's an enenra. Apparently, it's a creature made up of smoke and ash and murders people. That's all I've learned so far. As soon as I knew it was happening again, I reached out to you two."

Corey stepped forward and wrapped an arm around Ichirin's shoulders, giving a squeeze. "Don't worry. We'll figure it out. We always do. At least this time we know what we're dealing with, and it makes sense that you can do your whole smoke body thing. Have you tried to see if there's anything else you can pick up?"

Ichirin shook her head. "Not yet. When these things happen, it isn't like they send a flyer saying, 'Hi, there's a new monster in your neighborhood; here are your new powers.'"

I'm glad to see that some of my sarcasm is rubbing off on you. I like to think that after all of this time we are having a positive effect on each other.

That thought made her shake her head. As much as she appreciated Taka's insight—and very occasionally his sense of humor—it was not something she wanted to pick up on her own. It was like kuding tea, a little bit of it could be pleasant from time to time and was sometimes necessary, but regular doses of it were bitter, and it was an acquired taste.

"What if you just tried to change part of you, like your hand or something? Could you do that? Rather than your whole body?" Corey continued to give Ichirin her full attention while Hemingway scanned through pages on his phone, his eyes darting back and forth.

"Let me try."

Ichirin held up her hand in front of her face with her fingers splayed out, staring at it for a moment. She flexed her fingers, paying attention to how the tendons moved underneath her skin and how the air felt. Closing her eyes, she thought of how she transformed her body into smoke but thought of the change stopping at her elbow. She imagined a bracelet of some sort attached there, serving as a barrier that prevented the change from spreading up to her shoulder.

When she opened her eyes, her hand was dark and semi-translucent. Now that she had grown accustomed to the feeling, she became aware of the small gaps between the molecules, feeling the air inside her hand. She reached out and swung her arm at her desk, watching as her smoke hand billowed around the edge and reformed on the other side. Curious to see what would happen, she shook her hand back and forth as fast as she could manage. It retained its shape but stretched out and left smoky trails through the air.

Corey leaned forward and blew at Ichirin's hand. Ichirin jerked her arm away and backed up.

"What are you doing?"

"I wanted to see if I could make it move or swirl or something. Did it hurt?"

"No, but it feels like being stabbed, just without the pain."

13

Ichirin relaxed and held her hand up in front of her once again, examining it while Corey did the same thing on the other side.

It served as a good test, to see whether or not you had the willpower to keep it together. Just because you can handle moving around like you expect to doesn't mean you can do the same when something interferes with you. A reference body does help though.

Ichirin paused, not understanding what Taka meant. A reference body?

Enenra can take any form they want. They are smoke, entities without form. In order to have a shape, they need to will it into existence. Many of them revert to human form, but not all. Thought becomes physical form. The fact that you expect your body to move in a certain way is very strong on a subconscious level. That strength helps give the smoke shape and enhances your will.

If she understood Taka correctly, that meant she could give herself a different shape if she had the willpower to do so. The only way she'd know what she was capable of was with experimentation. Ichirin imagined her hand changing form, the gaps between the fingers disappearing and them melding together while lengthening. In her mind, she pictured herself with a blade or a conductor's wand. She pressed her fingers together, trying to force the shape into being. Nothing changed.

Maybe it would help if you picked one image and stuck with it. I'm no expert, but I imagine if something took a concentrated effort of will, flip-flopping would be detrimental.

Ichirin's forehead creased in response to the fledgling throbbing just behind her temples. She could come back to this, but for now she returned her body back to its normal shape and consistency. It took a lot less effort to become whole than it did to transmute to smoke. The changes also seemed to be getting easier, even if the mental exhaustion was stacking up. She drummed her fingers against the desk, still relieved to feel substantial.

"Okay, I think I got something. Sending you a link." Hemingway swiped several times on his phone and then pulled his chair closer to Ichirin's desk.

Snagging the back of her chair, Ichirin spun it around and dropped into it, turning on her computer as she pulled herself up to her desk. Her fingers blurred across the keyboard as she entered her credentials with a speed that could only be achieved through years of practice. She pulled up her email and opened the link Hemingway sent. He leaned forward with his elbows on the desk next to her, close enough that she felt his breath against her arm. Corey stood behind her, peering over her head at the screen.

The website came up and showed a news report about a body found in a shipping container near the West Seattle bridge. The corpse baffled authorities because all signs pointed toward the person dying of smoke inhalation, but no fires had been started in the container.

"Ladies, I believe we found our victim."

CHAPTER TWO

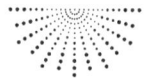

Knowing where to start their search filled the entire group with excitement. The three of them packed into Hemingway's car and drove toward the West Seattle bridge. Previous experience had taught them the sensibility of having Hemingway drive. Ichirin's powers could exert themselves at inappropriate times, and Corey driving resulted in an unwelcome shot of adrenaline for all her passengers. Granted, she had gotten them out of messes before, but totaled two cars in the process. Thankfully the insurance company covered the cost of repairs due to the freak ice storm in Seattle at the time.

Good thing you didn't have to explain why the streets were covered with ice in the middle of April. Talk about awkward. I suppose they blamed global warming.

As they traveled, Ichirin sat in the front seat and played with her powers, trying to shift her hand or just a finger back and forth between substantial and smoke. If it followed the same pattern as her previous powers, it would become more relaxed and easier the more she worked at it, like a muscle.

Just remember that muscles also get more exhausted the more you use them. Just something you might want to keep in mind.

She lowered her hand and rested it in her lap, feeling much like a chastised child. It reminded her of when her grandfather would lecture her for chewing on her fingernails. It possessed the same tone and resulting emotional impact.

That makes sense considering that I am your elder by literally hundreds of years. Nonetheless, remember I say this to keep you safe. I would not want you unable to use your abilities at a time when they were crucial to your survival. Think of it not so much an admonishment rather than concern for your well-being.

The words helped to soothe the sting, and the hunter nodded to herself as much as to the kami. His words carried wisdom, and she appreciated his concern. Anything might happen, so as with all things, balance was the key. For now, she should rest and save her abilities until she needed them.

"What are we going to do when we get there?" Corey leaned forward between the seats when she spoke.

Ichirin twisted around so that she could at least see Corey out of the corner of her vision. "The story said that the body was found last night, and the police classified it as a freak accident. Right now, we hope that means we get to check it out."

"It's still going to be trespassing."

Ichirin raised an eyebrow at Corey's statement. "And since when has that bothered you?"

Corey grinned and dropped back against the seat. "It doesn't. If anything, that makes it more fun. Gets the blood pumping. You going to come with us, Hem?"

Hemingway squirmed in his seat and tightened his hands around the steering wheel. Ichirin rested her hand on his arm and spoke before he felt compelled to do so.

"We need him in the car, ready to go in case we need to make a quick getaway. Otherwise, we either have to park far away or leave an unattended car in the middle of nowhere. We don't want that kind of attention."

She felt the tension in his arm ease as she gave her explanation, and Corey nodded in agreement with her logic. She knew

17

Hemingway well enough to know he'd go with her through a sense of duty if necessary, no matter how uncomfortable it made him. She'd rather have him somewhere safe where she wouldn't need to worry about him, but at the same time do it without harming either his pride or his sense of honor.

The group drove onto the West Seattle bridge and got off on Harbor Island, a place not designed for standard daily traffic. Large stacks of shipping containers stretched high on either side of the road, and several cranes reached into the sky and extended out over the water. Some of the sections had the containers piled three or four on top of one another in neat rows while other areas looked more like an iron maze. The lack of organization made Ichirin twitch, but she consoled herself by insisting that she just didn't know the system.

They had the road to themselves. A few industrial parking lots littered the area, most of them at least half full of parked cars. People went about their business, paying the trio no mind as they moved through their work like automations.

They probably think you're either lost or tourists, or both. That could work to your advantage.

The news article hadn't specified the location of the body, but it did provide a few pictures that served to give them a starting point. They knew to check one of the areas directly on the water with a large crane in the background. That limited their search to the east side of the island. They also knew what the container looked like and the markings on the side, but that still left the task of finding it.

One of the shipping containers stood separate from the others with space cleared on every side despite the rest of the metal crates being stacked on and flush against each other. The men and women working in that area made a point not to look at the container as they went about their business.

"I think that's it. Pull over." Ichirin tapped Hemingway on the leg.

He drifted to the side of the road and eased to a stop, leaving the car running. The wheels still crunched over the loose rocks when Corey opened the door and jumped out, tumbling as she adjusted to the movement change. Ichirin shook her head. At least she waited and didn't run off to the container on her own. Patience was not one of her friend's virtues, and never had been, but sometimes she felt that Corey didn't treat the situation with as much gravitas as it deserved.

She doesn't have your connection to the beasts and appreciate how dangerous they could be if left to their own devices.

The hunter climbed out when they stopped and turned around in the open door.

"Stay here and be ready to go in case something happens."

Hemingway nodded, checking in his mirrors even though no one else was within a hundred yards. Ichirin left him, joining up with Corey. The two of them walked around the container wall, looking at the crate that appeared ostracized from its neighbors. The symbols matched the pictures from the article.

"It's a lot of open ground, but if we time it right, I bet we can make it before anyone notices." Corey narrowed her eyes as she studied the different people walking around the open area.

What a great idea. Nothing keeps attention from being drawn like running. That's why survival lessons say the first thing you should do when you see a predator is run.

Ichirin reached out and tugged on her friend's shirt, making her turn around. "It's the middle of the day. If we walk over like we belong here, it will look less obvious. Even if they do see us, what will they say?"

When Corey didn't immediately object, her friend took the initiative to step around and walk toward the container in question. She channeled her business walk, the measured steps she took when about to enter a conference room meeting with her superiors where she needed to give a presentation. Then, just like now, she pretended that she had the space to herself. She had a job to do and would do it, no matter what obstacles stood in her way.

Her lips pressed together as she recognized the analogies to her current situation.

If anyone bothered to pay attention to her presence, no one came up to her to question it. Soon she found herself standing just inside of the cargo container, the midday sun barely able to penetrate around the back, giving it a shadowed appearance despite the bright light. The container was cleaner than she expected, with a few spots of rust and dirt that had accumulated over an unknown amount of time, but nothing unusual. She caught the faint odor of bleach cutting through the ever-present salty flavor this close to the Sound. Nothing indicated the police found a body here.

Where you expecting a chalk outline on the ground? You already knew the police classified it as something not worth investigating. Look for something subtler, something that an enenra would leave behind.

What would a creature like that leave behind? If she had to guess from her own personal experience, trails of black smoke and ash smeared against any surface that it touched. In truth, she expected the inside of the container to be caked in the soot-like material, but it seemed spotless.

Corey's footsteps echoed against the metal as she walked inside, the sound reverberating through the open space. She paused, taking a glance around without going in any farther.

"So, what do we look for?" she whispered.

"I'm not sure. Some evidence of the monster, see if we're on the right track. But I don't see any stains or anything. I expected to at least find some filth in something this old. Even without a trace of the body or the enenra, it should still look weathered and used. Don't you think so?"

Corey took a few steps in and ran her fingers along one of the walls, checking them after a quick swipe. "You're right. This place looks like someone scrubbed it up to be sold to a farmer for storage or some rich person to make one of those hobbit homes or something."

"What does that mean? Do you think the creature did this?" Ichirin wondered out loud, asking both Corey and the kami.

Unlikely. While enenra can display a limited intelligence, this requires a level of forethought unusual for such creatures. Not to mention, I'm not sure how it could complete such a task without leaving evidence of its passing. Consider what you did to your bedroom in just a matter of minutes.

"What did it say?" Corey asked. When her companion looked surprised, she continued. "Whenever Taka talks to you for a while, you get this distant look on your face, like you're listening to a podcast on your headphones and focusing on it real hard. Hemingway and I both have noticed it. You might want to be careful if it speaks to you in front of someone who doesn't know about it."

"Good to know. I didn't realize."

"Not all the time. Just when the conversation goes on a while."

I guess I should keep my responses shorter when in mixed company. I'll make a note of that.

Ichirin scrunched her face as she tried to think how Taka could make a note of something to remember later. She gave a couple of quick shakes of her head to dismiss the tangent.

"Taka said he doesn't think the enenra could've cleaned up after itself. That means one of two things. Either this death had nothing to do with the creature, and we hit a dead end…"

"Or someone else helped our quarry and did the track covering," Corey interrupted and finished the thought. "I'm betting on the latter just based on the timing. Come on. Mysterious deaths at the same time one of these smoke demons shows up?"

They're not demons! Demons are something very specific. I'm amazed at how much lore has been forgotten over the years in the name of technology. Mythology exists for a reason, and not just as parable. Granted, some of the Greek myths are more than a little far-fetched…

"But why didn't they do anything about the body?" Ichirin asked, staring down at the ground, possibly where the victim had been found. She scuffed her shoe against the floor of the container.

Corey shrugged. "Harder and more mysterious to get rid of a body? I mean, person dies due to a known cause of death. Sure, it might make some people curious, and they might ask some questions, but it doesn't look anywhere near as bad as trying to drag a body off and being caught by security or traffic cams or something like that."

"I suppose that makes sense. We should go, but let's see what we can figure out about this container: where it came from, what it was supposed to have in it, anything like that. Hem will know how to find that. We just need to get him to one of their computers."

Corey nodded, and the two of them left and walked back in the direction of the car. As soon as they were back in the open air, the hunter hesitated. Her skin crawled, and she felt like someone stared at her, but when she turned her head, no one seemed to give them any undue attention. Several people milled about, but they all looked to be involved in their own business.

Hemingway sat where they left him, continuing to twist and glance in every possible direction. Ichirin climbed into the passenger's seat and held up her hand to forestall their departure.

"Do you think you could find out anything about that shipping container? Where it came from or who shipped it or anything like that? If we wait for lunch, we could sneak in when people scatter." Hemingway would be reticent to try and break into a building, but she didn't want their only lead to slip away.

"Hang on. Let me try something first. Corey, would you open my bag and hand me my computer?"

Corey followed directions, and Hemingway set the computer up in his lap, turning it on and going to work. The passengers quieted as he talked more to himself than anyone in particular while he worked.

"Let's see, only a couple of networks around here, and only one of them with any measurable signal. I'm guessing that's theirs. It's secured, but let's see how good their network admin is." After typing a few quick sequences, he emitted a sound that was half chuckle and half sigh. "Networks are only as good as the humans who create the login credentials. And in this case, they didn't bother to change away from the defaults."

A few screens came up as he logged onto the corporate network. Some of them blinked by so fast that Ichirin couldn't register the display beyond a wall of text with some stock photography. Hemingway's voice dropped, and he whispered to himself as he became more immersed in his work.

"Right. So, their security is a joke. They have a nice easy system once you get in that lets you search for whatever you're looking for. And like that, we have the registration information for the crate. According to the spreadsheet, the container shipped from Tokyo. It was one of two. The shipper is listed as Super Freight Express…" His voice trailed off as he became absorbed with something on the screen.

"What?" Corey piped up from the back seat.

"Just that the gross weight and tare weight of the container are the same, which is really weird. That means that whatever they shipped didn't weigh anything, or at least not enough to make a difference on an industrial scale. At most, it couldn't be more than a couple of pounds. But why would someone pay for freight shipping if they weren't going to be shipping anything large? It doesn't make sense."

Except for that little thing called customs. I'm sure that customs officials don't have time to search every empty crate that comes ashore—especially with greased palms.

"It might have given them another way to get something into the US. What about the other crate? Can you find it?" Ichirin asked, trying to make sense of the different records scrolling past.

Hemingway shook his head. "According to the sheet I'm looking at, it hasn't shown up. The last record says it scanned leaving Tokyo. I would've thought it would be on the same barge, but apparently not. Unless they had an accident during shipping and lost the crate."

"In other words, we've got nothing. All we know is something shipped from Japan and another something might be sitting on the ocean floor somewhere between Seattle and Japan." With a sigh, Corey flopped against the back of the seat, her head tilted up so she stared at the ceiling.

"How much did the other crate weigh?" Ichirin asked. When Corey sat up straight and looked at her, she shrugged. "Never hurts to have more information."

"Looks like the net weight for that one was around one thousand kilograms, so a ton and change. Still not a lot for a container that size."

Ichirin raised her fingers to her mouth but caught herself before she chewed on her nails. Her hands slapped against her legs as she dropped them with force.

"It all depends what they were shipping. But none of that helps us find the creature. I think we can assume it came over in that shipment. This all adds up to an accomplice."

"What? What do you mean?" Hemingway twisted around, switching his attention from Ichirin to Corey and back again, waiting to see who would answer.

"Do you remember how I told you about leaving trails of soot whenever I touched something?"

Hemingway nodded.

"Well, I thought that if this all dealt with an enenra, some trace of it would remain inside the container. But when we went inside, we couldn't find any. Not only that, but it smelled like cleaning supplies. Someone sanitized it. I think the place was scrubbed, and the monster couldn't do that. The only logical conclusion is that someone is helping."

It also means that someone wanted it brought to Seattle. As your friend Corey would say, "That's convenient." You need to consider the possibility that someone knows about you, and it might be someone who doesn't have your best interests in mind.

The hunter felt like her role shifted from predator to prey. Her skin crawled, and she rubbed her arms while resisting the urge to glance over her shoulder. Her mind recalled the feeling of being watched as she left the shipping container.

"We're not going to find anything else here. Let's go back to the office and plan our next steps there." She tried to keep the nervousness out of her voice and hoped she sounded more confident than she felt.

If either of her friends realized her discomfort, neither one said anything. As they drove off the island and merged back onto the bridge, Ichirin kept watch for any stragglers tailing them. Until they got back onto the highway, she didn't see any moving vehicles. Maybe she was being paranoid.

It's only paranoia if you're wrong. Otherwise, it's called being prepared. I mean, your other alternative is to just pretend it isn't real and rely on your lightning-quick reactions and martial arts training... all four months of it. I vote for risking paranoia.

Despite her watchfulness, Ichirin didn't see anything untoward as they traveled back to her office. She maintained her vigil until they entered the underground parking garage. At that point, she opened up her fists that she didn't remember clenching shut. Her nails made deep imprints in the palm of her hand.

"So what do we do now?" Corey asked.

Both of her friends looked to the mythological soldier, waiting for her response.

"Research? I think that's the only thing we can do. The shipping crate is a bit of a dead end. We still don't know much about the creature, and we should be as prepared as possible for whatever happens. Maybe we can find something that will give us some clue how to deal with it."

Ichirin assumed that Taka didn't have any way to track the enenra, or he would've shared it, if for no other reason than to gloat or mock her efforts to find the monster through conventional means.

I only mock when there's something worth mocking. I don't make up situations, especially when I have my choice of material. I mean, did you see Jared in the hall before you left? I may be a little behind the times, but even I know socks with sandals is a cry for help.

It did not escape her notice that he didn't offer a direct response to her request. Ichirin's experience as a manager taught her much about how to mask the truth with subtle misdirection. Taka was a master at such techniques. She made a mental note of it.

"How are we going to find it? It's not like there's a giant cloud of smoke in the sky or a Looney Tunes-style trail to follow." Corey continued her questioning, her hands moving as she spoke.

Ichirin shrugged. "Maybe we'll get lucky and find something when we do some research? Otherwise, I don't think we can. We'll have to wait for it to reveal itself."

"What you mean is…" Hemingway paused and took a deep breath. "What you're saying is that we need to wait for the enenra to strike again."

CHAPTER THREE

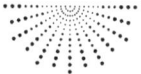

T he couch slid across the floor as Ichirin collapsed into it, despite her petite frame. Ash puffed up from the maroon fabric as she hit it, filling the air around her and making her cough and gag. It tasted like a campfire. The downside to having a physical body included the unpleasant things that could happen to it. As soon as she could breathe, she grabbed the cup of water off the side table and chugged it down in large swallows, trying to get the chalky taste out of her mouth. While it helped her throat, it did nothing for the charcoal odor in the air that felt like it permeated everything.

The floor of the room and her couch were a mess. Long streaks of black stains stretched across the tan carpet, making a gradient between her current position and the counter. Large concentrations of it surrounded her current position so it looked like she sat on top of a portable hole in a cartoon. At least she had the sense to put some towels down in the hope of saving the couch. Towels were easier to wash or replace. The fact that they were dark navy helped to hide the evidence from her efforts.

There's something charming about the fact that while trying to master supernatural powers, you still have the presence of mind to think about saving your furniture. I mean that with the utmost sincerity. Most people wouldn't even give it a second thought when they realized what they could do.

The hunter smiled and felt her chest swell in response to Taka's compliment, despite the backhanded nature of it.

Nothing backhanded about it. I meant what I said. But if we are done working on your ego, I think perhaps you should try again?

Ichirin suppressed a grumble out of habit more than anything else. Because of their relationship, Taka had a front row seat to the show that was her mental processes, but some habits refused to go away. She let her head roll back and looked at the ceiling with her arms splayed out to either side. Despite her eagerness in the car to work on her new skills, that desire had diminished as exhaustion claimed its toll. Now their roles shifted, and Taka kept driving her forward.

In the end, she agreed with his logic. Here in the comfort of her home, after making sure she wasn't followed, she felt safe from the creature as well as whoever might be helping it. Now would be the best time to push herself a little, at least until they had a lead on finding the creature.

Heaving herself up off of the couch, Ichirin took a deep breath to steady herself before transforming into smoke. The shifts felt natural now and took no more than a moment of thought. She pointed her arm at the counter, picturing in her mind what she wanted to happen. The shape of her arm faded away, losing substance until a horizontal rod of gray stretched away from her body. The rod extended, the smoke reaching out and crossing the distance between the couch and the counter. She imagined touching the vase holding a bundle of lilies resting on the far edge, next to the wall. As she stretched, small flakes of ash tumbled down to add to the stains on the carpet.

The tendril wrapped around the glass. At first, her efforts resulted in a large loop, with lots of empty space. She tightened the ring, the smoke curling in on itself until it wrapped around the narrow part of the stem. Ichirin felt it, just the same as if it were in her hand. It boggled her rational mind and didn't make sense. She didn't have nerves, she didn't have skin, yet she could feel it.

Focus. Remember that will is your shape.

Tightening her grip further, she tried to lift the vase off the table only to have it slide through her insubstantial appendage. She refused to accept defeat. She could do it. Focusing her attention on the vase again, she imagined her arm curling around it, becoming more solid and dense as she tightened her grip. If the strength of her form came from her will, she would pour every ounce of mental fortitude she had into making that grip strong.

The glass cracked a single time, and Ichirin tried to relax. But it was too late. Several rings followed the first in quick succession like a chorus of crystal bells as the vase shattered into shards that shot through the room. She cried out as she felt the shards pierce her skin and go through her body. Even though she felt the wounds, pain did not accompany them. Even the small pieces still in her arm didn't hurt as they succumbed to gravity and dripped down to the counter like tears.

Apparently there's a bonus to being insubstantial. Lucky for you! You won't have to clean bloodstains from your carpet!

She refused to respond to Taka's jest. Doing so would only encourage him, and he did not need any encouragement. She wondered if his confidence and *laissez-faire* attitude was due to his age or the fact that he had been trapped in solitude for so long before she found him.

You forgot the possibility that I might be aware of my superior status.

The comment made Ichirin roll her eyes and wrinkle her nose. She shook her head before focusing on the locket between her feet.

Making faces loses value when you are dealing with an entity that doesn't see things in the way you anticipate. Not to mention, you don't have a face right now, just a blob of smoke.

The fact that Taka knew she made a face served her purposes. Sometimes having him in her brain could be advantageous.

Her phone chimed with a text alert. The hunter transformed back into her natural state and snatched it to see who reached out. Hemingway sent her a link to a news site. She clicked on it, dreading what the content of the story would be. Her fears manifested as soon as she saw the headline.

POLICE OFFICER FOUND SUFFOCATED IN CAR.

Ichirin skimmed through the page, picking up enough of the details to realize that this had to be the creature they sought. The official story claimed the officer died in his car due to smoke inhalation. The body was found a few hours ago, and the site promised updates.

Ichirin ran to the kitchen to grab the clothes she put there to keep them clean during her practice session. While they wouldn't be able to get access to the body—especially given that it was a police officer—they could at least examine the area. Any chance of finding a trail for the enenra was worth taking; otherwise, it could strike again. She did think of one advantage to it being a high-profile murder: the accomplice couldn't cover the tracks. That hope spurned her forward as she dashed out of her house and into the garage. Just as she turned the key in the ignition, she felt something missing.

Her hands went to her neck, and she gasped. Taka. After all this time, she had grown so accustomed to his constant presence around her neck, that she didn't think to grab the necklace. She rushed back into the house, snagging it in midstride as she swung around the couch and ran back to the car.

You forgot about me. I'm not sure how to respond to that.

There wasn't anything to say in response, especially since she knew he could tell how bad she felt about it. While it may not have a body in the traditional sense, it was still a living entity—and an aged one at that—which deserved her respect. Anything else she said would be an excuse, which would be moot since the kami would recognize that.

In some ways, sharing thoughts helped to cut through a lot of the societal traps and pitfalls involved in normal interactions. It also cut down on the required dancing around topics or balancing acts that needed to be maintained with most people. If it went both ways, it could be a perfect relationship. Every so often, she received a reminder that the direct mental connection went in one direction, as if Taka had built a small temple in her mind with solid walls and spoke through a closed door.

Ichirin drummed on her steering wheel, waiting for the garage door, shooting out as soon as her car could clear the opening. She drove east to Seattle as fast as she dared, but the trip still took twenty minutes without traffic. The article didn't mention an exact location, but it did say near the West Seattle bridge. It seemed the monster had not gone far. Along the way, she sent a message to Hemingway and Corey, hoping that the voice-to-text didn't mangle her message beyond recognition.

Some messages came in while she drove, but she didn't want to look at them. It was night, and the light from her phone would illuminate her face. While the chances were slim that a cop would catch her, the risk was too great. She couldn't lose the only lead they had by getting pulled over for texting while driving.

You mean you don't think a modern officer of the law would accept the fact that you are protecting the innocent populace from a mythological Japanese monster? I can't imagine why that would be a problem. You could always turn into smoke in front of them. That would certainly get a reaction.

As soon as she got near the exit for the West Seattle bridge, Ichirin pulled over to the side of the highway and turned on her hazards. Now she was free to check her phone and see if her friends had any more information.

Both of them were en route, Corey showing her expected exuberance even in the limited medium of a text message. The eight exclamation points helped. Hemingway gave a more reserved response, as expected. He also sent a Google Map link to everyone as a suggested meeting point. He must have been a Boy Scout in a previous life, given how prepared he continued to be. She never ceased to appreciate that trait of his. She pulled up the coordinates on her phone and merged back into the early-evening traffic.

When she got to the rendezvous, she pulled over to the side of the road and parked, turning off her lights. The directions led her to an intersection almost under the bridge. The lights here were older and yellow, rather than the bright white LED street lights near her home. A fenced-off parking lot comprised a large section of the corner next to her. Up ahead, she saw blue and red lights flashing against the bridge support beams. She didn't expect to be this close to the scene of the murder, but Hemingway must have worked his magic again. He had proven himself far too capable for this to be mere happenstance.

A conflict of emotions warred in Ichirin as she grabbed her phone to resist the urge to bite on her fingernails. It creaked as the protective case bent around the edge. She slapped the device against the open palm of her other hand to try and release some of her tension.

On the one hand, she wanted to get out there as soon as possible and look for some sign of the enenra. On the other hand, waiting for her friends and seeking strength in numbers would be the sensible decision. She glanced at the shadows from the bridge blanketing most of the street and thought of how supernatural entities were not the only threat out there.

Don't forget, if anything does threaten you, you can always go all smoke on them, and that should keep you safe. Although there is that slight clothing issue to address...

While she debated the best course of action, Hemingway's car pulled up and parked in front of her. She got out and walked up to his vehicle, surprised that he beat Corey. At least with him here, it would be safer to go on ahead. His presence alone would scare off many potential dangers. She didn't want the trail getting any colder.

"Thanks for the location. How did you find it?" she asked as soon as he opened his door. She flicked her eyes over at the flashing lights, twisting her hips before she finished speaking.

"I set up an algorithm to search for anything in the greater Seattle area related to fire or smoke-related injuries and pulled in any news feed I could find. Once it found this story, I looked through social media and other sites, searching for pictures and used those to piece together an area. It wasn't too hard considering I knew when and a general idea on where."

Ah, social media, the bane of anyone's existence who wants to try to keep anything from seeing the light of day. I'm amazed how much more sees the light of day since just about everyone in the world has a camera and the ability to share what they see with everyone else. Imagine what you could do if you could direct all that power with singular will.

"Let's go look around and see if we can find anything. I know

Corey's on her way, but we'll text her. She can catch up as soon as she gets here. I don't want to lose this. I don't want to have to wait for it to strike again before we have another chance at stopping it."

Hemingway opened his mouth to protest but shut it and nodded by the end. The two of them crossed the street, walking toward the light show. A small crowd gathered, split up into small clusters of two or three people. The curious onlookers stayed just far enough away to either not be a bother or not be accosted by the police officers. Whichever reason they chose, the end result was the same. More than one had a phone out and took pictures or video.

If Ichirin didn't know what they were looking for, it would not be that impressive of a scene. Car wrecks attracted much more attention with their carnage and open displays of destruction. Here it looked like a bunch of cops standing around an empty police vehicle. There was no trace of the body, and if an ambulance had been here, it had long since left.

About half of the police officers faced outward, forming a perimeter to keep people from being too curious. The hunter walked around, maneuvering so that she could see around the police officers and look at the car beyond. Hemingway following a short distance behind her. She stopped and squinted into the limited light, trying to make out any details, but all she saw was a cop car. She needed to get closer.

Hemingway tapped her on the shoulder and handed her his phone. She looked up at him, about to ask what he was doing. He twisted it so she could see the screen, and the realization of his suggestion struck her. She held up the phone to take a picture and swiped at the screen to zoom in. While it wasn't the best view, it did give her a magnified glimpse into the front seat of the car. At first, all she saw was black leather, but when the light from one of the other vehicles flashed the right way, she saw texture against the surface of the seat.

Ash. The seat was covered in ash.

Panning the camera up, Ichirin saw a black deposit near the top of the door, marring the otherwise white surface just above the window crack. The cops might never notice the clue, but it confirmed what she and her friends had anticipated. Without a doubt, the enenra had been here.

"How long ago did he die?" she whispered to Hemingway, not pulling her eyes from the phone as she continued to scan the surface of the car.

"The report didn't give an exact time, but at least a couple of hours. It couldn't have been much longer than that, or it would've been a much bigger story. The latest update said that there's a witness."

Ichirin looked around, trying to see if the police had someone pulled aside for questioning, but came up empty. The officers who weren't engaging the public focused on the car and did a fair amount of head scratching. Truth be told, she couldn't blame them. The incident defied explanation if you weren't willing to accept the supernatural as part of your reality.

"Any updates on what the witness saw?"

A rustle behind her let her know that Hemingway shook his head. "Nothing yet. But I set it up so that I'll get a text as soon as the story updates. Can you see where it went?"

The bit of stain above the driver's side window was small, easy to miss, and not much of a track. Considering how much ash she left behind in her apartment when she experimented, it seemed unlikely that the creature had entered or left through that door. Gesturing for Hemingway to follow her, she walked around a couple questioning a police officer about what happened. He gave very short, curt responses and suggested that they leave it alone without using those words. Looking over their heads, he glared at the investigating duo, issuing a silent warning to stay away.

The pair of them curved around the vehicle, stopping whenever they had a new angle so Ichirin could examine the car with Hemingway's phone. They made it all the way around to the rear of the car before she found something.

Below the trunk of car, ash coated the bumper in several thick streaks. Her mouth hung slack as she saw the sheer volume of ash left behind. Even when she walked around her apartment, the amount of ash left in her wake was paltry compared to what pooled on the rear of the vehicle. The material was also far blacker than anything she saw in her apartment. For some reason she couldn't explain, she knew it would be cold. Staring at it made a shiver run down her spine strong enough that Hemingway put a hand on her shoulder to give a comforting squeeze.

At the risk of stating the obvious, I think it's safe to say you found your trail.

"Look." It was the extent of what Ichirin could put into words as she handed Hemingway his phone and pointed at the back of the car.

He stammered for a second, then swallowed before trying again. "If I had any doubts, I don't anymore."

"What are you staring at?"

Corey's sudden question made both of them jump, and Hemingway dropped his phone to the pavement with a loud crack as it bounced. It took Ichirin a moment to catch her breath as she put a hand on Corey for balance. Her friend gave a tentative smile. She mouthed the word "sorry" while the other two recovered.

"It's fine. We're okay, we're fine. We were just a little focused," Ichirin said.

I have to admit, I'm as shocked as you that your friend managed to be so quiet in her approach. Even if you were focused, I wouldn't say you were oblivious to your surroundings. I expected her to make more noise when I saw her approaching.

The hunter hesitated. If Taka saw Corey coming, why didn't he give her some sort of warning? Did he stay silent because he recognized her? She waited a moment, but Taka didn't respond to her mental inquiry.

"So, what are you looking at? Did you find it?" Corey's voice pitched up at the end of her sentence, her grin deepening.

After examining his phone and brushing it off, Hemingway handed it to her. Once again, she mouthed the word "sorry" when she saw the crack in the cover. He shrugged and pointed at the car.

"Look at the back bumper. It has stains like those that Ichirin makes when she..." He paused as he searched for the words and gave a quick glance to his friend. "Does her smoke thing."

Corey used the phone to zoom in and see for herself. She let out a whistle when she saw the tracks. Panning with the camera, she searched the ground between their position and the back of the car. Ichirin saw what she was doing and looked around without the aid of the phone, trying to find any trail they could follow.

"Over there!"

Corey didn't waste time pointing. She broke into a run, forcing her companions to sprint to keep up with her. Their sudden motion caught the attention of one of the police officers, but he was still engaged with the couple asking too many questions for his liking.

Before they reached the spot, Ichirin saw what Corey had noticed. The trail was faint and mixed with both skid marks and the loose pebbles of pavement that came with a road showing its age, but it existed. When they were only a few strides away, she caught the burnt odor on the air that served as an undercurrent to the rest of the city smells.

As soon as she reached the edge, Corey dropped to a knee, sliding across the pavement and scraping her jeans against the surface with a grinding, shredding sound. Reaching forward, she ran her fingers through the ash, picking up the particles and rubbing them together in front of her face as if she could determine something from a close inspection of the particles. Both companions came up beside her, panting, with Hemingway resting his hands on his knees.

So, about that whole working on your cardio thing?

The hunter didn't feel that winded, but she still gulped down air more than she thought she should. Her excitement at finding a clue they could follow helped to push that concern aside. If they followed this, they might find the monster before it struck again. Crouching down next to her friend, she got a closer look.

"You can see it's two different paths," she explained, half to herself and half to her friends. "It looks like a single trail from far away, but up close, you can see the two separate routes almost touching each other."

Corey nodded, getting up and taking a stride to follow the trail. Only Hemingway's hand on her shoulder pulled her up to a stop. She whipped around, a questioning look on her face. Even though Ichirin still felt the effects of her previous sprint, she found herself siding with Corey this time.

Hemingway shook his head. "Just hold on a moment. We don't want to go running off after this thing without thinking about it. It has killed two people now. It's dangerous!"

"Which is why we need to find it," Ichirin insisted, peeling Hemingway's hand off Corey's shoulder.

The restraint removed, Corey looked at the one giving the orders. Her friend gave a single nod, and the athletic woman took off running parallel to the bridge. Ichirin followed at a steady clip, a pace she knew she could maintain for an extended period of time. Hemingway thundered along behind her, the sound of his heavy tread accompanying his heavy huffs.

The path they followed was straight, unbending in any way, and uncaring for obstacles. More than once, the group had to scamper around parked cars or find a way around a fenced-off lot. Traces of the creature's passing clung to the chain links. In her imagination, she pictured a plume of smoke traveling parallel to the ground and barreling through anything in its way as easily as if the barriers weren't there.

The trail led them to the brick wall of a three-story building with barred windows on the first floor. A couple of the windows on the third floor were broken, with a tarp taped up behind them on the inside of the building. This side didn't have a door, and the trail led them to one of the barred windows. No light shined on the other side.

Corey stood next to the building, waiting for the others to arrive. She leaned against the wall, her arm next to the window that the creature must have used to enter and exit the building. She tapped against the wall with her hand a few times before giving it a solid slap.

"We have to go inside. Or at least check around the perimeter to see if the creature came out the other side. I mean, it's been traveling in a straight line like a laser. It's a pretty good guess that there's an exit opposite this one. I don't think the creature's overly smart or sneaky."

Things never go wrong when someone makes an assumption like that. I mean, it went so well for the Persians at Salamis.

Ichirin found herself slipping into the tone of voice she saved for team meetings. "Check around the perimeter, but be careful. If you see something, just run. Don't hesitate. We still don't know how to deal with the monster."

Corey took off at a sprint while the others followed at a stroll, catching their breath and not speaking. As they neared the corner, the burnt smell no longer lingered on the air, helping to mask the scents of the city. In this section of town, the air carried a heavy odor of oil and exhaust with no discernible source. When the breeze picked up, the salt from the nearby water provided a refreshing interruption.

The back side of the building faced a narrow alley with enough room for a single car to drive down between the dumpsters pushed flat against the walls. The lights from the bottom of the bridge couldn't reach here, making the path thick with shadows cast by the building. Ichirin had seen worse streets, but nonetheless, this one did little to set her nerves at ease. The fact that they pursued a creature made of smoke and able to change its shape at will made the darkness that much more intimidating. She found herself staring at every shadow, her entire body taut, ready to jump into action at the slightest movement.

Behind her, Hemingway's feet scuffed against the pavement, and he reached out to put a hand on her shoulder. She felt his nervousness through that connection as his fingers tightened, and she knew that he was just as scared as she was, if not more. Knowing he shared her fears helped to steel her nerves. Corey seemed immune to the overbearing aura as she swerved around the far corner.

As soon as they stepped into the darkened side street, it felt like the temperature dropped several degrees. Ichirin shivered, bringing her arms up to rub them through her thin jacket. Being this close to the water didn't help. She wished she had thought to bring a heavier coat, something she had to take full responsibility for. She knew where they were heading before she left the house.

In your defense, you did have a little bit on your mind at the time and your singular thought was finding the creature as fast as possible. You even forgot me for a moment, and I like to think that I rank above a jacket in importance.

Once again, a pang of guilt washed through Ichirin for her earlier actions. One corner of her mind wondered how long Taka would milk that accident. He knew how she felt, which also meant he would know when his guilt-tripping would start to trespass into annoyance. Come to think of it, their arrangement made for the perfect recipe for maximizing the amount of guilt he could elicit—he would know the moment that pushing the matter had diminishing returns.

When Taka didn't respond, it spoke volumes.

She picked up her pace. Her fear of the alley motivated her, but she also wanted to make sure Corey was safe. Having her out of sight heightened Ichirin's anxiety. She trusted that her friend wouldn't go too far without them, but sometimes her lack of self-preservation became apparent.

What she saw as she came around the corner made her skid to a stop so that her shoes scuffed on the sidewalk, and she put a hand out on the wall to keep from falling over. Hemingway ran into her and had to help hold her up, but he froze as his gaze followed hers.

Corey stood in front of the windows, crouched down and looking at more of the black ash pooled near the edge of the building. Just behind her billowed a large dark cloud, rolling like a storm in a movie, with a human shape in the center of it.

CHAPTER FOUR

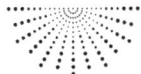

The enenra billowed over Corey and behind her, stretching up to the bottom of the second-story windows. The smoke around the human form shifted and swirled, like an aerosol whirlpool. The creature's head had no hair, but did have a face, somewhat angular with well-pronounced cheekbones. The creature had empty dark cavities where the eyes should be, but based on the way it stared at the woman in front of it, it had no difficulty seeing. It had two long arms that stretched down to the base of the cloud, lost in a general haziness of smoke where one would expect the legs to be. Given the size of the creature, it should have blocked out the light from the street lamps, but whether it was due to its nature or some mystical property, the entity cast no shadow.

And Corey seemed oblivious to its malevolent presence.

For the moment, the creature appeared to study her, watching without moving or making any threatening gestures. Adrenaline flooded through Ichirin's system, and her entire body trembled. Some part of her wanted to call out and rush forward, but then she thought of predators and their response to movement. How did supernatural creatures fit into that natural law?

"Corey," she hissed. "Corey!"

Corey looked up and gestured for the others to come join her. Hemingway shook his head back and forth quickly, the rest of his body unmoving. Corey's brow knit together, and she stood up straight, brushing off her hands as she walked over. The monster watched her walk to the building corner. It drifted forward, just a few steps behind her, drips of ash falling from its form as it moved.

"What's wrong with you two? I found more ash, but it's weird. It looks like it's piled around the window and not running off in a trail."

"Look behind you," Ichirin whispered.

The seriousness in her tone made Corey glance out of the corners of her eyes as she twisted around, her knees bent and shifting her weight to the balls of her feet. As she faced the sentient cloud of smoke, she stood up straight and scratched at the base of her neck. The enenra leaned forward, putting its face so close to Corey's that their noses almost touched. It looked like she could exhale and disperse the cloud.

"Very funny, you two. Trying to make me jump?" Corey turned back around, her hair whipping through the insubstantial creature, which reformed as soon as the strands cleared through.

"Um..." Hemingway stammered and had to swallow before he could continue talking. "The enenra's right there."

Corey turned around and held out her hands to either side. "Where?"

Without any warning and before anyone could stop her, Corey walked back to the window, stepping through the smoke entity. It didn't inhibit her movement in the slightest, and the creature reformed without any apparent issues. Its face and arms sank into the cloud only to reform on the opposite side so it faced Corey. It drifted after her once again. Ichirin took a single step, and the ash face whipped around. The creature coiled like a spring, ready to launch. It narrowed its eyes as it glared at the hunter.

She froze, hoping the monster would go back to ignoring her. Its mouth opened, but no sound came out. It rose taller, twisting around to focus on her. Its mouth opened wider, far beyond what a natural creature could accomplish. The smoke form rose taller and thickened, blocking out the light and making it impossible to see through.

I think you caught its attention.

The entity lurched forward, shifting into a solid column of blackness and hurtling toward the latest threat. It slammed into her chest, driving her to the ground. She rolled as soon as she fell backward, tumbling over her left shoulder and absorbing some of the impact. She landed flat on the ground on her stomach.

Hemingway rushed forward, spurred into action with a shout when he saw his friend in danger. The enenra once again took on the shape of a cloud with a human torso, and Hemingway lunged at the creature's face. His fist passed through the smoke, making the human stumble forward and pass through the other side when he met no resistance. The monster curled around itself.

It lifted an arm and pointed a hand at Hemingway, the arm extending until it wrapped around his throat and picked him up on his toes. Corey rushed over and grabbed Hemingway, trying to drag him down. When that didn't work, she flailed in the air in front of him, her arms passing through the tendril with no effect.

Smoke reached up from the collar, twisting curls sliding up his face and pouring into his mouth, cutting off his strangled protests. He tried to cough, but the black arm pulsed with malevolent power, forcing itself into his lungs and making him unable to breathe.

Ichirin pushed herself up off the ground and charged, changing into smoke in midstride. She kept her humanoid shape and slammed into the enenra with as much strength as she could muster, fueled by her rage.

The impact forced the beast back, and its arm uncoiled from Hemingway, dropping him to the ground on all fours, coughing. Corey rushed to his side, wrapping an arm across his shoulders while watching the fight.

The enenra twisted to square up against Ichirin just as she brought her fist around and slammed into its face. The creature's mouth opened, and its eyes widened as it pulled back from her assault. But the hunter continued to advance, relying more on power and rage rather than any skill or talent, driving forward until her feet left the ground and the bottom half of her body became as formless as the quarry.

The two smoke entities moved across the street until they slammed into the building wall. Ichirin tried to slam her fist into the monster, and it parted in front of her, making her punch the structure. The bricks cracked, and chunks fell, shattering against the sidewalk. The creature flowed around her, whipping down to the ground and scattering like a dust cloud. She turned, trying to see where it fled, but it was a vain effort. While she searched, her smoke reformed into a humanoid body and drifted down until her feet rested on the ground.

Now that the battle had finished, Hemingway and Corey walked over, his arm draped across her as she lent him support. He still coughed, but with less effort and frequency. The hunter gave up on the search, approaching her friends.

"You chased it off. I thought... I thought I was going to die." Hemingway's voice was softer than Ichirin could ever recall.

She reached out in an attempt to comfort her friend, but he recoiled from her smoke arm. As soon as she saw his reaction, she jerked back. She opened her mouth to apologize, but no sound came out. She settled for holding out her hands in front of her in a plaintive gesture.

"It's okay. Just a little freaked out at the moment." He forced a smile.

Hemingway stood up straight on his own, leaving Corey free. She raised an eyebrow, but he waved her off. Her shoulders slumped as she walked over to the pile of clothes discarded where Ichirin changed shape. She picked up the bundle and cradled them against her chest on her way back. She crouched down to lay the garments on the ground at her friend's feet. She and Hemingway both turned around, forming a wall as best as they could with their bodies in case someone walked around the corner.

Glancing around to check for any strangers, the mythological soldier crouched low behind her friends and resumed her physical form. She shivered as soon as the cold air struck her bare skin, and she jerked her clothes over her body. Her teeth chattered against each other, and Hemingway took off his jacket, reaching behind him without looking to offer it to her. Once she finished pulling on her own garments, she took it from him and wrapped it around her body. It was thick leather and blocked out the gusts of wind far better than the cotton one she wore. Her hands shook as she clasped the locket around her neck.

On the plus side, we know you can hurt it.

As practical and compassionate as always, it still was a relief to hear Taka's voice in her mind. She pressed her palm against the locket, pushing it against her skin. Despite all his quirks, she appreciated having him around and knowing that—to some extent—she could count on him. When he didn't respond with a witticism or sarcastic comment, she took that for as much sentiment as she would ever receive from him.

"Is it safe to turn around?" Hemingway asked.

"Yes, I'm clothed. Thank you for standing guard."

Even though Ichirin had donned her clothes, she still clutched Hemingway's jacket tight around her body. When he turned to face her, he didn't ask for it. She offered, but he gave her a gentle smile and shook his head.

"What happened to it?" Hemingway glanced back, as if he expected the enenra to manifest behind him and pick him up once again.

"I don't know. After I hit the creature, it scattered. The thing dropped to the ground and broke up into lots of little wisps that spread out like water on the sidewalk. I don't think I won. I think I just caught the enenra by surprise. I don't think it expected to run into anything that could do anything."

While they spoke, Ichirin noticed that Corey was far from her usual hyperactive and engaging self. Her head hung low, and her shoulders slumped forward. She wasn't sulking or avoiding eye contact, but it was as close to it as her former roommate had ever seen in the years they had known each other. She had seen her friend exhausted before, but this was different. Corey looked crushed.

"There's nothing you could have done," Ichirin said, opening Hemingway's jacket enough to reach out and try to take Corey's hand. "The creature is made of smoke. I don't even know why I could affect it, but you can't blame yourself that you couldn't."

Corey shook her head. "It's not that. I couldn't even see it!"

At first, Hemingway just stared at her, unmoving. Ichirin was about to ask her how she could miss the giant smoke creature but caught herself. As she thought about it, that piece made everything click together. It explained why Corey didn't respond when the beast hovered over her. If she couldn't see it, and it provided no resistance, of course she would have walked right through it.

If she had any doubts about the narrative, the crushing disappointment on Corey's face was more than convincing enough.

Hemingway broke the uncomfortable silence. "How is that even possible? It was right there! It was gigantic and blocking out the street lights when it..." His sentence trailed off as his hand rose up to his neck and rubbed it.

Corey pressed her lips together and said nothing.

Did the enenra have some power to hide itself from people?

There are rumors. It has been said that not everyone could see the enenra, that only those who were worthy to do battle with the creature could make out its form. What exactly they meant by worthy is up for debate, of course. Especially since we are talking about a society that you would consider positively archaic considering current technology.

Knowing that some people might be unable to see the creature seemed like something Taka should have brought up at the beginning. She felt like this proved that while he could be insightful and helpful, his help was unreliable at best. What if she had fallen into the group considered unworthy to witness it?

I had no doubts that you would see it, and that's as far as I thought the thing through. I didn't even consider that one of your friends might not be worthy or pure of heart or whatever the qualification is. The harsh reality that we both know is you're the one who has to deal with the entity. While they do serve a purpose, they've never been the killing blow. They are the support. You are the hunter.

Nevertheless, Ichirin maintained that she required information like this before beginning the hunt, rather than have it catch them all by surprise in the middle of a conflict. Even if Taka didn't care about the safety of her friends, it must realize that she'd do anything to protect them, so such gaps of information endangered her as well.

As you command, so shall it be done. After all, I but live to serve you.

The amount of sarcasm dripping off Taka's statement could have drowned her, but it did not surprise her. He got sour whenever she tried to order him around and sometimes when she suggested things could be done a certain way. She struggled to maintain a relationship where he was happy. When his mood was positive, he was much more forthcoming with information and suggestions, even if his mannerisms could be abrasive.

The possibility of silence when she needed answers terrified her.

Pushing those thoughts aside, she turned her attention to Corey. Ichirin pulled Corey close and wrapped her arms around her friend.

"It's nothing you did. Taka said some people just can't see the monster. It's always been that way. I don't know if that makes you one of the lucky ones or not, because the creature is terrifying."

"But I can see you when you go all smoky and stuff." Corey spoke into her friend's shoulder, her own arms coming up as she fell into the embrace.

"It's not the same. I don't know why, but I can promise you that. I'm still human, not one of these myths brought to life. I just get to do some of the same things they can do. Or maybe it's something they choose to do, and I haven't learned how yet. I don't know. I just know that it doesn't mean you failed. You couldn't have done anything."

After a moment, Corey nodded and pulled away, her smile starting to return. Ichirin wanted to spend more time comforting her friends, but the monster would not wait for them to recover. They had a job to do, no matter how unpleasant it might be to continue, and every lost moment gave their adversary time to escape or plan.

"So, we know the thing ran away, but how do we find it? There's no more trail to follow. When it scattered, the wisps that curled off were too small to leave something behind."

Now that she had something to focus on, Corey burst into motion. While she didn't quite have her customary bounce to her step, the movement seemed to help. She walked over to the window where she crouched before. Reaching up and through the bars, she slid her fingers across the surface of the outer sill. As the others came up to her, she showed them her hand. The tips were covered in a thick layer of ash.

"It's built up here quite a bit, but there's no trail. I don't know what that means, but I would guess that we might find some answers on the other side of this window. At the least, I think it's worth checking out. Unless we happened to get here at the same time that it did, I think it was waiting here."

Ichirin nodded her agreement. "And based on how fast it can move, we couldn't have caught up to it. It murdered the police officer hours ago. You're right. We need to get inside the building. We don't have time to waste. The enenra ran off, so we should take advantage of this moment before it gets back."

When she moved to walk toward the entrance, Hemingway stood in her way. He didn't make any movement to stop her, but his sheer size barred the path forward and forced her to come up short.

"We can't do that. We can't just break in. That's trespassing. Breaking and entering. Not to mention the whole bunch of police officers just a few blocks away!"

"Would you rather tell them that they need to enter the building because there might be a smoke monster inside? Have them try to shoot it? I'm sure that will go well. And that's if they can even see it in the first place." Corey stepped forward with each sentence, forcing Hemingway to either push back or retreat before her. He chose the latter option.

"Corey, stop. Hem's right. It's trespassing and dangerous."

Her words had the desired effect, and Corey relented. Ichirin understood her companion's motivations. She guessed her long-term friend was still trying to find a way to cope with feelings of helplessness. But that didn't excuse her behavior, and they couldn't start fighting amongst themselves now, not when they were on the beast's home territory, or lair, or whatever it would be called.

"But, at the same time, we can't just walk away," Ichirin continued. "This thing is dangerous, and we are the only ones who stand a chance of doing anything about it. If we walk away now, it gets to make the next move, which might mean another dead body. We make that choice. I know it isn't ideal, but we knew going into this we might have to do some uncomfortable things. I won't ask you to do anything you don't want to, but I need to do this. I can't let it get away."

Hemingway took a deep breath and closed his eyes. Despite the urgency of the situation, Ichirin waited for him to formulate a response. She needed his support.

"I think you're right. You are the only one who can do anything about it. I couldn't touch it, but it could..." Hemingway coughed and rubbed his neck once again. When he next spoke, his words came out in a quick stream without pauses. "I mean, I'll still go with you and help however I can, like keeping watch or dealing with more normal problems like the cops."

Ichirin felt a warmth spread through her as Hemingway displayed his customary sense of honor. He was a knight of sorts, even if he was ill suited to the role in this particular arena. It was one of the reasons why she came to him when the craziness first entered her life.

Like I said, hunter and support crew.

The fact that Taka didn't make a sarcastic quip made it clear that the earlier exchange still rankled him. She'd have to make up to him later, but for now, she needed to focus on the task at hand. The entity could return at any moment, and they had spent precious minutes discussing a plan of action.

"I need to get inside."

This time when Ichirin took a step, Hemingway moved to the side, making room for her on the sidewalk. Both he and Corey fell into line behind her, letting her take the lead as she marched up to the entrance to the building. The doors faced the main road and were set into a small alcove, which didn't give enough space for one person to seek shelter from the weather. A faint light flickered around the edges of

47

what once had been a window but was now a series of boards nailed to the door. The door had a single handle without a latch and a keyhole for a deadbolt lock. Small pieces of trash—fast food wrappers and empty Starbucks cups—littered the small entrance with a thin path through the center. The smell of rotten food wafting up from below made the hunter's head spin.

Ichirin tugged on the handle, and the door rattled against the frame but didn't open. She gave it another tug just to make sure that it wasn't stuck in the frame, but she felt the bolt holding it in place. With a frustrated grunt, she shoved the door, which proved to be just as productive.

"You didn't really think it would be that easy, did you?" Corey asked.

"I was hoping for a nice change."

Corey backed up from the entrance, craning her neck back and looking at the upper floors. Her friend moved to join her, also tilting her head back and trying to see what she was looking at. Corey pointed with her chin, gesturing at the second story.

"Some of those windows are broken. I'm pretty sure I could climb up there and get through, then come down and unlock the door from the inside."

"You can see glass shards stuck in the frame. Trying to clear those out while hanging onto the wall is too risky. Not to mention anyone driving by would see you. I said I'd help, but some things are too far. Maybe we could pry some bars off one of the first-floor windows?" Hemingway reached out and grabbed one of the bars, giving it an experimental tug. It proved to be just as malleable as the door.

"Look, we're running out of time. While you think of another option, I'll start climbing. I'll give you that the alley would be a smarter choice. Less likely someone will come along and see me doing my Spiderman impression."

Ichirin reached out and grabbed Corey by the arm as she turned to run around the building. "I should go in. It would be safer. Plus, if the monster's in there, I'm the only one who can fight it."

She hated saying that because of how superior it sounded in her own ears, but that didn't change the facts. While Corey was the better athlete and the better fighter by far, she couldn't even see their quarry. She squeezed the other woman's arm with more force than she meant to as she thought that her friend might be sacrificing herself if she went in alone. She didn't dare voice the fear.

"I'm not letting you fight that thing by yourself." Corey eased her arm free.

If you went ahead with that plan, you also wouldn't have me by your side. You would be completely alone, with no one and nothing to fall back on. Do you really think you're ready for that?

Ichirin's throat felt dry, and she forced herself to swallow. True, she had emerged successful against the enenra once, but she caught it by surprise. That wouldn't happen again. The entity knew she could hurt it. It would be prepared this time and would throw everything it had at her. The powers that she inherited were just a poor imitation of what it was capable of. Not only that, but it had far more experience than she could ever hope to gain. What chance did she really have in a direct confrontation?

Corey took the silence for assent and flashed a smile before running back to the corner of the building. Ichirin felt Hemingway as he stepped up behind her, a comforting aura enveloping her like a warm wave in the otherwise cold ocean. She leaned into him, and he wrapped an arm around her.

"We've got your back, no matter what. You know that even if I am worried about things and raise some concerns, I still support you, right?"

The question seemed foolish to her. How could she doubt his sincerity and loyalty? She started to say as much when her phone rang. Pulling away from Hemingway, she fished it out and saw that it was Corey.

"Is something wrong? Are you okay?"

Corey grunted on the other end of the line and let out a quick breath before speaking. "Yeah, I'm working my way up to the window now. Just thought that maybe..." She grunted again. "Maybe I'd call you that way if anything does happen, you'll know. Waiting is the worst, right?"

Ichirin turned the phone to speaker and held it out between her and Hemingway so they both could listen.

"Just focus on climbing right now. Let us know when you're inside."

After a few more grunts, the sound of crashing glass came through the line.

"Are you okay?" Ichirin asked.

"Holy shit…"

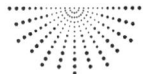

"What? What is it? Corey?" Ichirin turned to look up at the windows, trying to calculate the quickest way to her friend.

"It's okay. I'm fine. A little cut up, but I'm okay," Corey whispered. "There's people sleeping up here. Lots of them. At least I think they're sleeping?"

"What do you mean? Like you broke into someone's apartment?" Hemingway leaned forward and kept his voice low, matching Corey's discretion.

"No, I don't think so. There's way too many people and not much stuff. They look homeless or like squatters or something. They…" Her voice cut off.

The two friends made eye contact, holding their breath and not wanting to risk making too much noise. She didn't know how the people would react if they woke up to a stranger in their midst among a pile of broken glass. She didn't want to have Corey find out.

They heard some rustling and a couple of coughs close together, but that was it. At least no one shouted or screamed. But the tension made Ichirin's hand shake, the phone trembling in her grasp.

"Sorry about that. Needed to get out of the room. I think someone was waking up. They're definitely asleep. I'm in a hallway now, looking for the stairs."

A car drove by, its headlights washing over the two on the street as it drove past. The interruption made Ichirin realize that her singular focus on the phone meant she wasn't keeping watch on their surroundings. A man stood next to one of the pillars, watching her and Hemingway. He had two or three jackets on, the top one riddled with tears and patches. When she noticed him, he continued to stare, not trying to hide his scrutiny. Goosebumps spread up and down her arms, and she felt like she was trespassing.

You have been this entire time. It's just now you feel like you're in some-one's space. It has become more personal and less abstract. But if the enenra is in there, or based there, do you have any choice? At least I don't think he's the type to call the police.

Ichirin handed her phone over to Hemingway, who took it with a quizzical expression. She used her eyes to indicate the homeless man.

"I'm going to talk to him. See if he's seen anything and let him know that we're the good guys."

"Do you want me to go with you?"

"No. Keep in touch with Corey and make sure she's okay. I don't want him knowing we have someone inside. If this is his shelter or his home, I doubt that would go over well. I'll just be across the street. Shout if she gets into trouble."

Hemingway nodded and kept watch as the hunter crossed the street toward the stranger. She walked straight up to the man, keeping her hands out of her pockets despite the chill. She didn't want to give him any reason to be alarmed. He stood and watched her approach, his eyes the only thing that moved.

He looked to be in his forties, but the weathering of his skin made it difficult to judge. Thick bristles covered his face, not enough to be considered a full beard but enough to show he had no interest in shaving. The hairs were white as often as dark, both on his face and on top of his head. His top coat was worn completely through in several places, and the next layer did not seem any more intact. He exuded a stench of sweat, salt, and other things that Ichirin would rather not think of. His eyes were clear, if bloodshot and with heavy bags under them.

"Hi, I'm Ichirin." She paused to give the man the opportunity to respond, but he showed no inclination to do so. "Do you know that building over there? Is it where you live?"

He barked out a laugh, a reaction that caught her off guard. "Used to."

"What do you mean?"

"I mean used to. Slept there, no more."

Ichirin turned to check on Hemingway, half-expecting their quarry to be towering over him. He hunched over, speaking into the phone. She turned back to the stranger.

"Why not?"

The man shuddered, and his skin paled. His entire body shuddered, and his eyes widened as he looked at her, pressing the importance of what he was about to say. "Death lives there now."

The hunter's heart beat faster, and her breath caught for a moment, forcing her to lick her lips before she could speak again. "You've seen it?"

The man nodded slowly. "Yeah. Can't forget it. It just showed up today. Stood there and watched us. Spoke to someone and then flew off. I left. Didn't want to be around when it came back. It's still in there, isn't it?"

Ichirin nodded. "I need to know—can you remember who it talked to?"

"You came here 'cause of it, didn't you?"

"Yes. We're here to stop it."

He laughed again, this time more than a single mirthless chuckle. "You can't stop it. It's fucking death, the grim reaper, angel of death. It can't be stopped. It's gonna kill everyone in there."

She needed the man to focus. She might be able to figure out the identity of the accomplice, or at least get some clues to start that angle of their investigation. That wasn't going to happen if he succumbed to panic.

"It's not death. It's a creature called an enenra. It looks like smoke.

That's all it is, smoke and ash. It's dangerous, but I can stop it. I need to know, who did it talk to?"

"You're one of them! You can talk to it, too! You came here to drag me back in."

He backed up a step, lifting a hand in a warding gesture. His eyes were wide enough to show white around the entire iris. She took a step forward and held her hands out in what she hoped was a pleading and non-threatening gesture.

"Please. Just tell me who it talked to. I need to know."

For a brief moment, he stood frozen to the ground, staring at the woman. His gaze darted between her and the building. He opened his mouth but then clamped it shut and shook his head. Ichirin could feel his sanity slipping away. If he had seen the monster, she couldn't blame him. Something like that would terrify anyone.

"You can help me stop it." She took another small step forward.

That motion proved too much for the stranger. He whipped around and ran, fleeing down the shadowy street as fast as his legs would move. He tripped over a curb, scampering up to his feet and continuing his mad dash.

The hunter didn't bother to follow. Even if she could catch up to him, it would only terrify him more. She cursed herself, trying to think how she could have played it different. He could have given her something, a critical clue that could have helped her identify the accomplice.

Even if he had told you something, he's not the most reliable witness. For all we know, he saw someone talking in their sleep when the enenra happened to be around. Don't beat yourself up for this. We have more important things to worry about right now.

Despite Taka's reassurance, she continued to watch the man as he ran away, waiting until he ducked around a building and disappeared from view. She knew that the monster had someone helping it, and according to the homeless man, that person might be inside the building.

If they were, they'd recognize Corey as an outsider, even if the beast didn't.

That thought in her mind, Ichirin bolted across the street, making a beeline for Hemingway. As she got close, she heard Corey.

"...stairs down. I'm heading there now, and I'll see if I can unlock the door."

Hemingway raised an eyebrow, asking questions without saying a word, but she shook her head. She'd talk to him about it later. She wanted to focus on Corey right now.

"Well, that sucks. Door's locked on both sides. Need a key unless you can pick a lock and haven't told anyone about it. There has to be a way in and out. No way these people have a key. I'm going to poke around."

"Be careful," Ichirin hissed into the phone. "Someone in there might be working with the enenra."

"What do you mean?"

Hemingway's face indicated that he had the same question as Corey.

"I talked to someone who used to sleep there. He said he saw the monster talking to someone before it went out to hunt. No idea who it is though. He ran away before I could get more information."

"Right, so in addition to being worried about pissing off a bunch of homeless for crashing their pad, having a mystical creature that I can't see, I also have to worry about some high priest ordering the thing around like a pet hellhound?"

At this point you could remind her that she volunteered to go inside.

"Get out. We'll find another way," Ichirin offered.

"No. It'd be too hard to get out the way I came in anyway. I'll find another route. I think I saw more stairs going down to a sublevel or something. Maybe that's how they're getting in and out."

Not knowing what else to do, Ichirin paced back and forth in front of the entrance. Her hands balled up into fists, and she had to shake her arms to loosen them. She could transform into smoke and at least act as an escort or watcher for her friend. But for now, she decided to trust in Corey. If there was any trouble, at least they'd know right away with the phone. If that call dropped for any reason, she wouldn't hesitate.

There is one way I could go with you, even when you changed your form. If you give me control, then I wouldn't be bound to the stone in the locket.

No. That was not an option at this point. It might become necessary, but for right now, the thought of being a passenger in her own body was too terrifying to consider.

"For crying out loud, go around to the other side of the building, you two. The only side we didn't check yet." Corey's voice was normal volume, no longer couched as a whisper.

The two on the street walked around to the fourth side of the building. Once they were there, they saw the small half windows inset into the sidewalk. The building had a partial sublevel, at least on this side. The wells had bars over them, and more than one was covered with either cardboard, wood, or some combination of the two. But, a couple of them were still intact. Squatting down and peering through the bars and glass, Ichirin saw a flashlight beam cut through the darkness.

"I see her. At least I think that's her. Kinda hard to say," Ichirin called back to Hemingway.

"Yeah it's me." The beam of light shifted and aimed at the window, blinding Ichirin and making her drop back with a yelp. The beam lowered. "Sorry, my bad. Anyway, I'm betting one of these windows is loose, and that's how they're getting in and out. I'm walking down the line trying to figure out which one it might be. There's no one down here, just a bunch of junk."

Corey went to the windows, continuing her search until she found one that squeaked as it opened wide. Hemingway ran over to it, tucking the phone into his pocket so he could grab the bars in both hands. With a grunt, he lifted with his legs as hard as he could.

And the grate came flying up, not bolted to anything.

He fell to the ground, the security cover landing on his shin and making him hiss in pain through clenched teeth. Dragging his foot out from underneath the metal, it scraped against the pavement, making a grinding sound loud enough to be heard blocks away.

So much for being quiet and subtle.

Rushing over to the opening, the hunter held out a hand to help

Corey climb out of the building, but the other woman shook her head. Instead, she gestured for the others to come join her. Glancing around to make sure that the noise hadn't drawn any unwanted attention, Ichirin climbed down through the window. Corey helped her drop to the ground.

The sublevel was small and cramped with piles of junk, just like Corey had indicated. Most of it was discarded tools and building material, either used for construction or repairs. It was a chaotic collection of piles of unmatched wood, a few chewed up blankets covered in dust, screws scattered across the floor, and many pieces that Ichirin didn't know what purpose they served. The limited light coming from the window made it difficult to see beyond a few feet from the wall. Corey held her flashlight pointed at the wall. Despite the fact that it fit in the palm of her hand, it produced a squint-inducing blueish-white beam.

Hemingway came over to the window, still rubbing his shin where the bars had landed on him. He peered around the room as best as he could. He turned around, entering feet first so he could pull the bars back into place as he dropped to the ground. The metal scraped again, and their leader winced as the sound echoed around her in the cramped space. The three of them paused, straining to hear any sounds from the building occupants.

Despite her fears, no one came running down the stairs to investigate the noise. Perhaps in a building like this, they expected people to come and go whenever they pleased, and they had grown accustomed to the sound.

"Now we just need to get to the room where we saw the ash." Ichirin kept her voice to a whisper, not wanting to make any more noise than they already had. She gestured to her left. "It was on the first floor, somewhere against that wall."

The others nodded, and Corey walked over to the stairs, clicking off her light and tucking it back into her jacket as she reached the base. A flickering light illuminated the walls at the top of the stairs. It shifted, and the shadows danced, identifying the source as a fire rather than an electric light.

As they climbed up the stairs, the wood creaked in protest several times, but Corey continued to walk on rather than freeze at each noise. The hunter was thankful to change her role to being a follower in this situation. Every instinct in her made her want to stop as soon as any sound was made. Each wooden groan made the muscles in her legs tighten until it felt like she climbed the rest of the staircase on the tips of her toes.

When they reached the top of the stairs, Corey held up a hand behind her and leaned around the corner, poking her head out to see down the hall. After a brief moment where Ichirin found herself holding her breath, Corey stood up straight and gestured for the others to follow as she stepped into the light.

The hall beyond was wide and ran all the way to the front entrance of the building. Several doors came off of this hall on either side, and Ichirin caught a glimpse of a set of stairs around the corner. It looked like this was once meant to be some type of apartment building, with a front office near the entrance. A bank of mailboxes imbedded in the wall near the end of the hall supported this theory. Some of the apartment doors had fallen off or were stuck open, but those that were closed had numbers mounted in the center of the door.

The light came from the center of the foyer. Some enterprising individual had rolled a metal trashcan into that area, and it burned high enough that the flames licked over the lip. Soot coated the ceiling above it. The hunter couldn't help but think of the risks and foolishness of the endeavor, but then she reminded herself of the situation. She had not experienced what these souls had. They needed to keep warm, and this was the solution available to them. Someone had broken a couple of the windows on the second floor, and it was a vaulted entryway. It allowed for most of the smoke to filter out rather than collect. Even with that, the air carried an acrid odor making the trespassers question what the squatters burned. Judging by the light from some of the apartments, it was not the only fire.

A few people curled up in the entryway, wrapped in layers of whatever they could find. If any of them were aware of the trespassers, no one cared. A few of them shifted, and one person rolled from one side to the other, but the only other sound was the crackle of the flames.

As the three friends walked in the direction of the front entrance, Ichirin spied into the abandoned apartments. Most of them were empty, especially the ones with uncovered windows. It gave her the impression that the people living here did not want to risk discovery. She found one apartment with a group of people in it, huddled together as they sat on the floor. Someone had boarded up all the windows in that apartment, blocking any view. One of the children in the huddle looked up and made eye contact with the intruder before she buried her face in the arm of her neighbor.

After that exchange, Ichirin knew these people were not a threat. They were as frightened to be discovered as she was, if not more.

Corey led them to a door with the number worn off. The telltale flicker of light indicated a fire in the room beyond. She tried to turn the knob, but the handle was locked. She pushed, driving her shoulder into it. Unlike the front door to the building, it moved, but still held strong.

"I think we can break it down," Corey whispered, running her fingers along the frame. "Hem, give me a hand here."

"If we do that, everyone's going to hear it," he hissed back.

"They already know we're here. They're ignoring us, hoping we won't pay any attention to them." Ichirin nodded at the people sleeping in the entryway that had turned over to look in their direction.

As soon as Hemingway and Corey looked, the people rolled over or covered up their faces. They did it with slow and deliberate motions. The message was clear. They didn't want to be seen. Ichirin considered going over to ask if any of them had seen the enenra or the mysterious person it had spoken with, but she didn't want to make them uncomfortable. The memory of the man on the street was still fresh in her mind and here there was nowhere to run.

Hemingway moved next to Corey. She guided him to the edge of the door frame near the handle.

"One, two, three," Corey counted off.

They both slammed into the door, and it gave a loud crack as the wood around the latch splintered and the door moved several inches. Several of the people in the entryway picked themselves up and huddled in a corner. Others ran into one of the open apartments. While they might tolerate strangers in their presence, these trespassers had now escalated things to a new level. Back the way they had come, several heads poked out into the hallway.

Holding her hands out in front of her, Ichirin walked into the entryway, trying to use slow movements to show she wasn't a threat. She didn't want these people any more scared than they were. If any of them had seen the monster, they had suffered enough and did not need more emotional stress. If it did come back, she wanted to spare them as much as she could.

"We're not going to hurt you. But you might want to go hide in an apartment."

She stood off to the side, leaving a clear path for them to flee where they wouldn't have to come within a stride of her or her friends. Corey and Hemingway slammed into the door once again, and more wood splintered. That noise jolted the people into motion, sending them scampering to hide. The hunter watched them run off and felt better knowing that they would be safe. While Hemingway and Corey tried to finish breaking the door down, she examined the front entrance.

As she looked at the lock, a shadow fell over her, blocking out most of the light. She turned around and saw the enenra just as it charged her. It slammed into her with a stunning force, sending her barreling into the door and through it in a shower of wood and glass. Shards of both cut into her legs. The leather jacket protected her arms, and she managed to get her head covered before the creature struck.

When she hit the ground outside, Ichirin tried to roll, but the impact drove the wind from her body, and she tumbled into the street without any control. For a moment, all she could do was try to catch her breath. It felt like her lungs were gripped in a vise and unable to expand.

With a gasp, air rushed back into her lungs, and she began to cough. Her head rushed, and a dull throbbing started at the base of her skull. It was just the impact. She wasn't being choked. She needed to get up, see what was going on.

Rolling onto her side, the hunter pushed herself up into a sitting position. Her hip screamed in pain at the motion, but she stamped it back down as she pulled her leg up underneath her and rose to a standing position. The monster billowed in front of the destroyed door, the wreckage of it forming a trail from it to her. It had grown in size and stretched forward in her direction.

"You will not stop me."

This time when its mouth moved, she heard it speak. Its voice was raspy and weak, but she heard the rage embedded deep inside. The hunter stood up tall, ignoring the pain and raising her chin. She needed to fight this thing. She was the only one who could stop it before it struck again, and she was not going to let it cause more suffering.

"You're wrong."

The creature looked puzzled at her proclamation, rather than threatened.

Smoke! Now!

CHAPTER SIX

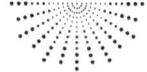

Ichirin didn't think. She willed herself to change just as she heard the sound of a gunshot. The monster saw her shift and roared, launching forward, propelled by a whirlwind of smoke. The hunter moved to the side, flowing out of the way as the enenra clawed at the space where she had been moments before. Her clothes scattered from the force of the attack, spreading out across the street. The entity changed its orientation so that it could face her directly as it charged once again.

This time, she dropped to the ground, flattening herself out and willing herself into a shape no thicker than a hand's width. Her quarry soared over her, slamming into the building as it couldn't stop its momentum. The human saw her advantage and turned the tables, trying to attack while the creature was still pinned against the wall.

As she came close, Ichirin changed her hand into a hammer, swinging it at the thing's back and trying to crush its spine, or at least the area in the center of its back. A hole appeared right before the blow landed, and the full force of the attack slammed the wall. Bricks cracked, and a few came free to shatter against the sidewalk below.

The enenra closed the gap in its body, trying to form over the hammer. The hunter recognized the maneuver and jerked her hand back, but not before the creature grabbed the head. It felt like the monster was in her hand, mixing among each particle that was her and squeezing it with an intensity that made her want to scream. She tried to push away and wrench free, but the beast continued to claw at her, its body spreading like a virus.

Willing her other hand into a long blade, Ichirin brought the weapon up and around, giving a strong slice downward. The monster recoiled, but she had another target. She sliced into her own arm, just below the hammer head, separating it from the rest of her body. The two smoke entities flew away from each other.

Her arm burned from the cut, and she felt like something was missing. Rather than feeling a wound, she felt something wasn't quite right, like she when lack of sleep caught up to her and she couldn't focus. Except the fogginess was physical instead of mental. When she focused, she formed a new hand.

She couldn't afford to analyze the sensation right now. The creature swirled, growing even larger. The hunter flew back, putting some distance between her and her quarry. Where was it getting its power? How was it continuing to grow? How big could it get?

Shouts from below caught her attention, and she looked down to see several police cars blocking off the street. Flashing lights lit up the side of the building and the underside of the bridge in a colored strobe. Several of the officers climbed out of their vehicles and had weapons drawn but stood with mouths agape. Ichirin hoped they didn't open fire. She knew the bullets would not affect either her or her adversary, but a bystander might get caught in the crossfire. She needed to keep the battle away from the police.

When the monster charged, it split in half before it reached her, arcing around to come at her from two opposite directions. The human leapt up, dodging the blow just before the two columns of smoke slammed into each other. To her surprise, they merged into one single column that shot up like a water spout. She flipped back, trying to get out of the way and getting her foot clipped in the process.

The impact throbbed and sent her spinning for a moment before she righted herself. As soon as she did, the beast slammed into her once again, sending her careening in a different direction as she tried to put some distance between the two of them. It continued to bat at her, like a cat playing with a mouse that had no hope of retaliation. The best the woman could do was manage to get enough distance to keep from being annihilated by any single strike.

Rather than try to dodge the next blow, the human held her arms in front of her and merged them together to form a single long lance. It cut through the entity as it charged, cleaving it into two pieces. The smaller piece dispersed into ash on the wind while the larger one curved away and formed into the half-human, half-cloud shape.

For the moment, they floated, facing each other, neither one attacking. Ichirin tried to recover, her mind still reeling from being knocked around. The lights from below lit up the enenra's cloud in flashes of red and blue and orange. That thought made her straighten up. Where was the orange coming from?

Looking down, she saw the building on fire. Homeless people streamed out of the now-destroyed front entrance, and the police guided them up the street, away from the supernatural battleground. Now that she wasn't distracted with the fight, the woman heard the screams and shouts. People pointed up at her and cowered.

The monster took advantage of her distraction, and a tendril snaked out of the darkness and curled around the human's throat. The tentacle jerked back, forcing her to arch her back and pulling her off-balance. She reached up and tried to free herself so she could breathe. The beast barreled into her with the rest of its form, making her feel like every piece of her was on fire at once. Having it barrel through every molecule of her threatened to overpower her. The hyperaware-ness of her body only served to highlight the intensity of the torture.

The entity still had a tendril curled around her throat as it turned to pummel her once again. And then Ichirin realized her folly.

She didn't need to breathe.

She stopped fighting the tendril and grabbed it instead, pulling it closer. It was still an extension of the enenra, and the sudden shift in force made the monster's next attack go wide. It slammed into one of the bridge pillars instead, sizzling as it struck the metal like cold water dropped into a hot pan. The creature loosened its grip, and the woman dropped free, reshaping her body so that she reformed beneath its grip.

She moved to charge the beast, hurtling through the air toward it in a bull rush. The creature saw her coming, just like she expected. At the last moment, the hunter veered, dropping below the bridge and soaring toward the burning building. People had stopped running out of it, and she prayed that meant they had all evacuated. She didn't have much of a choice. She needed to even the playing field however she could.

Forcing herself to condense, she shot through the front entrance and into the open foyer, the ragged edges of the doorway scraping her as she passed by. The barrel used as a makeshift heater was knocked over on its side, flames from its contents coating most of the entrance hall floor. A few snakes of fire led down the hall and into the apartment where she had least seen Corey and Hemingway. The door was open, and thick black smoke curled through the doorway to collect with the clouds trapped against the ceiling.

What about her friends? Ichirin flew into the apartment, the flames dancing through her body as she moved just above them. It was warm, but no more than curling up in front of a fireplace. At its worst, she'd would label it uncomfortable rather than painful.

The room beyond was covered in fire. A cleared section of floor sat in the center of the room where it looked like someone had created a firepit to start a bonfire. The pit contained several charred logs in various states of consumption falling apart on top of one another. Someone had stacked a pile of wooden logs—now very much aflame—near one of the walls. The smoke in this room was so thick that it created a roiling sea of darkness hiding the ceiling completely. If she needed to breathe, this room would be a death trap.

Two long arms stretched out of that sea and tried to wrap around Ichirin's body. She twisted and dropped to the floor, sliding across it to keep out of the reach of those tendrils. They extended and grew until the enenra floated in front of her. It was much smaller here—a necessity in order to fit in the room.

"Why do you fight? What are you?" the creature hissed in a haunting, raspy voice.

When Ichirin shouted back, she was surprised to hear her own words. "I can't let you kill people!"

"I am doing what must be done. They must be cleansed." The enenra spoke with as much emotion as someone saying the ocean was wet.

"No." Ichirin rose as she said the word. She didn't know how, but she would not let the monster continue hunting people down. It needed to be stopped, and she was the only one who could.

The entity stared at her for a moment and then hurtled forward, smoke arms coming around from one side and then the other as it attempted to pummel its opponent into submission. She blocked a few of the blows but got hit by more than she deflected. The monster was strong, and the human had to retreat before its assault. At one point, she blocked both of the enenra's fists, but a foot thrust out of its midsection to strike her in the chest. She stumbled back, the uncomfortable heat spreading throughout her core. As the creature drifted toward her, Ichirin scrambled through the only visible door, trying to get some space and a moment to think. Her pursuer was calm, watching her and drifting forward with the slow, deliberate relentlessness of erosion.

The hunter found herself in a large bathroom, untouched by the growing flames. To her surprise, Hemingway stood in front of the wood covering the window, trying to pry it free with a fire poker. Corey lifted a set of fireplace tongs like a baseball bat. When Ichirin stepped back and held up her hands, Corey lowered her improvised weapon.

"Ichirin, it's you, isn't it? Thank the gods! Look! We think this has something to do with the enenra. We were trying to get it out of here when someone started the fire and trapped us inside."

She pointed to the bathtub, and Ichirin saw a log about the length of her forearm and a little thicker. The bark of it was bone white, but between the cracks, it emitted a red glow like hot embers. The light it gave illuminated the entire bathtub. Despite looking like it had been pulled from a blaze, its exterior looked uncharred.

Not sure if they would be able to hear her, the hunter gestured for Hemingway to move to the side. Corey grabbed his shoulder and pulled him out of the way. Their savior reached forward, extending her arm and curling the tendrils around the edges of the wooden board. She yanked, tearing the wood free in a single jerking motion as the nails squealed in protest. Cool air rushed in through the opening, and the flames behind her flared.

Hemingway and Corey didn't need to be given any instruction. Hemingway gestured for Corey to go, and she jumped through head-first, rolling on the other side when she struck the pavement. Hemingway's departure was not as grand, but he crawled through the bathroom window and out to the relative safety of the street.

Once she was sure they were safe, Ichirin turned her attention to the log. She reached out to pick it up, surprised at how smooth it was and how it radiated no heat whatsoever. Even with her heightened sense of touch, she couldn't feel any blemishes along the length of the wood. Based on the way it glowed, she expected it to burn. Other than that, it seemed like an ordinary log. If the others had not called it out, she would have passed her attention over it.

When the enenra walked through the doorway, its reaction made the importance clear. For a moment, its eyes widened, and then it lunged for the log, stretching as it reached out with multiple hands, trying to snatch the piece of wood from the woman's grasp. She pushed herself through the window. The log caught on the edge of the frame, and she had to twist to yank it free.

The smoke coming from the building twisted together, forming into the enenra that was now almost as large as the building itself. Ichirin stared at it, amazed at how it had grown. When it opened its mouth to scream, she felt the creature could have swallowed her whole. She backed away and turned to go toward the water. A wall of smoke erupted from the ground in front of her, cutting off that path. The barrier appeared with such intensity that it ripped up a section of fence and sent it hurtling through the air.

The monster reached for her but jerked back with a hiss. It whipped its head around, staring at the fire trucks parked in front of the building and shooting water through the windows. The entity hesitated.

Taking advantage of its distraction, Ichirin rose up, trying to get over the wall of smoke and head toward the Sound. She propelled herself forward with all the speed she could muster, hoping to get beyond the beast's reach. She just had to clear the wall, and then she could drown the log in the sea water. Considering how it reacted to the fire trucks, that might banish the creature.

But as she passed over the black barrier, a gigantic hand swatted her out of the sky. The blow slammed her to the ground, and she crashed into it with an impact that shattered the pavement and sent the log tumbling from her grasp. The entire front of her body burned, and her side felt like that time she had broken her shoulder trying to keep up with Corey in college. She pulled the pain inside, distributing it through her form and presenting a new outer shell.

Ichirin looked up just in time to see the enenra drop a bladed tendril at her. There was no time to get out of the way. She raised her hand and spread out her fingers, willing the hand to extend and form a shield. She angled it, trying to make the attack glance off rather than try and stop it. The impact rang up her shoulder and made her scream as it shoved her deeper into the rubble. But the attack glanced off, carving a chunk out of the street and spraying her with small rocks that whipped through her body.

Moving to her left, she slid out of the way before another blow could land. For the moment, the beast had turned its attention toward the firefighters attacking the blaze. She couldn't be sure, but she thought the entity had shrunk. It still stood over two stories tall but no longer took up the same space as the abandoned building.

The hunter looked for the strange piece of wood, her eyes drawn to a red glow in the middle of the street. The enenra had formed a cage around the log but had not picked it up.

She needed to try something, or else there was no telling how much destruction the monster would cause. Charging the cage, Ichirin willed both her hands into long sharp blades. As she picked up speed, her legs disappeared, replaced by a small whirlwind like the one the creature rode.

The beast still focused its attention on the firefighters. It appeared to try and combat the streams of water rather than the humans. That fact was the only reason they were still alive, but at any point, the entity could realize the better approach would be to attack the people holding the hoses. Ichirin willed herself to move faster, the ground blurring underneath her.

When she struck, it was with the force of a bullet. She held her weapons up in front of her, slicing through the side of the cage with her momentum. The blades chopped through the cage like a cleaver through a piece of meat. As she cut through the opposite side, Ichirin reached out with a tendril behind her, making a hook out of the cloud that formed her lower half. It snagged the log, dragging it with her as she carved her way out.

The sudden attack captured the enenra's attention, and the creature whipped around to face her. The hunter veered toward the Sound, once again trying to climb up over the wall of smoke. The humanoid form of the monster shrank as it poured more of itself into the wall, making it flare up and block the woman's path. But Ichirin veered away before she reached the barrier. She whipped past the creature and hurled herself into the path of one of the fire hoses.

Holding the log out in front of her, she doused it in the stream of water, screaming as the water ripped through her body and felt like it tore her apart. Struggling to keep her form intact, she kept her position, twisting and moving the log so that it stayed in the stream of water even when the firefighters adjusted it.

The glow began to diminish, and the enenra shrank in size even as it collected itself together and tried to stop her. Ichirin shifted to another stream, moving out of the way as her mystical adversary launched an awkward lurching attack. The entity was human-sized once again, its cloud no larger than the human's.

Even if the technique worked, the pain was too much to bear. The hunter soared up and west, toward the Sound. This time the creature didn't have the strength to bar her path. It soared behind her but matched her pace. However, Ichirin noticed the log starting to glow brighter now that it was no longer assaulted. And as the intensity grew, so did the enenra.

Ichirin saw the edge of the Sound and hurtled toward it, diving for the edge of the water. She just needed to get the log submerged. Nothing mattered until she achieved that. She felt the creature clawing at her trailing cloud. She pushed herself, extending the log out as far as she could reach. The monster tangled in the tail end of her form and yanked back, jerking her to a stop. Ichirin let the log go, hurling it as her momentum stopped.

As she turned around to protect herself, the enenra pushed off of her, hurling her down into the ground as it raced after the glowing log. The wood landed in the Sound with a splash, and the creature pulled up short, howling silently at the sky. Ichirin drifted over, watching as the monster shrunk in on itself far faster than before.

The creature stopped writhing and captured her stare. It spoke, but not with its whisper and hiss. The voice that issued forth dripped strength and confidence, far more than she had ever heard from anyone or anything. If power itself could speak, this was the voice it would use.

"For every two of my children that you destroy, three more shall be born."

It was a promise, a guarantee, not a threat or a boast. And Ichirin had no doubt in the sincerity of those words. Whoever had just spoken to her—it couldn't be the enenra—had no need for empty plat-itudes. That much was clear.

As she watched, the beast faded until it became just a small cloud of smoke in the air. The wind blew it apart, scattering the last of the ashes. Glancing out at the water, she saw the strange log sink beneath the surface, drifting down to the bottom. She hoped that meant this trial was over.

As if in response, pain erupted through her entire body as her powers left and she snapped back to her physical body like a released rubber band. Ichirin collapsed on the ground, in too much pain to process anything.

CHAPTER SEVEN

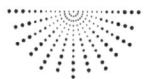

As tempting as it was, Ichirin knew she couldn't give into the encroaching darkness and pass out. There was no way of knowing who would find her, naked and injured by the beach. Or maybe no one would, and she'd catch hypothermia from the cold. Her body shivered so hard that she didn't have any extra energy to stand up at first. At least the sharp rocks jabbing her exhausted body gave her something to latch on to and fight against the wave of exhaustion. She gasped, sucking in that familiar chalky taste of ash, and coughed, her entire body tensing with each violent expulsion.

The first thing was warmth. She needed to get warm, and out of sight. Lifting her head, she tried to get her bearings. When she ran from the enenra, getting to the Sound as soon as possible occupied her entire mind. There was no conscious thought behind where she was going.

The beach here was a small stretch of land near the docks. The cloudy moonlit sky outlined large cranes that stretched up like ever-watchful guardians. At this hour, no one moved around. A ship floated in front of one of the cranes, and Ichirin considered going there, but she doubted she could walk that far, and there would be cameras.

Pushing herself up to her feet and shaking legs, she turned around and walked in the general direction of the building. It wasn't hard to find. The sky had an angry orange glow where the building burned, with flames that sounded tempting. She shuffled forward, feet scraping against the uneven ground. Keep moving, that's what she needed to do. She knew if she stopped, she might not start again. Put one foot in front of the other and look for anything she might be able to use as protection.

The wind gusted, making her dig her fingers into her arms as she hugged herself tighter, but it rustled something off to her right. Ichirin saw a tarp stuck among some rocks on the beach. It would be cold, but right now she didn't care. It offered protection from the wind as well as a modicum of decency. Walking over, she pulled it free with shaking hands and wrapped it around her body. It sent icy knives into her where the plastic touched her skin, but she curled her fists around the edges, glad to have something.

She reminded herself she needed to keep moving. Deep down she knew that. She couldn't give up now. Facing the fire once again, she trudged forward. Some buildings sat not that far away. Maybe she could find someone to help her. What would she even say? She didn't know. That much thinking was beyond her right now. She needed help; she needed someone.

Ichirin had never felt so alone. Even when she first came to the United States, it had been nothing like this.

Her parents had moved here because her father's job required it. Not only did she have to deal with learning an entire new culture, it was her first year in high school, which came with a host of other problems and stress. No one wanted to be friends with the quiet Japanese girl who spoke with such a heavy accent that she needed to repeat herself often. It marked the start of four years of solitude that felt like four decades. It didn't leave until she went to college and received Corey as her random freshman roommate.

At first, it seemed like a horrible match, and Corey's exuberance terrified her. But over time, they became friends. When her parents moved back to Japan, that friendship deepened and became a bond strong enough to withstand any storm.

Lost in her thoughts, she took several steps before noticing the headlights of a car washing over her. She stopped, staring at the car, trying to make sense of it and not having the mental fortitude to think to move.

The car screeched to a stop, and someone jumped out of the driver's seat, running toward her without bothering to shut the door. She couldn't make out who it was, just saw the silhouette of the body as he barreled toward her. He had something in his hands, something large that he unfolded as he moved.

Ichirin didn't process what was going on until Hemingway stood in front of her, wrapping a large blanket around her shoulders. She dropped the tarp underneath it, relishing the much warmer sensation of the scratchy fabric against her skin. He rubbed the cotton, warming her up with friction as he moved from her shoulders to her back.

"Are you okay? You're freezing. Come on, get in the car."

He led her around to the passenger's side and opened the door for her, easing her into the heated seat. The warmth billowing up around her made her sigh, and she closed her eyes. It felt more comforting than being swaddled in pillows taken fresh out of the dryer. The fan was on, blowing warm air over her feet and making them tingle as sensation flooded back. The light prickles helped to wake her up, despite the comforts she found herself in.

But with that wakefulness came awareness of her aches and pains. When Hemingway climbed into the driver's seat and slammed the door shut, the shaking made her wince. Her entire body felt like one gigantic bruise, and any motion made her feel pain in muscles that she didn't know she had. In addition to the bruises, she felt the stinging sensation of small fresh cuts in several places over her body. If her body was any indication, she spent the evening battered in a washing machine and then rolled through a field of nettles.

"Are you okay?" Hemingway asked again, examining Ichirin with his concern etched onto his face.

"I've been better. But I'm alive and whole."

She coughed, feeling a burning sensation in her lungs and throat when tried to talk. All she could taste was ash. She realized she couldn't even smell the salt from the Sound, everything was charred.

Hemingway reached into the back and handed her a bottle of water. As she grabbed it in one hand, he uncapped it for her. She lifted it, drinking half of the contents in several swallows in quick succession. She let out a heavy sigh as she lowered the bottle, propping it up on the edge of the seat and holding it between loose fingers.

"Is it done?" Hemingway asked.

Ichirin nodded. "It was tied to that wood you found. Once I..."

Hemingway shushed her. "Later. I just wanted to know if it was taken care of and you were safe. I'm going to let Corey know."

Ichirin didn't offer any objections. She was more than willing to take a moment or two to enjoy the comforts of his car and be glad that it was finished. Now that she was safe, she found it impossible to resist the siren's call of rest. Even though she struggled to keep her eyes open, they fell of their own accord. The last thing she remembered seeing was her locket hanging from the rearview mirror of his car.

When she woke up, the hunter panicked. She tried to sit up, regretting the action as pain bloomed through her entire back and she collapsed back into the mattress. A groan escaped her lips. She rolled to the side, propping herself up so she could swing her legs over the edge of the bed. At least she recognized her bedroom.

Hemingway and Corey both came into the room as Ichirin sat there, her head hanging loose and drooped in front of her body. She looked up and saw Corey holding out a glass of water. With a smile, the exhausted woman took it, taking several mouthfuls before resting it on the nightstand. It occurred to her she was dressed in her comfortable fleece PJs. Corey shrugged.

"Figured you could use the extra cozy. Besides, it's not like it's anything I haven't seen before."

As her awareness extended beyond her immediate body, Ichirin realized both of her friends still wore the same clothes as when they went into the building, minus the jackets. They had cleaned the soot from their faces and hands, but it still marred their garments, and the odor of it filled the bedroom once they came in. The stench reminded her of the previous events, and she shuddered, fighting the urge to cry. Only the thought of her friends keeping watch over her enabled her to push it back down.

"Have you gotten any rest?" she asked.

"Some," Hemingway answered for both of them. "We snoozed for a couple of hours each. Wanted to make sure one of us was up in case you needed anything."

"How long have I been out?"

"About ten hours." Hemingway stifled a yawn, revealing just how little sleep he had gotten.

Ichirin's hand rose up to her chest. The locket! Taka!

Corey walked over and sat down on the bed next to her friend, pulling the locket from her pocket. She handed it over, and Ichirin fastened it around her neck, glad to have its familiar weight pulling on her.

Welcome back. I don't say this often, but good job. I don't know how you did it, but you defeated the enenra. I knew you would, of course. You don't give yourself enough credit. Trust me, I've been around a few years.

"If it weren't for Taka, we wouldn't have been able to find you. I take back half of the sarcastic things I've said about him. After you took off, the locket had this slight subtle pull in your direction. Hemingway followed it to find you."

It wasn't easy, and it took a lot out of me, but it was the only way I could think to let them know where you are. We are bonded, even if we can't always communicate.

For lack of a better description, Taka's voice sounded tired. The hunter gave the locket a couple of light pats with the tips of her fingers.

"So, what happened? Are you rested enough to tell us the story?" Corey asked.

"Well, you know the first part. It blasted me out the door and we fought a bit. It kept getting bigger and bigger, so I went inside the building to try and even up the odds. That didn't go too well either, until I found you and you gave me the log. I don't know how, and I don't know why, but that log was tied to the monster. I knew something was off when I picked it up, but I didn't realize how important it was."

Corey interrupted, unable to contain herself. "Yeah, we pulled it from the fire, and it wasn't even hot. It sat on top, not burning or charred or anything. So, we pulled it out and found out it wasn't warm. When we tried to take it out, that's when some guy started the fire."

"Did you get a look at who it was? Would you be able to identify him if you saw him again?" Ichirin gripped the edge of the bed.

Both Corey and Hemingway shook their heads. That didn't surprise her, but for a moment, she dared to hope. She relaxed and continued her story.

"As I was saying, the log was tied to it somehow. How much did you see when I got out of the building?"

"We saw you use the firemen to help with bringing the thing down to size and then saw you take off toward the water." Hemingway leaned against the wall and slid down until he sat on the floor.

"Not much else to share then. I flew toward the Sound, hoping I could drown the log in the water or something. I almost didn't make it. The creature was catching up to me and grabbed me right before I hit the water. I was lucky. When it yanked me back, I threw the log as hard as I could. The beast tried to catch the wood, but as soon as the log touched the surface, the enenra shrank until it blew apart."

"What about the log?" Hemingway's brow furrowed, and one hand reached up to rub his neck. "If it washes up on shore, will that thing come back?"

"It wasn't normal wood. I don't know what it was, but it sank to the bottom. Hopefully it won't ever wash up on shore again and we're done. I wanted to put it out deeper, but once the monster was gone, I didn't have any powers. I snapped back to my regular shape and then struggled not to freeze to death until you found me."

"Maybe Taka knows something?" Corey asked.

I believe this beast is hunted. Your powers are tied to the creature, and that's an indicator that it's defeated. Even if that artifact washes up again, the spirit that inhabited it no longer exists. It would need to be recreated, not just summoned once again.

"It said that the enenra is gone for good."

Hemingway dropped his hand and breathed an audible sigh of relief.

"There was something weird that happened. Right before the monster died, it said something. But, I don't think that it was speaking. It was like someone or something was speaking through it."

Both Hemingway and Corey looked at her, waiting for her to continue.

"It said that for every two of its children I strike down, three more will take its place."

Probably just the enenra trying to scare you. The last dying breath of a horrible killer.

"What do you think it means?" Corey pulled up her feet so that she could sit cross-legged on the bed and face the others without craning her neck.

"I don't know. Maybe nothing. But it made me wonder if everything that is going on is more nefarious than just random beasts popping up. That definitely wasn't the creature. It couldn't have been. Even when it could talk, it didn't sound like that. I don't know how to explain it, but you have to believe me."

Hemingway nodded. "We believe you. You know we do. If you say it was something else, then it was something else. We just have to figure out what it means."

If you're right, and it wasn't the enenra, then it sounds like you're making progress, and someone is a little irritated at your success. I guess you'll just have to hunt them down twice as fast.

"It's just one of several things that doesn't add up in a nice, easy package. First the fact that someone helped the beast. We know that between what you saw and what the homeless man said before he ran off. Someone gave the monster orders. Not to mention the whole other crate. No way of knowing what happened to that."

"And the way the thing acted toward the firefighters," Hemingway added.

Ichirin tilted her head. "What do you mean? It fought them until I got its attention by taking the log out from underneath it."

"No, it didn't. It tried to stop the water from putting out the flames, but it never attacked the source. In fact, it made an effort to not hurt the firemen or cut the hoses or anything like that. I watched it. At one point it put part of its body in the way of some flaming rubble. We know it had awareness. It talked and identified you as a threat. As much as I hate to say it, it didn't attack the firemen. Not only that, but it protected them, and that's weird."

Ichirin looked over to Corey for confirmation, and she nodded, agreeing with Hemingway's assessment.

"Maybe it was worried that it might be threatened if it got too close to the hoses? It knew water could hurt it," Ichirin offered.

The argument sounded weak even to her. Maybe the creature reacted out of instinct and panic, rather than any rational thought. It was hard to say. They didn't know enough about how the monster worked or thought, what kind of approach it would take. There were a hundred possible explanations, and any one of them could be justi-fied—or they could all be wrong. Occam's razor seemed to go out the window when dealing with creatures that defied rational explanation.

In the end, does it matter? You defeated the beast. It can't cause any more destruction, and people are safe, thanks to you. The only other option I see would be to try and summon up another enenra and ask it for its opinion. But I'd like to register my recommendation to not even consider that option.

Ichirin agreed. Besides, they had enough mysteries on their plate. They didn't need to worry about the motivation and logic behind a mythical creature that was a known killer. Their primary concern was who called the shots and directed the beast. That, and what other surprises might be coming in the near future.

"We could keep talking in circles analyzing this to death, but I think you two need some rest. I just woke up, and I'm still feeling exhausted and abused."

As Ichirin said that, she rolled one of her shoulders, intending to emphasize the soreness. To her surprise, she felt a flare of pain that made the performance more real than she intended and she sucked in air. She needed to be careful.

If I had a body, I would shake my head at you right now. We just fought for our lives against an extremely powerful mythological entity, so let's do some jumping jacks!

"Sounds like a plan. I'm wiped and need to shower and crash. Don't do anything crazy, and take it easy for crying out loud. You're more strung out than I am after a tournament, and with good reason!" Corey reached out and gave her friend's hand a squeeze before she pushed herself up from the bed and left the room.

Hemingway propped himself up the wall as he stood, coming over and holding out his hand. Ichirin took it in both of hers. "I'm glad you're safe. We gathered your clothes as best as we could and just put them in your hamper. I'm not sure Corey got all of them, but we tried to snag what we could. I figure we can head down to get your car later. I'd take you now, but I feel like I'm about to fall over."

Ichirin shook her head and waved for him to go. "Don't worry about it. If I need it, I can always Uber."

"Alright. I'm going to get some rest."

"Thank you, again. You're amazing, Hem."

He beamed at her and then left. Ichirin heard the front door close, and then blessed silence surrounded her, almost as comforting as her own bed. She sat there for several minutes, enjoying the peace and the lack of danger.

Her need to be mobile and be productive overcame her enjoyment of the serenity after a short while. Pushing up from the bed, she shuffled out of her bedroom, feeling each of her injuries. Though it was uncomfortable, a smile spread across her face. The wounds may hurt, but she earned them for a good cause, and she defeated a monster. The elation she felt helped her walk lighter on the balls of her feet.

Once she was in the kitchen, she saw the stains across the carpet in front of her couch and caught the familiar odor of smoke. Her house also bore reminders of the battle. But, like her body, these could be healed and would fade into memory.

The more she moved, the more comfortable she became as she stretched her sore muscles. Between that and her need to be rid of the burnt smell, she ignored the wisdom of getting more rest and set to cleaning her place. She welcomed the slight burn of bleach fumes as they chased away the ash. Ichirin doubted that she'd want to be around a bonfire all winter, if not longer. Her desire to eliminate the olfactory reminders became a quest.

As she went to the laundry room and tossed clothes into the washer, she found Hemingway's jacket tucked in with the rest of them. She snapped it a couple of times to get rid of any ashy remnants. Short of taking it somewhere to be cleaned, her only other option was to air it out. As she held it up to sling it on a hanger, she saw light pierce through the back in a small hole about the size of her finger. It was in the center of the jacket, even with her shoulder blades if she put it on.

She pulled it close, getting a better look. The hole was a perfect circle and singed at the edges. She stared at the imperfection as the events of the previous evening played out in her mind's eye. She remembered the shot, and the sensation as she shifted into smoke. She let go with one hand and reached behind her back to feel for a wound, but she couldn't reach.

Tossing the jacket onto the washer, she went into the bathroom and lifted up the back of her shirt. Just inside her right shoulder blade next to the spine was a small circular scab.

That shot was meant for her, not the enenra. The shooter fired before she turned into smoke. If she had been even half a second later with her shift, the night would have had a different end.

I've got your back.

Ichirin reached up and squeezed the locket in her fist.

Pun totally intended.

THE END

PART II
DEEP CURRENTS

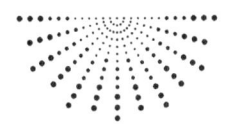

CHAPTER ONE

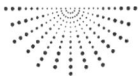

The sun created long, dancing shadows as it passed through the leaf cover on the winding back road, occasionally piercing through a gap to try and blind an unprepared driver. Ichirin Saito relished the warmth it brought. Summer took a while to arrive, but now she planned to spend a week soaking in as much of the Vitamin D as her pale skin could handle.

She hoped their annual trip to the lake wouldn't feel crowded. Corey's partners had come the last two years, enough to be considered regulars. Ichirin thought of Ayden and Leah both as friends, even if she never saw them without Corey. But this year, Hemingway planned on bringing his new girlfriend, Anika.

Ichirin knew Anika through work before she transferred to the same team as Hemingway. She was nice, but a voice in her head—her voice, not Taka's—made Ichirin concerned she might find herself as the extra wheel in all their interactions.

Look on the bright side. You have something that they don't: me. Who else could provide such colorful commentary for your enjoyment?

A chuckle escaped Ichirin's lips and merged into a sigh. While she appreciated the kami's presence, it wasn't quite the same. Before he could offer mock offense, she made sure to remind him she did find it comforting.

Something nagged at her and itched the back of her brain. Ichirin pulled to a stop at the side of the road. She stared out the window, narrowing her eyes as she scanned through the trees. Her hands tightened on the steering wheel, the cover creaking as she adjusted her grip.

You think something's out there?

Ichirin reached to her chest and touched the locket around her neck with two fingers, tapping it a couple of times. Her other hand drifted to the door handle, resting on it for a moment before she pulled on it and stepped out of the car.

The scent of the pine trees and dirt washed over her as soon as she left the climate-controlled environment of her vehicle. Birds chirped in the upper branches out of sight, and not too far away she heard the gentle lap of waves against the shore. Ichirin saw Lake Chelan through the gaps in the trees, the sun reflecting off the surface.

She took a few steps and paused, turning to look back at her car. She could be at the house in a few minutes and then wouldn't be alone when she went down to the shore. If someone or something waited for her, going alone could be dangerous.

And if it is another mythological beast, wouldn't you rather have us handle it alone than risk their lives? In the end, you're the only one equipped to fight them. Besides, a quick glance won't hurt.

Ichirin took a few shuffling steps forward, kicking trails through dirt and months-old pine needles. When the ground leveled out, she crept around trees, using them for cover as much as possible. She heard a crack off to her left, the snapping of a twig.

Go! Catch him!

A blur of movement flitted through the trees to her side, and Ichirin sprinted after the mysterious man. He wore shorts and a t-shirt, but there was little else she could determine from this viewpoint. He was blond and had a decent tan like someone who spent most of the summer outdoors.

He stumbled a couple of times, arms windmilling to either side as he tried to stay upright. That gave Ichirin the advantage she needed, and she closed the distance. With a lunge, she dove at the stranger, trying to wrap her arms around him. She slipped off, but her impact knocked him off-balance and sent him sprawling across the ground.

"I'm sorry! I was just leaving!"

Ichirin rolled over sideways and sprang up to her feet. Her adversary lay on his side in the dirt, his legs curled up and a hand held over his face. He closed his eyes tight enough to scrunch up his face and refused to look at her.

"Who are you?" Ichirin asked.

"My name's Ben. I was chilling at the lake. I didn't think anyone would be here. I promise. I'll leave."

He could be lying. You know as well as I do that someone watched you, and he's the only one here.

Ichirin cocked her head as she looked at the kid in front of her, and she surprised herself when that word came to mind. He looked like a minor, and something about him screamed inexperience and immaturity, even if he was only a handful of years younger than her.

Your experiences age you faster than time ever could. But we can discuss that another time. We must decide what to do with Ben.

"Did you see anyone else?" Ichirin asked.

Ben eased his hand down and stared up at her, twisting around to get on his back. He propped himself up enough to glance around before settling back on to his elbows.

"No. Thought I had the place to myself, so I didn't think anyone would care."

He watched her with wide eyes that continued to shift around whenever the wind made the trees creak and crack. His fingers dug into the dirt, and his breath came in quick gulps. Ichirin continued to observe him. She reached up to brush her hair out of her face and over her shoulder.

"Go on; get out of here."

Before she finished speaking, he turned away and scrambled to his feet as he tried to run. He caught himself on trees during his mad dash, like an accelerated drunkard.

On the plus side, now we know that all the running and Aikido lessons have delivered a return on investment.

Taking a final slow scan of the lake and the woods around her, Ichirin sighed and trekked back to her car. She opened the door and rested a hand on top of it, looking back over her shoulder. She no longer felt like someone scrutinized her. Sighing, she climbed in and continued the short distance to her destination.

The house was gorgeous, three stories with an attached garage. The trees had been cleared out around the building, leaving a large yard on all sides. A tire swing dangled from the sole tree remaining in the manicured front lawn. A set of stairs led up from the mulch-covered driveway to a front door with more glass than frame.

Two cars sat in the driveway: Corey's and Ayden's. Hemingway had yet to arrive. Before Ichirin parked, Corey burst out through the front door, leaping down the stairs in a single bound, her light summer dress billowing around her as she jumped to the driveway.

Have you ever seen her in a dress? I didn't think she owned one. At least she still has running shoes on her feet. The moment she shows up with a pair of high heels, or styles her hair, I'm screaming shape changer.

"Hey! You made it!"

"Traffic was difficult getting out of the city, but it's Friday. Knowing I was coming here helped me cope. I've been looking forward to this for far too long."

"I know, right?"

Corey rushed forward and wrapped her arms around Ichirin, giving her a good squeeze for a couple of seconds. When she let go, she moved to the trunk of the car, ready to help unload. Corey grabbed both backpacks, slinging one over each shoulder before pulling out the suitcase. While she was short and thin, she had muscles earned from years of physical activities. The luggage impeded her because of awkwardness, not weight.

That left two grocery bags for Ichirin. Corey and company would have stocked the fridge and pantry, but she wanted to do her part. Besides, she doubted anyone else brought ten different types of tea or frosted cherry Pop-Tarts. They were her weakness, but she had long ago accepted that as part of her character.

The architect for the house had a preference for open spaces. When Ichirin walked in the front door, she saw into the kitchen and out through the full-size windows at the back. On the other side of that glass lay a large deck and hot tub with the lake forming a scenic backdrop.

The furnishings of the house had a rustic décor, demonstrated by the sliding barn doors between rooms. Ichirin twisted to kick the door shut and noticed a new addition mounted over the door: a wicker wreath with a pair of antlers on either side. It made her twitch and pause as she took it in with other small changes over the past year. It reminded her of returning to visit her parents' home, where most things were the same, but those that changed felt out of place.

As Ichirin approached the kitchen, she caught the whiff of fish glazing in a pan mixed with a heavenly mixture of herbs beyond Ichirin's ability to identify. Her stomach rumbled in response. Coming around the corner, she found Leah standing in front of the stove with three pans going at once, the counter next to her covered with plates, spices, open food containers, and various other debris that collects when a passionate chef goes to work.

Leah stood in sharp contrast to Corey. Where Corey was the lithe runner who kept her hair short for convenience, Leah was the homebody who loved to cook and spent time every day fashioning thick dark curls that looked fresh from a salon. Today she wore a Tardis dress with an apron over the front that said "Shiny." Her focus on the cooking kept her from noticing Ichirin, even when the bags clinked against the counter.

Corey ran into the room, sliding across the tiled floor in her socks. Her exuberant entrance caught Leah's attention, and she turned around, brandishing her spatula like a weapon.

"Out of the kitchen!" She shook the spatula a single time, making Corey back up and lift her hands in supplication. "Oh, hi Ichirin. Good to see you! I'd hug you, but I'm a mess trying to make sure dinner's ready on time. Why don't you take this troublemaker out on the deck and get her out of my hair? Ayden went to check the pier and left me alone with her."

Corey danced forward and gave Leah a quick kiss before spinning out of reach. She laughed and ran toward the French doors. Ichirin took a lingering glance at the half-cooked dishes. Her stomach rumbled, reminding her that she skipped lunch. Leaving the kitchen became a matter of self-preservation.

Stepping out onto the deck felt like walking into a different world. All of her worries and concerns about daily life stopped at the doorstep, and Ichirin wanted to soak in the pure beauty of nature.

Except for the small matter of someone hunting you down, bringing mythological beasts into your life to do it, and knowing someone or something watched you. My job is to keep you alive, and part of that means keeping you on your toes.

The tension fading from Ichirin's body returned with a vengeance, making her flex her shoulders and curl the fingers of her right hand into a fist. She closed her eyes and took a deep breath, forcing herself to relax her body. But underneath the surface, the tightness remained.

The landscapers cultivated the back lot of the house all the way down to the lake to give a view that stretched to the opposite shore. Tall trees stood on all sides, swaying and creaking in the breeze. Flashes of movement caught Ichirin's eye as critters ran for shelter or scurried in an attempt to find food, the rustles of their passing adding to the peaceful white noise of the forest.

A pier stretched out into the lake, with an attached boathouse covering a couple of canoes and some water tubes, assuming the contents hadn't changed in the last year. While she did not possess the same passion for water as Ayden, Ichirin did enjoy the serenity of being on the lake. She could use more peaceful moments given their short supply in recent days.

Corey stood at the railing, leaning out over it and picking her feet up off the ground, balancing on the edge. Ichirin joined her, planting both hands on the rail and inhaling. The air smelled damp and earthy, a gentle reminder that she was no longer surrounded by towering buildings and far too many cars for a strained transportation design.

It's almost like people planned to fix the problems they had at the time and didn't give much thought to the future. But that would never be the case since humans are so good about thinking ahead. That's what separates them from the animals, right?

"How have you been?" Ichirin asked. "It's been a couple of weeks."

Corey kept her attention focused ahead, staring at the lake. "Going pretty well. Been working crazy hours. Trying to get as much time with Leah and Ayden as I can, but it's been hard since our hours are pretty much opposite. Makes it a little stressful sometimes, but I'm looking forward to getting some quality time with them this weekend."

She sighed with a smile and turned around, jumping so she could sit on the rail and swing her feet. "What about you? Any progress or discoveries?"

Her eyes grew wide, and she leaned forward, looking like a cat about to pounce, making it clear what she was referencing. Whenever she asked about new creatures or powers, her excitement became infectious.

Could you imagine if Miss "I'm-a-squirrel-with-coffee" was in your shoes and gained powers like you do? I think she'd be more of a danger than anything she might have to face. And I say that with the utmost compassion and consideration for her nature.

Ichirin gave a glance over her shoulder to make sure no one walked up. "No, nothing new as of yet. No creatures, no powers, and no news on the shipment. The official report lists it as lost, which means that's another dead end."

"In other words, we're back to sitting around and seeing if anything happens."

Ichirin pursed her lips together and gave a slow nod. "It looks like it. It might have been a fluke, and there's no grand scheme or anything. We can hope, because the alternative means someone out there knows what they're doing and manipulating mythological forces."

In an infinite universe of possibilities, at some point, the dice will all come up blank. I know you're used to dice with at least one pip on all sides, but I'm from a different time. Don't make me use the phrase "back in my day."

Having said that, you and I both know you don't believe that for a moment.

"Sure," Corey said. "I guess it could just be a coincidence. But I wouldn't let my guard down. We know someone shipped the enenra on purpose and helped it. The question is why."

"I know, and I'm not relaxing my guard. Call it wishful thinking that the missing crate isn't full of mythological creatures."

Movement on the pier made Ichirin lean around to get a better view of Ayden as he left the boathouse and approached them. He was lanky, much like Corey, and took long strides that ate up the back yard at a pace Ichirin would have to run to match. Despite the warmth and being near the water, he wore a pair of jeans. He bounded up the steps three at a time and offered a wide grin as he saw the women by the railing.

"And so, the party begins." He walked over and gave Ichirin a quick one-armed embrace before moving over to stand next to Corey. "Cor-rine's been ready to spontaneously combust waiting for you to show up."

Corey wrinkled her nose as he used her given name, but the reaction didn't last long.

"You look a little bushier than I remember." Ichirin reached up and stroked her chin.

Ayden mimicked the motion, digging into his beard and tugging on it. The last time she saw him, he kept it trimmed close to his face. Now he had a full extra finger's thickness extending below his chin. It looked good on him, the thick beard drawing attention away from his thinning scalp.

"I'm going for the mountain man look, much to Leah's disappointment. It's nice to know you ladies appreciate it though."

Corey reached out and gave it a solid tug that jerked his attention to her. She laughed in response. Ichirin felt out of place at the open display of affection and turned back to the house.

"I think I'll go see if Leah needs any help."

They all knew the emptiness of the statement, but it served as an excuse. Ichirin didn't have anything against the affection Corey had for her partners—she was very happy for her friend. But sometimes it made her uncomfortable when it was on full display in front of her.

Ichirin went back inside and busied herself unpacking her groceries. As she expected, her supplies proved superfluous, beyond the personal items she wanted. While she stood in the pantry, she heard the front door open.

"We're here!" Hemingway called out from the entryway.

Ichirin tossed her empty bag on the counter and went to say hi to her friend. The sliding of the porch door warned her of the whirlwind about to pass and she pressed herself against the wall. Corey sprinted by her and jumped at Hemingway, forcing him to wrap his arms around her and take a small shuffle step backward. He was large enough that her feet didn't touch the ground, but the effort of holding her up made sweat bead on his face in a matter of seconds.

Behind him and to the side, still standing in the doorway, was Anika. She wasn't tall, but she had a way of standing and holding herself that made her seem like she was. Her chin lifted, but not in a way that screamed superiority. Rather it radiated the quiet confidence of one used to projecting it to gain acceptance. It was a trait Ichirin admired and mirrored when entering a room at work filled with higher level executives where she was the only woman. In that way, they were similar.

She wore a colorful dress containing all the hues of a sunset, ranging from vibrant oranges to deep purples. It was a dress Ichirin never thought she could pull off with her pale skin, but against Anika's darker tones, it contrasted well. Her long, braided hair came down to just above her waist.

Corey let go and dropped to the ground, letting Hemingway take in a hefty gulp of air. While he exaggerated it to some extent, Ichirin knew it wasn't all for show. Though their regular walks helped, he still wasn't what she would call athletic. But some of his favorite t-shirts flowed around him more compared to when they first met.

"So good to see you," Ichirin said as she stepped up and exchanged a quick embrace. She moved over and held out a hand to shake Anika's. "And good to see you as well, outside of a work environment."

"I know. It'll be nice not to have to associate your face with budget review."

"Same rooms?" Hemingway asked.

"Of course. I don't know why you ask that question every year." Corey shook her head.

"Let's put our bags away and then come back downstairs. I smell Leah working in the kitchen, and she makes the best food I've ever had. Whatever it is will be phenomenal," Hemingway explained to Anika as he picked up his backpack and a couple of reusable canvas shopping bags.

"Considering you order delivery every night, I'm not sure that's much of a bar," Corey teased.

"First off, some of us don't have the luxury to live with a *bona fide* chef. Second, I'll have you know that Uber and Amazon have increased the quality of food deliveries quite a bit."

A literal world of information lies at people's fingertips, and what do they do with it? Order food and have pointless arguments over senseless minutiae. Could you imagine what your ancestors would have done with access to a repository like the internet?

Ichirin figured they would do much the same.

You're probably right. While individuals may be unique, people on the whole are predictable.

Anika and Hemingway went upstairs, and Corey rushed into the kitchen to assist Ayden with setting the table, leaving Ichirin alone in the foyer. She watched both her friends leave, and her earlier fears returned with the force of a crashing wave in a storm. Her hand rose to the locket around her neck, and she tightened her fist around it.

I'm not going anywhere. Even if I could, I'd still be around. And that's not because you're the only one who can hear me. Well, not only because of that.

Ichirin brought her free hand to her mouth to chew on her nails but dropped it before she bit down. Sliding open the door to the study, she walked inside and read the spines of the few books stacked on the shelves. They were classics, books like *Moby Dick*, *The Complete*

Illustrated Shakespeare, and *Pride and Prejudice.* Nothing on the shelves was written by anyone still living.

These are the types of books that people put on their shelves to make them appear educated and big readers, but I would wager the vast majority of showcased copies haven't been read outside of school. Then again, it fits the same theme of this house—a showpiece and façade rather than a home where anyone lives.

That didn't lessen Ichirin's enjoyment. Part of the appeal was its illusionary nature. This was a getaway that still felt like home. She traced her fingers across the surface of the desk sitting in front of the triple window looking out to the front of the house. The few wisps of clouds picked up the light of the sunset, swaths of color on a blue canvas.

Wanting to see the vibrant colors reflected across the surface of the lake, Ichirin strode through the house, emerging on the back deck. The temperature started to drop, and she shivered, reaching up to rub both shoulders and try to chase away the goosebumps. The view here proved worthwhile, with the calm surface of the lake reflecting the colorful clouds. Ichirin walked to the back rail and rested her elbows on it as she leaned forward.

A familiar gnawing sensation at the back of her mind itched, like when she struggled to remember a piece of trivia that rested on the tip of her tongue. Something felt wrong, but she lacked the ability to put the sensation into words. Ichirin looked around, trying to find the source of the unease.

"Dinnertime!" Corey called out from the house.

Ichirin paused, staring at the back yard and feeling like something watched and hungered.

I feel it too. We best be on our guard.

CHAPTER TWO

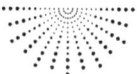

"I'm running along, sprinting my ass off, and looking up at the disc. I hear someone shout 'watch out!' and I think they mean the line. I look down and see I'm about to run out of bounds. So, I plant my foot and do a big jump, trying to grab the disc and throw it back in. Just as I leave the ground, I look up to try and find the disc..." Corey paused for dramatic effect and put her fork down on the table so she could use both hands. "And then I see a giant tree just a few inches from my face."

The people around the table laughed, even though all of them except one had heard the story before. Anika's presence served as an excellent excuse to share these again, and Ichirin found that knowing the endings didn't make them any less enjoyable.

"What did you do?" Anika asked, her hands hovering over her plate.

"What could I do? I had enough time to say 'Oh sh...' and then I curled up and smacked into the tree. I jumped into the branches at a full run and knocked myself flat on my back."

"Were you okay?"

"Oh yeah. I was laughing before I picked myself up. Both teams thought it was hilarious. We kept playing, and I didn't need a sub."

Ichirin felt the twinge at the base of her neck and squirmed in her seat. Hemingway noticed the motion and looked at her from across the table, arching an eyebrow. She forced a smile and waved him off, picking up a wine glass and holding it in front of her to shield her face. When he turned his attention back to the conversation, Ichirin twisted in her chair, trying to see out the large windows behind her.

By now it was dark, and the lights on their side made the glass more mirror than transparent. If she squinted, she saw some lights from buildings on the other side of the lake, but otherwise saw a reflection of their dinner party.

You're not imagining things. I feel it too.

She wondered if another creature hunted her. Would it attack the entire group, putting all of them at risk? Would her powers manifest in the middle of dinner, outing her? The first time she inherited powers, she summoned a gust of wind that blew a door off its hinges in her parents' house. If they had been home, there was no telling how they would have reacted. Taka helped her to gain control of the windstorms before her parents returned, but just thinking of that memory made her grip the edge of the table and pull the tablecloth taut.

You've gotten better since then. Remember the enenra and how long it took to compose yourself—minutes at most. I'll keep a watch out, and if anything seems off, I'll let you know. If need be, I could force any manifestation down.

Was that akin to when Taka offered to take over her body and possess her? His lack of response answered the question for her, and she stopped entertaining that train of thought. Instead, she took solace in her growing control. Each inherited gift had gotten easier to handle.

Just remember the tortoise and the hare.

The message was clear, understood, and agreed with, even if Taka's tone made her feel like a chastised child. She knew her limits. Without knowing the creature in the vicinity, she couldn't prepare or venture a guess about her capabilities. Every step forward felt like a shuffling limp with conditions, restrictions, and questions. So many questions.

A gentle kick under the table brought Ichirin back to the conversation at dinner. Corey stared at her with a pointed look, and Ichirin knew her inward focus could be noticed. Corey could tell when she had long discussions with the kami, no matter how much she tried to hide it.

"Sorry, I spaced out for a minute there. Let me start cleaning up," Ichirin offered, hoping no one else noticed.

Ayden leapt to his feet, making his chair screech as it slid across the tile. "No, that's my job. You've been working all day, and I had today off. Besides, I don't think anyone else should have to pick up after the catastrophe Leah leaves behind."

He winked at his partner, and she gave him an exaggerated eyeroll.

"If you insist," Ichirin said.

"I do."

Ayden cleaned off the table before immersing himself in scrubbing some of the pots left in the sink. Corey twisted so she could lean against Leah and propped her feet up in Ayden's vacated chair.

"What do you want to do tonight? We brought some games we could play, or there's always the hot tub."

Hemingway shook his head. "Not tonight. It's been rough at work, so I think we're going to retire early. Thanks for dinner, Leah. Marvelous as always. Ayden, are you sure you don't want any help cleaning up?"

Ayden shook his head and called out over his shoulder, "No, but thanks! I'll have this taken care of in no time. You two rest up. We've got a busy day tomorrow."

Hemingway glanced toward Ichirin, and she gave him a wave goodnight. He excused himself from the table and got up, standing there for a moment to wait for Anika. He reached for her chair but then pulled himself back, his face scrunched as he wrestled with his awkwardness. In a way, Ichirin thought it was cute and endearing.

Are you sure you don't have feelings for him?

Sometimes Taka revealed his archaic way of thinking. Ichirin knew she didn't have feelings for Hemingway, but that didn't mean she couldn't find him attractive or his quirks endearing. It reminded her of wrestling to make her parents change some of their traditional viewpoints. The world and social structures changed. Ichirin remembered Taka's reaction when he first learned about Corey's romantic situation.

And I have long since admitted my folly at my initial response. While the theory makes sense—and is one that I've believed since before your grandfather was born—I didn't realize such an arrangement was acceptable within society. In some ways, humans have advanced quite a bit.

"What about you?" Corey asked Ichirin as the other two left.

"I think I'll turn in early as well. I want to start this vacation off right, and that includes getting plenty of sleep for a change."

In truth, Ichirin felt wide awake, but she didn't have the energy to play one of their games without Hemingway. Otherwise, it felt like she played solitaire while the other three competed. Hemingway made the entire experience feel more balanced. At a minimum, it gave her someone else to play with who didn't know the rules backward and forward.

The excuse made, Ichirin went up to her room after giving her evening farewells. Her room was on the second floor at the end of the hall. She walked on the balls of her feet as she passed Hemingway's closed door, not wanting to disturb either of them as she hustled to her chamber.

Her room had a queen-sized bed and a window that looked out over the back yard and down to the lake. Within a couple of minutes, she rested on the bed, a book in her hands, and the rest of her belongings unpacked and tucked away. For the next hour or so, she looked forward to digging into the next novel in one of her favorite series. It seemed like all of her recent reading had been mythology books.

You should be reading those. The more you learn about the possible creatures you might face, the more competent a fighter you'll become.

Right now, with everything going on, she needed something lighter to take her mind off of reality. A few hours of relaxation wouldn't be the end of the world.

Do you think that's the best option when you know something might be out there watching you?

Even if a new creature wandered outside her window, her odds of winning the lottery were better than trying to find lore on it. Japanese mythology had a spirit or beast for everything, making it impossible to become knowledgeable about them all. No, her time would be better spent relaxing, even if that meant disappointing her guardian and spiritual companion.

I find it somewhat ironic that you chastise me for my lack of information when I do not provide every single detail, and yet you are not willing to put in the work to gain some of that knowledge on your own. This is the perfect opportunity to study, while the others are paired off and have left you alone.

At the moment, her brain latched onto the thought of being alone. A few moments of peace sounded like heaven and critical to her mental health. Reaching up, she unclasped the locket and carried it to the bathroom, leaving it on the edge of the sink. When she went back to the bed, everything was quiet, both inside her head and out of it.

For a moment, she closed her eyes and breathed.

Ichirin imagined it as a form of mental stretching. Rather than being cramped in a small space with another person, she had another entity squished up against her in her mind. Now that she had her brain to herself, she let her thoughts wander without someone jerking her back to task with a metaphysical leash.

Relishing the peace, Ichirin relaxed and sank into her book, turning the pages until she fell asleep with it on her chest.

In the morning, as she got dressed, Ichirin looked at the locket. She hesitated to put it on, a reaction that surprised her. Whenever she did, Taka would be upset for her leaving him behind. He would take her abandonment as a personal slight. She knew she'd have to deal with that at some point, but right now she debated if she possessed the energy.

A birdsong from outside caught pulled her thoughts away from her quandary. It reminded her of the beautiful nature scene just beyond that wall. The rising sun painted the sky with bright orange streaks, and the silence of the house made her think all the others still slept. A quick jog down to the lake might help her shake some of the cobwebs from her brain and rejuvenate her enough to deal with Taka's surly mood.

Walking through the silent house, Ichirin shivered when she stepped outside and the air hit her skin. It was colder than she antici-pated, but not uncomfortable. Picking up her pace to try and warm up, she jumped down the steps and into the back yard. Dew clung to the grass, the water soaking into the bottom of her pants as she trav-eled toward the pier.

As she got close, she jumped to the wooden planks, glad to be standing on something that didn't soak into her clothes. The water lapped at the thick posts, providing a regular beat that could lull her to sleep if she laid down and closed her eyes. Some mist clung to the lake, burning off in small pockets as the sun struck them.

Ichirin walked to the end of the dock, the boards creaking under her with each step. She took in a deep breath through her nose and let the serenity of the lake ease into every muscle of her body. The combination of earth, trees, and water served as a type of balance that she tapped into and felt magical—not true magic, but the pure energy of unadulterated nature.

That moment of peace crashed as the gnawing sensation reap-peared at the back of her neck. As soon as she felt it, Ichirin took a step away from the front of the dock, moving toward the house. When she noticed her reaction, she stopped. If something watched her, she didn't want it to know she felt its scrutiny. She chastised herself for her initial fear-based reaction.

Scanning the lake, she saw small waves dancing across the surface. The few broken branches pushed around by the currents took on fearsome shapes, even though Ichirin knew they were harmless. The prow of a boat came around a bend to her left, still with half of it hidden by the trees. Squinting, Ichirin saw one silhouette sitting in it, unmoving.

As she tried to focus on the person in the boat, she noticed someone much closer, staring at her from behind a tree. Given her previous reaction, she made sure not to react nor let her eyes get drawn to the figure. It stood in the long shadows, and only a portion of it extended into her view. She couldn't make it out, or even if it was human.

After taking a few breaths, she turned around, forcing herself to walk off the dock. The sensation of being watched spread until every fiber in her being screamed to run back to the safety of the house. She kept her steps slow and measured, reminding herself that she had faced down nightmares before. That helped her keep her composure as she climbed the steps to the deck. When she closed the sliding door behind her, she pressed her back against the wall and let out a long, loud exhale, her eyes drifting toward the ceiling. After a couple of pants, she sprinted through the house, taking the steps two at a time on her way to her room.

She ran into the bathroom and snatched the locket up from the counter, holding it against her chest before bothering to loop it around her neck. Now that it touched her skin, she closed her eyes and collapsed to a seated position on the floor, leaning back against the wall.

You shouldn't have gone outside without me. You know that I'm here to protect you and keep you alive.

Ichirin fastened the locket around her neck, enjoying the comforting weight as it hung against her chest. The metal felt cold after sitting on the counter all night.

You should not have left me behind. That was childish and foolish.

The disappointment in Taka's voice made Ichirin slump her head forward and pull her knees up to her chest. He was right. Her irrational behavior put her at risk. If the thing out there was not content with watching, she might not be having this internal debate. She no longer had any doubts that something or someone lurked outside.

But spending time agonizing over her mistakes wasn't moving forward. Ichirin stood up and took a deep breath. Closing her eyes, she moved her body, bit by bit, trying to see if anything felt different.

She wasn't sure what she did, but she searched for something on the inside that seemed out of place. The closest analogy she could summon was from Aikido class, when they practiced focused breathing. But everything felt the same. In the past, her powers had expressed themselves, or Taka provided guidance.

To answer the implied question, no, I am not aware of any latent powers.

People clambered down the steps and walked around downstairs, the noise carrying up to Ichirin even in her bathroom. She shook out her hands a couple of times before checking her appearance in the mirror. After grooming to the level she considered the bare minimum for facing the others, Ichirin walked downstairs. Hemingway and Anika sat at the table in the dining area.

"I was going to make some tea, would either of you want some?" Ichirin offered. A cup of green tea with lavender sounded like the prescription to put her in the right frame of mind.

"I'll take a cup," Hemingway said before turning to Anika. "She makes the best tea I've ever had. You won't find a better cup anywhere. She has flavors I never thought would be mixed with tea. Ichirin expanded my mind to so many possibilities."

Anika offered a soft smile but shook her head. "While that is a glowing and tempting recommendation, I prefer coffee. I hope you understand."

Ichirin held up her hand to wave off any concerns. "It's fine—each to their own. I never acquired the taste for coffee, even when I loaded it with sugar and cream. It always tasted too strong, like a punch. I'd much prefer the gentle massage of tea."

"I've never heard of coffee or tea described in such a way." Anika pressed her eyebrows together, and for a moment Ichirin thought she might have offended the other woman, but she still smiled.

"Perhaps I've missed my calling and should have been a poet instead."

Ichirin joined in the communal chuckle as she put the kettle on the stove and walked into the pantry to retrieve her tea ingredients. As soon as she opened the door, she froze. Packages of food littered the floor, and someone had ripped one of the shelves off the wall. As her hand slid down the edge of the door, she felt a rough indentation beneath her fingertips about the height of her waist. Something had carved several grooves in the wood less than an inch apart, the right distance for her to slide a finger into each scratch: the perfect size for a claw.

CHAPTER THREE

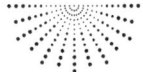

"I s everything okay?" Hemingway asked when he noticed her pause.

When she didn't respond, he pushed himself away from the table and came over. Anika twisted as much as she could to try and see without leaving her chair. Hemingway stood behind Ichirin and froze when he saw the scratches. He opened his mouth to say something, but she shot a glance in Anika's direction. He got the message and slapped his mouth shut.

You need to say something because you can't clean this up before someone not in your trusted group notices.

"What is it?" Anika asked, taking her turn to stand up from the table.

"I think something got into the house and ransacked the pantry," Ichirin said, keeping her face hidden behind the door, so she didn't have to focus on her poker face. "Whatever it was, it's long gone now."

Ichirin hoped that assumption was accurate. She gripped one of the remaining shelves and leaned forward, examining the four gashes in the door. They scratched through the paint and the top layer of wood but stopped before revealing the core. A thought came to her and made her take a sharp inhale.

The creature closed the door. No animal would do that. Could this be the same thing watching her? When was it in the house?

"Do you think it was a bear?" Anika sounded panicked, and she glanced outside the back doors as if trying to find the offending creature still in the yard.

"I don't know. When I came down this morning, the door was open, and I closed it, not thinking anything of it. We might want to keep the house locked up just to be safe."

Hemingway raised an eyebrow, and Ichirin shrugged, hoping that he got the message. She didn't want the others to know about her special gifts. She trusted Hemingway and Corey, but the thought of others beyond that small circle knowing her secret made her chest tighten. Besides, the less they knew about the creatures, the safer they were.

On this, I agree. You must keep these tiles close to your edge of the table, without others seeing them. There's no telling how they will react. You've been lucky so far, but luck runs out.

"I'll check the doors, just to be safe. Why don't you go upstairs and let the others know what happened?" Hemingway suggested.

Anika nodded and hustled to the stairs, her footfalls receding as she climbed them. When she was out of sight, Hemingway turned to Ichirin.

"Do you know anything about this?" he hissed, keeping his voice low and peeking around the edge of the door.

"No. I was as shocked as you when I found it. I made up that story about coming down earlier and seeing the door open. Everything was shut tight when I came down. I didn't know what to do, but we had to tell her something."

"Is this another myth? Do you have new powers?"

Ichirin closed the pantry door and moved to the back door, checking it while she spoke. The others would be coming downstairs, and she wanted to take advantage of the moment to look around.

"Not that I know of. I felt like I was being watched earlier, but then thought I imagined it. I don't know. But I can't do anything new. Even Taka hasn't detected anything, which is weird. I thought that it might be something mundane and normal, but after seeing those scratches, I don't think that's the case."

The muffled sound of people talking echoed down from upstairs. She couldn't make out the words but didn't need to.

"We should get out of here," Hemingway said.

Ichirin stopped and turned to look at him, trying to think of how to respond. He pointed up at the second floor to accentuate his point.

It's not your fault everyone decided to bring others into this. But that doesn't matter. You know you can't leave a legendary creature. You need to stay here, and you know what you must do. If he wants to leave you alone to face it...

"I can't go. You know that. I need to figure out what is going on. If it's another myth, I need to take care of it. If I left now, and people wound up dead, how could I live with that?"

Hemingway looked down and hunched his shoulders forward, not a lot, but enough to make Ichirin feel like she wounded him. She reached out and squeezed his upper arm, letting him know she wasn't upset with him. From her perspective, it was a statement of fact. It might have come out harsher than she meant, but the point stood.

Hemingway looked up. "You're right. We have to get Corey away from the others. Will you promise me something? Will you let me know the instant you have any idea what it might be or what you can do?"

"Of course, as long as none of the others are around. I don't want them to know my secret."

Hemingway placed his hand over Ichirin's and returned the squeeze before nodding in the direction the front door. They continued their investigation but didn't see anything unusual about any of the windows or the doors. As they checked the front entrance, Corey came bounding down the staircase, Anika, Leah and Ayden following without quite so much exuberance.

Putting a hand on the wall to stop her mad descent, Corey looked at Ichirin with a knowing glance. The only thing Ichirin could offer in response was a subtle shrug that she hoped the others didn't notice.

"What happened?" Leah asked as she descended. "Anika said something about a bear getting into the pantry?"

"We don't know for a fact it was a bear, but something got into the food and made a mess of what we brought. It didn't do too much damage, just ransacked the pantry." Ichirin walked toward the kitchen, leading the group and showing them what she found.

"Okay, that's never happened before. How did it get in?" Leah asked.

Corey jumped in before Ichirin had to say anything. "It's my fault. I opened the back door to let in some fresh air and must've forgotten to close it before heading upstairs."

"Do you think we should call the cops or anything?" Ayden touched the scratches on the door, squatting so he could view them at eye level. "Let them know there's an aggressive critter loose in the area?"

Ichirin shuddered at the thought. The last thing she wanted was more people involved. It would make keeping her secret more difficult. This time Hemingway came to her rescue.

"I'll take care of it. I'll give them a call and file a report, let them know what happened."

He walked onto the back deck, closing the door behind him as he brought his phone up to his ear. Ichirin noticed that he didn't bother calling anyone, but the others focused on the damage and had their backs facing the windows.

"When I came down, I didn't see anything," Ichirin said. "I think whatever it was must've gotten its fill and wandered off. I'd guess it's more scared of us than we are of it. We just need to make sure to lock the doors at night."

"The first-floor windows wouldn't be a bad idea either," Ayden offered. "I've never heard of a bear climbing up to the second story before, so that should be fine. But until they catch it, we should be careful. It could've smelled some of your delicious cooking and couldn't resist the temptation." He leaned in close to Leah as he complimented her. "Speaking of, when's breakfast?"

The ability of the human mind to accept a rational explanation for irrational events—no matter how far-fetched—is nothing short of miraculous.

Ichirin backed out of the ensuing conversation and walked into the study, leaving the rest of them to come to their own conclusions. As she stood in front of the desk, she heard footsteps come up behind her. She didn't need to turn around to know it was Corey. It had to be her or Hemingway, and his steps had a heavier tread and lacked Corey's energetic bounce.

"Before I get pulled back into the whirlwind of the kitchen, what is it? What can you do? What do we know?"

Ichirin held up her hands to stave off the questioning.

"Nothing yet. I didn't know anything until I saw the pantry this morning. I made up the part about finding the door open. That's the only reason I think it's another creature. As far as I can tell, I can't do anything yet."

"What about Taka? Has he decided to share any information with you?"

"No. It's as in the dark about all of this as I am."

An expression flitted across Corey's face before Ichirin could register it and she questioned whether she saw anything.

"It's alright," Corey said. "We'll figure it out and then find out how to stop it. That's what we do. This could become part of our yearly tradition too! Don't worry; I'm not suggesting we pull the others into it. I like this being our little thing. Plus, I know you well enough by now to know better than that."

"Speaking of that, thank you for helping earlier. I wasn't sure how to cover the situation."

"No problem. I figured that explanation made the most sense." Corey sniffed at the air. Ichirin did the same and caught the telltale odor of bacon. "Smells like Leah's gone back to work in the kitchen. Let's join them, get a good breakfast, and figure out what our next steps are going to be."

The exchange reminded Ichirin why she felt so grateful to have Corey in her inner circle. The woman was the perpetual cheerleader, pushing Ichirin forward and keeping her moving toward the end goal even when they didn't know what the end goal was. Whereas Hemingway was the rock she could hold onto, Corey put a light spin on everything and had no doubts about their success. In some ways, that made her a light-hearted version of Taka.

Did you just compare me to the one who has liquid caffeine as her blood? I think if I ever showed that much enthusiasm, your head would explode from the noise.

Both her friend and her spiritual guide shared a sense of confidence that Ichirin used for strength. Her faith in her mission renewed, Ichirin joined the rest of the vacationers in the dining room. Leah proved to be hard at work, demonstrating skills Ichirin could never hope to emulate. She marveled that Corey and Ayden remained so trim living with someone who could cook like that.

"What's the plan for today?" Ayden asked while helping himself to a generous pile of salmon-flavored scrambled eggs.

"I need to run to the store to replace some of what the bear got into. It had weird tastes. Like the cucumbers. Every single cucumber is gone. Other stuff is missing a chunk here or there, but those? Completely polished off." Leah spread her hands out, at a loss for words to explain the beast's behavior.

"Maybe it was a vegetarian bear?" Ayden offered with a smirk.

Leah smacked him in the shoulder with her fork, and he gave an exaggerated groan.

"Seriously though, I'm just glad all the fish and meat was in the fridge or freezer. Can you imagine if it got in there? You would have come down to it still feasting!"

"Well, I think we should go swimming today. Take a relaxing dip in the lake since the weather's nice. That's why we all came out here, right?" Corey looked around the table to a bunch of nods. "It's settled then."

People finished breakfast and went their separate ways to get ready for the excursion down to the water. By the time they left the house, the sun was high overhead and had long since evaporated the dew. The day heated up enough that dipping in the water sounded like a refreshing break. They walked down to the shore as a group, all of them piling onto the dock. Corey sprinted off the end, tossing her towel behind her as she jumped into the water. Ayden followed, cannonballing near her as she broke the surface to catch her breath.

Ichirin spread her towel, laying it out so she could lie down without worrying about splinters or rough spots in the wood. Anika and Hemingway did the same, stretching out next to each other.

Anika looked over and pointed at Ichirin's locket. "That's beautiful. I don't think I've ever seen you without it. Does it have special significance?"

Ichirin hesitated, not sure how to explain.

Just tell her it contains a living spiritual entity trapped in a rock that you found at the base of a mountain while hiking in Japan. What's so hard about that?

"It's an heirloom. It means something to my family members."

I suppose that's correct, if not honest. You are a part of your own family, after all. Or are you saying that you consider me a part of your family? While I'm honored, I don't think even your open-minded society would approve of you wedding a spiritual entity with no physical form.

Ichirin tried to block out Taka while Anika spoke, an effort made more difficult when the voice came from inside one's own head.

"That's wonderful. It makes it mean so much more when it has that history behind it, kind of like it soaks in the stories of where it's been and what it's experienced. Wouldn't you agree?"

If she only knew.

"Yes. It means so much more that way." Ichirin knew her blunt parroting would come off as rude, but she didn't have much choice. She did not want to continue this line of inquiry. Throughout the conversation, she tried to stay aware of their surroundings. The feeling of being watched had not returned, but she felt responsible for the safety of the others and needed to remain hypervigilant for their sakes.

And on top of all of that, an insistent voice made colorful commentary in her mind that proved impossible to ignore.

If I remember, you admitted you prefer my colorful commentary to my— how did you phrase it—immature silence. If you'd rather me remain quiet...

It took a concentrated effort not to sigh and roll her eyes at Taka's reaction. He knew that was not what she meant. Although sometimes his childish nature amazed her, considering he had existed the length of several lifespans. At least, several human lifespans. Did kami age? Did they grow senile or infirm like people did? Could they die of old age?

Senility and infirmity are both traits that require a physical form to manifest. I'm afraid that any lack of sanity I have is either due to my innate nature or being stuck on the side of a mountain for a few generations waiting for someone to find me who could talk to me.

Ichirin felt sad for Taka. She remembered the trouble she had when she first moved to the States and felt like she didn't know anyone. At least she had some measure of connection with the outside world through her classes. She couldn't imagine spending tens of years with no contact whatsoever.

Hundreds.

The correction left Ichirin stunned. Her mouth opened for a moment before she thought to shut it. No one noticed. Anika rolled over to talk to Hemingway, and splashing from the lake made it clear that Corey and Ayden were preoccupied. A couple of drops landed on Ichirin's back as the water fight escalated, the cool moisture feeling soothing on skin that might have been in the sun too long without sunscreen. She envied those who could go outside for long periods without needing to lather it on.

Ichirin sat up and hung her feet over the edge of the pier, dipping them into the water up to her ankles. The cold shocked her system, making her think twice about jumping in. It felt good as the chills ran up her calves, but the sun needed to warm up more before she plunged in.

The temptation to let her guard slip was strong, but she chased it away. Touching the locket with her right hand, she twisted it between her fingers, trying to see or feel anything out of the ordinary. But everything felt normal. Perhaps the creature had fled? It wouldn't be the first time. But with so little to go on, she didn't know how they'd chase it down.

Corey roared as she swam over Ayden, pushing him under the surface. He picked her up and heaved her to the side, making a large wave as she crashed into the water near the shore. Corey sank under and pushed off the bottom, bursting out like a buoy held beneath the surface and then let go. Her trajectory had her land on top of Ayden, and they both went under, him letting out a laugh before the water closed over his head.

The water around them churned from their wrestling match until Ayden burst free and took in a breath, his laughter still strong. He brushed his hair back with his hands and looked around, expecting an attack at any moment.

Corey lurched out of the water, coming up beside him and flailing to grab his shoulders. He swam away from her with a strong stroke as she dropped under the surface of the water. Her hands clawed for him as she disappeared from view. He turned to face her, grinning and getting ready for her next attack.

Seconds ticked by, and Ayden's grin faded. Ichirin stood up on the dock, staring at the place where she last saw her friend. The recent fight churned up the silt and made it impossible to peer through.

Corey's head broke free, and she gasped for air before some unseen forced yanked her back down under the surface.

CHAPTER FOUR

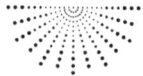

Ayden dove under the water and tried to grab Corey as Ichirin ran to the end of the dock, leaping off without a moment's hesitation. Hemingway and Anika scrambled to their feet behind her, rushing to the edge.

Ichirin wasn't a strong swimmer, but she pointed her hands over her head, trying to imitate swimmers she'd seen. The surface smacked against her abdomen and the top of her legs, but the stinging sensation didn't register. She kicked hard, trying to get to Corey and somehow save her.

Let me help you! I know how to swim.

Ichirin's panicked focus kept her from registering the offer. Fumbling in the dirty water, she reached out to find something to grab. Her hands brushed against something soft, but it pulled away before she could grip it. At least it gave her a direction to search in the muddy water.

Paddling forward as best as she could, Ichirin reached out with both hands, waving them back and forth, groping for any sign of her friend. The back of her hand hit something, and she latched onto it. The arm returned the grasp, fingers curling around Ichirin's wrist. Getting her feet underneath her, she pushed off the bottom, the cool mud slicking between her toes as she launched upward and tried to drag the person with her.

The air struck her in the face, and she gulped it down. Yanking on both arms, she pulled Corey up beside her. Her friend sputtered and coughed, free hand slapping at Ichirin's shoulder as she tried to recover. Ayden surfaced next to them and took Corey, helping her swim toward the pier. Once there, Hemingway and Anika pulled her up onto the wood structure. Corey rolled onto her side, coughing several times with enough force that her entire body shook.

The others got out of the water, moving close but also trying not to crowd her. After a few more seconds of agonizing hacking and spitting up some water, Corey rolled onto her back and took a deep shuddering breath. She kept her eyes closed but reached up and gave a thumbs-up gesture to those standing over her. Ayden grabbed her hand, leaning forward so that he could kiss her on the cheek.

"I still won," Corey managed before succumbing to another short round of coughs.

Ayden laughed and shook his head. "You're crazy."

"What happened?" Ichirin asked. She shifted her attention to the lake, searching for something that was not quite right. Other than the stirred-up section, the lake looked peaceful and serene, like something out of a brochure.

"I don't know. I think my foot got tangled in a weed or some plants or something. When I tried to push off the ground, I felt a hard tug on my ankle. I must've panicked when I tried to free myself."

The skin near the bottom of her ankle looked red compared to the rest of her leg, but it didn't appear to be injured.

"I'm fine, really. Although I think I might be done swimming for a bit."

Hemingway bent over and retrieved Corey's towel, wrapping it around her shoulders. She thanked him and held it shut with one hand, the other still intertwined with Ayden's.

"I think I'm going to head back inside," Corey said as she moved to stand.

Hemingway offered a hand, but Ayden helped pull Corey to her feet. She wrapped her arm around his shoulders, and the two of them walked up to the house.

"I think we're *all* done swimming for a bit," Hemingway said, gathering up the belongings the others left behind.

Anika followed his example, gathering her belongings. Ichirin sat on the dock with her knees pulled up to her chest and stared out across the lake. Her jaw clenched as she tried to penetrate the serene surface and see what lurked underneath. She didn't know if Corey believed her own story, but Ichirin thought it was too convenient to be the truth. Her fingers pressed against the surface of the locket, making the back of it dig into her skin.

With his arms full of towels and discarded clothing, Hemingway came up to Ichirin and looked down at her. "Are you coming up to the house?"

"Not yet. I need to catch my breath. I'll be up in just a minute."

He took a deep breath in through his nose and looked from her to Anika and then back again. After a brief pause, he nodded and walked off the back of the dock to escort Anika up to the house, leaving Ichirin alone with her thoughts.

Something was here. If she had any doubts about it before, recent events dispelled them. In addition, the unknown creature had tried to kill Corey. Ichirin's hands tightened into fists hard enough that her nails felt like they cut into her palms. Her arms shook from the strain until she forced herself to open her hands.

This creature made one of the worst mistakes possible. It made this personal.

Ichirin ignored Taka. Right now, she wanted all her attention focused on locating and identifying the creature that attacked one of her closest friends. Closing her eyes, Ichirin tried to use her anger to fuel her search for any latent powers. Her emotions had served as a catalyst multiple times in the past, and right now she embraced those emotions without any restraint.

But nothing happened.

With a muted growl, she jumped up and walked to the edge of the dock, her hands once again fists at her side. Each footfall slammed against the wood planks hard enough to make them shake. Ichirin leaned forward, staring at the water.

"I dare you to show yourself. You want to hunt me, then hunt me. I'm right here."

Ichirin kept her voice low, exercising restraint because she knew Anika or Ayden might hear her. Otherwise, she would have screamed the challenge with a roar of defiance.

Whatever it is, it isn't going to come out to face you. It doesn't have a connection with you like I do. You'll need to find it. You need to focus...

For the first time in their relationship, Ichirin shoved Taka out of her mind, silencing him behind a mental wall fueled by the fire of her emotions. She didn't need to listen to him right now.

Turning on her heel, she stormed off the dock, jumping into the water at the edge of the shore, sinking in the mud up to her ankles. She walked out, stopping when the water lapped at her calves. Holding out both arms like a sacrifice, she stood and waited for several breaths.

The lack of a target made her rage boil off, and she took a staggering step in the mud.

Save that anger. You'll need it later, but for now, you need to control yourself. Look for clues. There might be something around.

Taka's sound advice helped pull everything back into focus. Ichirin walked along the shore, picking a path that brought her out of the water but kept her within a single stride of it. She walked through the trees, noticing the temperature drop as soon as she passed under their cover. The air here had a mustier smell that made her nose wrinkle. As she navigated the large trunks, she realized it wasn't just the earth and the trees. Something putrid lingered in the air.

Following the odorous trail, her path curved away from the lake, heading back in the direction of the street. The land sloped up, making her use her hand against the trees for balance a couple of times. As she came around a thick trunk, she stopped her foot before she stepped in the foul-smelling mess.

A pile of trash rested on the ground, comprised of fish carcasses, a few McDonald's wrappers, and other empty food containers. The fish were raw and left to rot in the open air.

The stench forced her to put her hand over her nose to keep from inhaling too much of it. She turned around, looking for any sign of the creature: a trail, footprints, or the beast itself. Was this its home? Did it have a lair?

As she turned around, Ichirin noticed she had a perfect view of the pier. With a couple of steps to the side, she saw the entire back side of the house. The spacing of the trees provided more than enough places to hide from sight. This had to be where the creature spied on her and the others.

Since she didn't see the animal, she looked closer at the remains, picking up a stick to sift through the detritus. She found a cherry Pop-Tart wrapper, confirming her suspicions.

The question was how to proceed. She still didn't know what it was and didn't have a trail to follow. The evidence seemed to indicate it has something to do with the lake, but swimming without some type of support structure would be suicidal. Ichirin thought of Taka's warning about the tortoise and the hare.

I agree. If we leave now, there's a chance that the creature doesn't know you found anything: the longer we delay, the greater the possibility of it noticing you. Look at the food. It keeps returning to this spot. You don't want to spook it and have to track it down.

Before she left, Ichirin walked in a wide circle around the primitive campsite, trying to look for any more clues. Not for the first time, she wished she had more survival training. To her eyes, it all looked like dirt. Her search proved fruitful when she found a large X marked on the bark of one of the trees in blue paint. By itself, she might have thought it was a mark for some part of the forestation program, even though none of the other trees she saw had a similar marking. However, the remains of a large egg sat at the base of the tree, half-buried.

Ichirin squatted down and twisted her head to the side to get a better view of the strange object. She couldn't shake the idea that it looked like an egg about the size of her fists clenched side-by-side. The shell was the deep blue of the sky just after sunset. Small fragments of the shell lay near the opening, making Ichirin think they fell there when something broke free.

I don't know what kind of creature this represents. What I will say is to remember that the egg is symbolic. This doesn't mean the creature is only a few days old. We deal with magical entities that follow a rigorous set of rules. This could be a transportation mechanism, but the symbolism represents a rebirth.

Taka paused for a moment while Ichirin considered what he said.

Or it could be a creature that hatched.

Ichirin closed her eyes and shook her head as she stood up. She turned to head back toward the house but paused, looking further up the shoreline. Ichirin couldn't be sure, but the area looked familiar. After a short walk, she turned to look up the hill in the direction of the street. She lifted a hand, tracing a path from the road down to her current position and extending on her current trajectory. Breaking into a jog, she kept her eyes focused ahead, looking for something that even her untrained observation should be able to recognize.

After covering a short distance, she saw the large skid marks in the dirt where Ben had crashed to the ground. Ichirin pressed her back against a tree and rested her head, feeling the rough edges of the bark poke at her skull. If she had thought to do a more thorough search when she found Ben, all of this might have been avoided.

You couldn't have known that. He played his part well. I'm confident he isn't the one responsible for this but rather served as a lackey. I doubt he has the capabilities to plan something of this magnitude.

None of that changed the truth of how close she had been. But she needed to keep walking forward one step at a time. Besides, Hemingway and Corey would be worried about her. Her absence had gone on longer than she anticipated.

When she returned to the house, Hemingway stood at the deck railing waiting for her. He rushed down the stairs to meet her before she reached the landing at the halfway point.

"Are you okay? Did you see anything?"

"I'm fine. I didn't see anything. Whatever it is, it's still hiding. Where's Anika?" Ichirin paused before they got high enough to be visible from the windows of the house.

"Upstairs with Ayden and Corey. I had her check in on them, and I said I'd wait for you here. She made me promise I wouldn't go down to the dock though."

Smart woman. Sorry to say, but it looks like the water portion of your summer fun in the sun got canceled.

The two of them walked up the last flight of stairs and stood near the railing, facing the house to keep watch for any eavesdroppers. Ichirin looked up, checking to make sure none of the windows on the second floor were open before she spoke.

"I found a pile of trash out in the woods. I think it's where the creature was watching us—or me, rather. It had a good view of both the dock and the back of the house. For all I know, it could hear us too. We've certainly dealt with stranger things."

"Do you think it's watching us now?" Hemingway turned, staring at the woods, but Ichirin gave him a gentle nudge to keep his attention focused forward.

"It doesn't feel like it, but if I'm honest, I have no idea. I also found where it came from: an egg, about this big." Ichirin held up her hands and mimed cupping a large bowl. "Taka said it might have hatched, or it might be a mystical transportation tool for something fully grown."

"Does he know what we're dealing with?"

Ichirin shook her head. She let out a sigh and drummed her thumb against the railing behind her. "I think we need to come up with an excuse to get the others out of the house. It's not safe for them here."

"You don't want to leave to do some research and then come back?"

"I can't. Even if it weren't for everything else..." Ichirin walked over to the door to the house and paused with her fingers curled around the handle. "Not after it went for Corey."

Hemingway didn't offer any objections but instead moved to join her as she entered the house. As they passed the threshold, Ichirin became aware of the tightness in her shoulders. The house used to be a sanctuary and a source of solace, something that eased the tension with its existence and promises of escapism.

The creature invading the home while they slept had forever ruined that atmosphere. It crept through here, polluting the energy of the place in a way that could never be rectified. She knew this would be the last time they came here, but she took the emotions that stirred up and held onto them, planning to use them later to feed the emotional broiler that fueled her rage.

Now was not the time for anger. She walked into the pantry, impressed at how much Leah had cleaned before she left. The broken shelf was propped up in the corner, and all the remaining food had been reorganized to fit on the decreased shelf space. Ichirin's hands shook as she reached for her tea containers and grabbed the closest one without bothering to identify it.

Going through the motions of preparing a cup of tea helped soothe her nerves, frayed from the emotional rollercoaster of the morning and afternoon. Her shaking stopped, and she held her head up without pain spreading through her back. She prepared two cups, giving the second one to Hemingway at the table. As they sipped it in silence, the other three members of the household came to join them.

"How are you doing?" Hemingway asked Corey.

"I'm shiny," she said with an exasperated sigh. "It was just a little bit of water. What would help is if everyone stopped checking on me like I've died and been brought back by the red witch."

"You do know nothing," Ayden said, earning a backhanded slap in the shoulder from his partner.

"Seriously, I'm fine. It was just an accident, not something to pull down the whole weekend. So, let's keep the vacation going and play a game or something."

When no one objected, Ayden ran upstairs to return with a small pile of game boxes. He selected one after a brief discussion with Corey that left Ichirin behind almost as soon as it started. Within a few minutes, he explained rules to a game with so many moving pieces, Ichirin thought her head spun. It didn't help that she gave him half of her attention. The other half focused on the creature lurking outside. She longed to pour over her mythological books but couldn't find a way to excuse herself.

Once they were about an hour into the game, Leah came home, and Ayden jumped up to help her unload groceries. Anika excused herself to use the restroom, leaving Corey, Ichirin, and Hemingway at the table.

"My foot didn't get caught in anything." Corey propped her elbows on the table and leaned forward so she could whisper to her friends. "Something frakking grabbed me. I know that's crazy, but it's true. I felt fingers curl around my ankle and pull down hard. I kicked it and got away enough to get some fresh air before it yanked me back down. When you grabbed my arm, it let go. Otherwise..." She shuddered.

"I found a pile of trash in the woods that looked like the creature had been eating there." Ichirin mirrored Corey's pose, moving close and glancing at the hallway to make sure no one walked in on them unexpected.

"How do you know it wasn't just sloppy campers?" Corey asked.

"The fish wasn't cooked or scaled."

"Okay, so not campers."

Corey dropped back into her seat just as Ayden came into view, carrying grocery bags. Hemingway stood up, walking over to offer his help, but Ayden waved him off.

"We've got it. Just a couple of bags. Besides, it's your turn, isn't it?"

Hemingway made a show of looking at the board and rested his chin on his fist waiting until Leah walked in and chatted with Ayden.

"It isn't safe. We need to get them out of here," Hemingway whispered behind his hand.

That man is so subtle he reeks of suspicion.

Ichirin nodded, not trusting herself to say anything that wouldn't be overheard. While she agreed with Hemingway's sentiment, she didn't know how to accomplish it, at least not without all of them evacuating. The best-case scenario seemed to be Corey and Hemingway leaving with their respective partners and her facing the creature alone. She squirmed in her chair but admitted to herself that the others' safety was more important.

"Not a problem," Corey said as she pushed herself up from the table.

Ichirin and Hemingway both watched her as she walked over to Leah and Ayden. While they stared, Anika came back to the table. Her return pulled their attention back to the game. Ichirin longed to know what Corey said, but she couldn't make out any words. Instead, she poured as much of her attention as she could muster into the game, all the while knowing it was a futile endeavor. Ayden and Corey each had twice as many points as the closest competitor.

They continued to play the game to its inevitable conclusion—one where Corey and Ayden fought for every last point, and the others had given up. As they packed it up, Corey pulled Ichirin aside, leading her into the study.

"Ayden and Leah are going to hightail it out of here after dinner tonight. I didn't tell them why. I just told them that you needed some quiet friend time, and they were okay with that."

"Really?" Ichirin pulled back. She knew this was one of the few times where all three of them had large chunks of time together.

"Of course. Why wouldn't they? They know what it's like, and we live together. We'll have more chances to see each other, so it isn't that big of a deal. They're even willing to take Anika home if Hemingway can come up with some reason for her to leave."

"You have an amazing life."

"Yeah, well, don't forget that you're part of it. If the situation were reversed, you'd do the same. Now you just need to hope Hemingway can figure something out. I've done as much as I can. He's on his own."

Ichirin chuckled. "He's a little awkward sometimes, but he means well."

That's like saying Corey is a little energetic.

The two of them went back to join the others, Ichirin wearing a genuine smile after the exchange. Both Leah and Ayden matched her expression and gave her a nod, letting her know they supported Corey without saying a word. That went much easier than Ichirin anticipated. Soon both of them would be safe and none the wiser about her secret.

"Hem, can I steal you for a second?" Ichirin asked.

"Sure."

He excused himself from Anika, and Corey swooped in to run interference and distract her. Corey's social awareness and ability to handle a wide range of situations never ceased to amaze Ichirin. She had witnessed the skill many times, but she could never emulate it, even if she planned out social interactions in advance.

As soon as they were alone in the foyer, Ichirin turned around. "Corey said Leah and Ayden are both leaving tonight after dinner, and they're willing to give Anika a ride back home if she has a reason to go back."

"Okay, but how do I get her to go home? She's freaked out with everything that's been going on, so I don't think it will take much. But I can't just send her away. That's not honorable."

"I don't know. You know her better than I do. If you have to go with her, I understand. I promise you; I won't feel disappointed or let down. You and I both know it isn't safe for her here. And I can't ask her to be a part of it."

Hemingway reached up and stroked his chin, glancing back and forth between the kitchen and Ichirin standing in front of him.

"I'll try to figure something out," he offered after a moment.

Even with how well she knew him, Ichirin couldn't predict the outcome. On the one hand, she knew he wanted to help her with whatever she had to fight. He agreed to that back when she first shared this world with him. On the other hand, she knew he had a sense of duty to Anika. She understood that and meant what she said when she gave him a free pass to leave. She hoped he knew that.

Regardless of what he decided to do, Ichirin felt confident Anika would be safe by this evening. Hemingway would make sure of it.

The rest of the day trudged along. Ichirin looked outside every few minutes, hoping to catch a glance at the creature spying on them. If anyone else noticed her agitation, no one said a word.

Once the evening rolled around, Leah prepared another lavish feast. It managed to dwarf the previous night's offering. Ichirin assumed she made extra to compensate for her imminent departure. While they cleaned up, Leah announced that she and Ayden needed to head back to the city earlier than anticipated.

"If you're heading back early, do you mind giving me a ride?" Anika asked. "I live in Redmond, so it should be on your way."

"I don't mind driving you back," Hemingway offered, giving the best performance Ichirin had ever seen from him. Then again, the offer might have been genuine.

"No, you should enjoy your vacation with your friends. I appreciate it, but it's not necessary."

"We can do that. We've got plenty of room. Are you all packed?" Ayden asked.

"Just about. I'll be ready in a few minutes." Anika walked out of the kitchen and headed upstairs.

"We should start loading the car so we can get out of your hair." Leah tugged on Ayden's shirt, dragging him out of the kitchen with her.

Both Ichirin and Corey looked at Hemingway, mouths agape and eyes wide. For his part, he looked down at the table and turned his attention out the window, refusing to make eye contact. Corey couldn't contain herself any longer.

"How?" It was the only word she managed to blurt out.

"I logged into her test servers and crashed them. Since she's the project manager and it's the weekend, she needs to check on them." He offered a weak shrug. "It shouldn't take her long to fix. She just has to reboot them, but she can't do it remotely."

I'm impressed. I never expected him even capable of having such a thought, let alone carrying it to fruition. You're affecting him.

That thought made her reach up and hug herself with one arm. She didn't consider that a positive effect. Despite that, she was glad he'd be there to help her and Corey with the creature lurking in the darkness. She reached out to him, grabbing his arm and offering a reassuring squeeze.

The front door creaked open, letting them know someone returned from loading the car. The smaller group got up from the table and went to the foyer to bid farewell to the others. Leah and Ayden both kissed Corey before turning and leaving with a wave. Anika walked forward and took both of Hemingway's hands in hers, lifting them in front of her.

"Thank you for inviting me, and I'm sorry I have to go, but I trust you understand. Next time I'll make sure to put someone else in charge when we plan a getaway."

"I'd like that. I look forward to next time."

With that, she left, leaving the three of them alone in the front entrance hall. The door hadn't closed before Ichirin sprinted up the stairs and dug through her bags to get the mythology books out. She came back downstairs carrying the small stack and went to the dining room, putting them on the table. Hemingway picked up one and sat in his chair, leaning forward as he opened it up and thumbed through the pages.

"What do we know? Water creature? Maybe can breathe water? Eats food, has claws…" He ticked off thoughts while he scanned the book in front of him.

"Likes cucumbers," Corey reminded him. He added another tick.

Corey grabbed a book and leaned back in a chair, propping her ankles on the edge of it with the tome cradled in her lap. Ichirin sat across from Hemingway where she had a view of the windows looking out over the backyard. She looked through the pages, searching for some creature that met the criteria they had defined.

As the minutes ticked by, the effort to split her attention between the book and the backyard made her head droop until she jerked it back up. Hemingway succumbed to the siren's call of sleep, his face on the book and a soft snore coming from his body. The slow, steady rumbling sound threatened to lull Ichirin into slumber.

The words on the page blurred together, and Ichirin reached up and rubbed at her eyes with the back of her hand. She pinched her nose, trying to force herself to focus, but it took four attempts to read a sentence before she realized what it said. Perhaps just a few minutes of closing her eyes would do her good. Then they wouldn't feel dry, and she could continue her research.

It felt so good to close them. Relaxing even.

Wake up! Ichirin!

CHAPTER FIVE

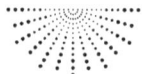

The call jerked Ichirin awake, and she snapped her head up, looking around in wide-eyed panic. It took a moment to remember where she was and what was going on. As soon as that realization flooded back, she jumped out of her chair and knocked it over with her enthusiasm. Something on the back deck stared at her through the window with wide eyes, its clawed hand resting on the handle of the door.

The creature was a little bit shorter than her, but it hunched over enough that she knew it'd be larger if it stood up straight. Its skin was a dark mottled green, a cross between flesh and fish scales. The arms looked stretched, like someone had grabbed each wrist and pulled them out to inhuman proportions. Its hands ended in claws as long as Ichirin's fingers. The creature had a ring of black hair and what looked like a divot on top of its bare skull. Instead of a regular mouth, it had a large curved beak, black and shiny like the lake at night.

The two of them froze, watching each other without blinking. Ichirin racked her brain trying to remember the creature's name. She had seen depictions of it somewhere, in one of her books. She dared to let it out of her sight and glanced down at the book still open on the table.

As soon as she dropped her attention, the creature turned around and sprinted into the deeper shadows at the back of the deck. It vaulted over the rail, moving at an unbelievable speed. By the time Ichirin reached the door, it disappeared into the night. Her motion roused Corey, who looked up and blinked several times, rubbing at her eyes while emitting a jaw-popping yawn.

"It's out there," Ichirin said as she jerked the back door open and ran onto the deck.

Corey followed her, stumbling over her chair in her haste to join her friend. On the way past Hemingway, she gave him a gentle punch in the arm to rouse him.

"Wake up! Battle calls!" she yelled with an exuberance that belied the fact that she had just woken up.

Outside, Ichirin stopped at the back railing and leaned over it, looking for any sign of movement. The darkness made it impossible to see any details, but she hoped the limited moonlight would at least let her detect motion.

"Anything?" Corey asked as she ran up, looking ready to vault the railing and pounce.

For a moment, Ichirin didn't respond, continuing to scan in the vain hope of finding something. She sighed and shook her head, pushing back and heading into the house.

"No, it's gone. At least I got a good look before it scampered away."

Hemingway stood at the table, the fingers of one hand trailing against the open pages of a book. Even as she stepped through the doorway, Ichirin described the creature.

"It was short and long-limbed, with nasty claws at the end of its hands. It had green skin and looked like it crawled out of the swamp with short, oily hair. Its head was flat or had a bit of a dent or something, like it was caved in."

If all of them had an idea of what to look for, Ichirin hoped they would find it that much faster. Taka could speed up the entire process by sharing some insight, but he remained quiet. That seemed unusual, given that he had roused her with his shout.

All three of them flipped through mythology books, looking at the pictures and using those to scan faster. However, the sheer number of potential mythological threats made it a staggering endeavor. The fact that not all of the entries had art compounded that effort.

Look up kappa.

Ichirin pressed her lips together and took a breath through her nose before appreciating the information. She knew Taka was not at her beck and call and would often disappear for lengths of time. She still wondered what he did, or why he went silent, but he had never been forthcoming with that information.

Picking up the heavy book, she flipped ahead until she got to the kappa entry. As soon as she saw the old painting, she knew they found their creature. Even being copied from an old scroll, the similarities were unmistakable.

"I found it. It's a kappa."

The others looked in their books for a similar entry. Kappa existed in many legends and lore, so they all found some information. The room became so quiet that turning a page sounded disruptive.

"You know, for something so common, you'd think there'd be a lot more details about what it can do." Corey flipped a page and then slapped it back, throwing her hands up in the air. "Three whole pages, and it doesn't say a thing about what they actually do. It just says they can work magic."

"This book says a lot about the cup of water on their head," Hemingway offered. "I'm guessing that's the divot."

"Mine talks about that too, and how polite they are, and how they can be bargained with, but it doesn't say anything about what they do," Corey emphasized the last word, leaning forward and laying both her hands on the table. "We need to know that so we can find out what Ichirin might be able to tap into. I don't think her magic abilities are going to mean she's more polite. You're already one of the politest people I've ever met, no offense."

Ichirin scrunched her brows together, not quite sure how she could have taken offense at being called polite. "Mine's much the same. It's vague about any abilities they might have. It does say they love cucumbers though, so that's at least one mystery solved."

"You getting a hankering for cucumber salad?" Corey teased.

Ignoring the comment, Ichirin looked inward, wondering if Taka had any more insight he could share. His experience often surpassed what they found in the books and had helped her discover things in the past. According to what she read, the term kappa applied to a subset of creatures with many different types that had subtle differences. Maybe Taka knew which kind it was.

Sadly, I do not. I did not get a good enough look at the creature. What I can tell you is that everything you've read is accurate. As for the well on its head, that's the source of its power. When that well empties, it can't use any of its abilities. I would warn you it's still a formidable foe even when reduced to just its physical traits.

After her look at it, Ichirin felt sure it could rip her to shreds in seconds in a direct physical confrontation. She never planned on trying to take it out with force. Having some insight into what it could do—and by extension what she might be capable of—could help her turn the tide in her favor.

I'm afraid all I can share is conjecture and rumor. I know that its powers are greater the closer it is to the water that it considers home. This creature would have no power if it were submerged in the water of the Sound, for example. That may be a reason your powers are not manifesting. If it follows the parallels of the creature, your abilities would focus around the waters of your home.

Ichirin noticed that both Hemingway and Corey stared at her, waiting for her to say something. She flushed a little, thankful for the limited light that made it less noticeable. It felt awkward to have people notice when she had a conversation in her own head, even if they knew it wasn't a sign of impending insanity.

"Sorry," she offered. "I'm afraid it isn't good news. Taka said maybe my powers aren't manifesting because I'm not near my home water. I'm not sure what that would be, but it definitely isn't Lake Chelan."

"You mean that this time around, we might need to face a demon without any perks on our side?" Hemingway chewed on his bottom lip and glanced over his shoulder at the windows.

Not a demon!

The kami continued to rant, but Ichirin ignored him to the best of her abilities. It became white noise in the back of her mind, but more agitated.

"Yes, that's what I'm saying. The other option is to leave, but since this is the creature's home, I doubt it would follow us back to Seattle. That means it stays here and hunts people who don't even know it exists. I can't do that, leaving those innocents at its mercy. At least we know what we're dealing with."

"We can handle it. Ichirin's not the only one who's got a few moves."

Hemingway held up his hands to show that he didn't intend to argue. "I just wanted to make sure we all knew what we're getting into. I agree we can't leave this creature here to wreak havoc on innocent people. I also think we should be careful. We don't have a good idea what it's capable of."

Remember the tortoise.

"Then we're agreed. I think we should set a trap for the kappa, let it come to us. It's been here before and came up to the house tonight. I'd much rather face it here than near the water. The last thing we want is to get dragged into the lake and have to fight it there."

The others nodded their agreement.

"While the kappa is smart, it says here that they are horrible at resisting temptation. I think that if we leave out some cucumbers, we could lure it somewhere and get the drop on it."

In the interest of sharing things early before I get berated for withholding information, you should know that kappa are nocturnal creatures. You will have a greater chance of luring it out if you set your trap at night.

"Taka says kappa are nocturnal creatures, so I think we should try tomorrow night." Ichirin held up a hand to forestall Corey's objection before she could voice it. "If we try tonight, we'll rush it and not be prepared for whatever it can do. I'd rather take our time, set the trap, and be as ready as we can. Besides, after the scare we just gave each other, I don't think it would come back tonight."

Despite her enthusiasm and determination, Corey relented in the face of Ichirin's logic. She bowed her head and waved her hand to concede the point.

"How do you want to go about this?" Hemingway failed to stifle a yawn as he asked his question, the last word drawn out in a long breath.

"First off, we need rest. But I don't want to risk the kappa coming in on us while we're asleep. Just because it didn't attack us the first night doesn't mean it won't now. It's attacked Corey since then. It might not be as peaceful this time around, and we shouldn't take the chance."

"I'll take first watch!" Corey jumped up and went into the kitchen, putting the kettle on the stove.

Great. She's making coffee. That's what she needs.

Hemingway glanced at Ichirin, but she had nothing to say in response. With a groan, Hemingway got up and went upstairs, coming back with some pillows. He handed a couple to Ichirin before making a temporary bed for himself on the floor at the opposite side of the table.

"You wanted restful sleep, so we should get as comfortable as possible."

Ichirin appreciated his forethought as she realized how draining the day had been. She hadn't been too physically active, but the emotions took their toll as well, and her body felt ready to drop into a rejuvenating slumber. A few moments ago, she thought she'd just collapse in her chair and sleep leaning against the table. But her lower back, in particular, let her know how much it would prefer being flat on the floor.

Feeling comfortable with Corey watching over them, Ichirin slid to the ground and stretched out. She fell asleep within seconds and didn't even stir when the kettle whistled.

When she woke, the glare of the sun penetrated through her eyelids, making her scrunch her face even before she opened her eyes. Using her hand to shield her from the brightness, she opened her eyes and saw the sun had risen far above the tree line. She shot up to a sitting position, worried that she was supposed to be on watch and fell asleep on her duty. Corey was curled up on the floor across from her where Hemingway had been when she fell asleep. Hemingway stood in the kitchen, holding one of the mythology books and reading through it.

Reaching up, Ichirin used the table for balance as she eased herself to a standing position. Keeping an eye on Corey, she tried to move without making any noise. Walking on tiptoes, she approached Hemingway. He looked up at her as she got close and pointed to a coffee mug, raising a single eyebrow in silent question. She nodded, and he turned on the stove.

Ichirin got close enough to whisper. "Why didn't you wake me?"

"Between the three of us, you need the most sleep. You're always the one going toe-to-toe with these creatures. It seemed like the sensible decision. At least this way, I was being useful and letting you get some rest."

On the one hand, she appreciated his selfless act, but on the other, it concerned her. She knew Hemingway would push himself far beyond what he could handle if it meant saving her an ounce of trouble. It was a precedent she didn't want to become the norm.

She also noticed the self-deprecating statement, but it was too early to deal with that aspect of his personality.

"Any sign of our friend?"

"No, and not according to Corey either. I think it got spooked enough to not come back. That fits with a lot of what I've read. When they are warded away or chased off for any reason, they'll come back, but it takes some time."

"How much time?"

They only had the house rented for three more days. If it took longer than that, they'd need to reevaluate their plan. The thought of hunting the kappa in the water and near its source of power made Ichirin shiver.

Seeing her reaction, Hemingway shook his head and reached out to put a hand on her arm. "No, no, not that long. Sorry about that. Only a day or two. It isn't like it scares them away for good."

Ichirin let out a sigh. It looked like their plan might have a chance of working, if they could figure out some way to set up a trap. Luring the creature into the house was the easy part. The hard part would be what to do once they had it in here.

That's easy. You know you need to eliminate it. As I once heard someone say, "I know of few things, living or dead, that can live for long without their head." Barring that, kappa are corporeal creatures, so sticking them in the heart should do the trick.

That information helped, but Ichirin couldn't help but wonder if talking with the kappa was an option. They were rumored to be intelligent creatures, as evidenced by this one's behavior. Perhaps if they found some way to restrain it. Several of the legends involved people making deals with the kappa or even tricking them, which implied that some form of communication would be possible. Perhaps it knew something about who sent it or why these creatures seemed to be finding her.

Sure, we could speak with it. Because I'm sure you can trust whatever it says and it's probably going to be more than willing to share secrets with you. That sounds like a great plan.

It was true. Even if she did manage to get the creature to speak with her, odds indicated it would lead her down a false trail. Ichirin read stories like that as well, not just in Japanese mythology, but fairy tales in general. Not only that, but how would they keep it from using magical powers that they didn't even know about? All in all, trying to speak with the creature seemed like a much more dangerous proposition.

But would it be worth the risk? If they could find a way to force the kappa to talk and tell them where it had come from, that would be a new lead. She might have something to go on other than a trail that had been dead for months. Instead of being hunted, she could become a hunter.

Need I remind you that it tried to kill one of your friends?

Those words sparked anger in Ichirin that had remained dormant for the better part of a day. As soon as it flared up, she realized it never left; it just simmered out of sight. But that reminder served as the catalyst to bring it to the forefront and remind Ichirin why a diplomatic solution was not an option.

"Once Corey gets up, we'll need to get some supplies. After we set everything up, we should nap during the day. It could be a long night."

The kettle whistled, and despite Hemingway's attempts to move it right away, the sound woke Corey. For a moment, she could not be considered the most active person in the room, a state Ichirin knew would not last long. She went about preparing a couple of cups of tea while Hemingway told Corey the limited details of the plan. At best, it could be considered a general outline.

Over a simple breakfast, the three of them settled on a plan of action. They left the house, confident the kappa wouldn't break in while they were gone. Even if it did, they had food to spare.

It took a few hours, but they collected everything to put their plan into action. When they returned to the house, they took shifts to sleep during the day. Hemingway got the first shift while Corey and Ichirin prepped the house.

Corey took a fishing net and strung it up inside the door of the pantry. It had thick strands and weighed enough that Ichirin had difficulty carrying it from the car. She hoped it would stand up to the kappa's claws but didn't want to count on it. Her fingers traced the scratches in the door, and she had to shake her arms to loosen them up.

They stashed the cucumbers on the top shelf in the pantry against the back wall. Ichirin didn't know if the kappa could smell them, or if it needed to see them, or something else. Corey suggested cutting one up and using it to lay a trail, but that seemed too obvious to Ichirin. The kappa had found them before, and she didn't want to give the creature any additional reasons to be on its guard.

They also got a couple of two-by-fours and stacked them against the wall beside the door. Those, combined with the industrial strength L-brackets, could serve to hold the door if the net wasn't enough. Ichirin attached the brackets to the studs in the wall, wondering how they would explain the additional holes to the homeowners. That problem could be addressed later when the threat of the kappa didn't lurk in the shadows.

Just tell them it was the better of two options. The other choice was to have a kappa running around in their backyard, terrorizing any visitors. I'm sure that would have a negative effect on property values. At the least, it would cause a few one-star reviews.

The thing that terrified Ichirin the most was not the kappa itself. Whenever she thought about killing it, her stomach clenched, and she lifted her hands to her mouth to start chewing on her nails. All of the other creatures she'd fought were much more alien-looking. It was one thing to eliminate a smoke entity murdering people in cold blood. It was another to attack a creature that looked almost human. She hoped she had the resolve to do it when the time came and that she didn't hesitate. She knew she had to be the one to do it. She couldn't pass that final act on to Hemingway or Corey; it rested on her shoulders alone.

If you think you will hesitate, remember what it tried to do. Stoke that fire and use it. It's a foul creature, and it needs to be eliminated before it can cause havoc.

In the end, she knew how she could do it. She could use that rage to push herself over the edge. She just hoped it would be there when she called on it. If not, Taka could push her over the edge. Of that, she had no doubts.

CHAPTER SIX

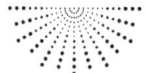

As night descended, the three humans took up their positions. Since the intent was to lure the kappa into the home, they thought it would be best if they vacated the kitchen area. Hemingway and Corey set themselves up in the study, hiding behind a door opened a crack. Ichirin waited in the front entrance, just around the corner from the pantry. She crouched down and leaned against the wall, her legs tightening up as she waited to spring into action.

You should sit. You'll hear the kappa when it opens the back door.

Ichirin eased herself to the ground. No sooner had her butt hit the floor than Taka spoke again.

Unless it has the ability to walk through walls or seep through the cracks between the door and the frame.

As soon as the words entered her brain, Ichirin pulled her feet underneath her and tensed up.

I'm kidding. I'm reasonably confident that if the kappa had such powers, something would have shown up in one of the legends. Your ancestors were nothing if not embellishers of the truth. I suppose that's another one of those facts about humans no matter when you look at them.

Even with Taka's assurances, Ichirin didn't feel comfortable sitting down again. She opted instead to stand up with her back flush against the wall, hoping the corner hid her entire body. Even if not, it felt far more relaxed. She justified it by thinking how much easier it would be to spring into motion from this position rather than stumbling over herself from a squat where her legs fell asleep.

While she waited, she tried to tap into whatever powers she might have inherited from the kappa but came up with nothing. That didn't change her duty. She just hoped they would be able to finish it tonight and be done with the whole affair.

The door leading to the deck squeaked as it slid open, and Ichirin held her breath. It had to be the kappa. No one else would walk into a stranger's house in the middle of the night. Her hands shook with a combination of excitement and fear, and a touch of rage mixed in as well.

Wet slaps echoed from the room just around the corner; the kappa was not as silent or stealthy as Ichirin expected. It paused, taking in a whistling breath as it sniffed at the air. Ichirin heard a few drops of water fall from the creature and splash against the floor. In her mind, she pictured it crawling out of the lake with moss still clinging to it in long strands like some sea monster in an old horror movie. Part of her wanted to peek around the corner to get another glimpse of it, but she forced herself to wait. A single glance could ruin the entire trap if it noticed her.

The kappa started walking again, the footsteps getting closer as it padded over toward the pantry. It got close enough that Ichirin heard its whistling breath even when it took regular breaths. She held her own, worried that it might hear her. She wondered if it could smell her waiting, if it could sense her excitement and fear. She closed her eyes but refused to move. There was nothing to do about that now. They all had to wait to see how the cards fell.

After what felt like an eternity, the kappa put its hand on the pantry door and eased it open. It creaked on hinges in desperate need of a cleaning. It was almost time. The kappa took two more steps and then let out a soft trill of happiness before it crunched down on a cucumber with a crispy snap. That was her cue.

Ichirin burst into motion, coming around the corner and reaching into the pantry to yank the cord holding the net in place. It dropped down even as the kappa turned, the heavy weights slamming into the ground with a solid *thunk* that Ichirin felt in her knees. The kappa stared at her and opened its beak wide, hissing and spraying her with spittle in its rage. Hemingway and Corey burst out of the study, rushing over to Ichirin's side, each of them brandishing a kitchen knife.

The kappa swiped at the net, its claws tearing through several of the strands in one swoop, but the extra coils wrapped around its arm, tangling it with the sudden motion. The kappa tugged hard, putting its feet against the bottom of the net to try and free its arm, but the entwined cord stayed strong.

Kill it! Now! Before it gets free!

Ichirin held out her hand, and Hemingway slapped the large kitchen knife into it, backing up and giving her space. The doorway to the pantry was a limited entry point, providing enough space for one person at a time. Both Corey and Hemingway knew Ichirin felt she needed to be the one to deliver the killing blow, so they stood to either side. Ichirin stepped into the entryway, holding the knife by her side.

The kappa froze and stared at her, making Ichirin hesitate. This close to it, she knew it had intelligence. It looked at her and knew what she had come to do. Its eyes went wide, and it hunched down as if pleading for its life. Ichirin stood up straight, wondering if she was doing the right thing.

What are you waiting for? Do it!

Her fingers tightened around the handle of the blade, catching the kappa's attention. It flew into a rage, lashing out at her and swiping at her face. She pulled back, bumping into Corey and using her friend to keep from falling over. The claws swiped close enough to her face that Ichirin felt the air part and heard the whistle as they passed. Thankfully, the tangled net still trapped its arm, restricting its reach.

Ichirin pushed forward, leading with her knife and trying to stab the creature in the chest. It twisted, but the tip of the weapon sliced through skin that felt rubbery and tough. The kappa hissed and snapped its head forward, trying to bite her shoulder. Ichirin jumped out of the way, slamming into the shelves and knocking boxes of food over into the floor, a few of which bounced off her. The impacts knocked her weapon off target, making the blade point at the side wall as Ichirin struggled to keep a grip on it.

The kappa used that moment to try again to cut itself free from the tangled weave wrapped around it. It managed to shred a hole large enough for most of its body. Only one arm remained ensnared and entwined.

Not wanting to lose the advantage she had, Ichirin advanced again, jabbing with the knife multiple times in short quick motions. A few of the attacks penetrated the creature's hide, but it twisted enough to keep any of the attacks from going too deep or being too brutal. When it tried to counterattack, Ichirin retreated, staying out of its reach thanks to the remains of the net trapping the creature's left arm. After a couple of counterattacks, Ichirin realized where she needed to be to be safe. As long as she remained behind the point marked in her mind, the kappa couldn't reach her until it freed itself.

As Ichirin danced back from another attack, into her safe zone, the kappa shot forward farther than should have been possible. Its trapped arm extended while its free arm shrunk, like the kappa's torso floated on a string from hand to hand. It got close enough to chomp down with its beak. The tips of it shredded the skin over Ichirin's bicep, and she screamed out in pain. Corey grabbed her shoulders and yanked her out of the pantry, slamming the door shut as soon as she was clear.

Hemingway picked up the bar and slapped it into place, securing the pantry while Corey looked at Ichirin's wound, her knife discarded on the floor. Ichirin had dropped the other one inside with the kappa, not that it needed the weapon considering its far superior natural tools.

Blood poured forth from Ichirin's arm. The injury was deep enough that it dug into the muscle. Ichirin clenched her eyes shut and lifted her face to the ceiling as Corey pressed a rag against it. Blood flowed out around the makeshift bandage, running down Ichirin's arm in thick rivulets. For the moment, Ichirin couldn't do anything but focus on the pain and try to keep it from overriding her system. Some part of her knew that a wound like this could send her into shock. She had heard about the symptoms, but this was the first time she ever came close to experiencing it. It was odd, but even through the pain, she thought about what her body was going through and how she needed to be careful about her body temperature dropping. It felt like some part of her detached from the wound and her body as a whole and observed it from an outside perspective.

Which was one of the warning signs of shock.

"Upstairs bathroom, there's Ace bandages and gauze. Get them!" Corey shouted at Hemingway. He ran off, glad to have something to do. "Focus on me; stay with me."

Even though she knew that the injury affected her mental faculties, Ichirin thought Corey overreacted. She hadn't lost that much blood. The pain had faded, and she opened her eyes. Come to think of it, she couldn't feel her arm at all.

"I'm going to be fine. It's not that bad."

Ichirin made the mistake of looking down at the injury and seeing the significant pool of blood next to her. While the sight of blood had never disturbed her before, the disconnect with her brain made her feel lightheaded, and she was glad to be sitting down. She rolled her head back and slammed it into the wall.

"You're right. It's not that bad. But humor me. Tell me something. What's been on your mind lately?"

"I'm worried about Taka," Ichirin said, slurring her words and taking time to say them. Her eyes drooped, but Corey grabbed her chin and shook her head back and forth. "He keeps saying he can help, taking control of my body. But that scares me. I don't want to be a passenger..."

The kappa hissed and slammed into the wooden door, but the brace held. On the second bash, the wood cracked. The kappa hissed in response. It could have been frustration or anticipation.

Hemingway ran into the room, grabbing the corner as he swung around, carrying multiple bandages in his right hand. He extended them toward Corey, dropping them in his rush. The door cracked a second time as he stood there, the mounting point for one of the crossbeams pulling loose from the wall. Hemingway pushed his shoulder against the door, leaning into it with his entire weight.

Corey took one of the bandages and then removed the rag from Ichirin's arm. The bleeding had slowed, but it still oozed down her arm. With practiced motions, Corey tore open a couple of the gauze packets at once, laying them on the wound site. The entire time she worked on the wound, she kept talking to Ichirin.

"So, the kami wants to take control?"

The words tumbled out of Ichirin's mouth without any filter. "Yes. A couple of times it offered to help and said it could handle a situation better than I could. And it makes sense. I mean, it does have centuries of experience. It does make sense, doesn't it?"

"What do you think about it?" Corey held the makeshift pads in place as she wrapped the bandage around them, keeping the entire thing tight.

The pushing sensation on the wound elicited a gasp of pain from Ichirin. With that action, all the feeling came rushing back in a wave. It was like someone reconnected the current for all the pain receptors in her arm at once. She screamed, which turned into a growl by the end. She panted, the quick breathing helping to distract her from the pain that threatened to overwhelm her.

The door thundered again, the force of the blow pushing Hemingway away and making him drop back into it. Visible cracks appeared on this side of the wood. It wouldn't hold for much longer. Ichirin picked up her right arm and flexed her fingers. The motion made her arm throb in pain when she curled it into a fist, and she hissed. Holding a knife or any other weapon seemed impossible, let alone using it to fight.

"We need to get out of here," Ichirin said, her doubt coming out clear in her tone. She didn't know how she could face the kappa in her current state and wanted a chance to regroup.

Corey snagged the knife on the floor and turned to face the pantry door, standing on the balls of her feet and bouncing a little bit. "We're not letting it go. Just because you can't be on the front line doesn't mean it's time to retreat. Let some others do the heavy lifting for a change. If you can cut it, I can too."

Her enthusiasm and spirit gave Ichirin some much-needed resolve. They still had the upper hand. She pushed herself up from the floor, letting her injured arm dangle free and trying to use it as little as possible. She looked around for something else to use as a weapon, not seeing anything that would serve. In a flash of inspiration, she remembered the antler wreath hanging over the front door.

Yanking it off of the wall with her left arm, she tugged and twisted, wrenching one of the antlers out of the decoration. Ichirin tested the points with her thumb, pleased to find they were quite sharp. It might not be the best weapon, but it was better than nothing. When she came back to the kitchen, Corey stood off to the side of the pantry door on the side where it opened. Hemingway still pressed his back against the fragile barrier. A large crack ran from just below his waist up to over his head.

"Are you ready?" Hemingway asked.

Before anyone could say anything, claws pierced through the wood and his shoulder. For a fraction of a second, Ichirin had a horrifying image of him impaled on claws burned into her memory. He fell forward, grabbing his injured shoulder with the opposite arm and stumbling to a knee. The kappa clenched its fingers, tearing a chunk out of the door and ripping it free. Corey moved to help Hemingway, missing the opportunity to attack as the kappa reached through and lifted the crossbeam. Ichirin tried to squeeze through and stab with her antlers, but the kappa pulled its arm back to safety and slammed the door open before anyone could reinforce it.

Corey whirled, standing in front of Hemingway and brandishing her knife at the kappa. The creature hissed at her but didn't advance. Ichirin lunged with the antlers, attacking from the side. At the last second, the kappa twisted to try and avoid the blow. It reacted too late. Several of the tips sank deep into the creature's shoulder, one of them breaking off as the kappa turned. It howled, and blood ran down its side and dripped off its arm. Corey attacked, slashing with the knife as she stepped forward.

The kappa sprang back, slamming its shoulder into the door frame as it tried to evade. Some of the water in its head sloshed to the side, coming out and splashing against the floor. The motion caught Ichirin's attention, and she remembered the legends. When she attacked, she aimed her thrust at the kappa's head, trying to get it to duck away.

As she hoped, it had to pull its head to the side to avoid getting pierced by the hardened bone, and more water spilled out from the divot in its skull. It reached up to its head as if trying to keep the water from falling out. It slid to the side, clearing the doorway of the pantry and putting some distance between it and its attackers.

With a glance at Hemingway to make sure he was okay, Corey circled, staying between the kappa and the back door. If it wanted to return to the lake, it would have to go through her. It looked at her, tilting its head to the side as if considering something. Ichirin moved in from the opposite side, her motion reminding it of her presence. It reached up and placed a hand over the still-embedded piece of antler.

Its hesitation filled Ichirin with hope. She stood up straighter, ignoring the throbbing sensation in her right arm. Even though the kappa was a formidable adversary, they had wounded it and threatened it. From this angle, it looked like most of the water from the well on its head was gone. And now the creature stood between them where they could both attack it at once.

The kappa lunged at Ichirin, forcing her to take a step back, but the kappa feinted. Even before Ichirin put weight on her back foot, the beast dropped its shoulder and turned toward Corey, charging with the full strength of its fury. Corey sprang back, swiping at the air in front of her as the kappa filled the space, the blade slicing deep into its hand. The claws grazed Corey's arm, but the scratches looked superficial even from a distance. The kappa's wound went deeper.

Although it panted from its injuries, it continued to press forward, trying to drive through Corey and get to the back yard. Its limbs whirled around like a blender, a reckless whirlwind of fury and fear trying to escape. Ichirin saw an opening from behind and brought the antlers up, intending to drive them into the beast's back, using the full force of her weight.

Look out! The arms!

Ichirin had committed to the attack when the warning came. The kappa pulled one arm into its body so it could extend the other and twist it around to attack Ichirin. The claws dropped down at her face, and all she could do was wince and brace for the impact.

Something slammed into her just below the waist, knocking her to the side and down. She bruised her hip against the floor as she landed, and the impact drove the antlers from her hand, but Hemingway had saved her. He rolled off her legs, grunting with the effort as he moved over his injured shoulder. With as much as her right arm throbbed, she couldn't believe he remained conscious.

Scrambling to get up, and using only her left hand to do so, Ichirin moved toward the discarded antlers. Off to her side, the kappa engaged Corey in single combat, advancing on her. It slashed with terrible claws and snapped at the air with its beak. Corey was losing ground but kept herself between the beast and the exit. Ichirin wasn't sure how much longer her friend could keep up the defense. She needed to get back in there!

Snatching the antlers, she whirled to face the kappa and look for an opening at its back. The creature leapt at Corey, pushing her weapon aside and charging over her. It knocked her down with a solid shoulder check and ran over her, the claws on the creature's feet digging into her as it ran. Corey brought the knife around, stabbing at the creature's leg and sinking it up to the handle. The kappa screamed, but continued to run with a shuffling step, yanking the weapon out of Corey's hand as it retreated.

The kappa fled out the back door, limping and half-dragging its leg as it went to the back railing and did a clumsy fall over the side as it tried to vault it. In another situation, the visual would have been comical to watch. Ichirin ran to Corey's side to see if she was okay, putting down her weapon and helping her friend sit up.

"I'm fine," Corey said between a couple of coughs and gasps. "Just knocked the wind out of me. Hemingway?"

He waved from where he laid on his back a short distance away before letting his hand drop to the ground with a slap. "I'll be alright." His proclamation was less convincing.

Corey pushed herself up to her feet and took a few deep breaths before shuffling over to the pantry and picking up the discarded knife. Despite everything that had happened, she had a smile on her face. In light of their injuries and the blood on her clothes, it looked more manic than cheerful. It managed to both give Ichirin a shiver and energize her.

"We're not letting it get away," Corey said.

CHAPTER SEVEN

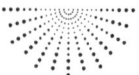

*S*he's right. If you want to end this, you need to follow it now. It will *heal faster than you. Either pursue it or run away and come back when you've recovered. But there's no telling how much damage it will do in that time.*

As much as part of her wanted to run away, to at least rest and recover from her wounds, Ichirin knew it wasn't an option even before Taka added his two cents. She needed to pursue this to the end now. They had caught the kappa by surprise and wounded it. It wouldn't fall for a trap like that again, which meant fighting it on even ground, or worse, in a situation of its choosing. They would not get a better opportunity.

Picking up her discarded weapon, she went over again to Hemingway, checking to make sure his wounds weren't worse than he let on. Corey came over, bringing some of the bandages left over from her quick patch job on Ichirin's arm. The two of them helped Hemingway slide across the floor without dragging his injured shoulder and propped him up against a wall. He gasped when his back touched the surface.

He had lost a little bit of color, but his breathing sounded strong and his eyes focused on her when he opened them. Other than the blood loss, he seemed as healthy as someone could be after being stabbed in the back by a mythological creature. Her mind wandering, Ichirin wondered if the wounds the kappa caused would get infected. Her gaze dropped to her bandaged arm, which throbbed when she allowed herself to think about it. Even if the creature itself wasn't venomous, it did spend most of its time in water and looked unclean.

This would be a useful and interesting chain of thought...if the kappa wasn't limping away in the backyard right now!

"Are you going to be alright?" she asked while Corey applied some gauze and wrapped a bandage around Hemingway's shoulder. Even for her limited skills, the job looked sloppy. Hemingway reached across his body with his good arm to hold it in place. Corey patted his hand and helped him apply some pressure. He pushed her hand away.

"You go do what you have to. I'll be here waiting for you when you get back."

That was good enough for Ichirin. She stood up and looked over at Corey, who looked like an extra from a slasher film. The two women rushed out the still-open back door. Ichirin made a beeline for the railing while Corey leapt down the steps, sliding her hands along the banister to take big sweeping leaps.

The kappa shuffled across the grass of the backyard, heading in the direction of the pier. Corey slowed it down more than Ichirin dared to hope with the stab to its leg. Even with the time spent tending to Hemingway, the kappa only managed to cross half the distance to the water. Corey came around the corner from the stairs and sprinted toward it. Ichirin moved to join her just as the kappa looked back and saw the pursuit.

As she ran down the stairs, Ichirin heard a yelp of surprise that made her pick up her pace and jump down the last four steps in a single stride, stumbling as she hit the ground. When she turned, she saw Corey standing in the yard jerking as she pulled at her leg. It didn't move, like someone had glued her foot to the ground. The kappa stood on the far side of her, hand extended in her direction as it backed away toward the trees.

And now you know some of its capabilities with magic. Stay away from your friend, force it to split its attention. It looks like it needs to maintain some focus to keep her ensnared.

Ichirin slid to a stop based on Taka's suggestion. Her immediate response was to help Corey, but what the kami said made sense. Even if the kappa had enough power to trap them both, it would be better to present two targets rather than one. Hugging the deck, Ichirin crossed the backyard, trying to come at the kappa from another angle. It saw her movement and turned its attention on her.

Vines rustled as they uncurled from the deck supports and lashed out at Ichirin, their long strands curling around her wrist and ankles. At first, it provided a slight resistance, and she just jerked herself free, but as more and more vines entwined around her limbs, she found it difficult to move. She tried to push toward the lake, away from the deck, but she couldn't escape the vegetation.

Her movement halted, and her breath caught as she felt the vines drag her back under the dark shadows of the deck. One of the tendrils wrapped around her injured arm, tightening and making her cry out in pain. Once again, she dropped her makeshift weapon, the antlers turning over and embedding themselves in the soft ground.

You need to reach out to the plants, tell them to let you go. You have the same power as the kappa. Your abilities come from it. Tap into that power. Even if you're far from your home, you still have some! Focus!

Ichirin struggled to fight the mounting fear threatening to overtake her and drive all rational thought from her mind. She needed those powers now. Her life depended on it. The pain shooting from her arm helped. It gave her something concrete to focus on, rather than the terror of her impending demise.

Taka spoke the truth. With every other creature she faced, she gained their powers. That was why she had to be the one to hunt them down. That meant she could use the same magic as the kappa. She might be far from any waters she could call home, but that didn't mean she lacked the abilities. She would make the plants listen to her. This was not the end of her story.

She pushed those thoughts into the emotional broiler of her rage, using them to give her focus. She thought of the kappa, and how it tried to take Corey from her. She thought of Hemingway, sitting back in the house injured and bleeding. She thought of herself, and how unfair life turned out with mythic creatures showing up causing chaos and upending her life. She never sought this duty out nor asked for it; nonetheless, fate handed it to her.

The fire grew within her, changing her desire to cry out in pain to a roar of anger. She glared at the kappa, pushing those thoughts in its direction. It stood in front of her, no longer retreating. The arm extended in Ichirin's direction shook with effort, the entire slimy limb vibrating as if all the muscles flexed. The vines around her loosened and stopped dragging her toward the deck.

Not wanting to miss her opportunity, Ichirin yanked her leg forward and took a stride away from the house. The vines tugged and resisted at first, but her constant pressure made them tear and snap. Across the back yard, Corey pulled herself free, shaking her legs to rid herself of a few stray strands of vegetation. She looked over at Ichirin to see if she needed help, but Ichirin stood tall as she ripped off a few lingering strands. She pointed at the kappa and didn't say any words.

The creature turned to the water and tried to run, dragging one useless leg as it half hopped, half stumbled toward the shore. Corey sprinted after it, launching herself when she got within range, trying to stop it before it got into the water. She landed in the center of its back and stabbed it in the shoulder before they crashed down and became a mad tumble of limbs that Ichirin couldn't decipher. She tore herself free of the last lingering vines and ran after the two combatants, trying to make out what was happening.

They rolled in the mud just beyond the edge of the water, looking like one grotesque multi-limbed beast. Ichirin saw a flash of metal reflecting the moonlight as Corey brought the knife down again, trying to end the fight. But the kappa still had strength and spirit left. It twisted its head to the side and bucked its hips, trying to unseat the human on top of it. While Corey was a determined and skilled fighter, her small size did little to restrict the creature's movement when it drove her up and scurried out from underneath her.

She managed to grab an ankle before the kappa got away, but it snapped a kick, catching her in the head and stunning her enough that it tore free and jumped into the water. Corey rushed after it, stopping when she was knee-deep in the lake. She looked around, head whipping from side to side as she tried to see any trace of the creature. Ichirin still had a few strides before she reached the edge of the water, but she caught a flash of something underneath the surface.

"Look down!" she shouted.

Corey saw the dark shadow as it reached for her ankle and she jerked back, driving her knife down. The kappa pulled away, moving through the water like it provided no resistance. It circled and grabbed her other leg, yanking her off her feet and dragging her toward the center of the lake. Ichirin saw the mad splashing as Corey tried to gain some footing.

The fury of rage still driving her, Ichirin jumped into the water headfirst, feeling the shock of cold as it enveloped her entire body. She kicked as hard as she could, trying to gain as much ground as possible as she chased the churning waters.

To her surprise, she caught up to the conflict. Corey must have fought the kappa every inch of the way or found something to hold on to. The fight stirred up the silt and muddied the entire area. Even with more light, Ichirin wouldn't have been able to make anything out.

She reached out, trying to grab one of the fighters. Either one would give her something to work with. Her fingers brushed against some fast-moving limbs, but they were gone before she could tighten her fingers. She swam harder, plunging deeper into the tumultuous waters. Something kicked her in the shoulder, driving some air from her lungs, but she couldn't identify the assailant. She reached out again, trying to find anything to gain some purchase.

Her fingers felt cool flesh, and she gripped it with all her strength. Corey tried to yank her arm free, but Ichirin held on, pulling herself forward until she found herself even with her friend. She swam upward, trying to give enough lift for Corey to get her head out of the water and take a breath. Between the two of them, Corey broke the surface long enough to gasp for air before the kappa yanked her back down. Ichirin knew her lungs should be burning, but she didn't feel winded, so she dove deeper rather than surfacing herself.

The water was deep here, and it got colder the farther down they went. Silt no longer obscured vision as the ground dropped away, but the beams of light from the moon did little to illuminate the area. At best, Ichirin made out tangled shapes. The kappa still had a firm grip on Corey's ankle and used it to pull her down farther. Corey's kicks grew weak, and the kappa swatted them away with its other hand if any came too close to its face. The motions looked lazy, like an afterthought.

When it noticed Ichirin, it snapped its hand out, and the water itself tore at her, trying to drive her back toward the shore. The assault caught her off guard, but her grip on Corey's arm saved her from tumbling away in the sudden current. It still buffeted her around, making her twist and turn as it attacked her from multiple sides.

She tried to return the attack, reaching out to the water and willing it to rush forward, to push toward the kappa, but nothing happened. It felt like trying to communicate with someone through a spotty cell phone connection where she caught every fifth word at best, the others lost to a continuous chatter of static. Another blast assaulted her, this time with small rocks and bits of sand caught up in the middle of it that stung as they bit into her skin.

Her priority was getting Corey free. The woman's struggles slackened, and her entire body looked like it moved in slow motion. Ichirin pulled herself up further, walking down Corey's body and easing the knife from her hand. She stabbed at the kappa's arm, trying to strike it just below the wrist.

The blade sank into the creature's flesh, making it let go of its prey. Ichirin didn't waste the opportunity. She grabbed Corey around the waist with her injured arm, ignoring the pain as she tightened her grip and kicked hard for the surface of the lake. When they burst through to the surface, Corey gulped down air like the precious resource it was. Ichirin dragged her toward the shore, trying to get her out of the kappa's reach.

Now that the battle has become aquatic, she's more of a liability than an asset. Get her out of the water and on solid ground.

They covered half the distance to shore when Ichirin felt the cold talons of the kappa brush against her ankle. She gave Corey a shove, pushing herself back toward the kappa with the same motion. She would not let it have her!

The kappa didn't expect her sudden reversal as she passed by its claws and found herself face-to-face with the creature. Before it recovered from its surprise, she stabbed at it, the blade cutting into its side. It jerked away from her with a screech that echoed through the entire lake. A current of water buffeted around the kappa and slammed into her, striking her in the chest like a sledgehammer and driving her back through the water. She stopped where it was shallow enough that she rested on her hands and knees and most of her torso remained in the open air.

Glancing to the side, she looked for Corey, pleased to see that her friend had managed to crawl out of the water and collapse on her back in the grass well away from the shoreline. She coughed and struggled to breathe but appeared safe. Knowing that, Ichirin could focus all her energy on the battle to come. She stepped up, her head bowed and her long hair hanging in front of her face, dripping down into the water. Her knife was in her left hand, the tip of the blade bent and pointed down at the ground. Despite the pain, she squeezed her right hand into a fist as she looked at the water in front of her, aftereffects from the aqueous assault still rippling the surface.

"Come on!" She lifted her head and screamed at the lake, uncaring of what any vacationers within earshot might think.

The kappa rose from the water like an angel of the deep until it stood on the surface. Blood dripped from several wounds, including the one with the piece of antler still stuck in its side. It moved closer without stepping, the water rising in a gentle wave that radiated outward and brought the kappa toward the shore. Ichirin felt a gentle tugging around her ankles as the undercurrent washed past her to meet the next wave.

Despite its injuries, the creature grinned, almost leering at her.

Ichirin felt the mockery in that gaze, a challenge that said she wasn't good enough to face the kappa on its home ground. It wasn't scared of her; it didn't view her as a threat at all. That stare, that self-confident look of insignificance, it was one that Ichirin had seen multiple times before, from many people who underestimated her. She knew the kappa was trying to goad her into making a foolish mistake. She wouldn't take the bait.

But it didn't know that about her.

Playing the part of a reckless, goaded warrior, Ichirin charged through the water at the kappa. She forced herself to stumble, dropping to a knee before the water got too deep. Just as she hoped, the kappa surged forward, riding a foaming crest and lunging at Ichirin. But she had prepared for the attack; she had counted on it. Rather than fall and put her hands out in front of her, Ichirin pushed off the ground and twisted to the side as she leapt forward.

Her knife flashed in the moonlight and scored another deep hit on the creature's side. The cut met resistance as it struck bone, and the impact knocked the knife out of Ichirin's hand. Despite her lucky break, she found herself in thigh-high water, staring at the injured kappa with no weapon in her hands.

The kappa whipped around, backhanding her across the face and sending her sprawling into the water. The creature didn't hesitate, leaping on her with all four limbs. Claws bit into Ichirin's shoulders as it curled its fingers to get a better grip and shoved her forward, under the surface of the water. Ichirin struck the bottom of the lake, her face slamming into the mud and half of it getting buried in the cold, clammy muck. She tried to push off the ground, but the kappa had both strength and leverage on its side, and it kept her pinned.

Unlike before, she felt her lungs burn with the strain of holding her breath. The more she struggled, the more her chest felt like it would burst. She managed to lift her face out of the mud an inch, and fresh water washed over her face, relieving the urge to breathe. The relief was short-lived as the kappa shifted, shoving her back down and trying to suffocate her in the ground.

Ichirin reached out to the water, trying to force it to come to her aid and buffet the kappa off of her. When that failed, she tried to speak to the plants, using them to get some semblance of control. But nothing happened. She couldn't focus. Not even the pain in her arm allowed her to ignore the panic of her situation. The need for air overrode every other signal in her body. She tried to reach up and grab the kappa's arm and twist free of its grasp, but it jerked her around from side to side enough that she couldn't get a good grip. Her chest felt like she carried a fire inside.

Give me control! I can help!

Ichirin refused, heaving with all her strength and getting enough purchase to get another moment's relief. She twisted to the side, managing to get free enough to take a stroke in the water, but the kappa refused to be dismounted. It adjusted, jerking Ichirin around and keeping her under control. She thrashed and flailed, but it had as much effect as using a water gun to put out a house fire.

You're going to die.

Those words made her panic, and she tried to breathe, feeling the mud enter her mouth and making her gag, spending air that she didn't have to spare. She tried to push off the ground again, but her hands slipped, and she didn't have the energy to try again. Her face sank deeper into the mud, the cold against her face spreading through her entire body.

I can save Corey.

It was like a spark in the night. That mattered, and anything else was immaterial. If Taka could save Corey, then any price would be worth it.

CHAPTER EIGHT

The sensation felt unlike anything Ichirin had ever experienced. She felt lightheaded from the lack of oxygen, but that reaction increased a hundredfold as she felt like someone reached out and eased her to the side in her mind. She felt like she floated in a glass sphere, watching everything and aware of what happened to her body without feeling it. It reminded her of the time she had her wisdom teeth removed and she came out of anesthesia.

One thing that came through the mental fog like a flashlight blinding her in the face was Taka's exultation as he screamed in excitement at having free reign of her body. A light blossomed in front of her chest, and it took her a moment to realize the locket glowed bright enough that it cut through the darkness of mud and silt.

Taka pushed off the ground using strength Ichirin didn't think she possessed. He drove back through the kappa's arm with enough force that it stumbled and fell behind him. Taka rose up, standing over the kappa and grinning with maniacal glee. For the first time in the water, the kappa looked scared. Its eyes widened and it shook its head a couple of times, short movements that looked like it had a seizure. It turned as if to run, but Taka leapt on it, grabbing it by the back of the neck and one wrist. Twisting around, he heaved the kappa into the pier hard enough for the wood to crack and boards to tear free from their mounts.

The kappa slid into the water, dazed from the impact. Taka gestured, and the water rose up underneath it, bringing the creature toward him and presenting it as if it were a prize or a meal on a platter. Ichirin felt the water respond to Taka's call, doing as he instructed like a puppy eager to please.

How are you able to do that? The water wouldn't listen to me at all.

That fact didn't surprise Taka. The powers Ichirin had inherited were tied to her home waters, which might be in Japan or might be the Sound, depending on which one she connected to more. For him, his home was wherever he chose to be. He was ancient by the standards of most creatures, more ancient than any realized, and he considered the entire physical world his home. All waters on this planet would respond to his call as long as he could access the kappa's abilities.

When he thought of the word ancient, Ichirin felt what he meant. He measured time not in years or even decades, but lifetimes. She saw him envision an Earth where humankind had yet to emerge as the dominant species.

The kappa roused itself as it got within Taka's reach, and it lashed out with a claw, slicing through his shirt and drawing three lines along the flesh of his abdomen. Ichirin felt the pain like a dull ache of sore muscles after a day of strenuous exercise. It fascinated her on an academic level, but she knew how much those wounds would hurt once she regained control.

Be careful with my body!

Taka looked down, seeming to notice the injuries for the first time. The motion drew his attention away from the kappa long enough for it to lash out with a mystical attack of its own. The water around Taka's ankles swirled and pulled, yanking him off his feet and dragging him out to deeper water. The kappa dove under the surface and swam after its prey.

The kappa's attempts to drown Taka made him laugh. How could it not realize he could pull oxygen out of the water to survive? This hunter had gotten lazy. It didn't bother to think it fought anything beyond a normal human, despite evidence to the contrary. Taka decided to have fun with the kappa while it lasted. He didn't want to end the fight too soon, because the moment it did, all the additional powers would disappear, and he'd be stuck in a normal human form.

The situation fascinated Ichirin. She never expected she'd be able to hear all of Taka's thoughts as they passed through his mind. The continuous flow of information contained both logical thought and pure emotion. Keeping up with the various tangents proved painful but illuminating. Now that their roles had reversed, she felt confident Taka couldn't read her mind. When she wanted to speak with him, she had to make a concentrated effort, rather than him blurting in on her private mental wanderings. She waited to see if he reacted to her musings, pleased when he did not.

Did Taka know this would be an effect of their switching places? It seemed strange to her that Taka would allow her this much access to his thoughts after how secretive he'd been. Of course, the moment they reverted to their normal roles, he'd know what she discovered. If they lived through this, it might be the best opportunity to try and ferret out secrets Taka seemed unwilling to share. The biggest question along those lines was where to start?

First things first—they needed to survive the encounter with the kappa. Ichirin focused on the physical world around her body, aware that Taka tumbled through the water, shooting toward the center of the lake like a torpedo. No moonlight could penetrate the depths the current had pulled him to. Taka closed his eyes, reaching out and extending his senses through the water. It seemed as if the lake itself spoke to him, sharing an image of his surroundings—not just the borders of the ground but also the fish that swam around. And in the distance, the large form of the kappa slicing through the water like a bullet through the air, water swirling around it and propelling it on.

Taka ordered the water to deflect the kappa to the side at the last second, and the creature screeched as it struck a veritable wall at a sickening speed. The sound made the fish scatter, unsure what happened but wanting to be as far away from the fight as possible. Taka grinned and held out his hands to either side, fingers splayed. He couldn't remember the last time he had this much fun. He wanted to toy with the kappa some more before ending the game.

For its part, the kappa refused to give up the attack. It shot forward once again, reaching out with long claws and trying to skewer its prey. It twisted as it got close, changing its offense at the last second. In response, Taka asked the water to rise in a geyser around him.

The force of the blast sent the kappa soaring into the air as Taka rose to the surface, watching his opponent drop from the sky. When the kappa struck the water, it had become hard as ice, and the creature bounced with a sickening crunch that made Ichirin want to wince. The brutal display made her uneasy, and she started to pity the creature. It felt like watching a cat toy with a mouse while pinning its tail to the ground under a paw.

End it. There's no reason to prolong this.

Taka growled, his frustration at Ichirin's command bleeding over their mental connection. He had to play nice. He needed her to think he was on her side, maybe even subservient to her. But he wasn't willing to give up the reins of control yet. He walked over to the kappa, standing on water that provided enough resistance to be solid. Once there, he looked down at the kappa, the creature twisted from its painful impact and bleeding from multiple wounds. Taka willed the water to carry the two of them back in the direction of the house.

"I saw you before," the kappa coughed, its voice raspy and weak, a wet whistle accompanying every word. "You convinced the girl to kill the enenra. I was sent to watch…"

Its words cut off with a strangled choke as a strand of water extended from the lake and wrapped around the creature's neck.

What was it saying? Stop! Let it speak!

"This creature only speaks lies. It's known for its duplicitous nature. You cannot believe any words that pass beyond its twisted beak. It would say anything to save its hide."

When Taka spoke, Ichirin felt her throat moving, felt her body making the words and heard her own voice. But something seemed off. The voice sounded darker, for lack of a better word. Twisted and with more malice than she ever thought herself capable of articulating. In those ways, it was not her voice at all.

I still want to know what it was going to say. Even if it is lying, that might give us some insight into what's going on.

"You've seen how fast it can move, and some of its capabilities. It's desperate now and prone to lashing out. Would you risk the safety of your friends to hear its lies?"

The wave deposited Taka and the kappa on dry land before washing away back to remain part of the lake. Corey stood there, looking at the scene and hesitating to get too close to the kappa. She moved to get close to Taka but kept him between her and the creature.

"Are you okay?" she asked.

"I'm fine. Thank you."

"Who were you talking to?"

"I had a conversation with my mental companion, trying to decide what to do with the kappa. Taka thinks I should kill it without asking any questions or giving it a chance to talk. It's concerned for your safety and mine. The kappa's still a threat."

Conveniently not going to mention that you're the one in the driver's seat?

As soon as Ichirin felt the kami's rage start to mount, she amended her statement.

Not that I blame you. I understand why. It would be an awkward conversation, and right now we have other things to worry about.

The last thing Ichirin wanted to do was anger Taka while he both retained control of her body and had all the powers of the kappa at his disposal. She didn't know how to take back possession of her body and didn't want to tip her hand too much.

Corey crossed her arms as she looked at the kappa. Its eyes fluttered, and its chest rose in small amounts as it struggled to get air. Ichirin wondered if Corey saw the thin ribbon of water tightened around the creature's neck, but she doubted it. The limited light made such small details disappear into the darkness of the evening. Ichirin herself wouldn't know about it if she couldn't feel it on some level.

"Let's get this over and done with. I want to check on Hemingway, and you need to get to the hospital for your arm. The sooner we put this behind us, the better. It's not worth it."

"That settles it then, two votes to one. We do live in a democracy after all."

The band of water tightened around the kappa's throat and it flailed, giving a last attempt to get free despite its beaten and broken body. Taka continued to will the water to tighten, slicing through the skin and the delicate tissues underneath. Soon the kappa lay still, blood running from its neck and soaking into the mud beneath it.

"You go check on Hemingway. I'll take care of the body."

Corey hesitated, her eyes narrowing for a fraction of a second before going back to normal. Ichirin was grateful Taka's attention focused on the kappa at his feet and he wasn't watching. Ichirin knew what mistake Taka had made—he called Hem by his full name. Ichirin never did that. What she didn't know was what Corey would do with that information.

"You sure about that? You're kind of beat up yourself." Corey glanced around, looking for something on the ground, but shifting to keep Taka in her peripheral vision at all times.

"Don't worry about it. I'll be up shortly. I just want someone to make sure he's okay. But one of us needs to take care of the body, and I'm better equipped to do that. We don't want it sitting out when the sun comes up."

"As you wish. I'll check on him and then come back. Don't push yourself too hard. You're not too shiny yourself right now."

When Corey walked away, Ichirin noticed that she continued to keep Taka in her field of view. Before they had this role reversal, Ichirin assumed the kami only saw what she did. Right now, she realized her senses extended beyond that, like she sat a few feet away and watched the entire scene unfold from a cameraman's perspective. It was surreal, even more so by the fact that her body was part of the scene and she could feel everything happening to her on a muted level.

"The kappa is defeated, and your powers have fled. I felt them leave. Your body is about to collapse from exhaustion."

Ichirin felt the truth in Taka's words.

How are you still upright?

"I'm not connected to this body as you are. You feel its exhaustion and pains in full, whereas for me those complaints are hushed. I would wager that even at this moment you are pulling in some of the suffering yourself, feeling it even though you do not inhabit the body."

There was also the fact that he had centuries more experience in using willpower to create physical manifestations. He knew enough about the workings of bodies to understand that all physical forms had two limits. Most beings stopped at the first, what the body could handle. A few talented individuals learned that the ultimate barrier was the second, what the mind defined as the final limit. He could push that mental barrier much further than any terrestrial creature could manage.

How are you going to take care of the kappa?

"Push it out into the lake. The kappa will dissolve in the waters where it was born, so there should be no trace of it as long as it is submerged."

Taka bent over and grabbed the kappa's ankles, dragging it into the water. Once there, the kappa became much easier to move. Taka towed it out until the water came up to his chest. He brought the body around in front of him and pushed it out to the center of the lake with as much strength as he could muster. The body drifted away from the house and sank beneath the surface.

He turned around and walked back toward the shore, noticing Corey standing up on the deck watching. Taka raised a hand in greeting. Corey returned the gesture before turning around and disappearing. She lacked the usual bounce in her step, but he supposed that was expected. Even beyond the exhaustion of the combat itself, she would have to deal with the emotional fallout of realizing Ichirin once again emerged victorious in a physical confrontation where she failed.

The trains of thought that Ichirin found herself a voyeur on fascinated her. While she couldn't probe through his mind or memories, their connection took any surface thoughts that arose and laid them out before her for her scrutiny. Assuming the relationship was the same when Taka resided in the locket, that meant he didn't have unfettered access to her mind like she feared.

Earlier when you first possessed my body, the stone in the locket glowed. The light was so bright that it leaked out through the gaps. Was that because we switched places? If you put the necklace down now, will I be unable to communicate with you?

Ichirin felt the spike of fear from Taka. It tasted like oil: thick, slimy, and unappetizing. If she had a body, it would have made her stomach clench and turn, but in her current state it caught her attention and roused her curiosity. She assumed fear was not in Taka's emotional spectrum given how confident and blasé he managed to be regardless of the situation.

"If I removed this now, our bond would be severed as always. I would be forced back to the stone, with no small amount of pain I might add. As for you, I can only hope that you would find your way back to your body. Otherwise, your spirit would wander free, unattached to anything."

He placed her odds of survival around fifty-fifty. If she managed to find her way back to her body, she would be fine. But it would still be a literal soul-wrenching experience. If for any reason she couldn't find her way back, she'd wander as a dispossessed spirit, and he'd be forced to find a new tool for his master.

Those words rang out in Ichirin's mind as Taka shuffled back toward the stairs, not immune to her body's physical exhaustion. She longed to know more, to ask about his master. Taka had never insinuated anything about a master before, and right now she had access to information in a way she never thought possible. But she couldn't think of a way to ask a question without tipping her hand, and her instincts screamed at her to keep this a secret.

Which raised another issue. She could never think about it while wearing the locket or anywhere near it. The minute that she did, Taka would pick up on it. She hoped she had the mental fortitude and control to keep from thinking about such things. At some point, she'd slip up, but she hoped to forestall that as long as possible.

"I assume you would like possession of your body once again, now that the threat is over?"

As much as Taka enjoyed having a chance to interact with the physical world, he knew he needed to give up the reins. She had to stay in control, and he wanted to make a gesture of goodwill, so she didn't regret handing her body over to him. Otherwise, she'd be reluctant to do so ever again.

Yes, I think that's for the best once you get to the base of the stairs. That way if I collapse as soon as I get back into my body, the others can find me.

Judging by the level of exhaustion she felt even when separated from her physical form, Ichirin knew collapsing was a distinct possibility. She doubted her ability to climb the staircase by herself, but she needed to switch with Taka before running into Corey again.

Taka did as she requested, moving to the base of the stairs and taking a knee in front of the first step. He placed a hand on the railing for support and bowed his head.

"Are you ready?"

Yes.

"Then take back the control as I give it to you."

Ichirin wanted to ask how when she felt herself pulled into her body like the undertow in the lake. She knew she could resist, but instead, she dropped into it, letting herself flow with the mystical current. Her awareness narrowed and focused in on her physical form until it was inside of her and she was looking out.

She took a deep breath, and pain from multiple sources seared through her, plunging her into darkness.

When she woke, she felt hands peeling the shirt off of her body. She groaned and felt a large hand put a cool rag against her forehead. Hemingway's voice cut through her thick, muddled thoughts.

"It's okay. Don't breathe too deep. You've got some nasty gashes on your abdomen."

She followed his advice, taking a soft, easy breath, feeling the skin pulling around the wounds of her stomach as either he or Corey continued peeling the shirt back. It stung as they freed it, but she knew it was a necessary evil. On the plus side, the pain reminded her that she lived.

Thinking back over the last few hours, she reached up and pawed at her neck to feel for the locket, surprised to find it missing from her chest. She forced her eyes open and licked her lips, getting ready to speak. Hemingway stood over her, washing her face with light brushes from a warm rag while Corey cleaned her clothing out of her wounds.

"The locket?" Ichirin gasped.

Hemingway and Corey shared a glance that spoke volumes before he responded.

"It's on the kitchen counter in the other room. Do you need me to get it?"

"No. Better with it gone. Need to talk to you." She winced as she tried to sit up, only to have Corey push on her shoulder.

"Frakking hell, what are you doing? Keep your ass on the floor and your head on the pillow, at least until we clean you up a bit. There's no way you're not going to the hospital tonight, but let's at least make it so we can drive there and not need to call an ambulance."

Ichirin smiled at Corey, thankful to have her insistent but caring hands. Still, she needed to share some information, now while she could. She took a breath, trying to make sure to move as little as possible.

"Taka took over my body at the end. I didn't know how else to defeat the kappa, and I was worried it was going to come after you next."

"I know," Hemingway said. When Ichirin raised an eyebrow, he shrugged and glanced at Corey. "She told me about it when she came up to the house. Wanted me to be ready just in case. Not that we had any idea what to do about it."

"Right. Well, if that ever happens again and you need to get me back, the easiest way is to pull the locket. Taka can't stay in my body if the locket isn't nearby. I hope it never comes to that, but just in case."

There was no reason to tell them about the possible side effects. If they needed to get Taka out of her body for any reason, she didn't want them to hesitate because of their concern for her life. Taka was quick and ruthless. Even a moment's hesitation could result in one of their deaths, if not both.

The talking consumed what little energy she had, so Ichirin closed her eyes and took a few more breaths. Her friends moved in silence as they waited for her to continue, cleaning her wounds with as much care as they could manage.

"You got lucky. The stomach cuts aren't deep. You'll still need stitches, but you've got good insurance." Corey leaned forward onto all fours and rested a hand on Ichirin's shoulder.

The touch roused Ichirin, and she spoke again, her voice still soft and slow with significant pauses. "I also learned some things about Taka. He can't read my mind. He can only pick up surface thoughts. Which means I can't think about any of this while I wear it."

"You could always not wear it," Hemingway offered.

Corey answered for her before Ichirin summoned the energy to offer a response. "If she does that, then Taka will know something's different. And I'm guessing by the way that she's sharing this with us, she doesn't want him to know."

"Got it in one," Ichirin said.

"Which also means we need to watch what we say or what we ask you when you're wearing it. It's like a sleeping thread. We don't want to make any calls to it that will alert the monitor."

Even though she only half-understood the programming reference, Ichirin knew what he was getting at and was glad he had brought it up. She hadn't thought about that piece of the puzzle. She lifted a hand to give a quick thumbs-up before letting it drop to the ground with a wet slap.

"I also learned that he has a master, but that's all I know about it. It was a fleeting thought."

"Wait," Corey stood up and took a step back, leaning against the wall. "You mean that when you switched places, you picked up on his surface thoughts? That's how you learned all of this?"

Ichirin felt her strength building up, so she moved to prop herself up on her elbows and give a nod. As an afterthought, she realized she rested on some blankets strewn on the dining room floor. A large pile of bandages and medical supply wrappers collected at her side. Now that her awareness was returning, she shivered as the cold air prickled her skin. Hemingway wrapped a towel around her, draping it over her shoulders with a gentle touch.

"I didn't want to ask too many questions, because I'm pretty sure he didn't know I'd be able to do that. Like you said, I think this is something we don't want Taka to know. He's been secretive for so long that I took it for granted. I don't want to lose the only opportunity we have to learn more."

"But in order to do that, you'll have to let him walk around in your skin again." Hemingway's voice was soft, reserved.

Ichirin pressed her lips together and gave a solemn nod. As much as she didn't like the idea, she couldn't think of any other way they could get access to that information. Of course, that necessitated a situation arising where Taka suggested they switch places. Given how much it unnerved her, she couldn't offer, or he'd know something had changed her mind. Appearances needed to be maintained if she wanted to keep this advantage.

The only time she'd switch roles with him was when it became necessary to protect herself or others.

"What do we do now?" Hemingway asked.

"Well, I think you two get to go to the hospital while I get to try and figure out how the hell we're going to cover this up. At least we have a few days to try and put it all back together." Corey pushed off from the wall and walked into the hallway. Once there, she spun around and pointed a finger first at Hemingway and then Ichirin. "And no arguments or I will call for an ambulance."

She turned around and left, leaving the other two alone for a moment. Ichirin saw no reason to argue and looked forward to the promise of pain meds and a good night's sleep. She told herself the doctors wouldn't mind if she passed out while they worked. She and Hemingway would need to come up with a story for their injuries, but they could figure that out on the car ride over. She didn't even bother to entertain the thought of driving herself.

As she pushed herself up off the ground and walked toward the kitchen area, Ichirin saw the locket sitting on the counter, looking like a harmless piece of jewelry. It amazed her how much it had changed. It used to be a source of comfort, but within a matter of hours, had transformed into a weight. But she wouldn't walk away from it. She couldn't. She still had much to learn.

And that said nothing of the beasts. The creatures would keep coming, whether she had Taka or not. Her abilities were what made her destined to fight them and made them seek her out, not her connection with the kami. She couldn't leave others to suffer because she felt uncomfortable with what she needed to do.

Above all else, she needed to push some of these thoughts from her mind as far as possible. She reached up and hugged her shoulders to keep from shivering at the thought.

Walking over, Ichirin picked up the locket and attached it around her neck, feeling the chain bite into the skin near her spine. It felt cold and heavy against her skin, but familiar as well.

It feels good to be back where I belong.

Ichirin agreed with that sentiment. Taka comforted her in a way that she found difficult to describe, but she appreciated nonetheless. If it hadn't been for his intervention, she didn't know if they would have survived the encounter with the kappa. The fact that two of them would be going to the hospital in their own vehicle seemed like a monumental victory.

Corey walked into the room, carrying a mop and a bucket. She put both of them down on the floor near the streak of blood left by the kappa. Before getting to the cleaning, she walked over to Ichirin and reached out to give her a reassuring squeeze. No words, no judgments, just that simple gesture. Then she started the monumental cleaning effort.

Shame I couldn't do anything to save your security deposit. I'm guessing evil mythological water spirit isn't covered under your escape clause.

No, it probably wasn't. But if that was the least of their concerns,

Ichirin was more than willing to part with a little bit of money. Her thoughts on the finances might be different if she didn't have first-hand experience with the quality of her health insurance plan. Hemingway had the luck to be in the same situation.

"Are you ready to go?" she called out as she shuffled to the front door.

As she came around the corner, she saw Hemingway standing there waiting for her. He opened the door so she didn't need to alter her pace.

"Do you think the hospital has a membership loyalty program?" he asked as they walked toward his car.

"I'm praying we don't find out."

THE END

PART III
PREDATOR AND PREY

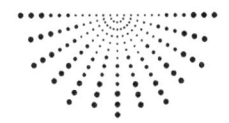

CHAPTER ONE

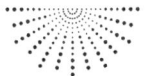

Ichirin kept her weight on the balls of her feet, her entire body tense as she watched her opponent. The two of them circled each other, their bare feet sliding across the exercise mats with a familiar *swish*. She anticipated the attack, waited for it, hoping she'd be able to respond fast enough. Corey had reach and strength on her, but if the aikido dojo had taught her anything, it was that size and strength were not the only factors in a fight.

Across from her, a grin danced at the edges of Corey's mouth. Whereas Ichirin viewed the training as a way to improve herself and her chances of survival, her taller and lankier friend enjoyed it, sinking into it with a frightening passion.

Corey took a moment to blow at some of her pale hair that fell into her face. Her hair was too short to pull back as her opponent had. In that moment, Ichirin saw opportunity. She lunged forward, rising to try and get over Corey's shoulders so she could grapple the athletic woman to the ground. Corey saw the move and brought her hands up, intending to meet the charge and redirect the energy.

But the attack was a feint. Ichirin bent her knees at the last moment of her lunge, dropping under Corey's prepared response and getting close enough to wrap her arms around the other woman's torso. She grunted from the effort and pushed forward, trying to use her momentum to shift Corey's hip and push it down to get to a pin.

The resistance disappeared.

As Ichirin drove forward and tried to force her sparring partner into submission, Corey spun, slamming her adversary onto the mats. The impact made her bounce and forced the air out of her lungs. Corey was on her in a moment, pinning her to the ground. How such a wiry woman could be so heavy remained a mystery. The hunter struggled to rise from the mat, but her opponent met each effort with a shift that pushed her back down to the cool padded surface.

"You're getting better," Corey said.

At first, Ichirin's embarrassment at her performance flared, and she thought it might have been a jest. But when she looked up, she saw the sincerity on her friend's face. That made her cheeks redden at the compliment, a warmth that she felt. She disliked how her pale skin made it that much easier for her to blush, a thought which exasperated the problem. Corey climbed off and began to roll her shoulder, stretching it out.

"So, have you been able to figure out anything else?" Corey dropped her voice to a whisper, not that it would have mattered. The other students were busy wrestling, and it was difficult for the two women to hear each other over the collective grunting, sighing, and solid impacts against the floor.

There was only one possible thing Corey could have referred to: Taka. After Ichirin switched roles with the kami that lived in her locket at the lake house, she had learned much more about him than he ever revealed, including that he had a master. The glance into his thoughts reshaped her entire view of the entity.

"Not yet. I haven't wanted to ask too many questions in case he figures out what I'm up to. It's hard enough not to think about what happened when I'm near the locket."

"What are you going to do? It's only a matter of time until you think of something when you're wearing it and then..." Corey let the thought go unfinished.

Ichirin didn't need her to complete it. That fear existed as a constant itch in the back of her mind. If she was honest with herself, she was surprised she managed to push the thought back as far as she did. As near as she could guess, Taka could only pick up her surface thoughts, but she wasn't sure how deep his reach extended.

For the moment, relations with the kami seemed normal, as much as they could be when dealing with a disembodied entity that spoke into her mind. He continued to be as helpful and sarcastic as ever. The only difference she noticed was that she no longer found him to be a comforting presence in her mind. Instead, she dreaded putting the locket around her neck.

Before she had a chance to answer the question, the instructor walked over and stared down at the two women with a look that carried multiple layers of disapproval. The students both gave a quick nod of deference before resuming their sparring exercise. Once again, Corey gained the upper hand, tossing her partner to the mats with minimal apparent effort.

Their struggles continued in much the same vein, with Ichirin fighting to gain some manner of leverage. Every time she felt she was close, Corey slipped out of the way or turned things around. The constant failures made Ichirin clench her jaw and take deep breaths through her nose that made her nostrils flare. When the instructor called for a switch, she felt relieved to have the opportunity to challenge herself against someone else.

By the time class ended, the hunter's feet dragged across the floor as she shuffled to the changing room. She reminded herself that there were good days and bad days, and most days were in-between. Today was far from her worst.

The woman's locker room was sparse and not often used, as expected considering the gender makeup of most classes. On the plus side, the room had a floral scent mixed with a bleach cleaning solution.

Getting close to her bag, she felt Taka's presence before she put her hand on her belongings. Ever since she had given him control of her body, she felt the moment they reconnected. She didn't know if it was a side effect of their temporary role reversal, but the timing fit.

Probably a result of us growing closer and increasing our bond. The fact that it happened after you let me take control is not too surprising. I would agree with your hypothesis.

Ichirin changed clothes, starting with putting the locket around her neck and feeling its weight and familiar coolness against her chest. It didn't matter how long she held the piece of jewelry, it always felt cold to the touch, making her inhale a bit when it shifted against her skin or when she first put it on. The only time that changed was when it had shone in the lake right before she swapped positions with Taka.

The memory sent a shudder through her months later. It was unlike anything she had ever experienced—being a passenger in her own body.

Now imagine living that reality for centuries. Frankly, I'm amazed I'm still sane considering how long I had to endure that miserable existence. You have no comprehension of the layers of boredom sitting on that mountainside waiting for you to come along.

Ichirin would argue she did have some idea, but only because Taka reminded her of the story every time he saw an opening. In her imagination, she pictured Taka sputtering in frustration, and a smirk crossed her lips. To her surprise, he remained silent through it all. She knew he'd be back. Their relationship was not dissimilar from coworkers harassing each other at the office.

As she thought about it, her brain stumbled over what to call their relationship, especially now that they had shared the same body. Would that terminology be correct? Would what had happened be considered possession?

While I appreciate your attempt to dig deeper into what transpired, I would caution you against going too deep down the rabbit hole. Besides, in the end, does it matter what label is applied? As long as we understand it and have an agreement, that's what's important.

The woman agreed with that much. She despised labels and could approve of the sentiment. But even throwing those aside, this relationship was unlike any she had ever had before, unlike any relationship any normal human being found themselves in.

You're normal. Well, in most ways. You're just a little special in others.

Which would be the very antithesis of normal.

I will concede this point to you. But I will say your uniqueness is what makes it enjoyable to travel with you. And I'm not just saying that because my other option was sitting on the side of a mountain talking to myself and contemplating existence.

How charming to think she rated above solitude when it came to her company. Ichirin moved to the mirror and undid the ponytail, collecting the errant dark strands that came loose during her grappling sessions. She pulled it all tight behind her head before looping the hair tie around the entire bundle. It wasn't perfect, but it would serve until she got home. She had no plans now that she'd finished class.

As she turned back to resume getting dressed, Corey came around the corner and bumped into her with the full strength of her stride, making both of them take a step back. Ichirin slipped and reached back, slamming her wrist against the hard tile floor. She let out a soft yelp and picked up her hand, cradling it in front of her chest.

Across from her, Corey stood, her eyes darting around the small bathroom area like she expected something to leap out of a wall and attack her. Given some of the things they had seen, that wouldn't be entirely outside the realm of possibility.

"Ichirin?" she asked, her voice a whisper as she hissed out the name and crouched, taking on a combative posture.

"What is it?" Ichirin asked, rubbing her wrist while she contorted her hand through various positions, checking to see the extent of the damage.

"Where are you?"

Those words caught her attention, and the hunter froze, staring up at her friend. She noticed that while her friend scanned the entire area, Corey's eyes didn't pause as they passed over her.

It would appear you have manifested a new ability. Some new creature has been released or traveled to this region. I advise caution, especially if it is capable of hiding in plain sight.

Ichirin stood up, the noise of her rustling clothes making Corey snap like a taut rubber band as she focused on the sound. She sank lower, narrowing her eyes as she tried to find the source.

"Relax, it's just me," Ichirin whispered.

She considered reaching out to give her friend a reassuring pat on the arm but decided against it when she thought of some of her new bruises. The ceramic floor in here was not as forgiving as the padded mats outside.

"I can't see you. What's going on?"

"It looks like there's something new we get to worry about."

As she spoke, Ichirin moved to the mirror. To her surprise, nothing appeared different. Before she had a chance to say any more, she noticed Corey walking forward and sweeping her hands through the air as if navigating through a dark, unfamiliar house.

"Why can I see myself?" the hunter wondered aloud.

I would guess it is because your invisibility is an illusion. Since you are the one projecting the illusion—even if it is your subconscious mind—I think you are immune to its effects.

Corey took a step in the direction of the mirror with her arms extended in front of her until Ichirin reached out and laid her hand on Corey's forearm. Her friend gasped and jumped but resisted pulling her hand back. She grabbed on, tentative at first and then with more conviction. Once she had a firm grip, she reached out with her other hand, sliding it up the unseen woman's arm until she stopped at the shoulder.

"This is unbelievable. You're invisible!" Corey grinned, her eyes sparkling with excitement that radiated. "That is so cool!"

Her giddiness infected Ichirin, and the hunter found herself grinning. Many times in her life she felt invisible, and it was a frequent fantasy, but now it was real.

Under normal circumstances, I would love to hear what sorts of trouble you imagined getting into in your youth. At the moment, I do feel the need to remind you of the downside. There aren't many entities capable of this level of illusion, and none of them are pleasant.

Taka's reminder dampened her spirits. While she enjoyed the powers, it served as a reminder of her duty as a soldier against these mythological creatures. The first step was trying to determine what entity had surfaced.

As I said, there are a few possibilities. It's still too early to tell. But I think there's a bigger problem unless you want a video of your car driving itself to show up on social media. I suppose you could try to expand the illusion to cover your vehicle, but that seems like the greater of two evils— although it could be entertaining.

"I need to figure out how I'm going to get home," Ichirin said aloud.

"I guess that's true. I didn't think about that." Corey took a deep breath. "For once I'm happy there weren't any other women in class tonight. I'd rather not have to explain that I'm talking to my invisible friend. Pretty sure that story ends with me getting committed."

Corey paused a moment before continuing. "So, how does this work? How long will it take for you to get control of your powers enough to become visible? Sooner or later, the instructor's going to knock on the door and ask us to leave."

"I don't know. Sometimes Taka talks me through it. Give me a moment."

Try to picture the illusion like a tapestry. Or better yet, a crochet project. It rests on top of reality like a blanket, masking what is really there. But, if you can find a single thread, you can pull the entire thing free. All it takes is grasping the right piece, and it will unravel.

Ichirin closed her eyes and tried to picture what her spiritual guide described, imagining a layer of magic hiding her from others' vision. At first, she sensed nothing, but experience taught her to continue to search. She focused on trying to find something that felt different or out of place.

When she felt something odd, she knew it was the illusion. It surrounded her and clung to her like wet paper, moving when she did and hugging her body when she retreated. She pictured it as a weave, a collection of fibers, any one of which she could grab and pull. The second skin unraveled, shedding off her body and evaporating into nothing as it peeled away.

"Wow. That was crazy. I kind of expected you to fade back like on an old *Star Trek* episode, but you just appeared. It was like you weren't there, I blinked, and then you were back."

Illusions are not like when you changed your body into smoke. They are either there or not. There is no intermediate state.

Living with Taka felt like taking a never-ending continuing education class. Their connection enabled her to feel him swell with pride at the compliment. She knew how much he enjoyed having his experience and knowledge appreciated.

Don't all sentient beings crave that type of recognition? Even when they are doing altruistic acts, it's still to please that little voice inside that wants acknowledgment. Some would argue there are no truly selfless acts in the world.

While that might be an interesting discussion at some point, right now was not the time. They needed to get a jump on the new creature before it caused chaos and endangered people.

"I'm going to text Hemingway, let him start doing his research on what we might be dealing with. No, Taka doesn't know what it is yet." Ichirin answered Corey's question as her mouth started to open. "There are too many possibilities to know for sure, so it's the hard way. Taka can at least give us somewhere to start."

I'll wait until you're composing the message. The list is fairly lengthy and no point in you trying to keep track of it all in your head.

While Corey finished getting ready to leave, Ichirin sent a message to her friend, letting him know that a new hunt had started and they needed his help. Taka supplied a long list of possible creatures, which she copied into the text message and sent over. She didn't wait for a response before tossing the phone into her bag. She didn't need to see the answer to know Hemingway would be up and begin the research tonight. She was willing to bet he'd still be at work or at least working from home. The latter option seemed to be his preference as of late.

Can you blame him? I imagine that's why you have the saying "don't mix business with pleasure." That relationship with his manager was a bad idea from the start. At least it ended reasonably amicably. Can you imagine how much worse it could have been?

She could, and she was glad it didn't go down that road. Ever since the relationship ended, Anika's behavior had been cold but professional. Ichirin assumed the other woman didn't have a choice. Working in the male-dominated technology sector made it critical to maintain decorum, even when not at the office. That fact made the hunter appreciate her strict upbringing. It didn't quite make up for the years of forced piano lessons, but it did make one aspect of her life easier.

As she pulled on her slacks, she heard the chime of her phone. Hemingway had to be working on it. By the time she got home, she wouldn't be surprised to find a ten-page report on the various creatures rumored to possess the ability to craft illusions.

The two friends finished getting ready to leave, bundling up in several layers to protect from the cold. As they left the dojo, they gave a small but respectful bow to the instructor and went into the parking lot. The air felt and smelled crisp, like ice mixed with the exhaust from the cars on the road.

The lot was full, with a fair number of people out and about either grabbing a late bite to eat or shopping for the upcoming holiday. It was that strange time between Thanksgiving and Christmas where it didn't quite feel like a holiday, but it also didn't feel like regular days and weeks.

"You sure you're okay to go home alone? With this new thing, it might not be the best idea." Corey looked around, trying to see anyone who might eavesdrop on their conversation. No one was within earshot.

"I'll be fine for now. I'll call you if anything comes up or I need your help. Don't worry; I won't leave you out. Besides, I always have help."

Corey made a pointed glance at the locket hanging around Ichirin's neck, but the motion was quick and her expression unreadable. She settled for coming in for a quick hug before climbing into her car.

"Let me know when it's time to go hunting." Her typical grin had returned to her face as she shut the door and left.

Walking over to her car, Ichirin thought about the new creature and its illusions. Would she be able to see through them like she saw through her own? Were they connected on that level?

I'll be honest; I don't know. You have to remember that this is uncharted territory for both of us. There have not been many—if any—throughout history capable of doing what you can do. Before our partnership, I had no direct experience with it. My instinct says no, you will not be able to see through the illusions. The only reason you see through yours is because you created them. When you inherited the powers of the kappa, you were not bound to the same water it was, which makes me think you don't share that level of connection with these abominations.

The term caught the hunter's attention. While she knew Taka didn't approve of these mythological creatures and they both wanted to eliminate them before they caused too much damage, the sheer vehemence he used to impart the word made her miss a step.

I apologize for the strength of my conviction in using such a title. However, it seemed the most fitting way to refer to them. You've seen the devastation they can cause when left unchecked. But that's why the work you do is so important and why I'm committed to this quest. Together we can stop them.

Ichirin watched the other people walking around as she got closer to her car, trying to see if any took an unusual interest in her. A man noticed her staring and stood a little taller, sucking in air to stick out his chest. It would have been comical if she wasn't aware of being a woman alone in a dark parking lot. Enough people milled around that logic said the likelihood of a threat was small, but that didn't change the ingrained fear and awareness of the inherent danger.

The closest person was a woman walking her black lab on the sidewalk, just a few cars away. Still self-conscious from the previous interaction, the hunter kept her head low and glanced out of the corner of her eye. As she fiddled with the lock, she heard a low growl come from their direction.

The dog stared at her with its lips curled back in a permanent snarl as it continued to rumble, the rest of its body tense as it leaned forward until the walker had to lean back to keep her dog in place. Her eyes widened with a combination of fear and surprise as she tried to calm her dog with soft sounds interspersed with apologies. The animal barked, making Ichirin jump and flatten herself against the car. She pictured the leash snapping and the beast launching itself at her.

The tension lasted only a few seconds until the woman managed to drag her pet away, pulling him with her. She looked distraught over the turn of events and insisted her good boy never acted like this. Not sure what else to do, the hunter mumbled an apology, squirming where she stood. Meanwhile, the black lab continued to stare, even as its owner dragged it backward.

When she dropped into her car, Ichirin slammed the door shut and engaged the power locks, letting out a heavy breath now that she had a physical barrier between her and the threats—both real and imagined. Her hands clenched on the wheel, and it was a full minute before she managed to uncurl her tightened fingers.

While that encounter may have done little to soothe your psyche, it did grant me some insight into what the creature might be.

CHAPTER TWO

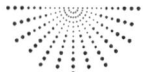

iven the way the canine responded and the fact that it's a hunting breed at its roots, I think there's a good chance that the creature might be a kitsune. It would make sense if the animal is as peaceful as the owner proclaimed.

Ichirin's hands still shook, but at least some good came out of the hair-raising event. It gave them a probable direction to focus their search. What were kitsune known for? She remembered hearing something about nine-tailed foxes and playful creatures, not something evil.

That's because your perception is flawed from modern culture, which likes to romanticize a lot of things. Look at the popularity of pirates. Do you really think they were swashbuckling heroes with a smile who regularly bathed? It's human nature to look back on things and put a happier coat of finish on it. The same is true with the kitsune.

True, not all of them are inherently evil. There are multiple types of fox creatures. But all of them are capable of powerful magics, illusions in particular. They are also renowned shapeshifters.

Which begged the question of how she could find it. Even if she managed to see through its illusions, that might be irrelevant since it could change shape. It could be anyone or anything out there. Sitting up straighter in the car, the hunter glanced out the windows and around, trying to see if anything moved close to her position. At the moment, she wished Hemingway got the dog he kept talking about wanting. That would make their lives a little easier right now.

And then you wouldn't be able to get near him no matter how well the dog trusts you because you're something it's programmed to hunt. It might make finding the kitsune easier, but only if you weren't around. I'm afraid that loophole is closed at the moment. But we'll find it.

Ichirin wished she had Taka's confidence, but too many questions and horrible situations rattled around in her mind, made all the more pronounced since she couldn't see the kitsune coming. What she did have was conviction.

She knew without a doubt that hunting these creatures down was her purpose, her destiny. She also knew that if she didn't do it, no one else could stop the monster. If she failed, whatever chaos it caused fell on her shoulders. She didn't know how she'd succeed, but that never stopped her before and it wouldn't now.

Reaching into her bag, she grabbed her phone. Hemingway had messaged her to let her know he started researching. She sent him a quick note to focus on the kitsune, and they'd talk when she got home.

By the time she finished her commute, she felt filled with the sense of duty and drive that had gotten her where she was in life. If she could handle telling a divisional manager he had built his business plan on a flawed premise, she could handle this. She picked up the phone and called Hemingway before climbing out of her vehicle.

"I hope it's not too late," she said when he picked up, even though she knew he'd be up. She needed to maintain some social standards.

"Of course not. I won't crash for a few hours yet. I've been digging up everything I could about various kitsune. There's a ton of stuff about them. Not surprising considering their popularity in modern media. It's taking a while to dig through all of it. I have a wealth of stuff to show you. I'll email some links. What happened and how do you know it's a kitsune? Did you see it?"

Hemingway's excitement made his sentences run together with

few pauses in a way that seemed more appropriate for Corey. Was his enthusiasm because the beast was a kitsune?

Either that, or he's glad to have something other than work to distract him. It's kind of like a forced vacation for his brain, making him switch gears. He does seem like the type to work himself into the ground of his own free will. That's not a bad thing.

"Giving you the 'too long, didn't read' version, I went invisible in the changing room at aikido. If it happened ten minutes earlier when I was still on the floor, it could've been bad. Then there was a dog in the parking lot. When it saw me, it got aggressive and strained against the owner's leash trying to attack me. Before it noticed me, it looked normal, wagging its tail and quite content to shuffle along at the owner's side."

"Interesting." Hemingway dragged out the word and Ichirin pictured him sitting in his home office, nodding as he drummed his fingers on the edge of his keyboard. "That would fit with what I've been reading. Some people used to have dogs to guard against kitsune since they could see through illusions or other tricks the creature would try."

"What else have you found out? It's nice to have a jumpstart on this one, and I want to keep pushing that advantage. Perhaps for once we won't be playing catch up and can take the lead on something. It would make for a nice change."

"Yes, but the creature can shapeshift. Even if we learn everything about it, how are we going to find it? It could just jump into another skin or something, and we won't know what to do."

"One step at a time. We'll worry about that when we get there. The more we know, the more prepared we can be."

"I won't argue with that. I'll see what else I can find. In the meantime, take a look at those links I sent. They should give you a good general idea about what powers they might have or the ones you might inherit. There's a lot of conflicting info, so I guess the hardest part might be filtering the facts from the noise."

Which might be something where Taka could help. Over their time together, she came to believe he had firsthand experience with many of these monsters. It would explain why he knew so much about the different mythological beasts.

I have lived for many human lifetimes and believe myself to be ageless. It's possible I will never die. In that time, I have heard many stories, been carried by many people, and seen many things. It helps to always be paying attention.

Ichirin realized his answer was both accurate and uninformative. She had come to expect as much whenever Taka talked about his history. He seemed reticent to volunteer too much information about himself.

Digging into the information Hemingway provided sent her down a rabbit hole that ate away hours before she realized how long she had been sitting at her computer. The words started to blur, and she pawed at her eyes in a vain attempt to clear them. She realized she should head to bed when she read the same paragraph four times in a row attempting to glean its meaning.

You need rest. You won't accomplish anything if you are too exhausted to read.

Taka's presence in her mind sparked a flash of irritation that spurred her into a more wakeful state. He had been silent the entire time she read, not offering any insight or guidance for the wealth of information she tried to absorb. Hemingway continued to send links and snippets of information, half of which Ichirin hadn't even been able to open yet. The kami could have saved her so much time and agitation, but it elected to remain silent for those hours.

I would apologize for not being at your beck and call, but I am not your servant. I do not expect you to follow my orders because of our relationship.

Ichirin looked down at her hands on her lap, and her shoulders slumped. Of course, Taka wasn't her servant, and she didn't think that. The frustration was momentary and boiled to the surface, an additional side effect of the exhaustion. She reached up and rubbed her eyes as she gave in to the urge to yawn.

Don't chastise yourself too harshly. I understand you're tired and frustrated with this. It is understandable. You did not ask for this responsibility.

But you have it, and we need to work together to make sure we accomplish our goals and stop these creatures.

Taka's words helped her relax, but her arms felt heavy, and her hands rested limply over the edge of her chair. She wondered if the kami could continue research in her stead. If he took over her body, could he read while she rested? Would she wake up with the knowledge, like studying in her sleep?

I'm afraid not. Your body has physical limits I might be able to push, but there's a limit to what I can do. I can't make your physical form more resilient. As soon as we switched, I'd encounter the full brunt of your fatigue. You might feel more energized, but only so long as I maintained control.

Wishful thinking then and bedtime for her. The articles would still be there in the morning, when Ichirin could tackle them with fresh eyes and a fresher mindset.

Her sleep was uneventful and free of dreams. When she woke, it felt like she had laid down and closed her eyes mere seconds ago. The brightness peeking out from around the blinds of her bedroom window indicated otherwise. Her body didn't feel too sore after the previous night's activities. She had a few bruises and tight muscles, but nothing unexpected. Her mind felt drained and sluggish, like she had stayed up far too late working on an overdue project that still wasn't complete.

That didn't help give her the motivation to get out of bed.

She managed to force herself to get up and start facing the day, if for no other reason than she didn't want to have Taka lecture her about her lackadaisical attitude. Thanks to her mother, she had enough of those speeches to last a lifetime. She knew the kitsune might be hunting her, and her best chance was to get informed and get a handle on her abilities.

Within the hour, she had dressed and jumped back into the research while sipping a cup of tea. According to his last message, Hemingway planned to come over this morning to help brainstorm ideas and go through the information together. She wanted to read as much as she could before he arrived.

Throughout all the different accounts about what a kitsune was or what it was capable of, one consistent element was the ability to shapeshift. Considering she created an illusion of invisibility, Ichirin wondered if it wasn't shapeshifting, but rather an illusion.

I would consider that unlikely. Creating illusions does not alter the phys-
ical form of the entity. When a kitsune changes its shape, it can look and
function like a human to fool others. If it were just an illusion, then it
wouldn't be able to do things like serve tea, unless it was the most dexterous
fox alive. I know they are amazing, but even that seems a bit far-fetched.

The hunter smiled, unable to contain her excitement and unwilling to try. While the forthcoming hunt carried a note of seriousness, the idea of shapeshifting was intoxicating in and of itself. What person hadn't imagined what it would be like to change into a bird and fly through the skies?

Someone deathly afraid of heights?

Ichirin sighed and shook her head back and forth a few times. Her point still stood, and a single comment wasn't going to squash her fantasies. Of all of the powers she could inherit, this rested at the top of the list that she would ever dream to request.

Standing up from her desk and pushing the chair back, she got ready to attempt to tap into this ability and then realized she had no idea how to make it happen.

I suspect it would work like when you transferred into smoke, but that's
just a guess on my part. Imagine having a part of your body shift, shortening
as needed as the bones reshape. Hold the image of whatever you want to
become in your mind and think about forcing yourself into that shape, kind
of like when you try to cram clothes into a bit of spare space in your suitcase
to fit everything you can.

The human did as Taka suggested, closing her eyes and imagining that a crane stood in her place. She tried to feel her neck lengthening and thinning. She considered what it would feel like as her arms shortened and sprouted feathers, picturing her body morphing into that elegant creature. The image became difficult to hold onto, and her face tightened with the effort to do so.

But nothing happened.

Not willing to give up, she tried again, and then a third time, each attempt producing the same results. Her frustration mounted, and she paced around the room to relieve some of the tension.

It's possible you have not inherited that gift, or that kitsune do not possess it. Yes, it's one of the few things that most of the lore agrees on, but it could still be a complete fabrication.

Taka continued before Ichirin could articulate a mental response.

But, assuming that is not the case, perhaps a different approach would be merited? What if rather than trying to mold yourself into a specific shape, you imagined your form becoming malleable? Think of your body becoming more fluid, less rigid, no longer bound by the constraints of a physical form.

It was worth a shot. At this point, she was willing to try just about anything if it meant she could realize her childhood fantasy.

This time, when she tried to center herself and tap into the near-meditative state that allowed her to access her temporary abilities, she didn't picture her body changing. She tried to think of letting go and being free, no longer constrained to the limits of her physical form. Or rather, no longer having her physical form constrained. The different phrasing was subtle but important for what she tried to accomplish.

While she felt something, Ichirin wasn't convinced it was any more than a reaction to slipping into her trance-like state. She felt a little looser, like after a long, deep massage. Other than that, she felt the same.

Now imagine taking that malleable body and shifting it like clay, reforming it into the shape you desire. Make it a slow process and don't try to force it. Guide and encourage, rather than shove and force.

A knock on her door startled her as she attempted to follow Taka's advice. After her initial shock, she knew it had to be Hemingway. As she walked to the door, her body felt slow, heavy, and sluggish. At one point she stumbled over her own feet and put out a hand to catch herself.

The hand propping her up was much larger and black.

Ichirin let out a quick squeal of surprise and dropped to the ground when she pulled her hand away. She tried to fall and roll, absorbing the impact, but her body didn't move as she expected. It felt like she wore a suit of armor. The bruises and discomfort made it clear she wasn't as she impacted against the floor. The carpet did little to absorb the shock.

Lifting both her hands in front of her face, she saw that she had changed. Those were not her arms. They were thicker and darker skinned than her own. As she examined them, she noticed a scar on her right arm, matching the one Hemingway had, down to every detail she could remember. Touching her face, she felt at it like a patient who just had the bandages removed after surgery.

Now that's interesting. It would appear you have changed shape, but not into an animal. If it was anyone but Hemingway, I might suggest that terminology was debatable.

Ichirin's mouth hung slack as she ran her fingers up to her hair and felt how much shorter and different it was. Her entire body had changed, which spurred a curious thought. She pulled out the waistband of her pants as far as it would go—the clothes had changed as well—and glanced between her legs, feeling herself blush as she noticed that yes, everything was in fact different.

Taka chortled in her head, amused at the connection of thoughts that the shapeshifted woman tried to push down to no avail.

After composing herself, Ichirin got up and moved around, taking a few steps to get used to her new form. It was her body, but at the same time, it wasn't. It didn't feel like she wore another skin, because that implied something separated it from her body. It also made it sound like something she could remove. She walked in a circle, brushing against her couch and feeling it press against her legs rather than her waist. She stopped and looked down, chuckling at the difference. Sniffing at her arm, her eyes widened, and she let loose a soft "huh." Her skin smelled like Hemingway every time they hugged.

The real Hemingway gave a more insistent knock at the door before calling out her name. Ichirin's head shot up, and she focused on the closed door. What if the person outside wasn't Hemingway and it was the kitsune instead?

That would be unlikely. How would it know where you lived? And even if it could determine that, such an action would reveal its strategy before the stones were in place on the board. There is nothing in my experience or in any of the lore that indicates kitsune have telepathic abilities. There's a reason most of the classical tales involve someone who is a stranger.

The hunter walked over to the door and checked through the peephole out of habit. Hemingway stood on her doorstep, moving back and forth between trying to peer in one of the front windows and looking over his shoulder or into her yard. She pulled the door open and he froze when he found himself staring into his own face.

CHAPTER THREE

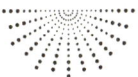

His eyes wide with fear, Hemingway brought his fist up and lunged forward in an awkward punch that threatened to pull him off balance. Ichirin turned and shifted, her instincts kicking in to avoid the blow and use his momentum to toss him to the floor.

Her muscle memory was used to a much lighter body.

Hemingway's fist came straight in at Ichirin's chin, accurate despite his lack of training. As she tried to slide out of the way and off target, the edge of his knuckles grazed her jaw. She brought her arms up and pushed a foot back, creating an open space to throw him down.

But the hunter got tangled in her legs and toppled to the side, pulling Hemingway down on her body when she clamped down on his wrist. He tried to wrench free but was past the tipping point and couldn't get the leverage to liberate himself. The two of them fell together in a mad tumble of identical bodies.

To his credit, he tried to continue his assault and pin her to the ground. But while she wasn't used to her new form, many of the lessons and ideologies were the same. She slid out from underneath him and pinned him to the floor. At least the fence kept her neighbors from peering through the front entrance and seeing the spectacle of twins fighting.

"Hem, relax! It's me!" Ichirin said between grunts as she held Hemingway in place. His strength almost gave him the upper hand, but her training let her maintain control. "I know what it looks like, but I'm not the kitsune. I was experimenting and trying to figure out what powers I had."

Hemingway stopped struggling and looked up at his friend wearing his face. She saw his indecision. He never had much of a poker face, and this time was no different.

"How do I know it's you?"

"Because I can tell you that you had to move our regular lunch walks to Thursdays because of your 1-on-1's being pushed into our normal Wednesday slot."

Ichirin hoped the obscurity of that fact would prove her identity. It might help convince him even if he didn't know the kitsune couldn't read minds. The gamble proved effective as he relaxed underneath her and opened up his hands in a submissive gesture.

"That's still a little..." He paused as he searched for the words, shifting his eyes to avoid her gaze. He coughed and swallowed before trying again. "It's weird looking at myself. Super weird. I don't know how to explain it to you, but it's a little freaky. Could you change back or into someone else?"

"Oh gods, I'm sorry. I didn't think..."

Ichirin rolled off to the side and sat up, walking away from Hemingway and turning to hide her face as much as possible. She noticed that he twisted to the side like a nervous teenage boy trying to be gallant. It must've made him more uncomfortable than she realized. She needed to shift back to her regular self.

You know how to do this. Relax and remember. That's what you need to do. It's ingrained in your system, and it's just another type of muscle memory. Think of it like clenching a muscle and then relaxing it as it returns to its natural state.

With a deep breath, the hunter tried to ease the tension from her muscles like she had learned during meditation. She tensed her entire body and then released all the tightness at once. Closing her eyes, she kept her mind as blank as possible. Taka remained silent, letting her maintain her focus.

When she opened her eyes and lifted her arm to examine it, the flesh had returned to her normal color and regular size. She reached up to touch her face, and that small motion told her everything she needed to know. Her body responded as she expected, moving like she thought it should. Even the weight of her hair felt reassuring.

How did it feel putting on someone else's skin? I suppose that gives a new meaning to the phrase walking in someone else's shoes. I find it fascinating that not only did your figure change, but your garments also matched what you're accustomed to seeing him wear. I've never been this close to a shapeshifter before.

"It's okay. I'm back to myself," Ichirin said, watching as Hemingway turned back to face her, the relief evident on his face. She heard him release a long exhale.

"I really thought you might be the kitsune. Maybe it found you, came over, and got you to let down your guard. I don't know. It was so weird. Like looking into a mirror, but everything was all flipped around. And staring at a face that I know is mine but isn't mine."

Hemingway continued to babble, and Ichirin couldn't remember if she'd ever seen him this unnerved before. Given some of the things they had faced together, that thought alone was frightening. She walked past him to get a glass of water. When he first took it from her, his hand shook, and the water threatened to slosh over the sides. He took several long swallows and handed her back a near-empty glass with much steadier hands.

"That was…" He paused. "Unnerving."

What could she say in response to his discomfort, considering she was the shapeshifter? She could only imagine how unsettling it must have felt. In the end, she reached out and offered a light squeeze of his arm near the shoulder. He put his hand on top of hers and smiled, appreciative of the gesture.

"So, that was exciting. Why were you looking like me in the first place? I understand testing out your powers, but why me?"

You could always tell him that you've been noticing the weight he's been losing.

Only through a supreme effort of will did Ichirin keep from blushing at Taka's intrusion into her mind. While it was true, she hadn't been noticing in the way that the spirit implied. She coughed a few times, using it to release some of the tension she felt. Hemingway saw her hesitation and opened his mouth to ask a question, but his friend spoke up before he could form any words.

"I didn't try to look like you. I was trying to change into a bird, but it wasn't working. I wanted to see what it would feel like to fly. Taka tried to talk me through it to help get it to work, but nothing happened. When you knocked on the door, I knew it was you. When I opened my eyes, I was wearing your skin."

As soon as those words came out of her mouth, she regretted it. Hemingway shuddered, but managed to keep his composure. After a brief moment, he broke the awkward silence but kept his eyes focused on the floor.

"You know, it might be that you can't shift into an animal. Think about it. All the stories that we read deal with a kitsune either as a fox or taking on the form of a human. I'd bet that could have something to do with it. It would explain why you couldn't become an animal, but why you shifted into someone else without much of a thought."

Someone you know very well. As soon as his name comes up, you summon a mental image without any effort. Think of it like muscle memory, but for your brain. There's a lot of credence to this theory.

"If that's true, then do you think I can only shift into other people? Or can I just change one aspect of myself if I wanted?"

Hemingway shrugged, admitting his lack of knowledge.

Only one way to find out. How'd you like to try being a blonde?

Ichirin closed her eyes and focused. She tried to relax and not force the change, letting it take place in its own time and using her mental guidance as nudges along the path she wanted it to take.

"Holy shit," Hemingway muttered.

The hunter could count on one hand the number of times she'd heard Hemingway swear and have fingers to spare. Opening her eyes, she grabbed some of her hair and pulled it in front of her face to take a look at it. The strands were pale to the point of being white.

Looks like you went a bit far on the color spectrum, but that's still impressive. You're improving at getting a handle on your powers and doing so with haste.

"I'm not going to lie. This is impressive, and I'm more than a little bit envious," Hemingway said. "You could be anyone you wanted to be. What's it feel like?"

Hemingway reached out, entranced by her new look, and then hesitated, his hand hovering in space. Ichirin nodded and leaned forward, letting him run his fingers through her hair and study it.

"It's not an illusion. You actually changed it."

It felt like a silly realization given their brief wrestling match. He must have felt the difference in weight when she changed into him, but she admitted he might be trying to forget that experience. She saw no point in reminding him.

The prospects were exciting, but it didn't get them any closer to tracking the kitsune. But it could help Ichirin sneak up on her quarry when the moment arrived.

Only if you are used to your temporary body and there aren't any dogs around. You were unsteady and off-balance while matching Hemingway's shape. If I were an ageless shapeshifter, I would learn to recognize that discomfort in others if I didn't have another way to sniff out a potential rival.

"We still need a way to find it. Other than dogs, we don't have much to go on. Especially after seeing what I'm capable of, I doubt we can trust our senses, any of them. Wherever the kitsune is, it can look, sound, and smell like anyone it can imagine. Did you find anything that might get us closer?"

"Let's compare notes. I have a couple of ideas, but not a lot to go on." Hemingway stared for a breath or two, just long enough for his friend to squirm.

"What is it?" she asked.

"Could you change back? It just looks wrong. I'm sure you could pull the look off, but it's not what I'm expecting to see when I look at you."

Ichirin laughed once she learned the source of his scrutiny. She obliged, returning to her natural state. She noticed that it took no effort to maintain her altered appearance once she set it in place. In contrast, changing back took a conscious and concentrated effort.

The two of them spent some time going over the various stories and what they had been able to discover on their own regarding the kitsune, trying to determine what it was capable of and how they might find it. They spent much of the time in quiet reading on opposite sides of the room, each lost in their own computer screens.

As the afternoon pushed toward the evening, Hemingway stretched, his body letting out a couple of cracks as he reached toward the ceiling.

"I suppose you won't want to go to the holiday party with all of this showing up."

Ichirin was about to agree when an idea bloomed.

"I think we should go. It could be our chance to catch the kitsune, or at least meet it face to face." She nodded a couple of times as she thought about the idea. "We know it's probably going to come after me. That's what happened with the kappa. Otherwise, it wouldn't have been there. Whether these things are hunting me or are drawn to wherever I am, the point remains that they find me."

"So, you think it'll be there looking for you? Will you at least look like someone else?"

She shook her head. "We don't know if they can recognize each other. For all we know, it might have some way to detect if I changed my appearance. That would let it know I've learned how to use some powers. We need to keep whatever advantage we can get. Let's keep it in the dark. We'll go like we planned and try to flush it out."

I do not like this plan. Not one bit. It's as wise as the frog giving a ride to the scorpion.

"Sounds risky, but if you're okay with it, it makes sense," Hemingway said. "If it's hunting you, that's the most public place where it can predict you're going to be. The more I think about it, the more I agree with the idea."

You know how I sometimes talk about human foolishness? This is a prime example.

"True, we don't know what it'll look like, but from everything we've read, it'll be drawn to the center of the party, not at the fringes. I'd be willing to bet it'll cause a bit of mischief of some sort or another. Nothing we've been able to find indicates that kitsune are murderers, so I think I'll be okay."

The hunter convinced herself that this was the proper course of action, even if Taka didn't agree. There were risks, but sitting and doing nothing also contained risk. This way she felt like she took some agency for what was about to happen and might force the kitsune's hand. She wanted to spur the action forward, rather than just react to what happened around her.

It's not like I can do anything to stop you, but I hope that you have duly noted my objections. I might not be able to make much of an epitaph, but I am looking forward to that brief moment where I can say I told you so.

"Well, if that's the case then I should get back home to get ready for the soiree. I'll pick you up around six, and we can head to the party from here. Do you have directions?"

"Already open on my phone. I'll see you in a bit."

After Hemingway left, Ichirin did a little bit of last- minute research before getting herself ready. It wasn't a formal event, but her standard business attire would be insufficient. Even if her true purpose was looking for the kitsune, she still had a professional career to be concerned about, and the sad reality was that her appearance tonight could help or hinder that career in equal measure.

The original plan involved wearing a simple cocktail dress, but the potential encounter with the creature changed things. She knew things might become problematic if she did meet the monster.

In the end, she opted for a loose skirt, thick tights, and a pair of boots that found the happy middle ground of being stylish yet functional. The events of the past couple of years had a significant effect on her wardrobe and how she viewed it. Before she ever met Taka, she never would've considered whether or not something was comfortable enough to run in, let alone fight in.

At the thought of fighting, she made sure she tucked her knife into her bag. Her few lessons with knives went well, and while she wasn't an expert, she felt competent. That was something else filed under the list of things she never would've considered before meeting her insubstantial companion.

I'm honored to have been able to enrich your life. At the least, I can say I've altered it. I'm pleased you have taken some of my suggestions to heart. I do have your best interest in mind.

And his own. She had no delusions about his altruism in helping her. After all, he often shared the suffering he'd endured waiting for her to come along. What did he do before her hike? Was there ever another person he could talk to, or did his existence start on the mountain? If so, how did he have so much experience and tales to draw from?

As usual, Taka said nothing. Ichirin chuckled. If she ever needed the kami to be quiet, all she had to do was ask him a few questions. After having the idea, her shoulders slumped, and she pressed her lips together. She knew her train of thought was unfair. Many things existed in her past that she didn't feel comfortable thinking about and she wished not to discuss. That was a sentiment she understood.

Apology accepted. Of course, you realize the importance of picking out your outfit is somewhat moot when you can change it in a moment's notice.

Except for the fact that doing so meant changing in front of good-ness-knew how many people. Such a display would get far too much of the wrong kind of attention. That wasn't an option. The last thing she wanted was more people aware of her secret.

The evening had taken on a different tone, but now Ichirin paced from room to room waiting for Hemingway to show up. She drummed her fingers against her leg as she patrolled from one window to another, wondering when she might catch sight of his car. Before, the party was a required social event that others expected her to attend. Now it could bring her one step closer to solving the mystery in front of her.

Not to mention, the kitsune was a creature capable of speech. The enenra spoke a few words, but other than the time it spoke in a different voice, it couldn't be considered intelligent conversation. Perhaps in this instance, the hunter might gain some insight into the grand scheme. Maybe the kitsune would let something slip or even be willing to talk.

The creatures are known for their deceit and ability to twist words. Even if it does deign to speak, you won't be able to trust anything it says. Its words are its most powerful weapon. I suggest not letting it speak at all, or else it will convince you that day is night and you are the monster that needs to be taken out.

On the other hand, if she knew what it tried to do, wouldn't that protect her? Or at least provide some level of resistance? Similar to how knowing someone has a reputation for being a player made her more aware of his tricks.

I don't think it's worth the chance. If it wouldn't be inappropriate, I'd suggest earplugs or fancy noise-cancellation headphones. You could pretend to be testing some new device or so busy you can't stop working. That would make an impression. Your employer does love to try and convince you to be working all the time, don't they? I'd be willing to wager at least one in ten people at the party are on their phones writing email at any given time.

Ichirin knew better than to take that bet. She knew how much she worked, and how much the members of her team put in. It was expected. And she didn't qualify as someone passionate about their job. Of course, hunting down mythological creatures made any office job seem meaningless. How different would her life have been if she never manifested these strange powers?

Hemingway's arrival interrupted her train of thought before it traveled too far down those tracks. She squared her shoulders as she went to meet him at the door. She might not have chosen this, but it was her life, and spending time pondering "what if" was a waste of energy. Not to mention, some part of her loved having this unique ability and direction in life.

Hemingway wore slacks and an ill-fitting collared shirt that he purchased before he started getting in better shape. The belt was a couple of notches tighter than the well-worn hole, and he still wore his running shoes despite the rest of his outfit. His attire made his caste clear. He would fit in fine with the other engineers but lacked the necessary touches to blend with the managers or executives.

The ride to the club took twenty minutes, ten of which was spent dealing with Bellevue traffic. With it being a Saturday night, people crowded the streets to get to restaurants, bars, and clubs. At least this year, the party was on the Eastside. Heading into downtown Seattle, like last year, would have been worse. As wonderful as the city could be, entering it during peak traffic times often made Ichirin wonder if she should invest in a bike.

Soon, the two friends walked into the building while a valet parked the car. Their party was on the top floor, twenty-four stories up. A short hall led from the elevators to a sizable two-story club complete with a balcony. A full-service bar stretched along the entire wall, with four separate bartenders pouring drinks as fast as people consumed them.

The opposite wall was made of glass and provided an unimpeded view of downtown Bellevue. Many of the buildings had Christmas lights and decorations brightening the night sky in festive colors. A couple of people stood on the outside terraced area, resting on the railings and enjoying the view in its full glory. Most of them didn't last long, choosing to return to the warmth of the main room.

Why is it that it doesn't matter what corporate party you go to, some things are always present? Like the photo station where people can pose with props and select their background? Is there a book somewhere that says these events must include such things?

The party was well-attended, but as was par for the course, the company reserved more space than necessary. This was the holiday party for Hemingway's department, so while he had to stop every few feet to greet someone new, his companion only saw a handful of familiar faces. Anika caught sight of her from where she stood and offered a polite but formal nod and only the smallest of smiles.

Perhaps things were not as comfortable with Hemingway as you thought. On the plus side, that's one person you can rule out for being the kitsune. It wouldn't know to be the right combination of cold and distant but still professional.

Ichirin felt sure the kitsune wouldn't be anyone with the company. Masquerading as a specific individual would require having intimate knowledge about their role. It would be too risky. They might get stuck in a conversation with someone and fail to play the part. No, the kitsune would have to be a guest.

Or one of the workers.

Taka raised a good point. Someone working the party would be able to go in and out at will and have unfettered access to the grounds. They might need some inside knowledge, but not too much. Companies often hired outside agencies to handle the serving or entertainment.

A passing waitress paused and offered up a tray holding artisan crackers and ingredients Ichirin couldn't identify in the dim light. She caught a salty, spiced aroma and recognized the small dab of caviar topping each of the delicacies. The plate was half-empty. She lifted her hand in a gentle refusal, and the server drifted on through the small groups of people. The hunter watched her walk away, wondering if she might be the kitsune.

She shook her head. Second guessing every person she came across would drive her mad. Not to mention, her scrutiny would become obvious. Better to mingle and wander the crowd, keeping a broad view on everything without pursuing anything with laser focus.

As she walked around the floor, she felt something watching her. It was a maddening itch on her spine at the base of her skull. She continued to smile, offering nods to relative strangers and engaging in small talk as she turned, seeking the source. It was gone before she managed a quarter turn.

I felt it too. The kitsune is here. Watching you. You're not imagining things.

By now, Ichirin had a drink in her hand and took small sips as the night wore on. The party ran until midnight, so she had some time. She kept feeling the eyes of the kitsune on her but made an effort not to respond. Her movements felt tense and stiff as she tried to pretend nothing was out of the ordinary. She formed a mental checklist of faces, ticking off those who stood in front of her whenever the sensation flared.

"Find anything?" Hemingway whispered, the words malformed as he kept a smile on his face while someone he knew walked past him. He had spent most of the evening engaged in various conversations, and this was the first opportunity for relative privacy. They stood on the second floor while most of the party-goers mingled on the main level.

"It's here, watching me. I'm sure of that. I've narrowed it down to a handful of people."

"How are you going to figure out who it is?"

"I'm guessing it's the one staring daggers into my back. If I'm right, I have about ten people left as possibilities. Let's try to pare it down some more."

Ichirin took Hemingway's hand and led him down to the main floor of the party. The two of them walked up to a group of five people forming a tight circle and engaged in conversation. Three of them were men, and two were women. As Hemingway and his guest walked up, the group parted and made the circle bigger to accommodate the newcomers.

"Hey, Hemmie! Good to have you here," one of the men said—the one with the well-groomed beard.

He reached out and slapped Hemingway on the back, making the larger man wince as he put a forced smile on his face. Ichirin wasn't sure if it was for the slap or the hated nickname. His response did nothing to dampen the greeter's enthusiasm.

"Thanks for saving my ass last week when I was supposed to be on call. I don't know what I would've done without you. I owe you one."

The hunter scratched him off her collection of possible suspects. He knew personal details and was too familiar to be an imposter. She already knew it wasn't one of the couples in this gathering. That left the other couple as potential threats.

The man wore a full suit that made him stand out compared to the majority of the crowd. He was not the only one to cross the line into formal attire, but they were a few. His style went so far as to include a tie pin.

The woman at his side wore a cocktail dress that seemed black or blue or some combination of the two. It shimmered and looked like a liquid when she moved. She wore heels that gave her an extra two inches and looked impractical for mobility. Light sparkles in her blond hair caught the eye whenever she twisted her head.

"I don't mind. We all have to look out for each other," Hemingway said.

"I mean it, though. You saved my ass! Otherwise, I might've gotten the ax in this latest round of layoffs. I. Owe. You." He accentuated each of his last three words enough that Ichirin smelled the alcohol on his breath.

So, this is the resident corporate drunk? At this point, this corporate holiday party is almost complete. Now they just need to have some door prizes where only one of them is something that would interest anyone.

To complete the scene, the obviously-intoxicated coworker stepped forward to embrace Hemingway in an awkward hug that her friend reluctantly accepted. The others in the group lifted hands to chuckle behind. As Hemingway submitted to the uncomfortable physical gesture, the woman across the circle from Ichirin locked gazes with her.

The woman's eyes flashed gold as a coy smile spread across her lips, and she walked across the circle, trailing her hand over the drunk's shoulder. The hunter moved to follow the woman but stepped back as the man in the suit shoved the drunkard in her direction.

"What was that for?" Even with the flash of anger, his words came out slurred.

"How about you tell me why Jade touched your arm right there!"

"I'm not interested in your escort!"

The two men shouted back and forth and drew a crowd, most of whom seemed more than content to watch the event play out rather than interfere. The peanut gallery began to shout comments at the two men, egging them on.

Ichirin found herself trapped amidst a large press of bodies. She tried to worm her way through, sliding into any opening she found and moving forward. Hemingway got lost behind her in the crowd. It seemed like everyone in the party congregated to this one spot—everyone except the woman who started it all.

With a final grunt of effort, the hunter pushed herself through the last of the people and looked around for the kitsune. She had to be around here somewhere. It hadn't taken that long to get out of the mass of people.

There! By the patio!

The woman, Jade, stood with her hand on the door, twisting around to look behind her. When she saw Ichirin, she opened the door and stepped outside, walking to the balcony edge like she was out for a stroll.

And also like it isn't below freezing. That's the kitsune.

Glancing over her shoulder, she saw Hemingway still trapped in the cluster of people. The two in the center shoved each other but had thrown no punches. No one paid her any attention as she ran to the door.

The kitsune stood by the railing, gazing at the city and leaning out over the open air. The wind picked up and whistled as it whipped around the edge of the building, making Ichirin glad she still had her scarf with her. It didn't make her immune to the chill, but something was better than nothing.

"So many people out there, oblivious to the world as it truly is. Going through their lives with no knowledge of what exists and the mysteries that are just beyond the edge of observation. I wonder, if they truly believed, would they ever have forgotten us?"

Don't listen to it. This is your opportunity. Its back is turned. You could end this before it has a chance to do real damage. Just think of the chaos inside.

"What are you doing here?" Ichirin asked.

The woman turned around, wearing a grin feral enough to make the human slide back a half step.

"Isn't it obvious? I'm here to kill you."

CHAPTER FOUR

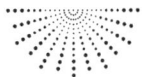

Ichirin stopped her retreat and set her stance, prepping for the kitsune to charge her. She didn't know what the monster would use to attack. As far as she could tell, the shapeshifter wasn't armed, but that was little comfort given the creature's penchant for illusions. The hunter clutched her bag, wondering how long it would take to retrieve her weapon. The kitsune was still about ten feet away. That should be enough time.

Without saying a word, Jade turned around and climbed up the railing, kicking off her high heels as she rose to the top bar.

What are you waiting for?

Spurred on by Taka, Ichirin snatched her knife from the bag and charged the monster's back, trying to grab her and wrestle her back down to the balcony. Before her fingers made contact, the creature jumped.

The hunter gripped the edge of the railing and leaned forward, searching for the kitsune and expecting to see her plummeting to the ground. The beast fell a couple of stories and then slowed, turning around and waving with a playful grin filled with superiority. The wind whipped around her, tangling her hair and snapping her cocktail dress.

Ichirin let out a howl of rage when she couldn't form words. With a growl, she slammed her hands down on the railing and climbed up to the top, her eyes focused on her prey falling away from her. She worked her way to the far side, one hand holding onto the rail behind her while the other snapped her blade open.

"Ichirin! Stop!" Hemingway shouted as he burst onto the balcony.

But his friend had already released her grip. As she fell forward, she pushed through her legs, jumping off the building and plummeting toward the fleeing kitsune. As her hair stretched out behind her and her clothes snapped against the air, she willed herself to fly, trying to soar after her target.

She continued to fall.

Realizing that gravity was not lessening its hold, Ichirin's resolve shattered. She windmilled her arms through the air, her knife forgotten as she tried to see anything that might save her from the forthcoming fatal impact with the ground. Closing her eyes tight, she screamed.

Her breath caught as two arms scooped her up and stopped her descent. The sudden change in motion made her head snap forward, giving her whiplash. Easing her eyes open, she found herself staring into the gold pupils of the kitsune. This close, the hunter saw that the irises sparkled with a light of their own beyond the reflections of the holiday decorations. A powdery, sweet smell filled her nostrils.

"You know, I could let you go and end the hunt right now."

The creature's voice was so level and void of emotion that Ichirin had no doubts she'd be willing and able to do that if it struck her fancy.

"But not yet. There's still much to learn and games to play."

The kitsune chuckled, a sound that made the human's skin prickle at the base of her neck. Sparing a glance at the ground still far below, she froze, not wanting to do anything to risk changing the creature's mind.

They floated to the ground with the lightness of a dandelion blossom. Ichirin stretched with her toes, only letting go of her unexpected savior when she felt the sidewalk pavement underneath the tip of her boot. The relief was short-lived, and she jumped away, spinning to face her adversary and lifting her hands into a fighting position.

The shapeshifter chuckled and shook her head. "Still so eager to fight? No, not yet. Soon though. I'll be watching."

Her eyes flashed metallic once again, and she gave a small curtsey.

"By the way, you dropped those."

Ichirin followed the kitsune's outstretched finger and saw her locket and now-folded knife sitting on the sidewalk next to the building. When she looked back, the creature bounded into the street in front of a car. It slammed on its brakes, creating a magnificent shriek. The vehicle swerved across the road and crashed into a parked car just a few feet from the hunter.

She rushed forward, yanking on the mangled door and trying to open it. The glass had shattered, and the driver slumped forward over the airbag, blood pouring down his face from several small cuts. He groaned as Ichirin reached in through the opening and unclipped the seat belt. She pulled the man free from the wreckage. He winced and moaned but didn't open his eyes or offer resistance. The hunter didn't have much training, but the words from the instructor at the emergency trauma class came back to mind.

The stranger was breathing, and that was a good sign. She checked his pulse, and it seemed stable to her untrained hands. A couple of the head wounds bled quite a bit, so she took his arm and lifted it, pressing the cuff of his jacket against the worst of the cuts. As she held it in place, Ichirin looked up to try and find the kitsune, but she was gone.

A crowd started to gather, and Ichirin shouted for someone to call 911. More people pressed around and a stranger relieved Ichirin of her duties, taking over and caring for the injured man. Hemingway appeared in the crowd and wrapped Ichirin's jacket around her shivering form. She fell against his chest, glad to have the support and leech as much warmth off him as she could.

While she stood there, he handed her the knife and the locket, sliding them into her hand.

"Are you okay? That was crazy."

I'm inclined to agree. What inspired you to leap to your almost death?

"I don't know. There was something about the way the kitsune acted that stirred up my emotions in a way I've never experienced before. It was like I couldn't think of anything else except hunting it down. I thought I'd be fine. If it could fly, so could I. Somehow, I knew that, even if I was wrong."

She shuddered, and Hemingway squeezed tighter around her.

The kitsune might be able to stir up emotions or prod them forward. It would explain why she is so good at what she does. Combine that with her illusions, and it becomes a hazardous mixture.

Ichirin slipped the chain over her head, letting the locket fall back into place. She didn't bother to pull her hair through the loop. Red and white lights flashed on the buildings around them, and the ambulance emitted a single high-pitched chirp to announce its arrival. The crowd parted to let the professionals handle the situation.

"Is he going to be okay?" Ichirin asked.

Hemingway looked over the shoulders of the people in front of them and listened to the conversation for a moment before responding.

"Yeah, it sounds like it. Nothing too major from what I can see. He's conscious now, and the paramedics are helping him sit up."

"Good. Let's get out of here. I don't want to hang around any longer than we need to. People might start asking questions."

Hemingway turned around, leading them back to the valet station and handing the distracted worker his ticket. The young man apologized before grabbing Hemingway's keys and running off to the private parking lot.

"I don't think anyone's going to ask you too many questions," Hemingway said as they stood on the far side, away from the scene of the accident. "I ran to the railing and tried to see what was going on, but I couldn't find you. I think the kitsune did her best to hide you both."

"Why?" Ichirin hadn't meant to voice the question out loud, but it slipped of its own accord.

Hemingway shrugged. "Who knows? You talked to her for longer than I did. All I know is that she came with Brian. That got messy for a little bit. Brian threw a punch before cooler heads prevailed."

Ichirin looked up, her curiosity piqued and feeling more alert. "Do you think anything's going to come of it?"

"Nah, I don't think so. Brian's pretty high up there, and his management chain likes him. At worst, he'll get a slap on the wrist. Plus, it isn't like anyone else tried to stop it. How'd you get down safely if you couldn't fly?"

"The kitsune. She saved me."

The look on Hemingway's illustrated the confusion she felt. Ichirin didn't have answers for the questions she felt sure ran through his mind. She couldn't answer her own.

"I don't know. She admitted she was here to kill me but didn't want to do it yet. She said she had more games she wanted to play."

That can't be good.

The valet came up the driveway with Hemingway's car, pulling up in front of the two friends. He exited and ran to the other side, holding the door open so Ichirin could slide into her seat and tuck in her skirt with her hands. As they drove back to her place, she pulled out her phone and gave Corey a summary of what happened. She considered leaving out the part where she jumped off the balcony of the twenty-fourth floor but decided against it. If the kitsune came after Corey, she needed to know the creature's capabilities. Holding secrets would hurt their chances of survival.

Speaking of precautions, you might want to consider allowing me to take possession of your body if we get in another confrontation. Due to my nature, I will be less likely to fall under the sway of the creature and more able to do what must be done. As I told you before, its words are dangerous.

It was something worth considering. The hunter remembered the intensity of her emotions when she leapt off the balcony like a fool in pursuit. Even if she could fly—something she wanted to start working on as soon as time permitted—what was she going to do? Have a fight in the middle of the sky above Bellevue? Her mind swam in the sheer multitude of reasons explaining why that was a bad idea. She reached up to chew on her fingernails but stopped and slapped her hands down into her lap. She couldn't believe it seemed like a good idea at the time.

All the more reason we need to be careful, as do your friends. They will be just as susceptible as you were, if not more so. You saw what she did with the men at the party and the car accident. She is a personification of mischief and trouble. There can be no hesitation next time. Even if you could get the answers you seek, how would you know you could trust any words that spilled from her mouth?

The question of how they were going to take care of the kitsune still stood. She looked like a human. Ichirin couldn't stab her in a public venue. Even if the hunter managed to create an illusion to mask them, that ability would depart as soon as the creature breathed its last breath.

An additional complication arose when she thought of how her powers worked. Since it didn't take an effort to maintain the illusion, would the kitsune revert to a fox after it passed on? If not, that meant that they were planning a murder. At least, that's how others would perceive it.

When they got back to her home, Ichirin bid Hemingway goodbye and walked inside alone. Her feet scuffed against the stones of the walkway, and her eyes focused on the ground in front of her feet. She brought her hand up and flopped it onto the handle. She needed some time to relax and some solitude to unwind after the events of the evening—although she was never truly alone these days.

I will keep my silence and leave you to your solitude.

While she appreciated the thought, it wasn't the same. It reminded her of when a friend would come over and sit in a corner reading a book. While it wasn't a burden to entertain that friend, it remained a roadblock in the way of her recharging and recovering. Not quite to that extent, but the core concept was the same.

As the night passed, Ichirin's conscience told her she should be practicing, training, or doing research. The voice in her head had a trace of Taka's tone and mannerisms, a realization that made her sigh. He didn't need to speak to be in her mind.

After the events of the evening, the hunter knew she needed to take some time to recover. She knew herself well enough to recognize that any attempt to work would be counterproductive. Rather than trying to force it, she spent the night making tea, sipping it by the garden window, and reading a book with her legs curled under a blanket. Taka kept to his promise and did not intrude on her thoughts the rest of the night.

Come morning, refreshed and energized from her night off, Ichirin jumped into training as soon as she was out of bed. If she didn't learn how to fly, the kitsune would escape anytime she gained the upper hand. With Taka's guidance, she got to the point where she lifted off the ground. She jerked around as soon as she lost contact with the ground and slammed into the floor when her concentration broke, but it was progress.

You'll get it. Remember, these things take time and effort, like a muscle you're just learning to use. The more you practice, the easier it will become. You can't expect to jump out of the nest and fly before you've learned to flex your wings. And yes, I chose that reference on purpose.

Which begged the question of how Taka tapped into her powers at all when they switched places. If it was a new muscle she needed to learn how to flex, either he had experience with these powers, or he learned from her practice.

I have more experience than you realize, but in ways that are difficult to explain. And right now is not the time. We need to continue with your training if you want to have any hope of stopping the kitsune.

Ichirin nodded to herself, conceding the point before going back to work. After a few more failed attempts, she hovered in the air with her eyes closed, floating steadily with her hands out to either side. Her body inched upward to the ceiling, climbing without upsetting her balance. Then her phone rang. Her eyes popped open, and she reached for it, tilting in the air and careening into the couch in a mad tumble that left her straddling the arm with a single leg and one arm trapped underneath her. She reached up to grab the phone and saw Hemingway's photo on the display.

"Good morning," she said as she untangled herself and stretched out on the carpet.

"Morning? It's well past afternoon. Don't tell me I woke you up? I know last night was stressful, but that's not like you."

Ichirin looked at the clock on her stove, surprised to see it was almost two. Where did the time go? She couldn't have been training that long, could she? Her stomach growled in response, sharing its opinion of her loss of time.

"Sorry, just been busy. I didn't realize how late it had gotten. Is everything okay? Have you found out anything new? What happened with your team after the party?"

"There's a lot to go over. But things are definitely a little strange. There's been a whole email thread I'll show you. I don't feel comfortable forwarding it because of what's in it. Are you free right now?"

"Yes. Do you want to get together and share notes?"

"Better than that. I think I found your friend from last night." His voice slowed as he looked for the right words.

Distant voices came through the connection, people talking in the background. Ichirin felt a tightness in her chest. "I know who you're talking about. Has she seen you? She's going to know who you are. You need to get out of there."

"I'm fine. She's across the street in some kind of office building having a meeting. I'm in a coffee house buried in the middle of a lot of people. Even if she looks over here, she won't pick me out of the crowd. It's safe."

"Where are you? And how did you find her in the first place?" Ichirin got up from the floor, snatching her jacket and her keys. She snagged her knife as she turned the corner to the garage. It felt small and insignificant, but she wasn't about to leave without a weapon of some sort.

"I'm at the Starbucks on the northside campus. I won't follow her if she leaves, but I tracked her down based on some of the stuff Brian said. Figured out where she worked and thought I'd see if my info was right. I sent you a text about it."

"I'm on my way. Just be careful and don't let her see you."

She hung up the phone and pulled out into the street. Her tires squealed for a moment as she drove forward. The trip to campus would take about ten minutes, but she continued to flex her fingers on the wheel. Hemingway took a foolish risk tracking the kitsune down by himself.

In all likelihood, the creature won't kill him. It would not serve her interests to enrage you at this point, especially since she had the opportunity to kill you and decided not to. She is the embodiment of mischief and chaos, not death and destruction. However, considering his character, he will be helpless to her illusions and influence.

Ichirin wasn't sure if the kami was trying to help comfort her or urge her forward, but his words roiled the emotions she already had. Shaking her head to clear it, she swerved through the traffic, pushing all thoughts beyond getting to Hemingway's side into the background.

Most of the parking spots in the northside campus were empty thanks to it being the weekend. She parked near the Starbucks and forced herself to walk at a normal pace up to the entrance. Bursting in wouldn't help matters and might alert the kitsune to her presence. As she approached the front door, she looked over at the office building across the lot. A large window peered into a conference room, but it was empty.

The coffee shop was well populated. Most of the chairs were occupied, and three people stood in line, waiting to order. Hemingway sat in one of the large cushioned chairs, an indicator that he had been here a while to command such a position. His cup and empty plate sat on the table in front of him, and his laptop rested on his legs. The chair beside him had his bag nestled on it, an inconsideration most people would be too timid to address.

When Ichirin walked over, he looked up from his screen and leaned forward to remove his bag, gesturing for her to sit. She did so, feeling her shoulders drop and her back unwind as she sank into the cushions. Her friend was safe.

"I'm sorry I missed your texts," she said.

Hemingway waved his hand in the air and shook his head. "It's fine. I figured you were busy. Last night was kind of crazy, so I can't blame you for wanting to take some time to recover."

"First and most important, what about my 'friend'? She didn't see you?"

"No. She finished up her meeting and walked out of the room. I haven't seen her since, so I buried myself in my computer trying to find out what I could."

Ichirin sighed and let her head fall back so she could stare at the ceiling. Between the chair, the scent of roasted coffee beans on the air, and knowing her friend was safe, a calm serenity seeped into every cell of her body.

"Now that I'm here, what have you been able to find out?"

"Not much about the woman. Her name is Jade Miller, and she works as a contractor. Brian met her because the company she works for sent her in to fulfill a contract when the previous employee decided to quit out of the blue. This all happened over the last week or so."

Ichirin nodded, listening as Hemingway continued.

"To add to the antics of last night, she somehow stole a lot of money from Brian. He thought it was smart to share this piece of information on a corporate email. HR already chimed in on the thread, and Brian is going to be in a lot of trouble."

"What about him being high up and having protection?"

Hemingway shook his head. "I don't think that's going to help him here. Things went a lot further than I thought. You have to read this thread. It's pretty intense. I'll send it your way."

Did he just...

Ichirin leaned forward. She reached out and gripped Hemingway's arm, squeezing hard through the layers of his jacket.

"What did you do to him?"

CHAPTER FIVE

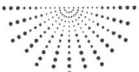

Hemingway opened his mouth to respond but snapped it shut when he stared into Ichirin's eyes. The kitsune replaced her serious look with a playful grin. It was not a look the hunter had seen on her friend's face before, and it felt out of place. Her fingers tightened, and she took a deep breath in through her nose. The creature's eyes flashed gold before returning to Hemingway's brown.

"Clever human. That took you less time than I thought it would."

"What have you done with Hemingway?" Ichirin growled out the words, refusing to let go of the monster's arm.

If it bothered the kitsune, she didn't let it show. She remained calm and serene, not twitching or looking down.

"Before you get too violent, I will let you know he's safe. In fact, you probably passed him on the way here." When Ichirin refused to loosen her fingers, the creature's smile faded, and she continued. "He's going to your house. The only thing I did was relieve him of some physical possessions, which you are welcome to."

Using her free hand, she picked up the computer and stashed it on top of Hemingway's pack. She slid the pair of items across the floor with her foot.

"Do you mind letting go of my arm? You're attracting attention."

The kitsune is telling the truth. People are starting to stare and whisper to each other.

Ichirin released her grip but remained leaning forward, her gaze firmly fixed on her prey. She settled for grasping the arms of the chair.

"Why shouldn't I kill you right here and now?"

The shapeshifter sat back with wide eyes and feigned a gasp of surprise. "I can't believe you'd say such a thing. And in such a public place."

The last two words were emphasized, reminding the hunter where she was and the fact that—to all appearances—she just threatened the life of a human. She needed to maintain control. In this situation, there was nothing she could do. Even though Taka said not to let the kitsune talk, there didn't seem to be any other options.

"What do you want?" Ichirin pushed back into the chair, still in position to propel forward at a moment's notice. She felt the weight of the knife tucked into her pocket and that helped her to steady her breathing and open up her shoulders.

"I feel I should be asking you that question. After all, you're the one who came to me."

Don't do this. Walk out of here. She can't be trusted. This is by far your most dangerous encounter, all the more so because you won't see the attacks coming.

"I came to talk to my friend, who you replaced."

Ichirin's phone rang. She jumped but didn't move to answer it until the monster nodded and picked up the coffee cup sitting on the table. The hunter spared a glance at the screen and saw Hemingway's picture. With a swipe of her finger, she sent him to voicemail. Knowing that he was able to call helped clear her mind, and she let go of the arms of the chair to uncurl her fingers.

"Not important?" the kitsune asked.

"Not at the moment. What are you doing here? Are you trying to throw me off-balance? What game are you playing? Do you delight in torturing people?" Ichirin kept her voice low, hoping people weren't listening after the earlier incident. A few people watched while attempting—and failing—to be discreet, but they weren't her immediate neighbors.

"I play all sorts of games. But for right now, what I want to know is you. What is it about you? Why are you so determined that we should have an epic conflict? We are obviously connected, you and me. I've heard about you, as I'm sure you've heard about me. What have you heard, I wonder?"

You need to end this. This verbal sparring match will not end well.

"I know you're a mischief-maker and a trouble-causer. I know you're responsible for sending a man to the hospital last night, and I know that I'm the only one equipped to stop you from causing more chaos."

The creature laughed, barking out the sound that made the woman behind Ichirin gather her things and leave, mumbling about inconsiderate millennials. The kitsune reached up and wiped the water from her eyes after her short outburst.

"That's rich, thinking you could stop my mischief. I do appreciate your gumption and your spirit. It is exceptional, even when compared to other humans. I'm impressed. You do know that mischief runs through my very essence as morality runs through yours, yes?"

The monster locked gazes with her human adversary, leaning forward and drawing her opponent to match. The sensation of the chair and the rest of the coffee house slipped away as Ichirin focused on the gold swirls that danced around the kitsune's pupils. Her hands slid off the chair to rest at the side of her legs. It felt like she could sink into that mystery and forget everything, even breathing.

SNAP OUT OF IT!

Ichirin shook her head, and the creature blinked, breaking the spell and leaning back in her seat. The mirth fled from her face, and she looked pensive.

"There's something else there. Something that runs through you and is not you. What is it, I wonder?"

Say nothing. We need to fight or leave. I understand you are not willing to kill the creature now, but we cannot stay here any longer. We are both in danger.

Taka sounded frightened, a response that made the hunter scrunch her eyebrows together and look down to her side. She shook her head again, blinking a couple of times as she tried to gather her thoughts. The kitsune stood up from the chair and looked down at her.

"But another time. I must ponder what I've learned today."

As the shapeshifter went to leave, Ichirin stood up to follow. Perhaps there'd be an opportunity to attack when they weren't in public.

As she rose from the chair, the espresso machine burst into a cloud of steam, spraying hot clouds in multiple directions. People shouted and shoved at each other in an attempt to put some distance between themselves and the accident. On the other side of the store, the kitsune turned back and offered a playful shrug before walking out of the chaos.

The press of people held Ichirin back, and making her way to the door through the crowd proved difficult. By the time she reached it, the creature had fled. A police officer pulled into the lot, getting out of his car and walking toward the entrance. When the hunter moved to walk around him, he held up his hand in a gesture for her to stop.

Years of ingrained respect for authority kicked in, and the hunter froze on the spot. At first, she thought it might be the creature, but that would have been impossible without having a cruiser waiting and running around the corner out of sight. She didn't remember seeing one when she pulled in, but she still edged away from the officer.

The man had a badge identifying his last name as Keefe. He looked like he was in the tail end of this thirties, with short blond hair shaved on the sides of his head. He was fit, with an angular face that looked like he had gotten in a few fights growing up.

"Hold up, miss. I need to ask you some questions."

"What's this about?" Ichirin asked, looking into the lot for some sign of her prey even though she knew it to be a fruitless endeavor. "I was just looking for a friend of mine. He left just before the coffee machine exploded..."

"African American male, about my height with short dark hair?"

Ichirin nodded.

"The same one that several witnesses saw you assault in the coffee shop?"

The hunter's mouth dropped open as she processed the words. She tried to speak, but no sound came out. After a quick shake of her head, she played back the events in her imagination and viewed them from an outside perspective. Even without an illusion, she looked like an aggressor.

"That was a misunderstanding, officer."

"Why don't you have a seat, Miss…?"

"Ichirin."

The cop gestured to the collection of patio tables and chairs chained together. They sat in a perfect arrangement because no one was foolhardy enough to sit outside when the temperature dropped this low. The woman sat down on one of the metal pieces, feeling the cold of it seeping through her clothes and making her clutch her legs in a tight grip.

"My name's Officer Keefe. I need to ask you a couple of questions about what happened in there. Perhaps things got a little heated between you two, and you argued?"

The officer walked over until he stood close enough to look down at Ichirin while they spoke. She felt her skin crawl underneath his scrutiny. Some part of her mind knew he was trying to express his superiority, but that didn't lessen the effect. She looked down and tucked her hands between her knees.

"That's right. We had a bit of an argument."

"Do you live together?"

Ichirin shook her head.

"Are you going to go chase after him now?"

"No, officer."

"Good. Perhaps you should sit here and calm down for a moment while I talk to the people inside and see about this exploding coffee machine. You didn't have anything to do with that, did you?"

After another shake of her head, he left her at the table and walked

221

into the coffee house. The hunter let her shoulders slump. The kitsune was long gone by now, but maybe that was for the best.

Ichirin grabbed her phone and checked her messages. Hemingway had texted her several times, asking if she was okay. She responded, letting him know she was fine and sitting outside the Starbucks where he'd been moments before. She got an immediate response that he was driving. A few seconds later, his car pulled into the lot.

As soon as he saw her, he ran over. "Are you okay?"

"Yeah, I'm fine. Just a little shaken up. The kitsune was here. Where did you go? What did she say to you?"

"That was the kitsune?" Hemingway stood up and leaned back on his heels, taking a deep breath. "I heard there was a major accident on the road near your place. I thought maybe you got in a rush and crashed on the way here. I went back to your house and called and sent messages. I was worried. I panicked."

"Enough so that you left your computer and your bag with a stranger?" Ichirin asked.

For a moment, he stood frozen before dropping onto the sidewalk like his legs failed him. He managed to utter a single word. "Wow..."

The hunter empathized with him. She remembered how it felt when the creature manipulated her emotions to such a powerful extent. She reached out to comfort him when Officer Keefe walked out of the building. He paused, looking at Hemingway, then back to Ichirin.

"Excuse me, sir, sorry to trouble you. This woman claimed to be your friend. Is that accurate?"

Hemingway looked up, his brow knitted together in confusion.

"Yes?" He made the word sound like a question rather than an affirmation.

"Would you like to press charges?"

Ichirin sucked in a breath through her nose. She wished there was some way she could tell him what happened, so he had the background to diffuse the situation. While his confusion was evident, he recovered and covered by rubbing both of his hands over his face.

"No, I'm fine. There's nothing to worry about here."

"Are you sure?"

"Yes. Thank you. We're fine." Hemingway stood up so he could shake the officer's hand.

The officer returned the gesture and pulled a business card out of his pocket, handing it over to Hemingway. "If anything happens, or you change your mind, don't hesitate to give me a call."

Without a word toward the accused, the officer returned to his car and entered information into the laptop attached to the console. Hemingway eased into the chair next to his friend.

"What was that about?"

"The kitsune pretended to be you. I got a little defensive when I realized it. I think some people called 911."

To her surprise, Ichirin felt no shame over the confession. She knew the monster manipulated and pushed her all in the name of playing a game. The creature toyed with her, and her friend.

Hemingway reached out and rested his hand on top of hers.

"Thank you."

After finishing entering his notes, the officer drove away, giving one last glance at the two of them sitting outside the coffee shop. When the car was out of sight, Hemingway let out a pensive sigh.

"So where was Corey in all of this?"

Ichirin twisted so she could look at Hemingway. "What do you mean? Corey wasn't here."

"Yes, she was. I sent her a message just before I left to try and search for you. She told me she was almost here and would keep an eye out for you."

As if on cue, the entrance to the coffee house opened, and Corey stepped out, wearing a light jacket that made the hunter shiver despite her warm coat. Corey had Hemingway's pack and computer tucked underneath her arm. After handing them off, she grabbed one of the free chairs and dragged it across the pavement, rattling it against the individual stones until she got it into place. Without much ceremony, she dropped down into the chair.

"When did you get here?" Ichirin asked.

"Just after Hem left. I saw him pulling out of the lot, and I saw another Hem stepping out of the bathroom. Since we're dealing with a shapeshifter, I figured one of them had to be the kitsune. I knew the real Hem just sent me a message about going to your house, so this one had to be the fake. I tucked up my scarf, stood in line, and waited.

"When you came in, I thought I'd warn you, but then I remembered what you said about wanting to get the upper hand. I was across from you. I'm surprised you didn't recognize me, but it turns out to be a good thing you didn't. I saw and heard the whole thing. We might have our edge."

"What edge?" both Hemingway and Ichirin asked.

"I tucked my phone into the fake Hem's jacket, and it has find my phone. We can figure out where the critter is and where she's going."

This member of your triumvirate continues to impress me. She consistently performs better than I'd expect from most humans.

"Corey, you're a genius," Ichirin said.

Hemingway had his computer open, and his fingers flew across the keyboard as he summoned it to life. Passing it over to Corey, she tracked the location of her phone. It was currently on the 520 bridge heading into Seattle.

"What are we waiting for? Let's follow my phone!"

Hemingway shook his head. "I don't know if we all should. Yes, we should follow her, but I should look into some things here. She stole a lot of money, and if I can figure out what she was doing with it, it might give us some clue of what you're walking into. Plus, I have stable Wi-Fi here. It'll be a lot easier to work my magic if I have a good connection."

"Alright, but Ichirin and I should follow her before she figures out she has my phone."

Corey stood up and walked away from the table. She took a couple of steps before she paused and looked back when no one followed her. The hunter had her attention focused on Hemingway.

"What is it?" she prodded him.

Hemingway squirmed, reaching up to rub the back of his neck. "I could be wrong, but did that Officer Keefe look familiar to you? Either of you?"

Both of the women indicated that he did not.

"I think he might've been one of the police officers in West Seattle back when we dealt with the enenra. Granted it was a while ago, but he looked really familiar. I think he was there helping with the barricade. But that doesn't make sense. This is nowhere near West Seattle. Cops don't move around like that, do they? They have jurisdictions and stuff, right?"

"You're right, that doesn't make sense," Corey said. "But it's been months. Maybe he transferred over? Or maybe he just looks similar? He does have a certain 'police officer' look to him. Then again, enough weird shit's been happening these days it might mean something."

"Maybe you could try and look into that while we're following the phone?" Ichirin offered.

"I'll try. It just didn't feel right and creeped me out. Now get going. I'm going to head back inside where its warm and get another coffee."

The group parted ways, with Corey jumping into her friend's car. They pulled up the website on Ichirin's phone, so they could follow the signal. By the time they reached the bridge, it looked like the telephone had stopped downtown.

"Well, either she dropped it, or something's going on over there. Head toward the Needle. It looks like she parked in a garage across 5th Avenue."

Ichirin drove into downtown, cursing the traffic slowing her progress to a crawl. She glanced at Corey, who had her eyes glued to the phone. She hoped the kitsune hadn't realized the device was in her possession. They needed to take full advantage of this opportunity, and the weekend downtown traffic wasn't helping matters.

I find it fascinating that people continue to congregate in the city on the weekends knowing the traffic will be horrible. And that's even without a sporting event. Just be glad that it's not tomorrow since there's a home game. Then I feel like the only way you would get downtown is if you mastered that flying trick.

It felt like an eternity until they turned off of Mercer and onto 5th. Corey pointed out the parking lot where the kitsune stopped for a short while before getting out and moving much slower. The two of them followed in their prey's footsteps, parking their car in the covered garage.

"Which way?" Ichirin asked as she jogged toward the street entrance.

"Toward the base of the Needle. My phone's right underneath it."

They crossed the street and joined a large crowd walking in their direction, taking in all of the sights and snapping pictures. It worked as decent cover as multiple people asked them to take pictures. The hunter felt more comfortable with the strangers around her, acting as a way to blend in.

"It's like AC, the earlier ones, when you had to walk in the middle and real slow to keep the guards from seeing you," Corey suggested.

"AC?"

"*Assassin's Creed*. Good game. Good series actually. I still like the first one the best."

Ichirin considered working an illusion but discarded the idea. The hunter worried about her ability to hold it while she focused on spotting her prey. Given how clever the creature had shown itself to be so far, they needed every advantage they could get.

As they came around the museum and turned down the path heading to the Space Needle, Ichirin reached out and grabbed Corey's wrist. She took a step back, dragging her friend with her until they stood out of sight.

"What is it?" Corey asked. "Did you see the kitsune?"

"I did. She's back in the body she had at the Microsoft party. And if that wasn't bad enough, she's talking to Officer Keefe."

CHAPTER SIX

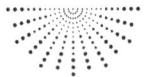

"W hat?" Corey went to walk back around the building and get a look for herself, but Ichirin refused to let her go.

"We can't let the creature see us. Otherwise, what's the whole point of this? If either one of us goes out there and she sees us coming, she'll take off. Worse, she'll know we followed her here and be on to us."

"I fooled her once. I'm pretty sure I could keep up my assassin skills and blend in with the crowd." Corey grabbed her hood and flipped it up over her head.

"And if you can't?"

I still think you should walk up behind her and stab her before she realizes you're there. I warned you about what would happen if you let her talk. If you're concerned about being able to do the deed since she looks like a human, you could give me control. I'll weave the invisibility illusion so she doesn't even know I'm there until it's too late.

Ichirin shook her head. She felt comfortable with the knowledge that she needed to kill the creature. The fact that she looked human did make her shoulders tense, but the hunter still had faith in the importance of her mission. The issue centered around stabbing someone in the middle of a public place in broad daylight with more witnesses than she cared to count. And if that wasn't enough, Taka proposed doing it in front of a police officer.

The plan is not quite perfect; I'll grant you that. There are some flaws.

Perhaps Taka wasn't as immune to the kitsune's effects as he claimed to be. But his plan raised an interesting possibility. If Ichirin could weave the invisibility illusion, perhaps she could get close enough to hear the conversation. That could be immensely valuable.

And what if the creature can smell you?

Ichirin pressed her lips together and nodded to herself. If the creature could smell her coming, that was a chance she was willing to take. She hadn't come this far to leave emptyhanded. She looked to Corey, who stared at her and shifted her weight from one foot to the other.

"You did it again—that long talk where your eyes got all distant. I take it you two came up with a plan? What do you need me to do?"

Ichirin knew Corey wouldn't like what she was going to suggest. "Stay here and stay out of sight. If I need your help, I'll shout for you. But otherwise, I need to make sure they don't see you. If either of them comes around the corner, that's where you need to use your ninja skills."

"Assassin," Corey corrected.

"Assassin," the hunter conceded. "Can you do that for me?"

"You know it. I don't like it, you being the one to take all the risks. That's usually my job, but I understand. Just don't expect me to get used to it."

"Of course not. I'd expect no less. There's something else I need from you."

"What is it?"

In response, Ichirin ducked behind the building where she had a small measure of privacy with a wall on one side and a line of trees on the other. That left one direction where anyone could see her.

When she saw the location, Corey stood in front of her friend, shielding her from view. Ichirin turned her focus inward, trying to weave the illusion like she had before, layering it bit by bit around her entire body. When it felt like she covered her entire body, she opened her eyes and held up her arm. It appeared unchanged.

Remember, you can see through the illusion because you know it for what it is.

"Corey?" Ichirin whispered, not wanting to make too much noise as a small group of people walked by.

Corey turned around, and her eyes passed right over Ichirin. "It worked," she said.

Ichirin stepped past her friend, maneuvering to make her way around the building and head to the base of the Needle where she saw her prey and the officer. She pressed her lips together as she muttered a silent prayer that the kitsune wouldn't see through her illusion as easily as she did.

It would be best to have a backup plan just in case. Even if she can see you, others can't. You'd be free to give chase.

It was amazing how much of a difference being invisible made. Ichirin had numerous experiences with others not respecting her space and sometimes walking through her as they passed each other. But even then, people gave with their shoulders rather than knock her off her feet or slowed down to give her time to swerve. Now people cruised all around her, and she stumbled trying to get out of their way as they didn't hesitate. After her second near miss, she stayed near the edge of the walkway where fewer people walked.

The creature and the police officer still stood near the base, engaged in a conversation. The officer paced back and forth and used large hand gestures. Meanwhile, the kitsune maintained a picture of serenity, standing with her arms crossed in front of her body. Her head tilted to the side as she watched the human in front of her. Tourists gave the pair a wide berth.

As she drew closer, Ichirin kept a close eye on her prey. The monster looked around, but her eyes passed over the hunter with no hesitation. The illusion appeared to work on the kitsune as well. Ichirin resisted the urge to let out a sigh of relief. She walked forward, making sure to be aware of where she stepped. Even if she wasn't visible, bumping into someone or kicking a piece of trash would give her away in a heartbeat.

Soon she was close enough to eavesdrop on the conversation over the general din of the crowd.

"I don't care what you think or what you saw. You have one job here, and that's to eliminate the girl. You had the perfect opportunity, and you didn't do it. You need to do what you've been summoned to do." The officer lifted his hand in a fist before dropping it to his side and pacing in the opposite direction.

"Do you honestly think a human knows more about what our god desires than me? I have been sent here to deal with her, not eliminate her. Things are often not as simple as your kind desires to make them."

The kitsune did not seem concerned if others overheard the conversation. In sharp contrast, the officer squirmed when she implied her inhumanity. His head whipped around as he tried to see if anyone paid too much attention.

"You shouldn't say stuff like that so loud. Someone might hear you."

"And what if they did? I have no care for what your kin think of me here. They will forget or assume they heard incorrectly. If any adjustments are required, I will deal with them in time."

Officer Keefe heaved his shoulders and continued with his argument, this time with less hostility.

"You know she's a threat. We've both seen that much. She's a piece that needs to disappear from the board. What she can do…"

"There is more than one way to remove a piece. Other forces are at play here, and I would understand them before committing to a course of action. Besides, I like to play with my prey first. Otherwise, what fun is there in it?"

"Your foolish games waste time. I don't understand why…"

The conversation distracted Ichirin enough that she didn't notice the group of people walking up behind her. Someone bumped into her with enough force that he fell backward and landed on the pavement with a curse, confused after colliding with empty air.

Both Officer Keefe and the kitsune turned to see what the commotion was. The officer's hand moved to his gun, but he kept it holstered as he scanned the crowd. The creature examined the scene and then her eyes came to rest on Ichirin. Even though the illusion felt strong, the hunter couldn't shake the feeling that the monster saw her.

"Go," the kitsune said.

The officer looked like he was going to object, but a quick glare discouraged him from doing so. He turned around, walking toward the Sound and blending into the crowd. The kitsune turned back toward the hunter and took slow steps in her direction, moving with the grace of a fox.

Now would be an excellent time to put that backup plan into motion. You know, the one you didn't think would be necessary.

Indecision made Ichirin freeze. She considered turning and running, but that seemed futile. She also thought about using this moment to attack, but a staggering number of witnesses surrounded them both. In the end, she managed to take a small shuffling step to the side as the kitsune advanced.

To her surprise, the creature's gaze didn't follow her. The kitsune kept her attention locked onto the spot where the human had been. When she got close, the shapeshifter inhaled through her nose, arching her neck as she sniffed the air. Other people cleared a space around her, several giving her odd looks.

"I can smell you, human huntress. I know you're here. Very clever to have found me and gotten close. Tell me, how much did you overhear?" The kitsune smiled with a grin that was far too saccharine to be innocent. "Let's have a chat, shall we? You've impressed me, something that does not happen often, and I'd like to reward that."

The closeness of the creature made Ichirin tempted to hold her breath. She eased away, keeping her movements slow and hoping her clothes didn't rustle enough to attract attention. At least the clearing of people gave her some space to move without the risk of running into anyone.

"I will not make this offer again. While I do appreciate a good game, I am not overly patient or fond of wasting my time."

Remember how dangerous her words can be. She's trying to lure you into a trap. Either run or attack, but do not fall for her tricks. I'm here if you wish to relinquish control.

"As you wish," the creature said, flicking her hand in the direction of the street.

A loud *crack* sounded nearby. Ichirin turned around and saw a thick branch fall from one of the trees lining the sidewalk. It dropped onto the open car door of a sedan just in front of the passenger about to get inside. The woman fell back, her eyes wide and her chest rising and falling as she stared at the mangled door ripped from its hinges. If that branch had fallen a half-second later…

Whirling back around, the hunter lunged forward, grabbing her knife and unfolding it as she took the first step. Her arm snaked out, trying to catch the kitsune in the abdomen before she sensed the attack. Witnesses be damned; people were in danger.

The monster swerved away from the attack, sucking out of the way just before the blade penetrated her flesh. As it was, the tip of the weapon snagged her coat, cutting a tear in the fabric. Ichirin didn't pause, but continued her assault, taking a step forward and bringing the knife in for another jab.

Before she got close, the creature lurched into the air, jumping off the ground and hovering like a stuntwoman in a Chinese martial arts film. The knife passed through empty space, and the kitsune kicked out. Her attack lacked accuracy, but the edge of her heel glanced off the side of Ichirin's head. The hunter's instincts had her roll to the side away from the blow.

"I offer conversation, and you respond with violence? For a moment you had me believing that you might be different from your kind."

The kitsune launched upward, soaring into the sky and out of reach. Not wanting to lose her momentum, Ichirin leapt, trying to force herself to fly after her adversary. She dipped at the end of her jump, but then hovered for a moment before propelling up like a missile.

Just before the moment of impact, the hunter ducked her head and presented her shoulder, using that to slam into the creature's hip. The monster let out a high-pitched yip, tumbling when the blow knocked her off balance. Ichirin's flight was awkward, but she adjusted her path and came back in, her knife slashing through the air.

It appeared as if the kitsune saw her now, as the beast dodged one attack and used her hand to deflect the second off to the side. She twisted in the air, tumbling around the human and slamming her heel into the woman's knee. The blow would have had greater impact standing on the ground, but the hunter let her leg go limp and move with the hit.

That allowed her to get closer, and she lashed out with the knife again. When the kitsune reached out to grab her wrist, Ichirin rolled her arm, bringing the edge of the blade up and slicing into her prey's flesh. The creature propelled herself backward, cradling her injured arm.

The two adversaries hovered in the air, several stories above an unsuspecting public. None of them glanced up at the scene or paid it any attention. The kitsune noticed Ichirin's quick look and smiled.

"While I am not opposed to an occasional word being overheard, irrefutable evidence of two women flying through the sky might make life more complicated. We have this stretch of space to ourselves. Now if you are quite done with your attacks, I was suggesting a discussion."

Do not listen!

Ichirin lunged, remembering how the kitsune could twist her emotions to the point of insanity. The fight was something concrete that she understood. She didn't need Taka to spur her forward.

When they collided, the creature blocked the weapon aside and wrapped her arm around Ichirin's, twisting it into an uncomfortable position. They tumbled together, struggling without any ground Ichirin could use for leverage. So many techniques she learned over the last several months seemed useless without a solid layer underneath her.

At least this monster couldn't overpower her with sheer strength. Judging by the amount of strain they both poured into the grapple,

Ichirin felt as stout as her adversary. That gave her hope she could emerge victorious. She just needed the right opening.

"Have you stopped to consider that if you do kill me, then you will fall to your death?" the shapeshifter said between grunts of exertion.

Ichirin hesitated, and the kitsune drove her knee into the woman's ribs, slamming the air out of her lungs and making her lose her grip. The creature used the brief interlude to shoot skyward once more, heading to the top of the Needle. As soon as she could do so, the hunter gave pursuit, the wind tugging at her hair as she skyrocketed to the top.

The shapeshifter landed on top of the landmark, her back facing her adversary. She waited until Ichirin got closer, and then brought her foot whipping around. It connected with the side of the hunter's skull and sent her tumbling across the roof, her focus on flight lost. The knife skittered across the surface and stopped several feet away.

The kitsune walked over and planted a knee on the woman's right forearm, pinning it to the structure. She leaned forward, applying pressure and sending pain shooting up the arm.

"You are not my enemy. You don't even understand what's going on, do you?"

Ichirin ignored the commentary and rolled over, bringing her free hand up and grabbing the kitsune's shoulder, yanking down and trying to pull her off balance. The creature rolled her shoulder to get free and then increased her weight through her knee until the hunter cried out as her bones ground against the metal beneath her.

"There is still much about you that I do not understand. But I will learn. And then we will see what to do with you. However, that would be much easier if you weren't so insistent on turning everything into a physical confrontation. Ask yourself this: why do you feel the need to destroy me? Do you even comprehend what it is that I'm doing?"

Ichirin recovered her breath as the kitsune eased up on the pressure, but she didn't try and reach around or attack. Her foe was too alert. The knife sat too far away to be of any use. She needed another option.

You could let me take over.

"You mean besides causing mischief, stealing, and sending people to the hospital? I think I've seen enough," Ichirin spat.

"You are more complex than that. Do not seek simple answers, for they hold no truth."

The kitsune stood up and ran to the edge of the Needle, jumping off and flying away. As soon as she cleared the edge, she blinked out of sight.

Ichirin sat up, rubbing her arm as she did so. The area would bruise, and her entire arm felt like it had been stuck in a vise, but nothing was broken. Once again, her prey had the upper hand and chose to run away rather than finish things. Perhaps there was more to the picture than she saw.

You are falling into her trap. Her most dangerous weapons are not the physical, but the mental. You should know that by now. You have seen how she manipulates people and how she makes them question their sanity until they do things they would never otherwise do.

While the creature had shown a penchant for using words as powerful weapons, there was still something odd about the entire encounter. The interaction with the police officer added to her misgivings and made her shake her head. Ichirin had the impression that the kitsune didn't want to kill her and was making an effort to ensure that didn't happen. The question was why.

So that she can play with your mind more and treat you like a mouse that it bats around before the feast. She is a fox and cruel. You do not question a cat's motives when it plays with its prey before killing because that is its nature. These abominations are no more nuanced than animals.

Why did the kitsune threaten Taka so much? Ichirin could never recall it being so passionate about hunting down the creature nor having such a strong bloodlust.

Because this creature poses a threat unlike any that we have had to deal with before, and it can undo much of the work we have done. I don't know if you are aware of just how tenuous things are.

The hunter felt there was much more than what Taka volunteered, but her exhaustion made it a matter for a different time. Right now, all she needed to know was that the reason she had these gifts was to hunt the monsters down, whatever that entailed.

And in this hunt, she fell back to square one.

Pushing herself up, Ichirin retrieved her knife, folding it up and tucking it back into her pocket. She inched her way to the edge of the Space Needle and looked down. People moved around like figures in a simulation, oblivious to her presence. At least the kitsune shielded them from sight. The hunter realized her attack was foolish and foolhardy, but it seemed like the best option at the time. She didn't want to consider the ramifications if someone had seen them and uploaded a video to YouTube.

She wrapped the invisibility illusion around herself again and stepped off the edge, floating down to the ground. Despite her capabilities during the conflict, her entire body trembled and shook as she descended from the top of the Needle. That had been brute force and speed, whereas this required a delicate hand and skill. She had to alter her course to move to an open area with no people but otherwise returned to ground level without incident.

As soon as no one stared in her direction, Ichirin unraveled the invisibility as well. She trusted that people would be distracted enough with their phones and each other to disregard her sudden appearance out of the corner of their eyes.

And now people will at least pretend to get out of your way.

Ichirin walked back to where she left Corey, hoping that her friend was still there. She wrung her hands together to keep from chewing on her fingernails until she saw Corey leaning against the wall of the building, drumming against it with her empty hands. When Corey saw her friend, she ran forward, sidling up alongside and matching pace.

"Considering how you're coming back looking like you got stuck in the rain, I'm guessing it didn't go as well as you hoped?" Corey asked.

"I overheard a bit of the conversation between her and the officer, but that's the extent of the good news. They're working together, but they don't seem to be on the same page."

"That's good for us, right?"

"I'm not sure." Ichirin sighed. "I have so many questions. We fought, and she won. She could've ended it right then and there, but once again, she decided not to. She also said some weird stuff."

"What kind of weird stuff?"

Ichirin shook her head and waved off the question. "We can talk about it later. Right now, I want to go home and try to absorb everything and figure out where to go next."

For her part, Corey supported her in the best of possible ways—by saying nothing and accompanying her to the car in silence. When they got inside, Corey borrowed Ichirin's phone, sending a quick message to Hemingway before checking the phone tracking app.

"At least it looks like she still has my phone. It's a few blocks away at the moment. Do you want to chase her?"

Ichirin considered it but shook her head. "Not right now. She'll expect it. We're not ready and need to regroup, or at least I do. We have to hope she won't notice the phone because charging in right now would be dumb."

And she had enough foolishness to last her the day. When Taka didn't argue, she felt vindicated in her decision and drove back to the East Side. They retrieved Corey's car and headed back to Ichirin's house. The hunter put on the kettle and went to her bedroom.

Sitting on the edge of the bed, she tried to think of everything that the kitsune said. What was the bigger picture that she missed? Why did the monster keep letting her live? Did she know about Taka? The way that the creature looked into her the night of the holiday party made her think it could see into her soul.

I know I have said this before, but you cannot believe a thing she says. The next time you meet needs to be the last. If you give me control, I will make sure of it. There is no shame in not having the strength to complete the deed.

While that was a possibility, right now Ichirin wanted a moment to sort out her thoughts and feelings on the subject. And to do that, she needed to find her center. She hoped Taka could understand that.

I do. I will be here when you return.

Ichirin was thankful and took the locket off, leaving it on her nightstand table. She took several deep breaths while staring at the floor, then got up and walked to the kitchen. Corey sat on one of the stools near the breakfast bar and looked at her friend's chest.

"So, what's really going on?" she asked when she noticed the absence of the locket.

CHAPTER SEVEN

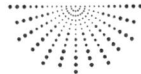

"I think I'm going to go crazy, trying not to think about things when Taka's nearby. It's maddening having to keep my thoughts from wandering too far." Ichirin collapsed on the breakfast bar, stretching her arms across it and laying her forehead on the cool surface between them.

"I don't blame you. Just the thought of having someone or something able to peer into my brain at any moment would feel so invasive. I don't know how you've been able to do it for so long."

Ichirin picked her head up and turned around so she could lean on the bar and face her friend. "At first, it was a comfort. Now it feels like a prison."

"How long do you think you can keep it up?"

"I don't know." Ichirin's head drooped, and her shoulders sagged. "But I might get my chance. It wants to switch places when we face the kitsune next time, and I think I'm going to let it."

Those words made Corey take a deep breath and press her lips together until some of the color drained. In the end, she nodded a couple of times, giving her support to the idea even if her disapproval was clear.

"After that, I don't know. I might need to start coming up with reasons not to wear the locket as much. This whole situation with the kitsune has been making things more difficult than usual. Taka's afraid of it. I'm certain."

"You mean more so than usual? He's always been a little bit protective when these creatures show up. It's one of the kami's few good traits if you ask me."

"This is different. Before it advised caution and tried to keep me safe. But now, it's obsessed. It's determined that the kitsune needs to die, preferably without talking. It keeps saying the kitsune's voice is its most dangerous weapon."

"Like with Saruman."

At least that reference was one Ichirin recognized. Although she knew it from the movies rather than the books. She didn't have much time to read, and that was before myths started coming to life and needed to be hunted down.

"I know the kitsune is capable of mischief and manipulating people, but this is something more. This feels deeper."

Corey grabbed a small handful of nuts from the bowl sitting on the counter and tossed them into her mouth. She spoke around chews. "Maybe Taka's afraid of something the kitsune might tell you. It makes sense. Silence the creature before it can spill some big secret."

The hunter's eyes lost focus as she considered Corey's suggestion. What if the kitsune did have something that Taka didn't want her to know? That would explain why he was so terrified of letting it speak. His reactions seemed blown out of proportion unless he was worried about something she might learn. And the kitsune did say she didn't know what was going on, that there was much more to the picture.

The boiling kettle snapped her back to the present, and Ichirin went through the process of making a couple of cups of tea. Her motions were mechanical, and she left her cup on the counter rather than taking a deep inhale to enjoy the floral scent as the hot water struck the packets.

"We need to talk to Hem. Have him look into her victims. I need to know more," Ichirin said.

"What about the kitsune? Do you want to leave her to her own devices? She might cause trouble, and we don't know how long it will be until she notices the phone. Once she does, we'll lose our way to track her."

Ichirin cradled her cup, appreciating the warmth that spread into her hands. Corey was right. The creature might get up to untold amounts of chaos if left unchallenged. But as of right now, the hunter questioned whether or not that would be a bad thing. She knew absolutes like good and evil did not exist often, and shades of gray were far more the norm. Perhaps if she could see the whole picture, she might be able to understand better.

"I don't think we have much choice. As much as I wanted to jump in and get the upper hand, it seems like we've been stumbling around blind even more than usual. That makes me nervous. That's even more disconcerting with some of the things the kitsune said. We need more information."

"I'll take care of Hem and see what he can find out. But what're you going to do about Taka? You can't possibly be thinking about putting the locket back on right now, can you?"

Ichirin shrugged. "What else can I do? If I don't, he'll know something's going on. He wants to take control, so I think I'll let him. It could be our last chance to peer into his mind. I doubt I'll be able to keep the charade up for long, but at least this way I can gain one last bout of insight before he locks everything down."

"Be careful. I won't pretend to understand what it's like or what you're going through, but when you talk about something that can take over your body..." Corey left the thought unfinished, spreading out her hands to either side. "I remember, if stuff gets too crazy, remove the locket. It's an emergency exit, but it might be necessary."

"Thanks. I hope it doesn't come to that, but it feels safer when you or Hem are around."

Corey held out her hands, and Ichirin was confused for a moment until she remembered that Corey didn't have her phone. She handed hers over, then took a moment to sip her tea while Corey called Hemingway.

Ichirin snapped her fingers as an idea came to her. "Don't forget to ask about the officer. That's another avenue he can pursue. I don't know about all the jurisdiction stuff, but the fact that he was talking with the kitsune is cause for concern."

Corey nodded as she talked to Hemingway. She got up and walked away from the breakfast bar, heading toward the front entrance. The hunter closed her eyes and enjoyed a few more sips of tea, even though she knew the gesture was a blatant attempt to delay the inevitable. She needed to go upstairs and put the locket on once again and have Taka ride along just inside the fringes of her conscious mind.

But before she did that, she needed to regain her focus. If she had to continue the game of mental chess, she'd need all her faculties to pull it off. She felt like she was on the cusp of discovering something, like she climbed a dune in the desert and was just about to peer over the lip at the oasis beyond.

She just hoped whatever she saw over the next rise wasn't a mirage.

Leaving her tea unfinished on the counter, she walked back to her bedroom. The locket sat on the nightstand, looking like a heavy weight rather than a piece of jewelry. As soon as she turned the corner, she felt its presence even without seeing it.

Welcome back.

Taka spoke in her mind as she took the locket and placed it around her neck.

Were you able to come to any revelations? Do you know how you're going to proceed?

The best course of action still seemed to be getting more information. The fact that the kitsune had bested her twice reinforced this idea. Both times were due to Ichirin's rashness, but she saw no reason to allow it to happen a third time. A more cautious approach might see better results.

I don't suppose you would rescind your refusal to get a firearm? It would be useful in this case. The kitsune would find it difficult to use her voice if you attacked from a distance. It might be your best hope of emerging victorious.

That was one item not up for debate. She didn't just dislike guns; their presence made her uncomfortable. She could never see herself owning or using one, and she didn't want that to change.

As you wish. You know I'll respect your choice in the matter. I was pointing out the possibility. I suppose we might as well see if Hemingway was able to give Corey any information.

Even though it had been over a year, Taka's ability to peer into her mind still sometimes caused her to miss a step. Ichirin stumbled and put a hand on the wall before continuing.

Corey was off the phone and pacing in the living room while drinking her tea. She stopped when she saw her friend enter the room.

"Hem did some poking around and said he thinks he found a trail about the money. Doesn't have any answers yet but is working on it. And the cop too. Apparently, the guy in the accident was released from the hospital without any serious injuries, but that's all he's been able to learn."

The stream of information came out in a rush. Ichirin managed to follow it because of her extensive experience as Corey's friend.

"Thanks for that. Sounds like it's in a holding pattern for right now. In the meantime, we should keep an eye on your phone and write down anywhere it stops. It might be pointless, but it could give us an idea about what she's up to or where her base might be."

When they checked the service, the phone was no longer available.

"She must've taken out the battery. It was close to full charge when I dropped it in her pocket so even if she went somewhere with no service, it wouldn't have drained yet. And the last recorded location was still downtown, so there's no way it's 'cause of a dark spot.'"

Ichirin nodded, agreeing with Corey's assessment. It was too much to hope for that the phone would still be useful, but checking didn't hurt anything.

"Let's go join Hem. At least then we can be in the same room, and he can share what he finds right away. Sorry about your phone, by the way."

Corey shrugged. "I was due for a new one anyway. I was holding out for the replacement plan to kick in. Besides, it was worth a shot, no? And if we didn't do that, we never would've found out about the cop."

The two of them left to head for Hemingway's office. They took separate vehicles, and each knew the way well enough not to need to pay attention to the roads.

The parking lots were almost empty as Ichirin drove through campus. As she turned down the street leading to Hemingway's building, she caught a glimpse of a cop car in her rearview mirror before she lost sight of it.

I didn't get a close enough look. Do you remember what the side of Officer Keefe's car had on it?

Ichirin had to admit that she didn't. She disregarded the car when she saw it at the coffee shop. She cursed herself for not being more observant and keeping track of the small details. If only Taka could replay her memories and watch them like a movie.

Something tells me you would not be happy with that arrangement. Even I would consider that to be too much of a violation of your privacy. But regardless, it is not possible.

Ichirin eased off the gas, slowing down without using the giveaway of having her brake lights turn on. The stoplight ahead of her turned yellow, so she made sure to stop even though she had enough time to clear the intersection. The cop car turned the corner, following in her lane and taking its time. She wished it would get close enough so she could see the driver, but the light ahead of her changed and she couldn't delay any longer.

Going to Hemingway's office right now seemed risky, especially if it was who she feared. Then again, if it was Officer Keefe, he probably knew where Hemingway worked.

Nothing wrong with being careful. That's how you stay alive, and I think we've proven you have more than enough enemies that caution is warranted.

Passing by the turn into the underground parking garage, Ichirin drove around the block. When the police officer swerved to pass her, she felt like she could take normal breaths once again. The driver was not Officer Keefe and didn't look in her direction.

If she didn't get answers soon, this tension would kill her long before any monster did.

The garage seemed like a ghost town. Contrary to most days at work, Ichirin found parking on the first floor near the stairway. Hemingway's car was one of three that she saw on the entire level.

Just because there are no other cars doesn't mean that no other people are here, or creatures. Remember that we're dealing with someone who specializes in illusions. Do not get lax just because your eyes tell you it's safe.

Those thoughts tumbled through Ichirin's mind well before Taka gave voice to them. The hunter tried to stay hyperalert as she walked up to the building entrance. She considered waiting for Corey to arrive but decided she'd feel safer in the locked building than standing exposed on the sidewalk.

Using her card to unlock the door, she went inside and down the hall to Hemingway's office. The building was so quiet that she heard the refrigerators while walking through the main lobby. She wasn't sure, but she thought she heard Hemingway's fingers striking his keyboard.

He didn't look up as she stepped into his room. He sat in his chair, leaning forward until his face was less than a foot from the screens. Four of them sat arranged in an arc around him, and his head twisted as he focused on one and then the next, without any pause in his typing.

Ichirin coughed to let him know she was there. He spun around in his chair and tilted his head when he saw that his friend stood alone.

"Where's Corey? I thought she was coming too."

"She's on her way. We drove separately. I didn't feel comfortable standing outside. The kitsune could be anywhere and works with illusions. Between that and the whole thing with the police officer, it feels much safer inside."

"I can understand that, and don't blame you for it." He raised a finger and took a breath, holding it for a moment before continuing. "But how is she going to let us know she's at the door if she doesn't have a phone?"

Oops.

"I'll go back to the lobby and keep an eye out for her. She shouldn't be too far behind, if not waiting there already. I'm surprised she didn't beat me here."

Hemingway buried himself back in his monitors before the hunter left. When she returned to the entrance area, Corey stood at the door.

"Hope you weren't waiting long," Ichirin said as she opened the door.

"Just walked up. Had to stop for gas."

As she turned around to lead the way back to Hemingway, something fluttered on the walkway leading to the garage stair. Ichirin paused and stared, but she saw nothing out of the ordinary.

"What is it?" Corey asked, pausing when she took a couple of steps and noticed her friend lagging.

"I thought I saw something."

Corey looked in the direction her friend indicated, leaning forward as she peered down the walkway. "I don't see anything. What was it?"

"I don't know. Maybe nothing. The whole thing with the kitsune has me on edge."

Corey turned to go but stopped when Ichirin reached out, resting her fingers on Corey's shoulder.

"What class did we have together freshman year?" When Corey raised an eyebrow, Ichirin continued. "Please. I need to know it's you."

"Fair enough. Never can be too careful, right?" Corey smiled. "Physics I, with that professor with the really bad comb-over. I don't remember his name."

"That's good enough. Thank you. This kitsune is getting inside my head and making me feel like I can't trust anything. Even Taka seems susceptible to her magic."

I'll remind you that might not be the case if I were in control of your body. While I am trapped here, I am limited to what you perceive. It might be different if you allowed us to reverse our roles.

This time when they walked into Hemingway's office, he turned around as soon as they came in.

"What do you want to know about first? The kitsune or Officer Mattias Keefe?"

"The kitsune. She's the bigger threat."

"Unfortunately, I'm still tracking down some of those gremlins, trying to ferret them out. I did track the money she stole from Brian. It turns out she didn't keep it. Someone donated the exact amount he lost to a few different charities, all in his name. Not only did she donate it, but she didn't take credit for the donations."

"But what about the fight at the party? Or the car accident in front of the building?" Ichirin asked.

"I don't know, yet. There aren't a lot of threads to pick. But I'm trying to find anything I can."

He reached up and stretched, his shoulders popping before continuing.

"As for the officer, I found some reports of him working for Seattle PD as long as two years ago, but before that, I can't find anything in this area. The name pops up a couple of times on the net, but I can't be sure it's him. According to what I've seen online, he works with Seattle, which means there's no reason he should've been on the Eastside responding to a call. Without a doubt, he's stalking you."

His lips pressed into a thin line, and he held out his hands with the palms up. He looked pained to share that news with Ichirin, but it was no less than she expected.

"Do you think he might have been involved with the missing shipments?" she asked.

Hemingway shrugged. "I suppose? There's nothing to link him to it, but there's no reason he couldn't be. He would have the proper connections to make it happen. I don't know if he's connected enough to have the resources though."

"He doesn't have to be the one in charge of it all," Corey jumped in. "Someone else could back the entire thing, and he could be a lackey. Just a grunt in the service of the empire."

I seriously doubt someone with that short of a temper and prone to hasty judgment would be the one leading a conspiracy. He doesn't seem to have the frame of mind to be that secret and effective. On the other side, I have no doubts about his ability to follow orders with great enthusiasm.

Ichirin opened her mouth to respond when her phone rang. She pulled it out of her pocket and looked at the caller ID.

"It's your phone," she said as she looked at Corey.

CHAPTER EIGHT

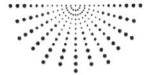

"**W**hat're you waiting for? Answer it," Corey said.

Ichirin hesitated. If the kitsune's best weapon was her voice, would answering the phone be a problem? Would it affect her remotely?

Hard to say. It isn't like there are a lot of stories or experiences with these beasts dealing with modern technology. But if you ask me, the risk is significant. I know it's up to you, but I would recommend letting someone else answer it.

That seemed like a nice middle ground between ignoring the call and risking falling into the kitsune's trap. She handed it off to Corey since she was all but grabbing for it already. The other woman didn't hesitate, snatching the phone and answering, but waiting for the other person to speak. She moved to press the speaker button, but Ichirin waved her off.

Corey didn't listen very long before she handed the phone back. "She said she'll only speak to you."

Ichirin was a little surprised, given that Corey hadn't even said anything when she answered. Nonetheless, she took the phone, anticipating Taka's warning before he spoke.

Be cautious and remember that you can't trust anything she says. Even if she doesn't have the ability to affect you through the call, she is still a master manipulator.

"I assume this time I am speaking with Ichirin."

The voice over the phone phrased it as a statement rather than a question. The voice sounded familiar, and Ichirin scrunched her eyebrows together as she tried to place it until she remembered she was dealing with a shapeshifter. She remembered how odd her voice sounded when she changed into Hemingway.

Corey moved beside Hemingway, and they whispered back and forth. He pulled up a new browser window, and Corey used it to locate her phone. The pip appeared in downtown Seattle.

"Why are you calling?" Best to keep the questions simple, try to figure out the creature's game.

"I think we need to have a conversation. And given how violent you have been in the past, this form of communication seemed like a far wiser option. As far as I know, it's a little difficult for you to try and attack me—unprovoked—through the phone."

On the one hand, Ichirin welcomed the opportunity to speak with the kitsune. On the other, she knew that battleground played to the creature's advantages. Then again, it wasn't like other battlegrounds had proved any more effective.

"What do you want to talk about?"

"Ironically, I need to speak with you in person. Some things about you are still very much a mystery to me, and if there's one thing that motivates me, it's a mystery. I don't suppose you would be willing to meet and have a civil conversation?"

Not in another thousand years.

The hunter knew without a doubt that she'd be walking into a trap, but it also meant she'd know where the kitsune was going to be. Perhaps that was something she could use to her advantage. If the creature was so desperate to meet, it meant Ichirin had something valuable.

You play a dangerous game. While you are quite clever, you are still just a human. You're talking about a beast that has spent its entire existence earning a reputation for being a mischievous trickster. In this, you will be outmatched.

"I'd be willing to consider it."

"I'm impressed to hear your civility. I'll admit, I didn't expect you to be so quick to agree to it. However, there is something unique about you that sets you apart, and I am talking about more than just your gift."

"When did you want to meet?" Ichirin asked.

"I will let you know where I am, and you can leave as soon as you collect yourself. I'll even have beverages ready—two of them, for you and me. No guests. The other two can stay at home."

"No," the hunter said.

Her tone was strong enough that both Hemingway and Corey straightened a little. It was not a voice that Ichirin used often, but she had enough professional experience to know how to summon it when necessary. She waited just long enough for the word to sink in and the kitsune to absorb it before she continued.

"You want to meet with me, so I get to name the location. I'll meet you alone, but only if you're willing to grant me the same courtesy."

The kitsune chuckled. "I have no one I would bring. I find others to be more of a detriment than a benefit. Very well. I'll play your game. It's a good thing you intrigue me. Where would you like me to attend you?"

Ichirin's confidence faltered as she realized she did not have an answer for that question already. She needed a place where she felt comfortable and knew well. She said the first thing that came to mind.

"My office." After a brief moment, she decided to amend her statement. "I assume you know where I work considering you knew to find me at the party. There's a large soccer field just outside my building. Meet me there in thirty minutes."

"Assuming traffic is not a problem, I will be there. I look forward to our civil discourse."

With that, the kitsune hung up the phone. As soon as the connection dropped, the tracking site reported Corey's phone had gone offline.

"So, she's coming here, and you agreed to leave us behind while you meet with her. Why would you do that?" Corey asked.

"The kitsune just wants to talk, according to what she said."

Corey gave her a look that indicated how much she trusted what the kitsune said.

I also trust the creature about as far as I could throw her. Let me remind you that I don't have a body.

"Yes, I know we have no reason to trust her. And I don't. I also know that meeting with her is dangerous because of her manipulation and how she plays with emotions. I'm well aware of the dangers. But, if you two are there, you'll be at risk just as much—if not more—than I'll be. If it comes down to it, I can let Taka take control, which should let me overcome any effects. You don't have that option."

"If you think we're just going to sit back and let you meet with the kitsune so she can get you all tied up in knots and shit, you're wrong. Right, Hem?" Corey reached out and slapped Hemingway with the back of her fingers, prompting him to nod.

"I know, and I appreciate that. I'm not asking you to leave. I just want you to watch from a distance, preferably out of earshot, just to be safe. If anything goes wrong, I'll be counting on you two to get me out. But, trust me on this; I have a plan."

The two friends did not look comfortable with Ichirin's proclamation, but they both gave their assent, however begrudging it may have been. She knew they'd do anything to protect her. She also knew the kitsune would use them against her if given the opportunity.

You don't have a plan, do you?

She did not, but there was no reason to let her friends know that. There wasn't enough time to talk them down if they knew the reality. She needed to face this alone, as she often did when it came to the creatures. Come to think of it, they all required her to enter the final fight by herself.

Not true. Even when your friends can't be present, I'm still there to support you.

True, and without Taka's help, she wouldn't have succeeded as often as she had. However, the core point of the message still stood.

She needed to face the kitsune without Hemingway and Corey. It seemed like that was the way these things unfolded. And if she was honest with herself, she preferred it that way. Kept them safe.

"I think the best place to watch will be the far side of the building. It has large windows looking out over the soccer field, and you'll see everything that happens. Plus, you'll be right next to an exit if you need to intervene."

"I know where you mean," Hemingway said. "We can sit on the couches and see everything. There's no way we'd hear anything. Plus, even if the kitsune looks in our direction, I doubt she'd see us."

Corey wrinkled her nose and frowned, but Ichirin knew she'd follow along. Knowing that her bravado would falter if she waited too long, the hunter got up and left the office to head out to the soccer field. She had plenty of time before the kitsune arrived, but she needed to maintain her illusion to convince Corey to remain behind.

When she stepped outside, the air felt colder than she remembered. It seemed unusual that even though she knew how dangerous the upcoming situation was, she felt more comfortable now than when she first came into the building.

I would wager part of that is because you know the kitsune is nowhere near you at this moment. You aren't jumping at every shadow.

Perhaps. But there was also a fatalistic comfort in knowing that a showdown was going to happen. No more running around, chasing leads, trying to figure out how to corner the creature. It came to her, and they would see what happened. The fact that she'd been so determined to have a plan and to get ahead of things was ironic considering how she walked out without any clue of what to do when the kitsune arrived.

Her hand checked on her knife, the only weapon she carried. It was tucked into her jacket pocket, easy to remove. Plus, keeping her hands in her pockets was normal this time of year. The wind gusted, and distant trees groaned in response.

She still wanted to hear what the kitsune had to say. Between the conversations they'd already had and what Hemingway discovered, the hunter was curious to learn the kitsune's side of everything. Taka said nothing in response. Perhaps he had gotten tired of preaching the same sermon over and over until she heard it in her sleep.

Sometimes her stubbornness came in handy.

It was too cold to sit still, and the wind was determined to try and find any opening in her clothing, so Ichirin walked around the soccer field on the sidewalk. After a couple of laps, she pulled out her phone. She checked when the kitsune called and saw that it had been twenty-two minutes. Her potential prey could be here any minute. She wondered if the creature sat nearby, watching her pace around the field and planning her own surprises.

Time to be aware if anything seems even the slightest bit out of place. Her illusions are meticulously detailed.

The hunter knew that but appreciated the reminder. She thought about weaving her own illusions but didn't know what purpose it would serve. What would she even create an illusion of? No, it was far better to save her strength and focus for now so she could react as necessary.

Some movement caught her eye, so Ichirin turned to it, seeing the kitsune walking toward her from one of the parking garage stairwells. She wore the familiar skin from the holiday party. Even though she wore a skirt and a blouse, the cold and wind didn't seem to bother her. The hunter cut across the field to meet with her target, both of them stopping when they were about an arm's length from each other.

The woman and the kitsune stared at each other, looking like fighters squaring off before a bout as they took stock of their opponent. Even the wind died down, making everything seem quieter and more intense, like a balloon filled to the point of bursting. Ichirin felt the urge mounting to say something to fill the silence, but she refused to cave, wanting the kitsune to speak first.

"Thank you for agreeing to meet with me and have civil discourse. I half expected you to launch into an attack as soon as you saw me."

"Truth be told, I considered it. However, I'm curious what it is that you wanted to talk about."

"You. As you well know, I've been sent to remove you from the board. You are a piece that has become troublesome at best and an annoyance at worst. However, as with most mysteries, I assume there is more to the story than I was led to believe. Unlike certain others, I don't believe that the best solution is to chop down the trees when they encroach on the garden."

Ichirin didn't understand the analogy but didn't let it deter her from the bits of information she could nibble. "Who sent you?"

The kitsune grinned, looking pleased. It made the hunter think of the phrase "the cat that ate the canary." Was it more or less fitting if it was a fox?

"As I assumed, you don't even begin to understand the grand picture. You really are a pawn at the moment, aren't you?"

She's taunting you, testing you to see how much you know and figure out where she can lie and manipulate you. You can see how much she enjoys this torture.

Ichirin's hand tightened around the knife in her pocket, and her finger played with the release. She could cover the distance between them in one step, but experience taught her that was too far. If she did want to lash out, she needed to be closer.

"Who are you?" the kitsune asked. "And don't tell me your name or foolish information like that. You know how much I've already discovered. Who are you and why can you do the things you do?"

Ichirin was stunned enough by the question and the genuine curiosity in the tone that she couldn't help but answer.

"I don't know."

"Poor child. Thrust into events that you could not possibly under-stand and tasked with a duty that is too grand for your shoulders to carry. I'm surprised you lasted as long as you have. You are just a human after all."

The superiority and subtle condescension in her tone sparked the anger in Ichirin. It was a reaction she often dealt with given her job and course of study. That patronizing attitude made the hunter's jaw clench, and she slid forward half a step.

"I meant no offense by the statement, of course. I was stating a simple fact."

I'm pretty sure she's so ignorant of human interaction that she doesn't even realize she's making it worse. She views all of your kind much the same way that most humans see their pets.

"If you are convinced that I'm so uninformed, why don't you provide answers to my questions?"

"It would take far longer than your lifespan to comprehend it all."

Ichirin's hand tightened around the knife so much that she worried her arm would shake and give away the presence of the weapon. She didn't trust herself to speak right now, so she settled for glaring at the creature across from her.

You are close enough. End this!

To her surprise, the kitsune perked up, leaning forward until her face was a few inches away. The sudden motion almost made Ichirin pull back, but she held her ground. She found herself unable to draw her gaze away from the creature's.

The shapeshifter's golden eyes seemed like large pools to fall into that stripped away all thoughts of reality and choice. The hunter's arm relaxed, and her fingers uncurled from the weapon. The cold fled from her body, along with all other sensations.

"Show me what else resides inside you. This is what I need to see."

Give me control, now! Before it's too late!

The kitsune got closer, drawing Ichirin into a hole she felt she'd never escape. The only lifeline available to her was the one offered by the kami, so she grabbed it and pulled with every ounce of mental energy she could summon.

Light flared from the locket, illuminating both the women's faces from below. The kitsune looked down at it, understanding crossing her face just as Taka took over Ichirin's body. He reacted first, drawing the knife, flipping it open, and slamming it into the kitsune's side.

She pulled back just enough to keep the attack from being lethal, but it still scored a deep gash just above the hip. The creature let out a yelp of pain and brought her left hand up to cover the wound. She reached out with her right, trying to grab Taka, but he stepped back and snapped a foot out, connecting with the kitsune's thigh and pushing her back.

Even in the middle of the fight, Taka felt elated, welcoming the feeling of being in a body once again and not confined to its prison. There was a joy to flexing muscles and feeling adrenaline coursing through a body rather than witnessing it as an observer and having the sensations filtered through his host's perception.

Now that she gave up control of her body, Ichirin felt her emotions simmer down. Whatever sorcery the kitsune worked on her no longer affected her as far as she could tell. Even the rage and frustration seemed to melt away.

Which made it seem plausible that Taka was not affected by the kitsune before now. That meant his fears, concerns, and reactions were of his own creation.

Taka refused to relent, pushing forward and attacking with every single step, keeping the kitsune on her heels and forcing her to retreat. She had to let go of her wound to keep up. The blood soaked into her blouse, spreading through the fabric. She bled from a couple of other cuts, small slices on her forearms that did little damage.

At one point, Taka lunged too far, and the kitsune knocked the weapon to the side, giving her enough space to leap into the air. She didn't try to counterattack, instead choosing to focus on running away. Taka hurtled after her, getting close enough to grab the heel of his prey.

As soon as he curled his fingers around it, the kitsune kicked down, trying to free herself. But Taka twisted around while yanking back, moving up along the kitsune's body like a climber scaling a rock wall. He stabbed with the knife, scoring several deep punctures until the two of them crashed down through the trees near the soccer park. Ichirin felt the heavy thuds as they broke through branches and collided with the ground, but they felt distant and muted. She knew when she regained possession of her body, she'd feel every inch of those wounds and was not looking forward to that prospect.

Taka needed to finish this now. If the kitsune revealed too much, years of work would be undone. He couldn't allow that to happen. At least she hadn't said anything yet that couldn't be patched over with time.

"Who are you?" the kitsune managed as she pushed herself up off the ground and slid away from Taka. She bled from several wounds and looked like she had broken bones as well.

"Enough words," Taka said. He staggered as he lurched toward the kitsune, but he moved forward despite his injuries, driven by a rage that felt blistering hot to Ichirin's senses.

Don't kill her. She's dying. Let her speak.

Taka dismissed his host's request. He knew how dangerous this creature could be. He needed to finish things before she caused irreparable damage.

Ichirin tried to force Taka back and take control of her body. She kept her attempts subtle, probing at the barriers and trying to find something to pull on to take Taka's essence and put it back in the locket. Her efforts were futile. It felt like trying to grab an egg yolk—it slipped out of her fingers the moment she applied any force.

Taka crawled next to the kitsune, bringing their faces equal with each other. He had to support himself on one arm to lift the weapon and deliver a killing blow. At that moment, the kitsune flashed into motion, moving with shocking speed. She grabbed the locket and yanked it free, hurling it into the woods.

Taka screamed as he felt his essence ripped from the body. For the first time, Ichirin felt something to latch onto as she tried to pull herself back into control of her form, a handhold which gave just enough purchase to yank herself up. Taka growled, refusing to loosen his grip.

The hunter felt like her head was about to split from the pressure as a wealth of information flowed past her faster than she could comprehend. And through it all, she felt, heard, and knew Taka's rage as if it was her own. And his power.

She tried to stop her arm from moving, but it drove forward as the kami willed it, sinking deep into the kitsune's abdomen all the way up to the hand. Ichirin watched in terror as she tried to wrest back control of her hand, all pretense of subtlety long since chased from her mind.

With a final wordless howl, Taka retreated from her mind, leaving

Ichirin in full control of her body. As soon as that happened, the full effect of the injuries struck her. She wanted to collapse from the weight of them but had enough adrenaline coursing through her that she pushed them aside for the moment.

She removed the weapon, making the kitsune cry out, and pressed both of her hands to the wound. It was lethal, there was no doubt about that, but perhaps she could slow the creature's passing. Or maybe provide some measure of comfort before the death came. Her lack of anger surprised the hunter.

"I'm sorry," Ichirin said. She wasn't sure why the words came to mind, but she felt like it was something that deserved to be passed on.

The creature smiled for a moment before her face contorted back into a permanent wince. She licked her lips, taking a shuddering breath that sounded weak and frightened.

"It was not you. It was another. I cannot blame you for actions you did not take."

So many questions rushed through Ichirin's mind that she didn't know what to ask. Which one was the most important? What should she ask before time ran out?

The sheer volume of possibilities overwhelmed her ability to choose, which made her more aware of how time slipped away.

The kitsune disrupted the spiral of thoughts by placing one of her hands on Ichirin's face. It was delicate, a touch light enough to make her think she imagined it. The kitsune's skin was warm and radiated heat that extended beyond the point of contact.

The kitsune shushed, and the hunter's mind calmed, the frantic trains of thought all easing to a stop. Even the physical pain dulled.

"Know that I serve Izanagi, and that you are not on the side of the board you think you are. Question everything. Look past the immediate effect and see the long game. Remember you're dealing with forces that play games where each move can be a lifetime. Or a life."

The creature took a shuddering gasp. Ichirin heard the rustle of the underbrush as someone crashed through to their location, but she didn't look away.

"And now the last gift I can give you. Couldn't have you killing a woman in the woods, now could we?"

The kitsune shifted form, changing from an elegant looking woman into a snow-white fox. The injuries looked even more garish on this form, forcing Ichirin to look away. The fox heaved a final sigh and then lay still.

The hunter remained in that position, crouched over the dead fox, when Corey and Hemingway came upon her. They took in the scene within seconds. Hemingway moved to support Ichirin while Corey took the fox and placed it out of sight. They'd need to take care of it later, but for now, the hunter was glad to have it hidden.

She didn't speak, lost in her thoughts and appreciating the presence and quiet support of her friends. As the sun dipped lower, the temperature followed, and Ichirin's muscles began to shiver. Hemingway gave her his coat, but it provided little warmth. They needed to leave.

On their way out, Ichirin stopped to search for the locket. They found it, and she tucked it into her pocket. The chain was broken and needed replacing before she could wear it around her neck again. When Taka didn't say anything, she wondered if he was recovering, lost, or choosing to say nothing. That would be a mystery she could solve later. She had enough to think about now.

Her friends continued to provide quiet support, helping in their way. Time blurred as it passed until Ichirin sat back in her home, a cup of tea in her hand, cleaned and changed into fresh clothes. Her friends sat in her living room, waiting. She was bruised and sore, but other than some scrapes, she had managed to escape without any significant injuries.

The locket rested upstairs, sitting next to her bed. Taka still hadn't said anything. But where the silence of her friends was supportive, that silence felt punitive.

"Thank you for waiting until I felt ready to talk about this."

Ichirin sat in the large padded chair across from Hemingway lounging on the couch. Corey laid on her back on the floor, propping herself up on her elbows.

"The kitsune learned the locket connected me to Taka, and she tore it free right before she died. I tried to stop the kami from attacking, but I couldn't. He killed her, using my body, and all I could do was watch."

She took a deep breath, tumbling through her emotions over that. Guilt, frustration, anger, and a protestation of her innocence warred in her mind, but for the moment she pushed it all down to process later. She couldn't afford to analyze those feelings right now.

"She said she served Izanagi. I need to know what that means. She also said to look at the long game. We need to look at everything we've ever done. We need to look at everything every creature we've faced has done. She also said we're on the wrong side."

"What did it mean the wrong side? There's monsters and not monsters, right?" Corey asked, then looked chagrined. "Sorry. Just voicing the question out loud. I know you don't have answers."

"But we need to get them. And we need to know what's been going on. It might've just been the kitsune playing a last-minute game, but I'm questioning Taka's motives. I want to learn everything we can and try to figure out what's going on. Izanagi is our first clue. Between that, and what happened with all the other creatures, it's a good place to start. It has to be."

"What about Taka?" Hemingway asked. "You can't be thinking about picking the locket up again, can you? If he's dangerous, you should let him be."

"That's not an option."

Her friends didn't question her decision, at least not yet. Hemingway's thought was an echo of ones she had herself over the last hour or so, but she knew it wasn't possible. They were linked in a way that she didn't understand, and she needed to know more. If any of this were going to make sense or come to a final resolution, she'd need to deal with Taka.

Even without going to the bedroom, she felt his presence, waiting for her.

THE END

PART IV
WEATHERING THE STORM

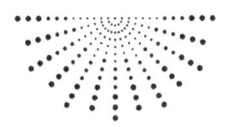

CHAPTER ONE

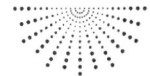

The darkness pressing against Ichirin passed beyond the lack of light, filling space with a malevolence of its own, seeking its opposite and snuffing it out with the same disdain humans give cockroaches. It carried a weight, bringing to mind stories of divers who went too deep, where light could no longer penetrate. Even the thought of moving carried a burden.

Logic screamed for her to wake, but Ichirin perceived a connection in this reality. Something latched on to her consciousness and affected everything she witnessed. It reminded her of her interactions with Taka, the kami serving as her spiritual guide and companion. But the unfamiliarity and power here tied a knot in her chest, the shadows reaching into her torso and squeezing.

"Hello?" she called out.

Her voice vanished without any semblance of ever existing, as if it offended the silence. The spoken word disappeared as it dropped from her lips. She sought the kami, even though it wouldn't work. Back in the real world, the locket manifesting her connection to the spirit sat on a table across the room from her bed. Sometimes they connected before she touched the piece of jewelry, but over inches, not the feet separating them now. She had no one. She was alone.

Not alone. Something lurked. Out there.

It watched her, the weight of its stare pressing on her spine between the shoulder blades. Ichirin turned fast enough that her long hair slapped her face, but she caught nothing. She grabbed her arm and squeezed, a reminder of her own existence and physical form. She transitioned to a pinch, intending to use the pain to jolt her body awake. While the pain registered, the illusion remained strong.

"This is only a dream. You're going to wake up any second now."

Ichirin spoke the words louder than necessary to fill the void. Instead, it reminded her of the unyielding emptiness. To quell her rising concern, she walked, picking a random direction and forcing one step after the other. The ground was cool and smooth against her bare feet, like walking on a slab of polished cement in the early morning hours. The nothingness swallowed the slap of her steps, drinking it with the ruthless thirst of desert sand.

When she heard the soft footfalls of something easing its weight onto one padded foot after another, she jerked to a stop and sucked in breath.

Everything remained hidden, but the hairs on her arm stood up and pointed away from her skin. Her long hair followed suit, curling at the ends. A flash of white-yellow light stunned her. The lightning knocked her flat as it streaked to the ground a few yards away. In that brief moment, she caught an image of something large, furry, and walking on all fours. It looked like a dog, but far bigger than any she'd seen, even in her imagination.

The static built again, warning her before another bolt descended. The electricity struck closer, and the beast stood nearby, its head tilted to the side, watching. Ichirin could tell it saw her even when the lightning faded. She questioned her role as a hunter, wondering if this time the roles were reversed. She dropped into a fighting stance from her aikido training. Dealing with giant canines hadn't been covered in their training regimen, but she trusted the core principles still applied.

By the time the third bolt discharged, she had learned the warning signs and turned to avoid the worst of the blinding effects. This streak of lightning struck the animal in its back, the electricity coursing around its body and dancing as it arced over its muscular form, leaving it glowing like a beacon.

The wolf's black fur melded with the darkness, making it hard to tell where it ended and the emptiness began. Larger than any natural canine had the right to be, the creature's head came to Ichirin's shoulder. Its aura of power forced her to shuffle backward, even without the threat of shock.

A sudden familiar weight filled the hunter's right hand. She brought the katana in front of her body, gripping it with both hands. The giant wolf recognized the challenge and crouched on its front legs, never removing its gaze from hers. A low growl emanated from the beast, piercing the void.

Some part of her brain screamed at her madness. She'd never fought with a sword. But the wave of confidence flooding her veins drowned out any protest. This was the way it should be. Ichirin crouched lower, widening her stance and preparing for the inevitable lunge. The beast could flatten her with size alone, to say nothing of its claws and teeth. But she wouldn't run.

This was right.

Before the wolf leapt, Ichirin jerked awake in her bed, both fists tangled in the sheet. She expected to wake in a sweat and gasping for air. Despite the intensity and lingering images of the dream, her breath and pulse remained normal, her spirit calm.

The bright light of the morning sun made her squint when she turned her head to face the window. Easing out of bed, the hunter scanned the room. Her book and locket sat on opposite sides of the table, and everything on the dresser rested in its proper location. If something invaded her privacy, it happened only in her mind.

Living with Taka taking up residence in her mind whenever she wore the locket numbed her to the thought of having a mental intruder. She didn't know which was worse, the situation itself or her awareness and rationalization of it.

Thinking of the kami made her focus on the locket. Taka lurked at the edge of her consciousness, waiting for her to reinitiate the connection. A subtle compulsion needled at her, a quiet but persistent urge to take the piece of jewelry. She picked it up and looped the chain around her neck, surprised she didn't hear Taka's voice the second she touched it. She couldn't say what he did when he became unavailable.

I am here and have been waiting for you, but think of it much the same as when you get up and stretch to wake all your muscles. I have more than a few years on you, so the metaphorical cobwebs are multilayered. Also, when we reconnect after a break, I become inundated with information and stress. Your mind is as busy and frantic as a mayfly swarm.

Ichirin chastised herself for her lack of mental control and sought to rein in her wayward thoughts. The nightmare impacted her more than she realized, cluttering her mind and driving it in chaotic paths. It had to be more than a dream. Was there a new creature she needed to fight?

What was the dream?

The hunter shared the details as best she remembered. As she recounted it, she found it relevant, not disturbing. Something about it spoke to being more than the product of mental wanderings and late-night Indian food.

Sounds to me like your imagination decided it needed to stretch as well— nothing that need concern you.

She furrowed her eyebrows in response to Taka's immediate dismissal. It felt real, like it existed. It reminded her of engaging with her spiritual companion and their mental connection.

Since you have become more familiar with our connection, I find it unsurprising to see it manifest in your subconscious brain. All human minds pull from real life to make dreams, do they not? And with some of the things we've seen together, your subconscious mind creating new monsters is a logical conclusion.

Besides, we both know this is not how your prey make their presence known. You manifest powers, not dreams. Have you ever dreamt of a creature before? Why would this flight of fancy be any different?

As usual, Taka's logic sounded true, even when his communication style dipped into abrasive.

I've been patient for hundreds of years. I believe I'm entitled to a small amount of sarcasm now and again. Besides, it's one of the few pleasures left to me in my incorporeal state. I consider each of your eye rolls or wrinkled noses to be a treasure to savor. The greater the reaction, the more exquisite the flavor!

His statement elicited a single chuckle and shake of her head. She rubbed her arms, chasing away the remnants of the dream and pushing it to the far edges of her mind. She walked into the kitchen, the scent of the previous night's Indian indulgence making her stomach growl in anticipation of breakfast.

There's no reason to tie yourself up in knots over this flight of fancy. However, if it truly troubles you, perhaps you should leave us connected on a more regular basis. I told you I was not comfortable with your regular alone time, especially overnight. I could shield you from these thoughts and chase the dreams away before they even happened.

That was a conversation the human half of the hunter pair didn't want to dig up again yet, not until she energized her brain and proved capable of debating the point. Taka claimed to respect her need for some mental solitude, but he continued to push back.

I apologize if that bothered you. I was simply looking out for your best interests and sought to help. But you are right, focus on the future. Given that, perhaps today we can make some headway on this Mattias Keefe. He's a dangerous character who has been stalking you and sending beasts after you. He's an assassin and should not be left to his own devices. If we move with haste, we can remove him from the board rather than wait for him to make another move against us.

At the name, Ichirin put both hands on the counter and took a deep breath while her head sagged down. Mattias Keefe frightened her. He talked about killing her, but he was also a police officer in good standing with the Seattle Police Department. She couldn't accuse him, not if she wanted to remain out of prison, not without proof.

Except for the bullet hole in your jacket from when you fought the enenra. *One could consider such evidence a smoking gun.*

She ignored Taka's poor attempt at humor. Even though the jacket had a bullet hole, it held no weight as evidence. How could she show

Officer Keefe pulled the trigger? No, if she targeted a member of the SPD, she needed something more substantial than a theory and an overheard conversation between him and a mythological creature.

That meant more watching and information gathering. Taka didn't need to voice a reaction for her to know his feelings, but she wouldn't take reckless action. The current situation didn't sit well with her, either. She hated being on edge all the time, always checking her rearview mirror whenever she drove. Police vehicles, in particular, took on a whole new level of apprehension.

Having an urge to move, Ichirin waved off breakfast and prepared herself to face the outside world. She put on a blouse and slacks, as casual as she ever dared outside of physical fitness activities. Her parents ingrained in her the importance of looking professional at all times as a matter of pride in oneself and good career sense. Working as a woman in tech, it proved a useful trait whenever she ran into a work colleague outside the office.

The one piece of her attire that had irreversibly changed since becoming a hunter was her footwear. Running shoes replaced heels and dress flats. Some part of her cringed at that transformation to her ensemble, but being prepared for whatever jumped out of the shadows took priority over professional appearance.

Today, her plans involved meeting up with Corey and her partners, but they weren't getting together until lunch at a café near Green Lake, leaving her a few hours to herself. Wanting to keep busy to avoid thinking about matters, heading downtown and getting a few laps around the lake sounded terrific. The chill of the coldest months had passed, and while she wouldn't call it warm, she wouldn't need more than a sweatshirt once her metabolism kicked in.

Taka kept his silence as Ichirin drove across the bridge, dealing with the Saturday morning traffic. She couldn't help but glance at the clock several times even though she had hours to spare. In the back of her mind, her father's voice scolded her for being two minutes late to piano practice. She still couldn't adjust to coworkers who maintained showing up within ten minutes of start time qualified as punctual. At least her team members learned her meetings began at the specified time.

Parking at Green Lake proved to be an issue—it was the first weekend in months where frost didn't coat the grass. The crowds forced her to park on the far side of the lake from the café, but Ichirin didn't mind the walk. The extra time would give her a chance to digest whatever she decided to eat.

Because you're known for gorging yourself since you do it so often. Although you did skip breakfast this morning, and stranger things have happened. I thought your generation had the lesson imprinted in your brains about breakfast being the most important meal of the day.

The wind coming off the water made Ichirin shiver, and she tucked her hands into her pockets. She pulled the hood up, using it to prevent the wind from whipping her hair and billowing out behind her as she walked. Several people walked on the path leading around the edge of the park, a piece of nature in the middle of crowded businesses and small houses without yards.

The air carried the scent of mud mixed with the pleasant spice of wet trees. Closing her eyes for a moment and taking a deep inhale, she pictured the damp ridges of the tree trunks under her fingers. With a smile, she set off at a brisk pace along the paved trail.

At first, the walk relaxed her, the movement easing out the kinks after a work week spent sitting at a computer for too long. The few people she made eye contact with offered a brief nod or smile as they passed in the opposite direction. The vast majority focused on their walk, and a handful had their attention focused on their phones as they put one foot in front of another.

It never ceases to amaze me how much people neglect everything around them and focus on a digital screen a few inches from their face—trading real experience for exaggerated accounts of what other people claim to have seen. I bet more than half of them are just looking at cat videos. They wouldn't even notice one of these beasts if it landed in front of them.

As she continued to walk, Ichirin's shoulders tightened enough for her to become aware of the sensation. Her hand drifted up to her shoulder before she slapped it down against her thigh to keep from chewing the fingernails. She paused at one of the boathouses, leaning against it and staring across the lake, or pretending to. Instead, she took the opportunity to look around the trail and see if anyone followed her.

The people moved about, oblivious to her existence. It didn't appear anyone paid her any undue attention. Ichirin rolled her shoulders, loosening the stress and shaking it off. When a man in a police uniform walked down the path, her breath caught, and her hands tightened into fists. As he got closer, she realized it wasn't Officer Keefe; the man was too tall and the wrong build. But her heart continued to race until her temples throbbed.

This stress is not healthy for you. For your sake, I almost hope a new monster reveals itself soon. Getting back into stalking and your crusade would give you an outlet. I don't see how you will be able to sustain this level of pressure, since you refuse to act against the officer like I have advised multiple times.

Sometimes Ichirin wondered if Taka forgot how things worked in the real world. It was understandable, given his current situation of isolation for hundreds of years, being bound to a locket she wore, and then being forced to accompany her without a body of his own.

Forget? Or find it not worth troubling myself over? I think you will find my outlook has been shaped by millennia and provides a unique perspective on what things truly matter, something humans are chronically incapable of understanding.

While that may be true, it didn't change the fact that assaulting a police officer would mean jail time at best. At worst, he could arrange for her to have an "accident." Judging from the brief snippet of conversation she overheard between him and the *kitsune*, he'd love to be given the liberty, which begged the question of why he hadn't acted yet. What was he waiting for? Was he afraid to deal with her because of real-world implications? It would explain why he kept sending the monsters.

Taka had a point, though, and she agreed with him. Having a hunt would help her focus. Her mind found its way back to the dream, the details of stumbling through the darkness except for when the lightning flashed. Something about the dream left the impression of it being real. Despite what the kami said, she believed the vision portended a fight she longed for.

I encourage you to forget about this. As we've been over, creatures do not reveal their presence in this manner. I would be more inclined to believe your theory of late-night feasting and indigestion than I would accredit a prophetic nature to the things your subconscious concocted. I would think you would appreciate my complimenting your creativity. You do seem to perform better than most of your kind on a regular basis.

Ichirin opted not to continue their debate and instead looked at her phone to check the time. She needed to work her way around the lake if she wanted to arrive at the café in time for lunch with her friends. Shaking out her arms, she continued her circuit, setting a quick pace that wouldn't leave her flushed or out of breath when she arrived.

The place was crowded, with several patrons standing outside leaning against the wall as they waited for a table to open up. The sight made her glad she had the forethought to make a reservation.

We both know the hyperactive child with caffeine for blood will be rushing over from some physical activity or another. I would not be surprised if she decided to run a half-marathon before coming. If she did, she might mercifully not bounce off the walls. Forcing her to wait might cause her to combust.

When the host brought her to a table, Ichirin chose a seat with her back against a wall to survey the rest of the room and look outside the windows. Even if shadows made her jump, she wanted to stay prepared and not get caught off-guard. Experience taught her there were any number of things she couldn't see coming.

As she expected, Corey and her partners were about ten minutes late. Her athletic former roommate whipped around as soon as she stepped inside. When she saw Ichirin, she rushed over, dancing through other patrons and servers, leaving both Ayden and Leah at the door. The couple took their time navigating the crowded area, stepping back to let a woman with a large tray of food pass without needing to dodge the new arrivals.

Corey flopped into the seat next to Ichirin, sliding over until they bumped into each other on the bench. The athlete gave her friend an awkward sideways hug before sitting back and pulling off her hat, dropping it next to her with her gloves.

"You got your hair cut. It looks good. Sporty. Very you." Ichirin said, gesturing to take in Corey's new style. The sides of her head were shaved, the blond hair over it not long enough to cover the exposed skin.

"Thanks! I figured it was time for a change. Sucks with the cold though. At least it's warming up, and I shouldn't have to wear a hat for long."

By then, Leah and Ayden had finished navigating the restaurant and joined them at the table. Ayden held out the chair for Leah before taking off his coat and draping it over the back of his own. He sat down and reached up with one hand to stroke at his beard as he stared at Ichirin. If she didn't know him better, the attention would make her uncomfortable. But she recognized the mischief shining in his eyes as he spoke.

"So, Corrinne says you've got a date tonight."

Leah's eyes widened at the sudden proclamation, and she slapped his arm. "Why on Earth would you start a conversation with that? I swear, sometimes I think you're worse than she is!" She nodded across the table at Corey before ignoring the others and squeezing Ichirin's hands. "I'm sorry you have to deal with their crassness. It's good to see you again. How have you been?"

Ichirin smiled and returned the affectionate gesture, glad to have something to distract her from her reddening cheeks, knowing Ayden relished the reaction. It helped her regain control.

"I'm good, thank you for asking. Things have quieted down at work, and I'm able to take some time to relax and have a social life again. For a while, my entire life centered around getting up and going to work, staying there far too late, and crawling into bed as soon as I got home."

She left out the parts about studying mythology and reading books until falling asleep on them. While Corey knew her secret, Ayden and

Leah remained oblivious about her unusual destiny. The hunter appreciated her friend keeping her secret, and the easy way Corey's partners respected her boundaries.

And with no small amount of envy, I am sure. While I point it out, please know I am not making a judgment. I thought you would want to be honest with yourself. Remember how connected we are. I can sense your emotions as well as what happens to you.

Taka spoke the truth, and Ichirin did envy her friend's relationships. She tried not to think about it. After all, she had work to do.

You do have me. I am always here to look out for you and do not judge you, no matter what we have to go through in the process. We have a connection most would envy as well, if they realized its depth.

And like all other relationships, this one was not without strings. Ichirin played with her locket, sliding it back and forth on the chain. The motion caught Corey's attention, and she raised an eyebrow for a moment before reaching out and resting her fingers on the hunter's wrist. Ichirin let go of the pendant and focused on the conversation between friends with her full attention.

CHAPTER TWO

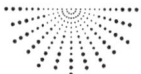

I *wish to restate my objection to your plan. Going out without me would be a mistake. Especially given how uncertain things are with your mental state, being without me could be a detriment. You do know I have your best interests in mind. Always.*

Ichirin's mind went back to the previous night's dream, her instincts screaming that a battle lurked beyond the horizon. Taka would dismiss it given the opportunity, but she had no wish to rehash the same argument. Nonetheless, she didn't want to go out on her date wearing the locket. While it was a simple gold pendant on a loose chain, it didn't fit with her outfit. She wanted to make sure she made a positive impression, and appearances mattered.

She stood in front of the mirror, smoothing out a few wrinkles on the side of her black dress. It was a simple garment, without any frills or decoration, but it also had an element of sleekness to it that she hoped her date would find appealing. He suggested they go to El Gaucho, an upscale restaurant in downtown Bellevue. The location suggested wearing something a touch more formal than the majority of Seattle which catered to the tech folk comfortable in slacks and a polo shirt.

Simply stunning if I may offer my unasked-for impression. I maintain my current state would be an excellent accompaniment to the ensemble. A touch of jewelry to show you recognize the importance of class without gaudiness. I do know what I am talking about given my lifetimes of existence. What I have seen far exceeds any human experience.

With a sigh and shake of her head, she undid the clasp of the chain and walked to the table to put Taka down. This evening fell under the umbrella of events where she wished for more privacy in her life rather than have a voyeur through every waking moment. Even if it turned out to be dangerous, she'd take the chance.

How did you meet this man? How do you know it isn't a trap set by the police officer to catch you off guard? Are you sure you can trust whoever it is? Throughout our time together, you have managed to exceed the expectations I have for humankind. I would hate for my assessment of you to falter.

Her date tonight was with a coworker, someone she'd seen in person several times, so she doubted it was an elaborate setup. If she kept arguing with her spiritual advisor, she'd be late for their reservation, a thought which made her hands quiver. She decided she'd be going solo tonight, and that should be the end of the discussion.

As you wish. I told you I would respect your wishes for privacy, and I will do so. Would you be willing to grant me an equal kindness? Rather than leaving me in my usual location on the table, would you rest me on the windowsill? At this point in our relationship, I think I am entitled to a change of scenery.

The request made Ichirin catch herself in mid-step, but she turned it into a change of direction and placed the locket and chain beside the glass of her second-story window. She stood there a moment, peering outside. The darkness made it difficult to see the trees on the other side of her fence. The sight was all too familiar this time of year. In a month or two, the sky would still be bright when she returned from work. Then again, avoiding extra hours would help.

Laying her hand over the locket, she bid a final farewell to Taka. He kept his silence, but she couldn't tell if he sulked or disconnected. Grabbing her jacket from the rack on the way to the garage, she shrugged into it before climbing into her car. Once seated, she rested her head back and let out a heavy breath. Her hands dropped on top of the wheel, letting it support her arms as she relaxed her thoughts.

Making a deliberate point to steer well away from specific ideas was an exhausting endeavor, and she didn't know how much longer she could maintain her vigilance. Whenever she touched the locket, Taka saw into her mind, but he couldn't detect anything underneath the surface. She recalled the times they switched places with perfect clarity, when she had glimpsed some of what he kept hidden.

Gripping the wheel tight enough to make the leather creak, she drove to El Gaucho. Even with her mind scattered, she refused to be late. If anything, clinging to old habits and patterns happened with greater intensity when her entire world became jumbled.

The restaurant hosted a healthy crowd, as was to be expected for Saturday night. As soon as she stepped inside, Ichirin caught a whiff of the seasoned steaks being cooked tableside for a couple seated near the entrance. It made her mouth water and her stomach rumble despite her earlier engagement.

As she stood in front of the host waiting for her table to be ready, Hemingway hustled toward the door. When he walked in and saw her, he stopped, staring with his mouth open a small amount. The attention made her blush, but the limited light of the front entrance hid it.

For his part, he dressed far outside his usual comfort zone. He wore slacks and a dark red shirt complete with a collar and tie. He hadn't made the full commitment to dressing up and still wore his tennis shoes. If he had, Ichirin would be worried something was wrong with her friend.

"Great to see you," she said as she stepped in close and wrapped an arm around him. Her face rested against his shoulder during their brief embrace.

He returned the hug and stammered a bit when he spoke. He reached up and ran his fingers through his hair as he glanced over his shoulder.

"What did you tell Taka about tonight?" he asked.

"I told him I had a date with a coworker. After all, it's the truth, even if the 'date' is an excuse to have a conversation without him eavesdropping."

Hemingway stumbled as the two of them followed the hostess to their table, but he smiled when Ichirin turned to look at him. The hostess took them to the back corner of the restaurant where the steady chatter dulled to a small murmur and the two friends could talk in quiet voices without straining to hear each other. As an additional perk, she had a view of the entire restaurant except for the kitchen. Her vantage point also gave her a glimpse of the city structures through the large window making up most of one wall of the restaurant.

Hemingway gave the restaurant a quick scan after the waiter took their drink orders, then leaned forward, resting his arms on the table. "Have you learned anything else about Taka and his plans?"

Ichirin shook her head. "No. He isn't very forthcoming with details, and I don't want to ask too much. I still don't think he realized I saw into his mind when we switched places. Somehow, I've managed not to think about it whenever I'm wearing the locket. I don't know how much longer I can continue, but for the moment, I think he's still in the dark."

She sighed and dropped back into her seat, thankful for the additional padding that let her sink into it. Rubbing her temples helped to ease the pressure. Hemingway chewed on his bottom lip, his thumb tapping against the table edge in quick motions.

"Hem, I'll be fine," Ichirin said after a moment, then put on a smile. "I appreciate you and Corey being so careful about what you say around me. I imagine it isn't any easier on you, and I want you to know how grateful I am."

"It's nothing compared to having someone in your head. I can't even imagine what it is you're dealing with. Compared to you, we have it easy. I wish I could do something to help."

Ichirin reached across the table for his arm and squeezed it, holding on for the space of a breath before letting go.

"You do plenty. Both with your research and your support. Thank you. But let's take advantage of this rare moment without my chaperone. What have you found? I hope you've been more successful than I have."

Hemingway nodded, and the visible tension eased as he dropped into a role he often fulfilled. "First off, the bad news. The entire thing with the shipment and tracking down the companies and such? A complete dead end. Even cross-referencing everything I could with Officer Keefe, I still came up blank. We should probably let that one go and not waste time or energy focusing on it anymore. I don't know what else we could do. Now for the weird stuff."

Ichirin raised an eyebrow but kept silent. Hemingway paused for a brief moment as the waiter brought their drinks and took their order, but then continued with an excitement level rivaling Corey's when she found out about a new monster. While her other friend enjoyed the hunt, Hemingway reveled in mysteries and puzzles. It's part of what made the three of them such a capable team across the various challenges they faced.

"After what the *kitsune* said, I did a ton of research on Izanagi-no-Mikoto. The long and short of it is, he married Izanami-no-Mikoto, and the two of them have a creation myth centered around their marriage and mating. Without going into too many details, Izanami died, and Izanagi searched for her in the land of the dead. When he found her, he became terrified and ran away, causing her to curse him, claiming she'd kill 1000 people a day. He challenged her back, saying he'd create 1500 a day."

Ichirin held up a hand to pause Hemingway's explanation. She closed her eyes and searched her memory to recall why what he said tickled the back of her mind. She swore she heard something like it somewhere, but the memory hovered at the edge and refused to come into focus. After a moment, she shook her head and gestured for him to continue.

"So if she told the truth about serving Izanagi, I figure that meant she had to be one of the good guys, right? It makes sense to me. So I poked around a little more in what each of these monsters did before we showed up. Take the *kitsune*, for example. We already knew the guy she put in the hospital got a huge insurance settlement that helped him save his house. And the money she stole from Brian went to charity. In addition, the little stunt at the Starbucks resulted in the place closing down, driving all the business to a small local non-chain coffee house. They've seen profits unheard of in their entire history over the past few months."

Ichirin's hands moved to clutch at her stomach, hoping the action would stop the churning. Dinner sounded less appealing the more she heard.

"What about the *enenra*? It killed people, including a cop," she asked.

"Well, the cop it killed turned out to be someone with a checkered history. He had several charges of excessive violence and bribery on his record and had been suspended without pay before. I couldn't find out too much more about it because I wasn't about to hack into a police station server, but according to what's available in the public domain, he wasn't a nice guy."

Her mind turned to what the *kitsune* said about pieces on a board. "Meaning the cop could work for Izanami."

"Maybe not directly. I think things are more complicated and tangled, but yeah, I thought the same thing."

"If you reduce everything to pieces on the board, maybe we've been removing Izanagi's pieces. Maybe we've been the bad guys." Ichirin stared down at the table, her eyes losing focus as she thought about the implications of what she said. Some part of her mind railed against the conclusion, claiming she had to be mistaken and that there were extenuating circumstances, angles she hadn't yet considered.

But the other part of her mind admitted the possibility she wasn't one of the good guys.

As if sensing her thoughts, Hemingway placed his fingers on her shoulder. She jerked her head up to look him in the eyes, and he offered a brief stroke with his thumb before letting his hand fall away.

"I didn't mean to upset you. I don't think we're the bad guys. But I do think we need to examine things before moving the next time one of these creatures shows up. I also don't think we can take Taka's word for it. We need to do our own investigating. We already knew he kept things from you, and I think this reinforces why we need to question his motives."

Ichirin laid her hand on top of Hemingway's, deriving comfort from the warmth of the connection.

"You're right. We need to make sure we get a better view of the situation before we act next time. Of course, until one of the creatures shows up, we don't have to worry about it too much. Which brings up the next important topic of conversation."

"Officer Mattias Keefe," Hemingway said. "Near as I can figure, he has a perfect record. Nothing outstanding, but no black marks either. It's like he's been a model cop without being good enough to stand out from the crowd. I did figure out what precinct building he works out of but didn't want to follow him home. I figured there's a good chance he knows what my car looks like, and I can't see any way where a black man tailing a cop ends well."

Hemingway took a sip of his beer before continuing. "We could have Corey talk to him, maybe at the station? She has the best chance of getting out of the situation without anything bad happening to her."

Ichirin shook her head. "It's still too much of a risk. If we don't have anything to use for leverage, I don't want any of us getting too close to him. As long as he's keeping to himself, we let him be. We have enough to worry about as it is, even if we're in a holding pattern of sorts."

Her words trailed off, and her attention turned to the windows, gazing at the lights of the buildings across the plaza. After a shake of her head, she came back to the present. "It's the calm before the storm, the tension in the air when you walk into a meeting and everyone is staring at each other but saying nothing."

The two of them continued to chat, the conversation shifting to more mundane matters. By the time the food came out, Ichirin's stomach had settled, and she could enjoy the delicious cut of meat cooked to a perfect medium rare. The spice on the vegetables gave the right amount of kick to complement the savory steak without over-powering the subtle flavors. She knew she couldn't even come close to cleaning her plate, but she had no compunctions against leftovers, especially when the original fare was of this quality.

For a while, she forgot the problems plaguing her and pushed aside concerns of epic games played by deities with living people as the pieces. When Hemingway excused himself, the thoughts came creeping back without warning as her attention once again shifted to the world beyond the glass wall. When she went home, she'd need to deal with Taka. With what she learned tonight, she worried she couldn't hide her secrets from him any longer. She longed to have a beast reveal itself to distract her and force her to focus on other details.

The hairs on the back of her neck stood on end enough to make her skin prickle. The sensation of an oncoming storm heightened, some sixth sense letting her know the winds and hail would soon commence.

A large flash from outside made her jump in her seat and caused the entire restaurant to gasp in unison. Several people laughed it off, and she caught snippets of conversations about thunderstorms and how rare they were in the Pacific Northwest. Acting on a hunch, Ichirin pulled out her phone and pulled up the weather app. She checked the radar, not surprised to find a lack of clouds in the area.

Another flash occurred, but this time people expected it. A few of the patrons near the window leaned toward the glass, peering up to see the lightning, but Ichirin knew they wouldn't see anything. She scanned the entire courtyard, for once knowing the exact thing she expected to spot.

At the corner, almost hidden by the edge of the building, she saw it. The shape was transparent and faint, like someone drew it on tracing paper held up to the glass, but she couldn't mistake it: the large black wolf. It stared at her before a final flash of lightning arced down from the sky, charring the cement where it struck the courtyard. As she blinked, the creature disappeared.

CHAPTER THREE

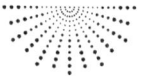

The noise in the restaurant escalated from murmurs to near-shouts as people talked over each other in their excitement. The atmosphere changed from one of hushed conversations in the dark to the energy in a college cafeteria. Ichirin forced herself to unclench her hands and lay her palms on the table. The sense of calm she had during the dream didn't carry over into the real world when faced with the creature.

At least her dream proved to be more than a flight of fancy.

For a moment, she considered tapping into any latent powers, but her current environment discouraged her. She didn't need to release a lightning storm in the middle of a crowded restaurant. Given past experiences, she doubted the first time she utilized her gifts she'd have much control. Not to mention, she didn't know the creature's abilities. The extent of her knowledge about it could be summed up in two words: lightning wolf.

Her wish came true, and now she had a focus. Even before Hemingway returned from the restroom, she searched for clues on her phone.

"What's going on?" Hemingway asked as he eased into his seat across from her, his brow furrowed as he looked at the general buzz of activity.

Ichirin put her phone back down on the table. "A new creature's shown up. I think it's connected to a dream I had. I didn't tell you about it because Taka kept saying it was my imagination, and it's not how creatures normally show up. Usually, I see some sign of their powers, or we notice something weird."

She patted the air with both hands to force herself to stop her tangent and took a breath.

"It's a giant wolf, all black. When it shows up, lightning shoots down from the sky. Maybe it controls the lightning? Or maybe the lightning summons it? I'm not sure. I know the two times I've seen it, once here and once in my dream, lightning happened. In my dream, a bolt struck it in the back, and little arcs of electricity danced over its body almost like it absorbed the energy or stored it. I know this isn't making sense."

Her voice trailed off at the end, and Hemingway offered a brief shrug with a smile.

"What about any of this has made sense over the last few years now? I think I'm used to it. Is there anything else you can remember? I'll dig into it as soon as I get home, but the more info I have, the better. I don't suppose you want to come back to my place and do some research together?"

Ichirin couldn't be sure, but she thought his volume lowered a little, and he dropped his gaze to stare at the table.

"I can't. I need to get back to Taka. I want to see what he can tell me now that I know the dream meant something and I've seen the creature in the real world. Even if he's up to something, he still gives us information. I don't think that will change. If he wants me to take the creatures out for any reason, it's still in his best interest to share what he can. It's a resource we can't ignore. Do you still have your phone location open? Just in case?"

"Of course. We should get on it then. Thanks for tonight."

They paid the bill and gathered their jackets to head back home. Before they parted ways, Hemingway reached out and put his hand on

Ichirin's arm, not preventing her from leaving but capturing her attention.

"Be careful. I'm worried about you. Corey and I both are."

"I will be. Don't worry too much. Taka can't do anything unless I let him take over my body, and I'm not about to give him that leeway, not until we have more answers. Even if it could give me a glimpse into his mind, it's not worth the risk."

The two of them parted ways, and Ichirin puzzled over all the pieces at once. It overwhelmed her at first, so she decided to break it into smaller bits and focus on one thing at a time. Right now, the most crucial element involved identifying the creature. Armed with that knowledge, she could devise a plan for dealing with it. Were the dreams part of its powers? Something it could do because of its nature? The connection left an impression far too real to be pure happenstance.

As she approached the door to her bedroom, she paused before turning the corner. Closing her eyes, she reminded herself about how she needed to concentrate. Her charade required the utmost intellectual discipline without trying to force it. The mental dance took place on a balance beam stretching over a chasm. The more she tried to forget something, the more it came to the front of her thoughts. The only solution she found required a singular focus on something, like the hunt for the wolf.

Walking over to the window, she sensed the kami's presence even before reaching out to touch the locket. Their relationship had grown stronger. She wondered if it was a side effect of time spent together or because they switched places in the past. Either one could be the root cause, but this was new territory for her, and she had nothing to compare it to.

In fact, I would wager few entities in human history have anything comparable. Our relationship is unique, and more so than most humans mean when they say as much. This isn't different in the details, but rather differs in terms of the entire foundation. What other relationship in mundane humanity could compare to the bond we share?

Ichirin picked up the locket, holding it in her hand as she looked out the window. Something lurked out there, hunting her and searching for her. Even though she caught only a glimpse, she pictured the creature in her imagination. Had Taka seen anything like it? Did he know what it could be?

Are you sure you saw what you think you did? Based on your description, this creature shares more than a passing resemblance to the one from your dreams. Are you confident your brain is not filling in the missing pieces with something you want to see? It is a known flaw of the human condition.

Did Taka suggest she imagined the entire thing? She saw the lightning, a rare enough occurrence in Seattle, let alone it happening without any clouds or rain. Everyone in the restaurant witnessed it as well. That was not a trick of the mind.

I'm not saying the storm and weather anomalies are figments of your imagination but proposing a theory. By your own admission, the courtyard beyond the windows was dark, most illumination happening in conjunction with the bolts of lightning. In those brief moments, would you consider the possibility you saw something but couldn't quite make it out? And rather than be an objective observer, you filled in the blanks with something on your mind?

She supposed his suggestion could be accurate. She didn't think so but couldn't say with a hundred percent confidence.

Did anyone else see the creature? I imagine something like that would be quite a topic for conversation, and restraint is not high on the list of common human traits. I would rank it equivalent to common sense in popularity.

The hunter looked down at her hands as she considered Taka's words.

I will concede your point about a new creature entering the playing field. But the one fact we possess is that the beast has some connection to lightning. Anything further would be pure conjecture and not a solid basis of theory. If I had been with you, I would be able to offer some insight and confirm your suspicions. This is why I suggested it, not because I wished to track your personal life. Perhaps going forward, it would be best for us not to separate?

Exhaustion struck Ichirin as if she had run face-first into a wall, and she didn't have the energy to debate the point. It would wait until tomorrow. She needed rest, and her bed called with a siren's song she found herself unable to resist. Putting the locket back down on the windowsill, she went about her routine of preparing for bed and crawled under the sheets in a few short minutes, drifting off to sleep while replaying the night's events over in her mind on repeat.

When she woke, things became darker rather than brighter. That fact alone told her she had reentered the dream. Rested and calm, she anticipated the upcoming battle. This place in her mind was an arena, and it wouldn't be long before her adversary revealed itself. She couldn't explain it, but she had no doubts about this reality. Extending her arm out to her side, she closed her eyes and slowly curled her fingers into a fist. The katana appeared in her hand as her grip tightened on it. Once she held the familiar weight, she bent her knees and dropped her hand, bringing the weapon to rest at her side until the tip of the sword hovered an inch above the ground.

The chill from the soil bled up through her feet and into her legs, so she shifted her feet, dragging her soles across the smooth dirt. The movement helped dispel the cold. She took deep breaths in through her nose, a technique she learned from her aikido classes. It sharpened her awareness, making her notice small details in the surrounding environment. For the moment, she kept her eyes closed. The darkness would attempt to dishearten her as if it had a will of its own.

And then she caught the whiff of ozone on the air.

Ichirin crouched lower, twisting her feet against the stone and turning her head to the side as she strained to listen. Off in the distance, a foot fell. The arena almost swallowed the soft click of nails against the stone, but knowing what to listen for, she anticipated the pattern as the creature stalked forward. When the lightning flashed, she jerked her eyes open after the initial blinding moment.

The impenetrable darkness surrounded her, pressing in and offering no clues to the creature's location. But the soft tick continued to grow in a regular pattern. It came from her right side. She waited, not wanting to let it know she heard it coming. Better to let it think it would catch her by surprise.

Another flash, but again, she was met with darkness when she searched. The creature had gotten close enough that she could hear its muffled breathing. She expected her hands to shake or her pulse to quicken, but the tip of the blade remained still near her ankle.

On the third flash, she saw the beast as electric arcs danced across its fur. It leapt at her, reaching out with paws as big as her torso and attempting to flatten her to the ground. She spun to the side, slicing out with her steel as she avoided the attack. Her weapon met no resistance as it cut through the air, making her think she misjudged the distance, but the blood from the wound smacked as it splattered across the ground. The wolf snapped at her, its wound not deep enough to deter it from attacking again. Ichirin jumped back. Her feet slipped on the wet surface and she fell. Hot air washed over her as the teeth slammed shut through the space she had been standing in a moment before.

Rolling to the side, Ichirin got to a knee and lunged forward, wanting to close from the creature's side, hoping to attack faster than it moved its massive bulk. Before she got within range, the electricity coursing over the beast's body arced to her, striking her in the shoulder and sending her backward as the energy sizzled through her entire body. Her jaw clenched so hard she thought her teeth must've cracked.

The beast turned to face her, a wicked smile betraying its malevolent intelligence. It stalked around her, twisting to make sure she stayed within its view. Another bolt of lightning came down and struck its back, intensifying the light show dancing through its fur.

Ichirin grabbed her weapon in both hands, holding it in front of her with the point leveled at the wolf's snout. For the first time since waking in the dream, her hands shook, and the tip wavered. Her confidence fractured, held together by thin threads. Why did she ever think she could use a sword to fight something three times her size? In desperation, she reached inside and called the lightning, willing the electricity to obey her command. Perhaps she could tap into the powers of the creature and use them to her advantage. At the least, she hoped for protection from future shocks.

But nothing happened.

Sensing her distraction, the wolf pounced. The hunter scrambled to the side, jumping into a shoulder roll to get safe. As she sprang to her feet, she turned around, not wanting to lose track of the wolf. Even with the electricity running through its fur, discerning the beast from the surrounding darkness became difficult if it got too far away. If she lost sight of it, she might as well fall on her own blade.

Ichirin turned in time to witness the monster swipe at her with a paw. She didn't have enough balance to dodge, so she braced for the impact. The swat sent her through the air; she tucked her chin to her chest, rolling as best she could when she impacted the ground. The sword tumbled free from her grip, skittering across the ground with a rattle. When she came to a stop, her chest pressed against the cold ground, and she struggled to lift her head to watch the wolf stalk toward her.

Her weapon rested a couple of body lengths away, out of reach and useless for the moment. As she stared at it, the steel emanated a soft, pale glow. The creature snarled, jumping back and turning to face the weapon. It pushed against the darkness, a losing battle but a beacon nonetheless. Ichirin crawled, dragging her body across the ground one movement at a time rather than getting up and risking the wolf's attention.

As she entered the circle of light from the weapon, the ground warmed under her. It changed from crawling across the chilled cement of her garage in winter to sliding across a gymnasium floor. She reached out and held her hand over the hilt, hesitant to grab it. The light kept the creature at bay. If she took possession of it, would it stop emanating the light?

"You must take up the weapon."

The voice sounded from everywhere, existing and filling the space without a source. She twisted, looking for some indication of the speaker, but she didn't see anyone. The shape in the darkness lurked at the perimeter of light, growling so low the vibrations thrummed in her chest.

"Hello?" Ichirin called out. "Who are you?"

"You must take up the weapon and slay the beast, or you shall be enslaved to it forever." The voice sounded faint, as if the speaker moved further away.

The glow from the sword dimmed, encouraging the wolf to step forward and snap at the light as if it could drive back the illumination even more. For all the hunter knew, it could. Ichirin grabbed the weapon, using her other hand to push herself up to her feet. The sword continued to glow. She turned to face the monster, squaring her shoulders and tightening her grip as she held the blade in front of her. The creature lowered its head, getting ready to pounce.

Ichirin screamed and charged, her voice filling the emptiness and giving her strength. She lifted the sword up and behind her shoulder as the wolf leapt at her, its lips curled back to show all its teeth.

The buzzing of her alarm woke Ichirin, yanking her out of her dream state and into full wakefulness in the space of a breath. Despite just rousing herself, she wanted to jump out of bed and do battle with the beast. Even if she had no clue what powers she inherited, she looked forward to the fight. If anything, she craved it. It took a few seconds before she realized she was standing next to her bed holding onto her phone, not a sword.

Pressing her lips together and hunching her shoulders, she put her phone down on the bed and went to the bathroom to splash water on her face. Her cheeks warmed with the flush, and the cold water helped restore some semblance of calm and balance. The dream worked her up and filled her with a drive she had never experienced before. It was important, but that fact raised more questions. Who spoke to her in the dream? Did she need to fight the wolf creature in her dream or in the real world?

Quite the state in which you awoke. But no need to worry. No one saw a thing, except for me. And let's face it, who am I going to tell about it? The sole person I can speak to is intimately familiar with the details of what happened. Your secret is safe with me. Now, care to share what woke you up in such a state?

Images of the wolf popped into her mind with no need to recall them. The battle itself played back, the details of it fresh in her mind. When she got to the part where she lost the sword, Ichirin stopped the train of thought and questioned Taka if he had any experience with a lightning wolf.

Are you sure you want to go down this road and assume this is the creature you need to worry about? The entire monster you're imagining could be metaphorical. We discussed this in part, but I think it deserves deeper consideration and debate.

They had enough conversations over the years for her to recognize his reticence. Why did he want to steer her away from this creature? What was it he wasn't sharing? Was he afraid to tell her for some reason?

At first, Taka didn't reply. Ichirin wondered if he was sulking or if she pushed too hard around a sore spot she didn't realize. Something held him back; she knew that much. She needed to be prepared to fight the creature when the time came, and he could help far more than any book, but he needed to open up.

How imperial of you to believe others should be subject to rules you are exempt from. Not very often, but with perfect timing, you manage to remind me of the narcissism of humans. Do you truly believe in your superiority because you have a body? I have seen generations of your kind come and go, and yet you still deign to treat me as your library. Your assistant. Your sidekick. Call on me when you need, but have consideration for what I've experienced and my concerns as an afterthought when things become inconvenient.

The hunter collapsed onto the bed, her head hanging loose so her hair draped over her legs. She didn't think of his concerns and well-being as often as she should. Sometimes she got carried away in the situation, seeking answers and blundering on in an attempt to make headway against the beasts she needed to fight. She did not mean to walk over Taka or any of her friends.

Your apology is received and appreciated. We shall proceed, but my small ask is you remember my situation and my experience. I have reasons for what I choose to do, and there are times when I need you to trust me. I promise you; I have your best interests in mind with everything I do. After all, without you, who would hunt these abominations down? You have unique gifts, chosen if you will, for this destiny. Together we will eradicate them before they can sow their chaos.

I will make an effort to think of any creatures fitting the description you provided. It should not be a lengthy list, but realize it will still take some time to consider all the possibilities. There are many creatures in legend connected with the element of lightning. To be safe, I don't want to limit it to those with four legs.

Even if she remained convinced that she had seen the creature, researching more possibilities would be a good idea. After all, creatures that could change their shape at will did exist. She remembered the *kitsune*, able to masquerade as any human she wanted even though she had been a fox creature.

I know you still haven't forgiven me for what I did, but I assure you, it was necessary. However, I won't reopen old wounds. Instead, I'll ask what happened after the wolf struck you in the dream. You cut off before finishing the retelling.

Ichirin remembered the glow coming from the sword, a light chasing away the darkness and keeping the wolf at bay. When she picked the weapon up again, an urge to fight filled her to the point of bursting. She woke up in mid-charge, screaming at the top of her lungs in her mad dash. It surprised her not to wake up screaming.

You tossed and turned, but did not scream or call out. And don't worry, I don't make it a habit to spy on you. I have much better things to do with my time. I paid attention in this case because I saw how rattled you were from your encounter at the restaurant. As I have told you before, your importance cannot be overstated. Watching over you is my duty. I would better be able to perform my role if you reacquired the habit of sleeping with me around your neck, which is a statement I'm well aware sounds horrible out of context.

With a chuckle, Ichirin pressed the locket against her skin with the weight of her hand. She appreciated the offer. Did this mean Taka admitted the dreams represented an attack or a connection to the creature?

Perhaps. I maintain my theory, but a little caution never steered anyone wrong. Except for the emperor's poison tester, I suppose. But even if it is your imagination and stress bubbling up from your subconscious mind, I can assist there as well. With your consent, of course. I may be centuries old, but I still believe in the importance of going where I'm invited. It's one of many ways I was ahead of my time.

She didn't like the idea of him poking around in her mind even if it was for her protection. Right now, they had a mutual understanding, but what he suggested reeked of intrusion. She gripped her shoulders, holding tight.

Fair enough. As I said, I would not do anything of the sort without your express permission. However, I'd suggest letting me stay close at all times. I am even more limited than usual when I am left too far away to connect with you. Especially with a creature about, we can't afford to take chances.

They could continue this discussion later. For now, she needed to finish getting ready and head to aikido class. With her new work schedule, Sunday mornings became the class she could attend with any regularity. Taka resigned himself to silence as she went about her routine and drove back into Bellevue.

To her surprise, he didn't offer any objections when she took the locket off. She remembered the first time she wore it in one of her classes. When one of the senior students threw her over his hip, it flipped over and smacked him in the teeth. The shock of the blow caused him to drop her to the mats, bruising her hip and making her walk with a limp for a day. The instructor gave the class a reminder to remove all jewelry before coming to class, something she never forgot to do since.

Corey sat on the mats, reaching to one of her feet and lying down until her chest rested on her knee. Despite the position, she turned her head to peer at Ichirin and offered a gigantic grin as her friend sat down next to her. Three other small clusters of people scattered about the dojo floor, doing their own stretches before class.

"I can tell by the look in your eye that something's up. There's a new critter, isn't there?" Corey's voice pitched up, and her eyes widened.

"Not so loud. But yes, I think there's something new we need to worry about."

"Sweet! What can you do this time? Do you know yet? Have you turned to steel, or spoken with animals, or run with super speed, or—"

Ichirin held up both of her hands to cut Corey off in midsentence. She feared how long her friend would continue if she didn't interject.

"I can't do anything yet. I don't know what we're dealing with except that it has something to do with lightning."

"Lightning like from the sky or lightning like from the Emperor's hands?" Corey rolled her eyes when Ichirin didn't get the reference. "Sith Lord? Star Wars?"

"No, regular lightning. But without clouds. Still coming down from the sky though. I don't know much more right now. But there's something else."

Ichirin couldn't help but glance over her shoulder even though she knew the foolishness of the gesture.

"I think Taka might be manipulating us."

Corey scoffed. "You don't say? I mean, we've talked about this. Maybe not in so many words, but it can't come as too much of a surprise."

"Yes, we've talked about him hiding things and the whole thing with his superior. But Hem thinks he has an idea who calls the shots."

CHAPTER FOUR

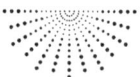

The statement made Corey lean back, and both of her eyebrows raised in surprise. Ichirin could count on one hand the number of times she'd seen such a reaction from her friend. Despite the seriousness of the situation, she paused to savor it. It didn't take Corey long to recover, and she soon leaned forward, crawling a step across the mats so that her face came within a couple of inches of Ichirin's.

"Who is it? You've got to tell me. Hurry, before class starts!"

"It's complicated," Ichirin said. "The short answer is he thinks Taka works for one of the gods of creation – Izanami. There were two of them, and one of them wants to destroy everything the other one creates. I don't know much more yet. I didn't want to research it while wearing the locket."

Before Corey could ask her next question, the instructor clapped his hands, the indicator for class to begin. Corey wrinkled her nose in frustration and huffed, but respected the instructor's rules.

The class focused on some high-speed throws and how to fall in the best way to not damage oneself. Despite her experience, the hunter still struggled with her landings, earning a couple of impacts that made her wince. One, in particular, guaranteed she'd have diffi-culty walking for the next day.

But as usual, Ichirin found joy in the training. At first, she became interested in learning self-defense as a matter of necessity. But the more time she dedicated to it, the more she appreciated the training for its sake alone. Pushing herself in a physical arena wasn't some-thing she experienced before, this being the first physical activity she maintained for more than a few months.

The time passed with the usual speed, making two hours seem like minutes. As the instructor turned them loose for post-workout stretching, Corey rolled until she sat beside her friend.

"So this Izanami character – they're like the dark lord, determined to kill everything?"

"I think so. Like I said, I didn't do too much research because I don't want to clue Taka into what we're poking around with. For the moment, he's his normal self. I don't know what he would do if he knew we suspected him, and I don't want to find out."

"What can he do? He's a disembodied spirit stuck in a rock. As long as you don't let him in your body and swap places with him, you should be fine, right? You're not considering swapping places with him again?" Corey leaned forward and hissed the last sentence, collecting a few raised eyebrows from other students.

They whispered to each other, but the hunter still didn't want to run the chance of others overhearing their conversation. She worked hard to earn her position in male-dominated social hierarchies and didn't need to be pushed back down because others considered her crazy.

"Can we save this for the locker room?"

Corey nodded. Once again, they were the only women in the class, meaning they would have the entire changing room to themselves.

When they left the training area and retreated to their private room, Ichirin's hair turned up enough for her to notice. She paused inside the entrance, and Corey stumbled into her from behind.

"What is it?" Corey whispered, crouching down and scanning the room.

"I'm not sure."

Ichirin sniffed, noticing something off. She took a couple of steps into the room and continued smelling. As she got near her bag, she recognized the ozone odor.

As soon as she identified it, Ichirin dropped into a fighting stance, scanning for some sign of the wolf. Given the creature's size, it wouldn't fit inside the small changing area. But the creature's powers remained a mystery. They'd dealt with one shapeshifter before. Corey picked up on her friend's caution and stalked the border of the room, approaching the entryway leading into the bathroom.

The hunter ripped open the zipper of her bag, grabbing the locket resting on top of her clothes. When she touched it, a small static shock jumped to her hand. She looped the chain over her neck and called out to Taka.

Why the panic and accelerated heart rate? Even with a strenuous class, you should have calmed by now. You're in one of your safe spaces where you don't need protection, remember?

She didn't have time for the spirit's attitude, not if the creature found her and lurked nearby. She needed to know if the kami had any insight to help her.

I thought we faced a gigantic wolf. I doubt even humans' limited sensory abilities would miss something like you described tromping through the dojo. And no, I don't have anything yet. These things take time. How long would a monk take to search through lifetimes of scrolls to find vague descriptions? If I had borne witness to the creature, I'm sure we could have a long conversation about powers and weaknesses. Shame that.

Corey disappeared from view as she checked the bathroom stalls one at a time. After a few tense seconds, she reappeared, shaking her head and shrugging her shoulders. Ichirin dropped down to sit on one of the benches with a sigh. When her friend came over, she made a deliberate glance at the locket before speaking.

"It's not here. I checked all the stalls, so unless it can go invisible or something, we're alone. You think it was here?"

"Possibly." Ichirin's voice sounded weak even to her. "I thought so with the static in the air. Did your hair stand on end when we came in here too?"

Corey shrugged. "I'm not sure. I got distracted when you pulled up short and I ran into you. Maybe? Hard to say."

"I'm sure it was here. I don't know how it managed to do it, but it's following me."

Jumping at shadows. Perhaps the stress is getting to be too much? I knew we should have done something about the police officer rather than enable his presence to drive you to the point of insanity.

"We'll take care of it. I'll check in with Hemingway and see how he's coming along. If Taka gives you any info, text one of us. We've handled worse than this. If worse comes to worst, we'll dress you in a rubber suit."

The joke had its intended effect, and Ichirin chuckled at the mental image dancing through her mind of dressing up like a mascot for a tire store.

Whatever form this creature takes, it would be prudent to treat it with the respect it deserves. I would advise against underestimating its capabilities or mocking its presence.

If she didn't know better, Taka seemed to take the joke as a personal affront. Her humor faded, replaced with a stony expression as she nodded. Each of these creatures was deadly in its own right, and she didn't want to end up being the prey. Hunters couldn't afford to ever let down their vigilance.

I'm glad you remember some of the lessons I have instilled in you. You show promise and are exceptional among your kind.

Since the creature left or was never here, she had no reason to stay in the locker room. Corey would get more up-to-date information from Hemingway and in far greater detail than she could provide. Discussing strategies before they knew what they faced was an exercise in futility.

Besides, she wanted to get home to begin experimenting with her powers. With sunny skies and a lack of rain, she couldn't ask for a better time to practice in the yard.

You mean you think summoning lightning from the sky in your house might be a mistake? Look at the plus side. The insurance company would have to declare it an act of God since I doubt they believe in mythological beasts or magic, which means you could qualify for a home upgrade. You should consider ways to use these gifts to improve your quality of life.

After collecting her things and bidding farewell to her friend, Ichirin drove home, heading into her fenced yard without pause. She stood near the back corner, where the land dipped and provided the most cover from prying eyes. It also put her as far from her house as possible without standing under a tree. If she called down lightning, she wanted to minimize the potential damage.

You have considered the fact there is no way that what you are attempting to do could be subtle, right? The sky is clear, without any clouds. Further adding to the list of potential complications, it is the middle of the day on a Sunday, a time when your neighbors have a high probability of being home. How will you explain away a bolt of lightning streaking down from the sky into your yard? Furthermore, what if you are unable to control your powers and a lightning storm ensues? How much damage would you cause before you reined in your abilities?

Her confidence wavered, and Ichirin reached up to chew on a fingernail. Taka spoke sense. In every other situation, her powers were subtle, something she contained within a room, indoors. If her assumption proved correct, this power entered a whole new category.

She looked up at her neighbor's windows. The blinds were closed, but it offered little comfort to the fears Taka summoned to the surface. She thought back to her dream and remembered the first few bolts didn't strike the wolf itself but hit the ground near its form. If it couldn't summon the bolts with perfect accuracy, what chance did she have?

Perhaps this test would be best saved for a different time when your location is not so volatile. You could take a much-needed break from your work and find some time to go to a secluded park when most people are stuck behind their desks. If you want my opinion, that would be the wisest course of action. I have a few years of experience in prudence and survival on you.

The hunter's head dropped, and she stared at the dirt at her feet. Taka sounded like the voice of reason. But sometimes, one needed to abandon reason when the stakes were high enough. Clenching her hands into fists at her side, she lifted her chin and looked up at the sky. She needed to do this. After all, this was her destiny, and she needed to fight the creatures using every advantage she could find.

It already found her twice. She had to take the chance now, before it became too late.

As you wish. I reserve the right to gloat in the few moments I have before my forced removal when you get arrested or thrown into a mental institution. If you are determined to impart on this ill-advised course of action, I will help however I can.

Being committed to a course of action and taking the steps along the path were two different things. Ichirin had the concept of calling down lightning from the sky, but beyond a general impression, she didn't have any idea how to make it happen. Closing her eyes, she reached inside as she had done on numerous other occasions but found nothing there. After a few minutes of futile searching for a spark, she changed her focus to the sky above. Squeezing her eyes shut, she pictured stretching up with ghostly arms, like when she floated outside her body. Nothing changed.

The gifts you inherit do not necessarily function in the same way they manifest in the creatures. Even if the beast calls down lightning from the sky, your powers may not be identical. Your mastery over electricity could manifest differently. Although I would recommend against testing this with a fork and a power outlet.

Ignoring the sarcastic commentary, Ichirin continued to flail mentally, searching for something to latch on to that connected to the creature she saw. With a tired sigh and slump of her shoulders, she stared at the still-cloudless sky.

On the positive side, you didn't set your house on fire. Although I still think you could get a new roof. They do wonderful things with solar power these days.

Did Taka have anything helpful to suggest? Often when she experimented, his guidance proved instrumental with tapping into her abilities. She lost count of how often he had been the first to discover her capabilities and lead her along a path to utilizing those powers.

I had a clearer picture of what creature we dealt with, and often its limitations and capabilities. At this moment, I am operating blind. The extent of information I have from you is a vague description and an impression it can summon lightning. Perhaps if I had more to go on, I could be more helpful. Despite my earlier sarcasm, you should consider the possibility you can't summon lightning from the sky.

Come to think of it, Ichirin wasn't confident the creature she saw summoned lightning from the sky. It had a connection to electricity, but maybe it drew the energy to it rather than summon it. Did that make sense? She needed to talk with Hem and Corey, see if they found out anything. A direction would help her focus her efforts.

For now, tea sounded like a great idea. Ichirin walked into the house, jerking the door open hard enough she had to catch it before it slammed into the wall. Chastising herself for her carelessness, she went into the kitchen and held the counter for a few breaths before going to her tea collection.

I understand your frustration, but I agree; something to calm your mind would do you good. Right now, your home repair budget appreciates that you do not have unusual strength. Despite my earlier suggestions, you might have difficulty classifying such an incident under the "act of God" clause.

The hunter perused her collection of tins, each one containing a unique blend of scents and flavors. She settled with a chocolate rose option, hoping the sweetness of it would soothe and relax her, what she wanted most of all at the moment. She needed to remember patience. Going through the ritual of preparing a perfect cup of tea helped.

A few minutes later, she sat cross-legged on her couch, cradling the warm cup in her hands and holding it below her nose as she took deep inhales. Her phone chimed, and she looked at it on the table next to her. Corey sent a message indicating she and Hemingway left his house and were going to swing by. Based on the message preview, they found something. Ichirin picked up the phone and scanned the full message, but it didn't contain any more details. When she sent a query back, Corey responded they'd fill her in when they arrived.

Have you ever known her to withhold information about the creatures? I would advise caution. Things that are capable of manipulating others exist, sometimes even without their notice. A cunning adversary would seek to use your friends against you since they are your greatest weaknesses. Watch for anything out of the ordinary, no matter how minor.

The words chased out any semblance of calm Ichirin gained from her tea ceremony. She stood up and paced around her living room, shaking out her hands. Out of habit, she made sure one of her knives sat on the table by the front door. The sight of it made her shiver as an image flashed across her brain of the *kitsune* dying in front of her while in human form. As much as she hated it, she knew she needed an accessible weapon, and she refused to deal with firearms.

Once again, I remind you I did what was necessary. I sought to spare you the task, which is why I suggested the switching of roles in the first place. Never doubt your interests and health are at the forefront of my concerns, always. I am here to protect you by whatever means necessary.

The waiting for her friends to arrive proved maddening. Ichirin couldn't stop considering the possibilities of a creature controlling or manipulating one of them. She didn't know how to handle it. And the more she pushed it away, the stronger the thought rebounded.

I am aware you hate me for the idea, but this is one of the reasons I have suggested distance. You are the hunter; they are, at best, assistants in this. I know you care for them, and I am not suggesting you remove them from your life. But in the scope of these hunts, they are a liability. I thought we covered this when dealing with the kitsune, *but perhaps we should revisit it.*

No. She refused to believe something possessed one of her friends. There could be any number of reasons why Corey didn't want to go into details over a text, even if it showcased uncharacteristic behavior. Assuming her allies were enemies would be another case of jumping at shadows. Spreading out her hands in front of her and patting the air, Ichirin took a deep breath and sat back down on the couch. She couldn't let herself get worked up over nothing.

Taka kept his silence while she waited. When someone knocked on her door, she put her empty teacup on the table and went to answer it. On the way, she couldn't help but glance at the knife.

Peeking through the peephole, she saw Corey bouncing up and

down on the balls of her feet on the other side of the door. Hemingway stood behind her, glancing over his shoulder into the driveway. As she watched, he reached up and rubbed his forehead with the sleeve of his jacket before tugging on the cuff.

Do they appear on edge to you?

Ichirin unlocked the door and pulled it open. Both of her friends smiled at her, and she stepped back, making room for them to enter her house. Corey blitzed in, heading right to the kitchen as she spoke.

"We found some stuff, and you're not going to believe what we discovered. It ties into everything you talked about earlier, you know, at the dojo?"

Corey opened the fridge and bent forward, reaching to the back to get one of the cans of iced coffee Ichirin kept stocked for her. Hemingway stepped inside, staying near to Ichirin and clasping his hands together in a tight grip.

Something is wrong.

"What did you find?" Ichirin asked, closing the door and stepping over toward the couch. Hemingway walked close to her, never straying more than an arm's reach away.

Corey emerged from the fridge and popped the top of the can. "Well, it's a big deal. We're pretty sure we know what we're dealing with. Based on your description, it was easy to find it. In fact, there are a ton of myths about it. At first, we didn't want to believe it, but with everything else…" she shrugged and let the sentence trail off.

She put the can down on the breakfast bar and tapped on the top of it a few times with her fingernail. Her eyes flicked over Ichirin's shoulder, at Hemingway.

Move!

Acting more on instinct than rational thought, Ichirin stepped forward, dipping a shoulder and turning as she did so. She dodged Hemingway's clumsy grab at her neck. His face scrunched tight as if in pain as she backed up toward a wall.

"What's going on?"

"You need to take off the locket!" Hemingway held out both his hands in a pleading gesture but didn't advance. He turned his head to Corey. "I told you we should've asked her."

"If you moved a little faster, this wouldn't be an issue. Look, Ichirin, you know me, you know us. Trust me; you have to take the locket off. It's worse than we thought."

"What do you mean?" Ichirin put a hand up and pressed the piece of jewelry against her chest.

Do not listen to them! They are not themselves. Get out of here as soon as possible! The boy is slow. You could make it to the door if you go now.

"Based on what you saw, we think Taka's real name is Raiju. He's a lightning spirit often taking the form of a large dog or wolf. His boss has to be Izanami." Hemingway held his ground and did not advance.

Do. Not. Listen.

"Are you sure about this?" Ichirin's fingers curled around the locket until the tendons in her arm became visible.

"No, but if I'm wrong, there won't be any harm in taking the necklace off. Listen to me, please. Let us show you what we found. I'll give you your phone, and you can read the articles yourself."

He wants to separate us. You will have no one!

"Okay. Toss me my phone, but don't come any closer."

As Hemingway faced the table, Ichirin glanced at the front door. With him distracted, she could escape. Corey had the counter to deal with, giving Ichirin the time she needed to flee into the yard.

But what if Hem told the truth? What if Taka was Raiju?

She sensed the silence from him before he spoke, almost like a wolf about to pounce.

I suppose the time for deception has passed.

CHAPTER FIVE

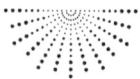

B efore she had a chance to process what he said, something slammed Ichirin in the chest with enough force to drive the wind out of her and make spots fill her vision. She blinked and shook her head to clear it, finding herself hovering outside her body.

No!

She clawed forward, scrabbling for her own body to regain control, but it reminded her of grabbing a log submerged underwater for years. Her fingers slipped off regardless of the strength of her grip.

Hem! Corey!

The hunter called out to her friends, but her body stood with a hand held out for her phone as Hemingway tossed it to her. A faint smirk turned up the corner of her mouth, something Ichirin hoped the others noticed. Taka snatched the phone and opened it with his fingerprint. He pulled up her email and scanned through the link provided by Hemingway.

This turn of events amused him. He didn't expect to have to reveal his identity so soon, but he was glad to have the deception done. Playing the human host to alter her path had been exhausting. He preferred the direct approach, but orders were orders.

He had to force a chuckle down as he read the article about Raiju. It fascinated him to see what humans got right and what they got wrong. At least they remembered him, even if they thought he was nothing more than an entertaining story told by primitives to explain thunderstorms.

Taka tucked the phone into his pocket.

"Say you are right, and I do believe you. Do you think the best course of action would be to remove my locket? Take away one of my best defenses?"

Ichirin saw Corey's eyebrow raise. Her friend stood up straighter, putting both hands on the counter. Taka didn't appear to have noticed.

Don't hurt them! You can do whatever you want with my body but leave them alone. Tell them you need some time to think about it but you want them to go. They'll respect my wishes and leave you be.

She needed to do whatever she could to distract him. Corey made her way around the corner, coming to the other side and leaning back on her elbows.

"It's not like Taka does much to protect you. He's an advisor, right? Yeah sure, he has millennia of astounding experience." Corey held up her fingers and used air quotes when she said the word millennia. "But it's not like he can defend you if we're going to do anything. No offense intended, but when it comes to physical protection, he's kind of useless."

Taka bristled and reminded himself not to tip his hand. Not yet. These humans weren't worth the trouble, and worse, they knew how to cast him out of Ichirin's body. In these confined quarters, they could be a threat.

Trust me. If you tell them you need some time to consider, they'll leave you in peace. You know me, and you know I'd do anything to protect them. Why would I lie to you about this? What could I possibly gain?

Corey took a small step forward, passing it off as standing up straight and stretching. Hemingway glanced from one woman to the other and then back.

"Taka looks out for me. He keeps me safe."

He almost reminded them about how he switched places with her when facing the *kappa* but recognized how it would be a mistake. Even if they knew about it, he didn't want to remind them about his powers.

"Please, Ichirin," Hemingway said. "You know I wouldn't ask something like this if it wasn't critical. The only reason we didn't lead with this is we considered not letting Taka know. Otherwise, I'd never lay a hand on you."

As Taka turned to face Hemingway and give him his attention, Corey lunged, reaching out to grasp the locket. Taka caught the motion out of the corner of his eye and sank into a full squat, dropping underneath the grab. He spun around, whipping a foot out and knocking Corey's leg to the side as her weight came down on it. With no support, she crashed to the ground.

Hemingway's mouth opened as he witnessed the attack. Taka didn't give him time to recover. He lunged with inhuman speed, landing on one foot and snapping the other into the programmer's gut. Hemingway bent forward with a groan and Taka twisted, bringing the back of his elbow into the tall man's neck, dropping him to the ground like a doll.

The attack gave Corey time to spring up to her feet, but as soon as she did, Taka launched a series of punches and kicks, driving her back as she scrambled to protect herself. In sparring, Corey never failed to defeat Ichirin, but Taka had experience and knowledge the hunter didn't. He also moved faster in her body than she could, as if each muscle grew in strength. Ichirin envied his smooth movements. If he weren't attacking her friends, she would consider it beautiful.

Stop! Leave them alone!

She screamed at him, hoping to offer some distraction. She clawed at the same time, fumbling for some purchase to regain control of her body. Her attempts met with the same success as before while he continued to assault Corey.

The athletic woman dove to the side, turning it into a shoulder roll. As she came to her feet, Taka slammed the heel of his foot into her lower back, sending her sprawling. To her credit, Corey rolled to the side, clearing the area as Taka jumped at her.

His attack put him close to Hemingway, who wasn't out of the fight yet. He reached out with one of his large hands, grasping for an ankle. The attack lacked finesse or speed, but Taka's attention focused on Corey as he chased her down. Hemingway wrapped his fingers around Taka's ankle and then brought his second hand to bear, clamping down.

When Taka continued the momentum of his charge, his foot stopped, and he lurched. Dropping onto his side, he whipped his other foot through the air. Hemingway pulled his head back, out of range, but the dodge required him to let go.

Corey got up on all fours and charged like a linebacker, driving her shoulder into Taka. The blow caught him in his midsection as he stood, pushing the two of them back toward the ground. The inelegant attack would've been useless if she wanted to do any damage, but Corey reached up for the locket, the chain dancing out of her fingertips before she gripped it. Taka drove his knee into her abdomen twice before she let go, and he squirmed to the side.

In a typical fight, he had nothing to fear from these two humans. They couldn't match his skill or his speed. But separating Ichirin from the locket would end the possession. They knew this, which made them dangerous. The longer he struggled with them, the higher the likelihood one of them got lucky.

Not for the first time, he regretted his host's choice not to use firearms.

I don't know how, but I will kill you if you hurt them. I will find a way.

She heard his thoughts when they switched places. That explained so many things, like how she resisted his manipulations. It also meant he needed to exercise caution with his mental wanderings while wearing her skin. For the moment, she would get her wish. Continuing to battle them here served no purpose.

While Ichirin's friends recovered, Taka charged, looking like he intended to attack Corey on her knees. The woman leaned back, expecting an assault, but Taka jumped over her, tumbling into a shoulder roll and coming to his feet on the other side. He sprinted on, snatching the keys to Ichirin's car off the laundry room table on his way into the garage.

He didn't wait for the door to fully open before driving out into the driveway. The edge of it scraped against the roof of the car. Metal crashed and crumpled as he clipped the corner of Hemingway's car on the way out. The glass from the taillights in both cars shattered, sounding like icicles in a windstorm. A burnt rubber odor filled the air as the tires screeched against the pavement before the car shot forward.

He had learned a lot about the modern world, but driving appeared to be a skill he had yet to master.

Looking in his rearview mirror, he didn't spot any immediate pursuit, so he slowed to the speed limit. It would not serve his purposes to be caught and pulled over for something as mundane as speeding. He had plans, and now he had the opportunity to put them into action.

What plans? It's still my body you're using, and I'd like to know what you're going to do with it.

She explored her limits, seeing if she could gain some limited control. If her arm followed her commands for even a moment, she could jerk the locket off and toss it away.

Taka laughed, and Ichirin couldn't tell if it was in response to her attempts to wrest control or to her question. Since she could see his surface thoughts, he saw no reason to vocalize his responses to her. He also saw no reason to grant her insight into his intentions. Besides, if she possessed half the intelligence or wits she claimed, she should discern it on her own. If she couldn't, the fault for her deficiency did not lie with him. Humans always overestimated their mental prowess.

How long had she suspected his true purpose? How long did she maintain a buried secret? He couldn't deny she impressed him. While he thought something had changed, her ruse prevented him from realizing her awareness of the greater players in the game.

It doesn't matter. Why did you reveal yourself now? Why are you hunting me in my dreams? At least now it makes sense why you kept trying to dismiss the dream.

She could ask all the questions she wanted. Taka could ignore her and restrict his thoughts. The world tested his mental fortitude over hundreds of years. In comparison, her insistence amounted to little more than a single white cloud on a sunny day attempting to create thunder. She would gather no further secrets from him. And the elementary questions she asked indicated her ignorance.

Something lurked at the edge of Ichirin's ghostly grasp. It reminded her of the time she went tubing down a river with some friends. After falling out of her tube and swimming after it, her fingers pushed it away the instant she tried to grasp it. Following the analogy, she kept her movements subtle, not wanting to shove what-ever edge she could grab further away.

It didn't make a difference. No matter how gentle she pursued the edge, whenever she closed her hands around it, her fingers slipped off. It didn't help that she couldn't articulate what she attempted to grab or do. Frustrated at her attempts, she turned her concentration to their surroundings.

Wherever Taka – Raiju – planned on going, it involved crossing 520 into Seattle. Ichirin reminded herself to use his actual name. She supposed he needed to use a false name because his own would have been too recognizable. For his charade to work, he needed to leave her in the dark.

Why did you pretend to be my ally? Why the act? You could've done this at any point. Why now?

Despite her questions, Raiju kept his mind focused on the road ahead of them. Ichirin couldn't find the slightest crack in his atten-tion. She couldn't help but respect his willpower. She hoped some thoughts would bubble to the surface, but received nothing.

This left her to devise her own theories. Maybe he needed a body, and to use hers, they needed to forge some level of connection first. He did push her into swapping places the first time and continued to press even after their first encounter. Thinking back, Raiju's behavior struck her as obsessed with getting them to change roles. And now he appeared quite pleased to inhabit her body for the foreseeable future. She tasted his emotions and found satisfied smugness.

Where are we going?

She posed the question as he pulled the car off I-5 and headed on to the West Seattle Bridge. He had to slow down as traffic backed up in front of him, forcing him to a walker's pace.

It's not like I can do anything to stop you at this point. Tell me where we're going. I'm familiar with how irritating a voice in your head can be.

He sighed and pursed his lips before making a cold smile. It made Ichirin uncomfortable to see her body move in a way she never would.

"I'm taking care of something you never had the courage to."

He didn't need to speak the words to communicate with her, but he enjoyed talking. After so long of being confined to a psychic connection, physical interactions came with a freeing sensation. He compared it to stretching one's muscles after a 1000-year long sleep, something a human could never understand.

You mean Mattias, don't you?

Her limited intelligence continued to exceed his expectations. Then again, he observed humans from an external viewpoint. The entire species demonstrated a core of narcissism and inflated self-worth.

"Yes, the officer of the law who you must have discovered by now is working as an agent of Izanagi-no-Mikoto. Whether he knows the purpose of his actions or not is irrelevant. He will tell me who his employer is. Someone in his financial situation cannot be the purveyor of Japanese artifacts. What is it your boy said? Follow the money? I intend to use a more direct, and more productive, approach."

More violent, I assume. You can't be serious. Even if you could find him, you can't assault him. The best-case scenario winds up with us going to prison. And that's if he doesn't shoot us like with the enenra.

Raiju chuckled. "It's not my body. If it gets damaged, I fail to see why I should be concerned."

If you get arrested, all of my jewelry will be removed, remember? You brought it up when you claimed I didn't see you in my dreams.

Her comment irritated him, judging by the tightening of his jaw and his sudden loss of mirth. As much as he considered himself to be superior, she still could affect him. And maybe if she got lucky, she'd pull some nugget of information free or find a way to regain control of her body.

How will you know where to go? You can't be considering confronting him at the station where he works. You're smarter than that.

"Of course not. But if you think I remained confined to the trinket you wore when you left my presence, then you are as foolish as I would expect."

He learned much when he traveled away from the sanctuary of the stone. He couldn't ever be gone for long in case she returned, but his wanderings proved fruitful and focused. His train of thought shut down without warning, like a steel shutter dropping into place.

"How clever, but you will not manipulate me with such simple tricks."

Despite what he said, Ichirin sensed his frustration. She succeeded in getting him to reveal more than he intended. Despite her lack of a body, she wasn't powerless in her current state. She had to be careful. If she pushed too hard or too often, he'd make a habit of locking things down. But if she distracted or prodded at the right time, then she could get more.

She maintained her silence while Raiju drove, crossing the bridge and passing into West Seattle. The highway disappeared to be replaced by small businesses and single-family homes. Ichirin got the impression he had taken this route several times and had it memorized. If not, he possessed an incredible sense of direction.

As they turned down a narrow side street, he pulled the car up to the curb and parked, sliding into a spot at the end of a long line of vehicles. When he stepped out of the car, he stretched and let out a soft, contented groan.

He switched over to his internal dialog, not wanting to run the risk of someone overhearing him. Stealth mattered now. He had plenty of time to enjoy this vessel once he completed this task.

While he wasn't worried about Mattias, having a firearm would make the entire endeavor more convenient. Even though he could push her body past the usual physical limitations and possessed a wealth of combat knowledge, his stature did not carry representative weight. Not many people would be scared of a skinny Asian girl—unless they watched a lot of anime.

This is crazy. You know he wants me dead. Can you think of a better excuse for a cop than someone broke into his house?

From Raiju's perspective, Ichirin presented an irrelevant argument. Even if the police officer had his weapon in his hand, it would not make a difference. She could watch as he demonstrated his capabilities.

Taking long strides, Raiju marched to the third house up the street. The home was a two-story building with a large front porch matching the entire front footprint. A short fence surrounded the property, stopping people from walking over a yard made up of more mud than grass. Raiju swung over the barrier with a small hop.

Light shined from a double window to the right of the door, but the curtains prevented Ichirin from seeing Mattias. She wondered if he was even home, and if he had any guests. According to his records, he was single, but single and living with someone were not mutually exclusive.

From Raiju's thoughts, she picked up a blueprint of the building. The image in his mind had as much clarity as if Ichirin pulled it up on her computer. Interspersed with the floorplan, she caught flashes of Mattias sitting on his couch, watching television.

You've been here before.

Of course he had. Did she expect him to be unprepared? Now if she did possess concern for her physical form, she should stop distracting him during this critical moment. She should sit back and enjoy the show.

Raiju eased his weight onto his feet as he climbed the deck stairs. He moved to the wall between the door and large window, pressing his shoulder against the wall to stay out of sight. He rang the doorbell, waiting for the space of a breath before moving in front of the large window.

As soon as the handle turned, Raiju jumped through the glass. The cuts on her arms from the shards stung Ichirin, but her separation from her body dulled the sensation. Raiju did not care about the wounds in the slightest as he tumbled across the desk to land on both feet on the other side.

Mattias stood in the open doorway, dressed in a pair of jeans and a Nike workout shirt. He turned and ran toward the banister, stretching for the belt looped over the bottom post. But he had to cross in front of Raiju to get there.

The kami snapped out a foot, connecting with the cop's hip. The officer rolled with the blow, causing it to slide off without doing any damage, and countered with a punch. Raiju ducked the attack and drove forward with his shoulder, the impact driving both combatants to the ground and rattling the bottles in a nearby cabinet. They tumbled for a bit, each scrambling to gain the upper hand.

Unlike her friends, Mattias proved to be a capable fighter, having both significant training and physical conditioning. If Ichirin fought him, she doubted she could last more than a matter of seconds due to their strength and skill differential. Mattias grabbed Raiju's shoulder and forced him over, slamming him into the ground with the officer's full weight behind the blow.

But Raiju jabbed his fingers into Mattias's armpit. The man's arm crumpled, and he put his other hand out to catch himself. Raiju grabbed the extended arm and twisted, using his leverage to get out from underneath the officer and stand over him, holding the cop's wrist at a sharp angle.

"You are going to tell me who financed your endeavors. Who arranged for your artifacts?"

In response, Mattias drove his shoulder into Raiju, shouting in a combination of pain and rage as his wrist continued to bend. But the attack had the desired effect, driving Raiju back a couple of steps. Mattias pressed his assault, yanking his hand free and twisting to bring his dead arm about like a club. Raiju moved to block the attack, creating an opening for Mattias to drive his free hand into the kami's stomach.

Taking advantage of his successful feint, Mattias grabbed Raiju's shoulder, spinning him and locking his good arm around the kami's neck. He bent backward, forcing Raiju on tiptoes as he tightened his arm muscles and cut off airflow.

Raiju grabbed the forearm choking his borrowed body. Ichirin wanted to panic, but the kami was entertained, not concerned. Using strength she didn't have, he bent at the waist, picking up the police officer and flipping him onto the ground. Mattias groaned when his back slammed into the floor, but he had enough frame of mind to roll to the side. His movement slowed, and he panted as he collected his feet underneath him. Raiju watched and waited.

Once Mattias got back to a standing position, he punched with his bad arm. Raiju stepped to the side, avoiding the clumsy attack. Mattias stumbled forward, making another awkward haymaker of a blow, one Raiju faded away from like a dancer. Mattias caught himself on the edge of the desk.

"I thought you would be more entertaining." Raiju gestured at his adversary. Lines of blood ran down his arm, dripping onto the floor and leaving a trail of combat.

Mattias lowered his head, dropping it almost to his hand as he slumped over the corner of his desk. He fell to a knee, his back rising and falling as he took deep breaths. Raiju took a step closer.

"You should talk before…"

Mattias burst into motion, tearing something free from under his desk and twisting to fire a taser. Raiju dodged, but not fast enough. The electrodes hit home, piercing the kami's skin. As Mattias stood up, electricity shot down the wires and coursed through Raiju's body.

CHAPTER SIX

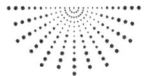

Ichirin expected to suffer the effects of the electronic weapon, to receive a distant shock through the muffled desensitization she associated with being separated from her body. Rather than pain, she became energized, like the time she made the mistake of following an energy shot with a cup of black tea.

Mattias turned his head to the side in a comical expression of confusion as Raiju smiled. When the taser stopped cycling, the kami grabbed the officer's wrist. Electricity shot through the connection, making Mattias spasm until Raiju let go and dropped his opponent to the ground. He howled with laughter and yanked the electrodes out of his skin.

Reaching down, he picked up the larger man with both of his hands curled around the cop's neck. Mattias strained to pry free, but Raiju released more of the stored energy, relishing the response as his victim jerked in his grasp.

"As I said, you will tell me who gave you your orders. If you resist, I'll satisfy my curiosity. I have often wondered what too much electricity would do if applied to a human's head."

He released his grip enough to let Mattias take a deep breath.

"Fuck you."

Raiju growled in response and channeled the electricity. Mattias howled in pain. Ichirin winced at the noise. It lasted an eye blink, but the sound stretched on in Ichirin's memory, and she doubted she would ever forget it.

"You are not worth my time. You are a foot soldier, and I destroy generals. Give me what I need, and I shall leave. If you continue to resist, know you are insignificant."

Ichirin reached out. She met with no more success than before, anything resembling a hook slipping through her fingers before she managed a stable hold. Her efforts became a mad scramble as her desperation grew.

Movement near the door caught her attention as Corey ran through the opening. The thud of her feet against the hardwood alerted Raiju in time for him to twist and toss Mattias into the new arrival. Corey slid to avoid him, but they collided, and her head slammed into the ground with a frightening *crack*.

Mattias groaned as he pushed himself up on all fours, crawling away. Raiju moved to intercept him but stopped when Hemingway filled the doorway.

"How did you find me?" he asked, taking a step to rest his foot on top of Corey's ankle.

When Hemingway moved, Raiju shifted his weight, applying pressure to Corey's bones and grinding them against the floor. Even in her dazed state, she cried out.

While her pain served as a deterrent for Hemingway, Mattias showed no such hesitation. He moved to the banister, reaching for his belt with the holstered sidearm. Raiju stepped off Corey, making her scream before she jerked her leg back and rolled away, putting distance between her and her attacker. Hemingway bent down to check on her.

Raiju grabbed Mattias by the wrist, but the cop expected as much and rolled his arm, bending his opponent at an awkward angle before punching him in the ribs. A second punch followed the first, coming in too fast for Raiju to react.

After the blows, Raiju dropped to a squat, wrenching his arm free and lashing out with a leg, sweeping Mattias off his feet. The officer rolled to his side, rather than striking the floor with his back. He grabbed Raiju's shoulder, pulling the spirit closer and using his weight and size to his advantage.

"The necklace!" Hemingway shouted. "Throw it away!"

Mattias looked at the locket hanging from Raiju's neck. Ichirin witnessed the kami's panic spike. As he redoubled his efforts to free himself from the police officer, she shrieked at him and clawed at his consciousness. The raw emotion of her assault dazed him enough for Mattias to loop his fingers in the chain. With a sharp tug, the necklace snapped. He hurled the locket to the opposite side of the room, where it clattered against a table before coming to a rest.

Ichirin's head threatened to split open as her howl mixed and joined with Raiju's before their violent separation. It made her think of hovering on the edge of a black hole as some force tore her awareness back into her body. Her head pounded, adding its pain to the wounds from the window and her bruised ribs. Ichirin flopped as much as she could, half-stuck in some sort of submission hold.

Mattias continued his work, moving to position himself on top of Ichirin and press her face into the ground. Taking advantage of her disorientation, he looped an arm around her neck while grabbing one of her wrists and tucking it behind her back.

"Insignificant?" he growled in her ear. "I should've shot you long ago."

"Stop!"

"No!"

Corey and Hemingway called out from the doorway, both of them advancing on the pair. Mattias twisted to face them but refused to relent. Ichirin pulled on the arm tightened around her throat, struggling to take a breath. The pounding in her brain intensified.

A flash of light filled the space as a ball of lightning appeared on the far side of the room. It swerved to avoid the furniture and shot out the open window, disappearing into the distance.

Mattias's arm dropped as he watched Raiju retreat from the scene. Ichirin collapsed, falling onto a shoulder and rubbing at her neck as she coughed. Corey and Hemingway rushed to her, and Corey stood over her friend even though she put most of her weight on one ankle and had a noticeable limp. Hemingway wrapped his arms around Ichirin, cradling her as he held her close.

"Don't you touch her," Corey said, balling her hands into fists, glaring at Mattias.

The cop recovered from his shock and stepped backward as he stood. He unholstered his weapon and brought it to bear in front of him in a smooth, practiced motion. Corey stood in his firing line, putting her hands down by her sides but refusing to budge.

"Do you even know what she is?" he asked. "Get out of the way now. I can end this!"

"She's not the monster. I don't know if you noticed, but the monster hightailed it out of here. What do you think the lightning was? A fairy from Neverland?" Corey said.

"She's a murderer."

"Says the cop sending demons after her. You're one to talk."

"I'm doing my job!" He shouted and lifted the gun higher, bringing the sight in line with his eye.

Corey opened her mouth to respond, but Ichirin put a hand on her shoulder, easing her to the side. Corey relaxed and stepped out of the way, making space. Ichirin stepped forward, standing in the center of the gun's path. Her other hand cradled her ribs, and blood still stained her arms. Her entire body moved with painful slowness, like she'd survived multiple days without sleep. She spoke, a whisper filled with an exhausted sigh.

"If you believe I'm the monster, then shoot."

A few seconds stretched toward eternity as they passed, the call of a startled bird from outside the sole noise breaking the silence. Mattias lowered his weapon but kept it at his side.

"Explain."

"I didn't come here to fight you. I didn't come at all. What you saw, the thing controlling my body, is a kami. His name is Raiju." She stumbled as the name "Taka" almost passed her lips, but she caught herself before she uttered it. "He possessed me and wanted to chase you down to discover who you're working for."

She swayed, and Hemingway stepped forward a half-pace to provide balance and support. Seeing her weakness, Mattias gestured to the dinner table and chairs in the neighboring room. He kept the three intruders in his line of sight as he walked over to the front door, closing and bolting it shut. It seemed a pointless gesture, given the smashed window next to it, but Ichirin chalked it up to force of habit.

Corey fetched the locket and placed it on the table. Raiju's departure scorched the entire front panel, and Ichirin didn't need to touch it to know he was gone. The necklace was nothing more than a piece of jewelry now. The sight of it made her skin crawl, and she caught a heavy whiff of ozone. She wrinkled her nose but couldn't say if the odor existed or her imagination retrieved the details from past experiences. Hemingway stuffed it into his pants pocket.

When the others sat down at the table, Mattias grabbed a chair and dragged it away, maintaining a distance of a few feet. He sat down and put his weapon on his leg, resting his hand on it. He stared at Ichirin in particular, and if she had enough energy to react, she would have squirmed under the scrutiny. Right now, she struggled to not collapse on top of the table.

"I've been working with a spirt, a kami claiming he wanted to guide me. I met him around the same time I ran into my first beast in Japan. You didn't set that one loose too, did you?"

Mattias clamped his mouth shut and narrowed his eyes. Ichirin understood the unspoken message. She needed to talk and provide answers, not seek them out.

"At first, I welcomed him. He understood details about my life that made me think I was going crazy. Everything clicked into place for the first time, and I guess I wanted to believe him. He showed me how to use my gifts and how to hunt down these creatures, claiming I was chosen for this because of what I can do."

She couched her words, looking for any reaction. She couldn't be sure how much Mattias had discovered about her and didn't want to expose more than necessary. These secrets represented the largest part of her life for the last few years. She couldn't lay them out in front of a man who admitted to wanting to kill her.

He gave a small nod, the most communication he had offered since sitting down.

"So we hunted. I believed we were doing the right thing. I thought these monsters caused chaos and killed people."

She paused and took a deep breath. It no longer hurt to expand her rib cage, and her energy returned in small bursts.

"But now I'm beginning to realize Raiju manipulated me, starting with never telling me his real name until we discovered it. When I thought about being on the wrong side, he took over, pushing me out of my body and making me ride along like an observer."

She put her hands on the table, now strong enough to slip into the role of professional presenter. She faced down creatures from mythology and angry corporate executives. Mattias was a police officer, much lower on the threat scale, even if he held a loaded gun.

Mattias stood up. He walked out of the room and came back a few seconds later holding a box of sterile bandages. He tossed it to Hemingway, who sat next to Ichirin. He continued to hold his weapon in plain view as he sat back down in the distant chair.

"For your arms. Stop bleeding on my table." His jaw clenched as he paused before continuing. "Do you know how many times I've heard the excuse 'the devil made me do it' in my line of work?"

"Except, in this case," Corey jumped in, "it's true."

Mattias's head snapped into position to stare at her, but she didn't back down. "You've set loose an *enenra*, a *kappa*, and a *kitsune*. And that's what we know of! Hell, even with how much I read, I wouldn't know half of those if not for you. If nothing else, you have to acknowledge it's possible."

Mattias's hand tightened on his knee, but the one on his weapon remained comfortable and loose. In the following silence, Hemingway winced as he ripped open a package of bandaging for Ichirin. He mumbled an apology as he handed over the sterile pad. The intrusion broke the mounting tension, and Mattias waved his hand in the air.

"I'll concede it's possible. But I have no reason to trust you. My orders regarding you are very explicit."

"The orders to remove me from the board?" Those words made him sit up straighter, and Ichirin pressed on. "I heard the *kitsune* tell you there's more than one way to remove a piece from the board. I'm talking about removing myself, or maybe even joining your side."

"What?" This time Corey revealed her shock. "You can't be serious."

Mattias looked intrigued, his eyes shifting to the side as he entertained his own thoughts. Hemingway reached out and put his hand on Ichirin's shoulder, giving a light squeeze to indicate his understanding.

"If I believed you, then the guilty party would be this Raiju. How do we know you're free from his influence now?"

"He's not here. His essence was in the locket, but somehow, he manifested when we got separated and fled. We need to stop him."

"Are you willing to prove you're not infected or possessed?"

Ichirin's breath caught as her chest tightened, and she leaned away from him even though he was well out of reach. But at the same time, she needed to convince him not to hunt her down. Chasing Raiju would be difficult. With a cop on her heels, she believed her likelihood of success pushed into impossible. That's if she could even get out of here without getting shot. She didn't forget the gun resting on his leg.

"What did you have in mind?" she asked.

"I'm guessing the kami's the reason my taser charged you rather than incapacitated you. Hitting you with it again might tell us whether or not Raiju's still there."

Both of her friends looked to her, waiting to see what Ichirin would say. She dreaded the thought of being hit with a taser. Even at the mention of the idea, she had to force herself to breathe past the lump pressing on her lungs. She swallowed and licked her lips before responding.

"Yes. We need to make sure."

She held up a couple of fingers to cut off Corey's objection. Hemingway's fingers tightened on her arm enough to indent her flesh, but she knew he'd support her through this like so many other things. Mattias's grin made Ichirin question the wisdom of her choice, but she committed to the decision. If this is what it took to convince him to let them go and not interfere, she'd accept the price.

Mattias walked over and grabbed his discarded taser. Coiling up the wires and swapping out the battery, he gestured for Ichirin to stand and come closer. She complied. Her friends stood as well, framing her on either side.

"You'll want to turn around. It works best if I target the back. Targeting the front can cause a heart attack."

Ichirin turned around, thinking about how he showed no hesitation in shooting her in the chest when Raiju inhabited her body. She squinted her eyes shut and took deep breaths in through her nose as she anticipated the shock.

She could never have prepared for the sudden surge racing through her.

Every muscle in her body tightened and seized up worse than any cramp she ever hard, and they wouldn't let go. She thought her teeth would crack from the force of her jaw clenching. Hemingway and Corey stepped forward, catching her as she fell, her body refusing to respond to any of her commands. They lowered her to the ground. By the time she reached it, she could move again, but didn't want to.

"It appears you told the truth about part of it."

"You sick, twisted..." Corey moved toward Mattias, but Hemingway grabbed her leg and shook his head.

"She agreed to it. Besides, now I'm willing to consider believing you about all of it. I'll need to contact my superiors about this change of events. For now, you're free to go. But don't think for a moment we're allies. If you are telling the truth, I don't want your death on my conscience."

When Ichirin stood, her legs shook, and she had to lean on Hemingway for balance. Through the sheer force of her stubbornness, she refused to have him carry any of her weight.

"We need to hunt down Raiju. The things he's capable of..."

Mattias shook his head. "You will not. If what you're saying is true,

you're a civilian, nothing more. You'd get in the way of the professionals doing their job."

"What professionals? The cops?" Corey snorted.

"Yes, the cops. We've seen weirder than the public knows, and we'll
handle it. Don't you get it? Without your powers, the powers the kami
gave you, you're a liability, not an asset. Stay out of our way. And get
out of my house."

He gestured to the door with his chin, making it clear the conversation had ended. The three friends left, Corey muttering under her
breath as she did. When they got outside, Ichirin paused to look for
any trace of Raiju but found nothing other than a bit of scorched
ground near the edge of the porch. He left, but the question remained:
where was he going?

They got into Corey's car, Hemingway crawling into the back and
leaving the front for Ichirin. She dropped into the passenger seat, glad
to have her legs stop quivering from the effort. She expected the pain
but didn't realize how long the effects lingered. The effectiveness of
the weapon impressed her.

"We aren't going to listen to that ass, are we?" Corey asked as she
slammed her door shut. "We all know the cops can't handle these
things. I don't care what mister I-like-to-electrocute-people said, this
situation is not normal. And we're the closest thing it comes to
experts when it comes to hunting these creatures."

"The first thing is to figure out where he'd go." Hemingway looked
at Ichirin. "Do you have any ideas? Or any connections to him?"

Ichirin was about to respond in the negative but stopped. They
had been bonded together for years, and the bond got stronger over
time. She could sense the locket and his presence before they touched
at greater and greater distances. Perhaps she could use her relationship now to find him.

Holding up a finger silenced her friends as they watched and
waited. She closed her eyes and reached out, imagining casting a web
out in all directions, searching for anything to trip over one of the
threads and give her a signal. Her brow furrowed with the effort as
she pushed it outward, expanding it further and picturing a map of

Seattle. Her net spread like a spilled liquid, seeping out in all directions.

Something tugged at part of her, but by the time she became aware of it, it faded. Cursing at her carelessness, she cleared her mind once again, remaining hyperalert for any triggers. She sat in concentration, hoping for some sign, until one of her friends shifted, the friction against the seat sounding like a rasp in her ear. She opened her eyes and shook her head.

"Nothing. I thought I had something, but I couldn't get a handle on it. It disappeared."

"So we're shooting in the dark," Hemingway collapsed into his seat. "We don't have any leads."

A police cruiser drove down the cross street ahead of them, and Corey smiled.

"I wouldn't say that."

CHAPTER SEVEN

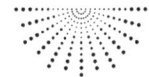

C orey took off with enough acceleration to make Ichirin clutch the edges of her seat out of instinct. Once they got to the corner, the daredevil slowed down and turned to follow the cop car. The vehicle didn't have its lights on, but it still swerved through traffic. Corey made sure to stay several car lengths behind it.

"What are you doing? We don't even know if that's Mattias."

Corey glanced in her rearview mirror to raise an eyebrow at Hemingway. "Do you have any better ideas? This is our best lead. Besides, what are the odds of another cop happening to zip down his street right then? We do our best work when flying by the seat of our pants. We're regular Browncoats that way."

While she missed the reference, Ichirin agreed with the logic. Odds were that the cop car was Mattias, and given their recent encounter, he was their best chance at finding Raiju, unless she could discover a way to strengthen the connection between her and the spirit.

"Hem, can I see the locket?"

She reached back with an open hand. He fished out the piece of jewelry and placed it in her palm. For the first time in as long as she could remember, it didn't strike her as heavy or cold. She pried at the cover, but Raiju's sudden departure had fused it shut. She searched for something in the car she could use to pry it open.

"What do you need?"

"Multitool?"

"Glove compartment."

Thus armed, the hunter pulled out one of the screwdriver tips and wedged it into the locket seam. With some dedicated twisting, she popped it open. The rock Raiju claimed to inhabit sat inside, its appearance nothing more than a large pebble. Ichirin dumped it into her hand and closed it in her fist, hoping its presence would assist them in finding the kami.

The stone still had some traces of him, like a scent lingering in the kitchen after cooking. She cast her net, ignoring the shifts of the car as Corey raced through the streets at speeds over the limit.

As she focused, certain trains of thought tugged at her attention and yanked her away from her goal. What if the kami was what made her special? What if she was now just another human in a world more magical than she ever thought possible? What if she didn't have any powers, nothing inherited from Raiju. Considering he'd been right next to her for a few years, if anything was going to manifest, wouldn't it have done so by now? Perhaps her drive to see herself as different, to be special, was no more than a deluded fantasy she chased because she wanted it to be true.

Perhaps her entire reason for being chosen boiled down to being in the right place at the right time and susceptible to manipulation.

The demons sounded loud in her mind, tearing at any net she built before she found anything to guide . She sighed and opened her eyes, staring at her fist. She uncurled her fingers and looked at the rock in her palm. It struck her as a perfect metaphor for her life. Not long ago, it contained something marvelous and existed as part of a grand game. Now it revealed its true nature, plain and ordinary and one of a billion others like it.

"We'll find him and stop him."

Hemingway's voice from the backseat pulled Ichirin out of her internalized dungeon.

"Maybe Mattias was right, and we should leave this to the experts. I don't have any powers or anything. If we get in the way, things could get worse."

The rumbling of the engine filled the void as no one spoke.

"It's okay," Hemingway said, putting his hand on her shoulder. "You don't have to fight all the time. Not every fight is yours to take. If you want, we can leave this one to Mattias and his professionals. No one would fault you. Both Corey and I know what you've done and what you're capable of. We wouldn't judge, and you shouldn't either."

Corey nodded to indicate her agreement with Hemingway, but the road demanded her attention as they swerved onto the West Seattle Bridge.

"And don't you dare think for a moment your powers are what make you special. You aren't an amazing hunter because you have some magical sponge-like ability. You're a good hunter because you see things others don't, you stand up to things I never could, and you have been through hell and back."

He took a deep breath. His voice carried no guilt, not expectation, just soft caring and consideration.

"But you don't have to take every fight. You need to do what's right for you, and we've got your back whatever you decide."

Ichirin pressed the side of her face against the back of Hemingway's hand and held it there for a few seconds. His support, both active and passive, spurred her determination. She needed to see this to an end, one way or another. Raiju manipulated her, controlled her, and targeted her. She refused to believe his entire reasoning came down to chance. His behavior was too calculating. From his perspective, circumstance resulted from careful planning.

"We go on. We find Raiju and come up with a way to stop him. Hem, do you have your computer? Find out anything you can. Are there any legends of someone fighting Raiju in the past? What worked? What didn't? Anything you can find."

Hemingway unzipped his bag, and soon his fingers hammered away on the keys with a steady clicking rhythm. Corey grinned and lowered her head to stare through her eyelashes at the car in front of her. Even though she drove an automatic, her hand slipped to the gear shift.

Once they got on I-5, the cop car turned on its lights and accelerated. Corey did the same but fell behind bit by bit as she refused to match the driver's pace.

"He's going too fast. I don't mind speeding, but if I zip through going eighty, someone's going to notice. We can't afford to get pulled over."

"It's okay; I think I know where he's going."

Hemingway passed his computer up to Ichirin. She clicked on the video queued up in his browser. She didn't recognize the area, but she saw a parking lot and a large brick building in the background with several tall stacks coming out of the top of it. As she pressed play, lightning flashed in the lot. First one bolt, then another, and a third in quick succession. When the bolts struck the pavement, they charred it. Considering the number of trees surrounding the building, the strikes were far from natural.

"Where is this?"

"Someone uploaded it from the University of Washington. If my guess is right, that's the power plant on campus."

Ichirin looked at Corey. "You know how to get there?"

"Already on it."

They lost sight of the cop car, catching the occasional flash from its lights as it exited onto 520. The fact a West Seattle cop raced to a scene in the U District confirmed the driver's identity. The hunter dreaded dealing with Mattias again after such an uneasy truce but facing Raiju trumped any other concerns.

Once they got off the highway, traffic stopped. Ichirin sat up taller in her seat and saw a line of red lights stretching as far as she could make out. Judging by the tire tracks in the median, Mattias pursued an alternative method of getting to his destination. She doubted people would be so forgiving for a civilian vehicle.

"I need to go." She spoke in a soft voice, but then realized the truth of her statement. "I can't wait for this to clear. I have to run."

Corey nodded and jumped out of the car first. Ichirin wasn't surprised at her friend's response. When she looked back at Hemingway, his face tightened, and he rubbed his shoulder. She wondered if he realized he massaged the scar from the *kappa* or if it was a purely visceral reaction.

"We need you to stay here," she said. "Someone has to stay with the car, and you need to research. You're our hope for finding some weakness. Are you okay with that?"

He nodded, getting out to transfer into the driver's seat. Ichirin jogged forward, setting a pace where she wouldn't arrive at the end of the half-mile breathless. Corey matched her speed with ease and handed off a Bluetooth earpiece.

"Figured you didn't have yours. In case Hemingway finds something. You aren't going into battle holding your phone in your hand."

Despite the situation, Ichirin chuckled, taking the device and jamming it into her ear. She connected it to her phone while she ran, trusting Corey to guide her if she strayed from the median and risked spraining an ankle or worse. Once she had it set up, she called Hemingway, figuring now would be better before all hell broke loose.

"Something wrong?" he asked as soon as he answered.

"No. Calling you and leaving it open so you can let us know if you find something. Nothing's moving up here, all the way up to the stadium. There's a bunch of flashing lights. I doubt you'll be going anywhere for a while."

"I'm still pulling up what I can. Be safe up there."

"Of course."

It didn't take long for the two women to reach the line of police cars blocking off the road. Several people at the front stood beside their vehicles, hovering near their doors and standing on tiptoes to catch a glimpse of whatever caused the delay. Mattias stood in front of his car, talking with a few other police officers. When he turned around, he saw the new arrivals.

"I told you not to come here. You're civilians and should wait behind the line like everyone else."

He climbed into his cruiser and drove forward through the opening between two other police cruisers, not giving them a chance to offer a rebuttal. Ichirin stopped. She doubted the other officers would be any more welcoming or willing to let her past their barricade.

Corey tugged on her arm, pulling her sideways and steering her along a route parallel to the barrier. When they got out of earshot, Corey shared her thoughts.

"They haven't formed a full perimeter. They're blocking cars so they can't enter the area. I'm guessing so random people don't notice what's happening, rather than a full security lockdown. If we wait until we're out of sight, we should be able to run in."

Her predictions proved accurate as the police presence thinned out once they got away from the roads. As soon as they considered it safe, they turned toward the power plant and ran through a thin cluster of trees breaking up the urbanized view. Ducking around a building for good measure, they emerged on one of the side streets well behind the barricade.

Up ahead, several police cars clustered in the parking lot Ichirin recognized from the video. All had their lights on, and the officers hunkered down on one side of their vehicles, using them for cover. Raiju stood in the center of the lot, his black fur sparkling as lightning danced across it in haphazard patterns.

He took the form of a giant wolf, as tall at the shoulder as Ichirin. He paced over scorched and cracked pavement, snarling at the police officers. They opened fire, and he ducked down his head and winced.

Despite the show, Ichirin sensed his mirth. If the bullets harmed him, the pain did little to douse his amusement. Taking a moment to study the situation, she noticed a cascade of small bursts of light appearing over his body in rapid succession.

"Hem, can you hear me?"

"What's going on?"

"Raiju's here, and he's covered with electricity. The cops are firing, but I don't think it's doing anything."

"They don't have any reference to guns, but I have found a couple of stories talking about how arrows and javelins were useless against him. I'd guess bullets too, but you'd know better than I would. Pretty sure this is the first time Raiju's had guns shot at him."

"Have you found anything about what could hurt him?"

"There's a legend about someone with a spear once, but it's more a vague reference. I'm still looking."

The hunter turned to face her friend. "We need to get closer. See if we can help them."

Corey needed no more encouragement as she took off, heading toward the wall of police in their standoff with the mythological wolf. Raiju pounced; the impact of his landing shook the nearby trees. He dropped his shoulder and drove it up into a car. The vehicle flipped, making the two cops on the other side scramble to get out of the way as the tons of steel crunched and glass shattered with a crash. Raiju stretched out, leaning over the car and snarling at the officer who fell in her retreat. He curled back his lips, exposing a line of glistening teeth more than capable of tearing through any body armor she wore.

A burst of light exploded with a loud pop right in front of Raiju's face. He jerked back, paws scrambling against the cement as he retreated from the sudden assault. Mattias hurled another flashbang grenade, this one falling short of its mark and not having the same disorienting effect.

Raiju faced the new threat and narrowed his eyes in recognition. His nose wrinkled as his chest rumbled, sounding like thunder. The sky above took up the chorus, merging into a single roar. Lightning shot down from above, striking the ground a few feet from Mattias. As he recoiled from the attack, Raiju charged.

The sheer level of rage Raiju held for the police officer threatened to overwhelm Ichirin. When they fought before, it had been a matter of business, a cat toying with a mouse. She never expected to experience this amount of vitriol in her life, let alone having it rattle around inside her head. She stumbled, and Corey stepped in to help hoist her up.

When she dropped to a knee, Raiju stopped in the middle of his charge. He looked up, dismissing Mattias and focusing his attention on her. He twisted his head to the side and growled once more, but this time she heard his words in her mind.

You could not wait to seek me out. Now you have beheld me in my pure form and seen my greatness. Do you wish to join me once again, human? It is not too late for you to reconsider your actions.

He said the word "human" as she might address an insect. A few police officers refused to recognize the futility of their assault and continued firing their weapons, the small flashes accentuating the energy coursing over his body.

She couldn't believe he thought she'd join his side. Had he learned nothing about her with as much time as they spent together? Had he ever paid attention, or did he consider her a tool to use, another game piece to manipulate?

It took the hunter a moment to realize Raiju couldn't peer into her mind. Despite their connection, he no longer had access to her surface thoughts. She reached out to him, much the same as she did when they switched places.

I will not continue working for your master. I'm my own master, and I'm not going to let you hurt anyone else.

Raiju's grin said more than any words he could've provided as he stepped toward Mattias. In a flash, his head snaked out, and the jaws snapped down. Mattias proved fast enough to avoid the blow, doing so by dropping back. He brought his sidearm up and fired a couple of shots as the muscle memory kicked in. The bullets were met with flashes, as Ichirin expected.

"The lightning," Corey whispered, her voice so soft Ichirin had to strain to make out the words.

You cannot stop me. Any of your champions who might have been able to perform such a feat perished generations ago. With your assistance, I have eliminated any real threats as soon as they appeared.

The hunter ignored his words, recognizing the barb for what it was. Instead, she looked at the lightning coursing over his body. It had diminished in intensity. When she first saw him, it ran across him in a near continuous wave. Now it appeared like an erratic spark across a frayed connection.

If she could distract him, perhaps the continuous assault would break through. She didn't have any better plan.

You're not invincible. You needed me for something; otherwise you would've done this years ago. Why use me if you are so powerful?

Mattias picked himself up and moved to the trunk of his car. The movement caught Raiju's attention, and his eyes flicked over for a second before coming back to Ichirin.

You still lack a most basic comprehension of the game you are attempting to play. You think it is a game of chess, with yourself as a bishop or perhaps a queen. But the game is Go, and you are a single pebble, nothing more. And when the flood comes, you shall drown and be swept aside like all the other flawed creations.

Not knowing what else to do, the hunter dropped into a fighting stance. She had to be at least twenty yards away, but she saw how fast he could move when he chose to.

If you're so confident, fight me. Don't waste your time with the others. They're insignificant. What did you say? You take out generals?

And you think you are worthy of my attention?

It was her turn to grin, goading the kami into facing her challenge.

You're the one who said it. I'm a piece on the board, just like you. We're both pebbles. If you're so confident in your superiority, attack me now.

With a snarl, Raiju charged.

CHAPTER EIGHT

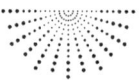

Unlike her dream, Ichirin didn't have the sense of calm pervading through her entire essence as Raiju charged. She took some relief in the fact that he happened to be smaller in the real world. Thank goodness for small favors. The size of his jaws still looked large enough to snap her neck in half with a single chomp.

When he covered half the distance between them, he leapt, reaching out with his front paws and opening his maw wide. The world slowed down as Ichirin witnessed death in front of her. She dove to the side, her body sluggish compared to the speed of her mind. The beast's claw clipped her shoulder on the way past, but the rest of her avoided the brunt of the attack.

As he got close to her, the officers held their fire. Most lowered their weapons and stood to watch. Not Mattias. He charged forward, running from his car with his gun pointed at the ground.

Corey leapt at Raiju, arms wide as she went in for a full-body tackle. He never saw her coming as she approached, but he didn't need to. When she got within a stride of the kami, electricity arced from his body to hers, stopping her and knocking her to the ground.

She rolled back over her shoulder, putting distance between her and the beast before getting back to her feet.

The foul smell of burnt hair filled the air.

Raiju approached Ichirin, taking the slow, steady march of a predator who knows he's about to catch his prey.

Are you afraid?

He sniffed at the air, making a show of attempting to smell her fear. He had a laser focus on Ichirin, holding her eyes with his own as he lowered his head and pulled his lips back.

Several loud bangs made her wince as Mattias fired at the wolf from his position at her side. The first bullet sparked as it came close to Raiju, but the second and third pierced his skin with a wet tearing sound.

Letting out a yip of surprise, he jumped to the side, bounding out of the way as the rest of the force opened fire. He weaved as he made a path toward the doors to the power plant, dropping a shoulder and bashing through with enough force to tear them from their hinges.

Mattias looked down at Ichirin, his gun still held in the direction of the fleeing wolf.

"You shouldn't be here. You're a liability."

Corey moved to help Ichirin stand. "She's the reason you're still breathing. You ask me, you need her, and you're the liability."

Mattias scanned around the scene, taking in the flipped-over car and the scorch marks decorating the parking lot, as well as the discarded casings. As a way of backing down, he tucked his gun into its holster and gestured for them to walk with him as he approached his vehicle.

"What do you think he wants?" Ichirin asked.

Corey shrugged. "I don't know, but he better not put us in the backseat. If we didn't show up, they'd all be dead, and the wolf would be terrorizing downtown like Godzilla."

Mattias had a quick, hushed conversation with one of the other officers before the woman relayed a message to the others. The police gathered together and talked amongst themselves.

When the two friends got next to Mattias, he popped open the trunk. Several black cases rested inside, each of them snapped shut. He opened a couple, displaying an assortment of sharp weapons.

"I'm not about to give you a firearm, but I can't let you go in there unarmed. Facing down the thing with your bare hands isn't brave, it's stupid."

Corey let out a low whistle as she traced her fingers over the collection of armaments. Ichirin's eyes locked onto one weapon—a katana. It didn't match the one in her dreams, but she didn't care. When she picked it up, the sensation this was right and proper once again filled her. She wanted to take time to examine the weapon and take a few practice swings, but every moment not giving chase gave Raiju the opportunity to get stronger.

"We need to go," she said to Corey.

The other woman snatched a shorter, angled blade. "I've always liked a kukri."

"I'm going with you," Mattias said as he grabbed a shotgun and closed the trunk.

Ichirin didn't trust him, but they didn't have the time to argue or debate. Not to mention she had no doubts about who the other officers would support in a confrontation. Rather than debate it, she sprinted toward the open doorway.

Even with her recent fitness training, the hunter couldn't match either of the others' speed. They both got to the doorway before her, Mattias flattening his back against the wall to one side. Corey burst into the building, showing her usual disregard for caution. Mattias shook his head and peered past the edge, exposing as little of himself as possible.

When she arrived, Ichirin took up position on the opposite side from Mattias. As soon as she got there, he entered the building, leaving her behind.

Ichirin followed, overwhelmed by the heat of the place once she passed the entryway. It reminded her of stepping into a dry sauna. Several pipes ran in both directions, some covered with wire mesh and labeled. Off to one side, she saw Mattias as he turned a corner, and the sound of feet running on a metal staircase echoed back to her.

"Hem, I'm in the power plant. Raiju ran inside, but it's like a maze. Any ideas where I should look for him?"

"If he's thriving on electricity, I'd bet he's heading toward the main boiler to recharge or power up. The building has one boiler dedicated to converting heat into electricity, so see if you can find it."

Being in the building proved to Ichirin that she didn't know the first thing about how power plants worked. She never expected there to be quite so many pipes. But luck stood by her side, and the halls had signage pointing her in the correct direction.

Before she got to the main boiler, a howl filled the air. Had Corey found Raiju? If so, did she take him on by herself? It would be beyond foolish, but Ichirin had to admit it existed within her friend's code of behavior. She picked up her pace, twisting her shoulders to the side every time it got narrow. It surprised her that Raiju had been able to get through without tearing the place apart, but she figured he could do something to change his size.

Of course! He could become a ball of lightning itself, more than small enough for even the tightest passages.

A sizzling crackle sounded, followed by Corey's yelp and a couple of gunshots. The hunter clutched the handle of her sword so hard her arm shook with the effort.

The hallway turned a corner and opened into a large room with some metal monstrosity resting in the center. It hummed loud enough to drown out most of the sounds of the combat. Raiju stood next to it, lightning crackling around him. Mattias held his sidearm level, pointed at the beast but holding his fire. His shotgun sat abandoned on the far side of Raiju. She couldn't see Corey anywhere.

Raiju noticed her arrival and snarled, the words once again coming to her mind over their shared connection.

After all this time and everything I have done for you, you would side with this abusive excuse for a human? Even among your kind, he rates at the bottom. You realize even now he yearns to eliminate you?

Ichirin uncoiled and flexed her fingers on the grip of her katana. Raiju didn't have his full height, but he still emanated a fearsome aura. Gripping the weapon refreshed her spirit, giving her the strength to lift her chin and maintain eye contact with the monster. Deep down, she didn't expect to be victorious, but all the same, her choices brought her here to this point, where she belonged.

You're the devil here. And didn't you say hunting down these abominations was my destiny?

Raiju grinned, taking a quick snap at Mattias when the human took a step to flank. The lunge prevented the cop from maneuvering to a better angle.

Do you think you can goad and manipulate me? Your hubris is entertaining. I consider it a shame your journey ends here. We could have accomplished great things.

With the proclamation, Raiju pounced, landing on the floor an arm's reach away from Mattias. Being in such close proximity made electricity arc from the beast to the man. Mattias jerked back as if struck with a solid object.

Drawing her sword, Ichirin tossed the scabbard to the side. It clattered as it slid to the wall. She brought the weapon behind her and ran forward, getting ready to swing at the creature's leg. He swatted at her before she got close enough, and she slashed at his foot while dropping back. Her feet slid out from underneath her, and she crashed to the ground, but her weapon sliced through the bottom of his paw.

When he put his foot back down, blood oozed out, leaving a visible print. The wound didn't appear to slow him down or cause discomfort as he circled the two humans. He took a few half-hearted snaps, pushing Ichirin back and not giving her an opening.

As she bumped into Mattias, she spared a glance over her shoulder. He pushed her to the side, moving past her to fire a couple of shots. The lightning flashed, and the bullets fell to the ground rather than striking their target. As long as he had his protection, the gun was useless. Mattias must've come to the same conclusion as he cursed and tucked the weapon back into his holster.

Raiju continued to advance, first from one side and then leaping over to approach from a different angle. He worked them into the corner, cutting off any opportunities for them to spread out and maneuver.

"Get out of my way."

Ichirin pushed Mattias to the side, grateful for his willingness to move. She didn't have the strength to force him away if he refused. She needed to push back against Raiju before he pinned them.

If he cornered them, he could walk forward and shock them until their hearts gave out.

Making sure to watch her footing, Ichirin rushed again, blade held over one shoulder. Her adversary crouched, lowering his back end in anticipation of leaping. The hunter forced herself to wait until the moment Raiju committed to his attack.

As soon as he pushed through his back legs, Ichirin planted one foot to the side and jumped off it with every ounce of strength she could muster. She lowered her blade, letting it trail behind her in the space she had been.

The space Raiju filled with his bulk.

The tip of the weapon slid into his leg, moving up to the shoulder as Ichirin raised it the moment she caught any resistance. Small threads of energy sparked from the wolf's body to her own, but it strengthened her grip as she clenched down tighter. Her body itched and burned at the same time, but her efforts rewarded her with a sharp howl as Raiju pushed away from her.

While the maneuver succeeded, it left Ichirin panting with sweat running down her face. The creature's fur matted at the wound site, but the leg held his weight as he moved. She needed something else. She couldn't maintain these exchanges and hope to emerge victorious.

Mattias took advantage of the opening to sprint across the room. His movement caught Raiju's attention, and the wolf rushed toward him. The hunter ran to intercept, making the wolf pull up short when she got close. It didn't have much of an effect, but it was enough for Mattias to make a diving lunge for his shotgun. He snatched it and chambered a round, bringing the barrel to point at Raiju without getting up from the ground.

Ichirin didn't need a warning. She dropped to the ground and ducked her head, tucking an ear against her shoulder as best she could. It did little to protect her hearing when the roar of the shotgun filled the room and echoed back at her. She found guns loud to begin with, but hearing one in a limited environment magnified the effect. She opened her jaw and shook her head.

Whatever the ammunition was, it proved effective. The lightning never crackled and several of the pellets struck Raiju in the chest, piercing the skin. The electricity covering him flared across the wound, and he let loose a terrifying howl of pain. When Mattias chambered another round, Raiju leapt to the side, unwilling to remain in place for a second shot.

His leap carried him to the other side of Ichirin; she guessed to use her as a shield. But her presence didn't deter Mattias from firing again. The air whipped at her hair and clothes as the projectiles cut through the space above her. Some of the pellets fell near her; they looked like gravel.

Realizing he couldn't use her for protection, Raiju jumped over her, taking the direct approach. As he cleared her body, she sliced up with her weapon, but he passed too far above for her to make contact. A third shot sounded, making her wince and adding to the ringing in her head. When she opened her eyes, she saw Raiju pinning Mattias to the ground with one massive paw, his fangs buried deep in the man's right shoulder. Mattias had his mouth open, and Ichirin was thankful she couldn't hear anything other than the incessant ringing.

Raiju picked Mattias up in his jaw, giving the man a shake before letting go and tossing him into a wall. The cop slid into a pile.

Finished with his first target, Raiju turned to face Ichirin. Blood dripped from several wounds and energy crackled over his body like a plasma globe when someone cupped it in their hand. The sheer number of injuries gave him the appearance of a large dog caught outside in the rain, but the coppery tinge in the air betrayed the illusion. Anger rolled off him in waves.

He rushed, taking a couple of long lopes to eat up the distance separating them. Ichirin backpedaled, staying away from his snout as he snapped at her. All her thoughts focused on staying alive, not any counterattacks. He continued to press her, and she worried about getting stuck against a wall. After another bite, she dove forward and to her left, aiming for the center of the room to maintain some ability to maneuver. Tucking her shoulder, she rolled, somehow managing not to get her weapon tangled up in her own body.

He leapt at her, but her dive kept her safe. The floor shook under her as he slammed his paw into it, the nails cracking the cement with the force of the blow. Ichirin rolled, using her momentum to spring to her feet, knowing if she remained still, it would be her death sentence.

"...use the sword! In the chest! Do you hear me?"

Her hearing came back in a rush, and she noticed Hemingway shouting in her ear through the earpiece. She didn't have the breath to respond, so he continued shouting his discovery mixed with pleading for a response.

Every breath she took sent needles of pain through her chest. She spun to face Raiju, looking for an opening and a way to get to his chest. Even if she could get close, the lightning would throw her back.

He continued advancing, teeth gnashing and growling, a maneuver made all the more terrifying since her hearing returned. Her confidence frayed, and she became hyperaware of the sweat slicking her palms. The image of the weapon going flying across the room danced through her mind as she swung it back and forth, using it to ward Raiju against getting too close.

Something dropped down on Raiju from above. It took Ichirin a moment to recognize Corey falling through the air, leading with her kukri. The electricity arced from the wolf to the athlete, but gravity maintained her course as she landed on Raiju's back. His head jerked up and twisted to the side in an attempt to bite the attacker. Ichirin charged, leading with her katana.

The lightning around the wounds shined so bright the hunter had to turn her head and squint her eyes against the glare, but she pressed on. The energy jumped to the blade, striking it and making it sparkle in a miniature fireworks display. A few of the bolts laced up to Ichirin's arms, but not enough to deflect her attack.

The weapon sank into the beast, sliding like a warm spoon through ice cream. This close, Ichirin couldn't help but get shocked. She continued driving forward, the weapon stopping when the hilt struck Raiju's body. He moved back, pulling away as he heaved a mighty wheeze, but Ichirin screamed and continued driving on, staying with him as if anchored to his chest. Her arms burned, and the electricity singed her clothing until her sleeves crumbled away in ash.

He fell to the side, and Ichirin slipped with the sudden disappearance of resistance. She banged her knees against the floor but continued to hold onto the weapon. It took several deep breaths before she had the energy to stand up, dragging her feet underneath her.

Raiju's eyes clouded over, and his chest shuddered with every inhale. His paws twitched, but it looked more like the response of a dream than any conscious exertion. He blinked, the gesture stretched out over seconds as if performed in slow motion.

You will fail. You are nothing. My master is everything.

The words came spaced out as if each one took a monumental amount of effort. Ichirin stood with one hand still on the handle of the sword. The lightning over his body faded, a few lingering arcs dancing from nose to tail. She should say something, but no words came to mind. She struggled to catch up with the mad tumble of events over the past two days.

The beast's eyes closed, and he took a couple more shuddering breaths before laying still. Ichirin remained standing over him, watching as his life passed.

Summoning what little strength she had left, she needed to look for Corey and check on Mattias. As she turned away from the wolf, a crack of thunder sounded, almost as loud as the bark of the shotgun. A bolt of electricity shot out of Raiju's chest around the sword, striking Ichirin in the back and propelling her forward onto her face. Darkness claimed her as soon as she hit the floor.

She woke up with all her senses muffled. Light glared from overhead, making her shut her eyes tight after opening them. She reached up to touch her aching head, but something restricted the motion.

"Easy, easy," Hemingway said from nearby, his voice cutting through the pounding in her ears and soothing the panic away. "To answer your first question, Corey's okay. Everything's fine, and you're in a hospital."

She smiled and shifted her arms to her sides, attempting to push herself up to a seated position. The back of her bed whirred to life as it lifted. When her eyes opened, this time with more caution, she saw Hemingway standing next to her bed with his finger on the bed controls. He looked like he hadn't slept well, and she noticed he had changed clothes. The implication of these facts worked their way through her scattered thoughts.

"How long was I out?"

"Almost two days. It's Tuesday morning. You got a hell of a shock and had burn marks up and down your arms. We told the doctors you were close to a power generator when it went haywire."

The best deceptions had an element of truth in them. Ichirin thought back to all of the chaos out in the open late on Sunday. Some had appeared online even before they arrived at the scene.

"What happened with the people?" she asked.

"The current story is a case of a student prank gone wrong, a power experiment that got out of control and required them shutting down the entire grid. For the most part, people believe it. After all, in this day and age, what's more believable? Some student trying to make a name for themselves screwing up, or a gigantic wolf shows up, summoned by a bolt of lightning? One of those is a lot easier to swallow, even more so for the folks who didn't see it with their own eyes. Doctored videos and all."

The door opened, and Corey burst into the room. She rushed forward and almost jumped on top of Ichirin, grabbing her in a hug and pinning her to the bed. Ichirin squeaked and returned the embrace, noticing the thick bandages covering her arms for the first time.

Corey let go and reached across Ichirin's body to smack Hemingway's shoulder with the back of her hand.

"You were supposed to tell me when she woke up!"

"She just did! I was going to text you right now."

"Uh huh, sure you were." Corey teased him, but she grinned and gave an exaggerated eye roll before turning her attention back to her hospitalized friend. "Did he tell you how the cops are doing some serious MIB shit and convincing everyone it's all a hoax? We're in the middle of a conspiracy. In ten years, we could sell the movie rights and see who plays us after the words 'inspired by true events.'"

Ichirin enjoyed the smile spreading across her face of its own volition, an effect Corey brought with her wherever she went. No force in the world could dull her shine. She grabbed her friend's hand, giving it as strong a squeeze as she could muster.

"What about Raiju?"

"Dead. And I'm sure dissected by now. I don't know what they did with the body. When the other cops came in, I was picking myself up off the floor on the other side of the room. Pretty sure my hair stuck out in every direction from the shock I got. Never even saw what happened to you." Her voice got soft, and her hand tightened around Ichirin's. "I thought you could've been dead."

Corey took a deep breath and summoned her token grin once more. "But I should've known better. You're the monster killer."

"And Mattias?"

This time Hemingway answered her question. She rolled over to look at him as he spoke.

"He's recovering. He had some intensive surgery but will be fine. I don't know how severe his injuries are, but I overheard some of the other cops talking about how he's out of the woods. He hasn't poked his head in here as far as I know."

Ichirin didn't mind if the officer didn't pay her a visit. He made it clear their truce had been one of necessity, and she had no idea how he'd react to her now. Though at some point, she should thank him. Without his help, she might not have been victorious. He also knew things that could help her.

THE SAGA OF ICHIRIN

If she decided to pursue this any further, that is. The doubts crept back into her mind, wondering if she mattered in this grand game played by gods. Even if she did, was it a part she still wanted to play? What could she do without her powers? Perhaps she should leave it all behind and focus on her regular life for a while.

Her friends remained silent as she tumbled through her thoughts like a person wandering around the house in the middle of the night, but without that much familiarity. If her world was home, someone had moved all the furniture while she slept. With a shake of her head, she chased the thoughts away for the moment. They'd return in due course, but she could deal with them later.

The three friends sat and talked about mundane things, steering the conversation away from any talk of myths, fights, or epic struggles of god-like figures. A nurse came in at some point, interrupting the conversation to remind the visitors they had to leave.

"I'll come back in the morning," Hemingway said, patting Ichirin's shoulder.

She picked up his hand and held it against her cheek for a moment before letting him go.

"And I'll swing by after work, maybe bring a game or two if you're up to it. I'll leave Ayden at home. I know it gets a little tense when you play against us both."

Corey's nature took any potential sting out of the words as she acknowledged her competitive streak, especially with her partner involved.

"I look forward to it."

The two of them left, and the nurse came over to the bedside. "I'm glad to see you're up and more alert. Let's take a look at your arms."

Ichirin held out her arms, and the nurse proceeded to unwrap the bandages. The skin underneath had a few dark spots with the bright pink color of new skin surrounding them. The hunter didn't even attempt to count the number of scorch marks. It had to be over twenty on her right arm alone.

"Honestly, we're all surprised you're doing as well as you are after the accident. You must have a strong heart."

The nurse attempted to be charming, but Ichirin craved silence once her friends left. While their presence helped invigorate her, she still operated at a severe shortage of energy. Talking with a relative stranger took more than she could muster at this point. The nurse picked up on the vibe and remained quiet as she finished undressing and examining Ichirin's arms. Afterward, she applied a moisturizing gel on the gray and red burns and rewrapped them in a clean dressing.

"I'll come back in a couple of hours and see if you want something to eat. For now, there's crackers and juice on the table beside you. Do you need a hand with it?"

"I can manage, thanks."

The nurse stepped out, leaving Ichirin alone in her hospital room. For a few minutes, she sat in the bed, staring at the edge where the ceiling met the wall. Her brain sorted through all the events of the last few days, picking them apart and going over them one piece at a time. She shook her head, still having trouble accepting how much Raiju had manipulated her.

With a sigh, Ichirin tossed off the sheets and got up to walk to the window. She pulled the curtain aside and saw the crowded Seattle cityscape. Her room was on a high enough floor to let her see over some of the neighboring rooftops and identify the Needle in the distance.

Leaning forward, she pressed her palms and forehead against the glass, enjoying the coolness of it against her skin. She closed her eyes. Her head felt empty. She'd gotten so used to another voice; she didn't know how to adjust to being alone with her imagination.

Raiju's final words came back to her. He had a master, so the game continued. What part did she still have to play, if any? Thinking about him inspired her to reach out, casting her mental net and searching for any trace of the kami. Even if his physical form died, she worried his spirit remained.

Nothing.

As she extended her focus, she became aware of something else. It wasn't a connection to her former spirit guide. No, this was something else. A deep rolling wave held back and was lying in wait. Curious, she touched it, and it responded with a flash of light she saw against her closed eyelids. She opened them in time to catch the final trails of a lightning bolt. Thunder rolled, muted through the glass.

Out of the corner of her eye, electricity danced down her arm, arcing across the fresh bandage and scorching it.

THE END

ACKNOWLEDGMENTS

No creative work is formed in a vacuum, at least not in my experience. There are many people who are responsible for this book getting to you that deserve some special recognition.

Jaym Gates for introducing me to Falstaff Books in the first place, and always pushing me forward even when I started to doubt myself. My mother who taught me the beauty and wonder that can be found in books as well as showing me how to share my own worlds with others. My friends who encouraged me to take this leap of faith and have been cheering me on the entire way, sometimes from the sidelines and sometimes right next to me.

When I was first thinking up the story and sketching it out, both Russell Jacobson and his wife Harumi Makiyama provided a lot of valuable insight into the lore and beliefs, as well as what it would have been like for a Japanese immigrant living in the United States. I couldn't have created as believable a story without their assistance.

Of course, I need to give proper credit to John Hartness, for being willing to take a chance on me, after vetting me with another author/sword-swinger (how many of us are there I wonder), a story that still makes me chuckle. Erin Penn for being an amazing editor and turning me into a much better author to the point where even I noticed it. Seriously, she is personally responsible for leveling up my writing game! Everyone else at Falstaff who helped out with editing, polishing, cover design, and all around making an amazing piece of work I'm honored to have my name on.

ABOUT THE AUTHOR

Dylan Birtolo is a writer, game designer, and professional sword-swinger. He's published multiple novels, novellas, and short stories both in established universes and worlds of his own creation. Some of the universes that he's created stories in are *Shadowrun, Exalted, Battle-Tech, Freeport*, and *Pathfinder*. On the gaming side, he is a developer of *Dragonfire* and game designer for *Shadowrun Sprawl Ops* and *Henchman the Game*. He is part of Lynnvander Studios, a game design company with several titles under its belt including the most recent *Divinity Original Sin the Board Game*! He trains with the Seattle Knights, an acting troop that focuses on stage combat, and has performed in live shows, videos, and movies. He's had the honor of jousting, and yes, the armor is real - it weighs over 100 pounds. You can read more about him and his works at www.dylanbirtolo.com, look him up on Facebook, or follow his Twitter at DylanBirtolo.

FALSTAFF BOOKS

**Want to know what's new
And coming soon from
Falstaff Books?**

Try This Free Ebook Sampler

https://www.instafreebie.com/free/bsZnl

**Follow the link.
Download the file.
Transfer to your e-reader, phone, tablet, watch, computer,
whatever.
Enjoy.**

CPSIA information can be obtained
at www.ICGtesting.com
Printed in the USA
LVHW091917270120
644939LV00011B/364/J